John K. M'Dowall

**People's History of Glasgow**

an encyclopedic record of the city from the prehistoric period to the

present day - Vol. 2

John K. M'Dowall

**People's History of Glasgow**
*an encyclopedic record of the city from the prehistoric period to the present day -
Vol. 2*

ISBN/EAN: 9783337225308

Printed in Europe, USA, Canada, Australia, Japan

Cover: Foto ©Andreas Hilbeck / pixelio.de

More available books at **www.hansebooks.com**

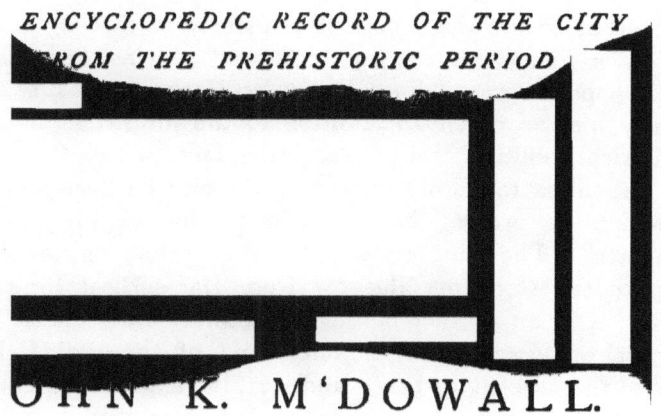

ENCYCLOPEDIC RECORD OF THE CITY

FROM THE PREHISTORIC PERIOD

OHN K. M'DOWALL.

T has occurred to me that there is a place among the histories of Glasgow for a history of the city compiled in classified form, and issued at a popular price. THE PEOPLE'S HISTORY OF GLASGOW is, consequently, not so much an addition to the multitude, as a précis of the historical, political, social, and other facts which "the man in the street" requires to know concerning the city he lives and labours in, and which at present he must grope for in big books and bigger reports. The aim of the present history is to act as a hand-lamp to the story of Glasgow from the earliest times to the present day; it is an extract of history, a short and concise account of the origin and growth of the city, and of the multifarious co-operations of the citizens in peace and war, in religion and commerce.

Accuracy and brevity have been anxiously studied. It is hoped that no fact, either of interest or of importance, has been accidentally omitted. Every effort has been made that all the information may be as correct as possible. I have found much divergence in facts and opinions in the historical authorities consulted, and some difficulty in reconciling conflicting statements, but in matters still in doubt, or under debate, the facts as given by a majority of the histories have been followed, except in circumstances where special information has been available.

"Who shall decide when doctors disagree,
And soundest casuists doubt like you and me."

It is only when one takes a bird's-eye view of the centuries during which Glasgow has flourished, and of the wide-spreading activities of the citizens during those centuries, that there can be obtained an intelligent grasp of the great part the city has played in the making of the nation and the empire, and in the civilising of the world. Glasgow has not been merely a city of shopkeepers, existing for private gain, nor has it been an accident. It was of set purpose that it put aside gentility for utility, and turned spears into pruning hooks in order to reap by the arts of peace a harvest for and from the world.

The story of Glasgow should be more correctly realised. I should even presume to have it taught in schools and colleges to its future citizens, who might thus learn to honour the spirit which gave Glasgow the ambition to be a hive of useful industry. If they knew of the life, the blood, and the treasure spent by the self-reliant and self-respecting generations of the past, and learned the lesson that the city's greatness has been due to corporate endeavour inspired by, and seconding individual effort, they would be incited to emulate and carry on those activities which have made Glasgow the first municipality in the world and the second city in the British empire.

J. K.

*1st November, 1899.*

## NOTE TO SECOND EDITION.

The First Edition of THE PEOPLE'S HISTORY OF wholly subscribed within a few days of announce Publishers have since refused many subscriptions apparent that there was a certain demand for the distinct from the desire to possess a First E Publishers decided to issue a Second Edition s respect to the first except that the size of the ma and that the book is unsigned.

*15th November, 1899.*

[ *The Cover is the work of Mr. John Duncan, late of the " Evening Ti Glasgow, and now on the staff of the " Graphic," London, and in combines the older style with the requirements of the modern Glasgow School. The subject is a decorative play on the Glasgow Arms, supported underneath by a couple of figures representing Romance and Industry.* ]

## PREHISTORIC and LEGENDARY.

THE history of Glasgow previous to the middle of the sixth century is a blank.

Undoubted remains of the Stone Age have been discovered on the Clyde, in addition to a number of canoes, of which five were found at Springfield, one near the Pointhouse, one near Clydehaugh, one at St. Enoch's Church in 1780, one at the Cross in 1781, one in Stockwell Street in 1824, one in the Drygate, one in London Street in 1825, and one at Victoria Dock in 1875. A large war canoe was also found last year (1898) in a crannog at Dumbuck.

During the Roman occupation of Scotland, 81 A.D. to 410 A.D., the valley of the Clyde, like other parts of Scotland, was covered with great forests, and the district from Galloway in the south to Perthshire in the north was held by a tribe called the Damnii, a handsome and warlike people, whose religion was Druidical, and who had a certain measure of civilisation.

From the death of St. Mungo, in 603, until the advent of the "Sair Saunt for the Croon," King David I., the history of Glasgow is legendary.

The British Kingdom of Strathclyde flourished until the tenth century, but in the reign of Malcolm II. it amalgamated with that of Scotland. Alclutha (Dumbarton) was the capital. The day of the Picts ended in 843 A.D., in the time of Kenneth Macalpine, when they united with the Scots. The Dane and Norsemen invaders were foiled by the Scots in their attempts to possess the country, and thus gradually the whole kingdom was brought under the subjection of the present race, which became consolidated under Queen Margaret and Malcolm Canmore.

## THE ROMANS.

When Lollius Urbicus, about 144 A.D., built a wall from Old Kilpatrick on the Clyde to Carriden or Blackness on the Forth, perhaps even when Agricola set up a chain of forts, about 84 A.D., the Romans had a small military station at Glasgow.

## ST. MUNGO.

**Parents.**—No reliable record exists regarding Glasgow's patron saint, St. Mungo. His father was said to be Ewen-ap-Urien, a prince of Strathclyde, and his mother Thenaw, a daughter of Loth, King of the Saxons of Northumbria—hence the origin of the name Lothians.

**Early Life.**—Kentigern, or Mungo, was born in 518 A.D. at Culross, where he is said to have been educated by St. Serf, who named his pupil Monghu, signifying "Dear One." Mungo became imbued with the spirit of his benefactor; tradition states he performed many miracles, such as restoring life, dividing the waters of the Forth, etc. Receiving a call from the Lord, he departed from Culross, and travelled *via* Carnwath until he arrived at a place called Deschu, on the banks of the Molendinar, in the kingdom of Strathclyde. At the earnest solicitation of the king and people, he agreed to make his abode with them. He was consecrated by a bishop, specially brought from Ireland, at the early age of 25 years, in A.D. 543.

**Preaching and Death.**—St. Mungo appears to have travelled about a great deal, preaching and doing good, going to Wales and even as far as Rome. His return from the latter place was made the occasion of great rejoicing. Addressing the people, as he could not be seen or heard by a large number of the crowd, he miraculously caused the ground on which he stood to rise into a mound. The spot is said to be the present "Dovehill." This incident gave rise to the motto, "Let Glasgow Flourish by the Preaching of the Word." St. Mungo died on 13th January, 603 A.D.

## ARMORIAL BEARINGS.

**Probable Origin.**— Several theories are put forward regarding the origin of the City Arms. I shall content myself with quoting one :—The Bird is St. Serf's robin, restored to life by Kentigern in his youth. The Tree, now fully developed, is the bough which, when frozen, St. Mungo blew into flame, and lit St. Serf's Monastery lamps. The Fish and the Ring are emblems drawn from an important episode in the life of Queen Langueth, who received the ring from her husband, King Rhydderch, but gave it to a soldier with whom she was intriguing. The King discovered the soldier sleeping on the banks of the Clyde, and slipping the ring off the finger of the unconscious son of Mars, cast it into the river. He then commanded his Queen to produce the tell-tale circle. The King's Consort, in her extremity, confessed all to St. Mungo, and besought his assistance. The Saint directed a fishing line to be cast into the Clyde. A salmon was caught, and the ring found in its mouth. The Queen then presented it to her lord, whose wrath was appeased, and the happy relationship renewed. The Bell is the consecrated one brought by St. Kentigern from Rome on the occasion of his last visit to that city. The Mound from which the tree grows is the ground miraculously raised by St. Mungo while addressing the people on his return from Rome, which gave rise to the motto "Let Glasgow Flourish by the Preaching of the Word." The following rhyme has been composed from the foregoing :—

Here's the Tree that never grew,
Here's the Bird that never flew;
Here's the Bell that never rang,
Here's the Fish that never swam.

**Present Form.**—The armorial bearings of the city were not registered till 1866. The want of an authentic crest had caused considerable confusion. It was remitted to Mr. Andrew Macgeorge, writer, who was an authority on the subject, to design an official crest for the city. The present well-known insignia is the result of Mr. Macgeorge's labour. It was

1866. The only important change is the curtailment of the motto, "Let Glasgow Flourish by the Preaching of the Word," to "Let Glasgow Flourish."

## GLASGOW SEE.

**Origin.**—Prince David, heir apparen and younger brother of King Alexander I. turned his attention to Glasgow in the yea 1115. He founded or restored the See o Glasgow according to the canons of the Church of Rome, and appointed his tutor and chaplain, John Achaius, to the bishopric.

**Prelates.**—The following held offic from the foundation of the See until th Reformation, viz.:—

543—St. Kentigern or Mungo, Founder.

His church was of wood and wattle.

The See was re-founded by David, Princ of Cumbria, who had, in 1115, ordered an Inquisition concerning the lands belonging to the Church of Glasgow, and who had i constituted a Diocese according to th canons of the Church of Rome.

BISHOPS.

1115-47—John Achaius.
1147-64—Herbert.
1164-74—Ingram Newbigging.
1175-99—Joceline.
1199—Hugh de Roxburgh, *elect*.
1200-02—William Malvoisin.
1202-07—Florentius, *elect*.
1207-32—Walter.
1233-58—William de Bondington.
1260—Nicholas Moffat, *elect*.
1260-68—John de Cheyam.
1268-70—Nicholas Moffat, *elect*.
1270—William Wishart, *elect*.
1273-1316—Robert Wishart.
1317—Stephen de Dundimore, *elect*.
1319-25—John Wishart.
1325-35—John Lindsay.
1335-67—William Rae.
1368-87—Walter Wardlaw, Cardinal.
1389-1408—Matthew Glendinning.
1408-25—William Lauder.
1426-46—John Cameron.
1446-47—James Bruce, *elect*.
1447-54—William Turnbull.
1455-73—Andrew Muirhead.
1474-83—John Laing.
1483—George Carmichael, *elect*.

ARCHBISHOPS.

On 9th October, 1488, the Pope erected the Diocese into an archbishopric, which made the Archbishop paramount over the Bishops of Argyll and the Isles, Dunblane

1484-1508—Robert Blackadder.
1508-24—James Beaton.
1524-47—Gavin Dunbar.
1548-51—Alexander Gordon, *elect*.
1551-1603—James Beaton, nephew of the Cardinal.

James Beaton was deprived at the Reformation, and retired to Paris, where he died in 1603.

### Protestant Archbishops.—

Although the Romish clergy had been deprived of spiritual privileges, they were still entitled to two-thirds of their temporalities in liferent if they were able to collect their dues. As James Beaton was, in the eyes of the law, still enjoying two-thirds of the temporalities of his see, four Protestants in succession were appointed "Tulchan" archbishops, in order to divert the revenues from him, while they had the spiritual oversight of their clergy. These temporalities were restored to Beaton by James VI. in 1588, and he held them until 1603.

1571-72—John Porterfield, *Tulchan*.
1572-81—James Boyd, *Tulchan*.
1581-85—Robert Montgomery, *Tulchan*.
1585-87—William Erskine (a layman), *Tulchan*.

In 1587 an Act was passed annexing the temporalities of all the Bishoprics to the Crown, a proceeding that practically uprooted Episcopacy by leaving mere names without corresponding revenues.

1603-15—John Spottiswoode, first prelate under the Protestant Episcopacy.
1615-32—James Law.
1633-38—Patrick Lindsay.

Episcopacy was abolished by the General Assembly held in Glasgow in 1638. For twenty-three years there were no Archbishops of Glasgow, but the Restoration, in 1660, brought with it the re-establishment of Episcopacy.

1661-63—Andrew Fairfoul.
1664-69—Alexander Burnet (deposed).
1670-74—Robert Leighton.
1674-79—Alexander Burnet (restored).
1679-84—Arthur Ross.
1684-87—Alexander Cairncross.
1687-88—John Paterson.

In 1688, at the Revolution, Episcopacy was finally abolished in Scotland, so far, at least, as State recognition was concerned.

### Restoration.—

In 1653 the Romish clergy in Scotland were reincorporated as a Mission, and governed by Prefects-Apostolic governed by a Vicar-Apostolic. The Roman Catholic Hierarchy, which was abolished at the Reformation, was restored on January, 1878, by Pope Pius IX., who appointed the Most Rev. Charles Eyre, D.D., Archbishop of Anazarba, Apostolic Delegate for Scotland and Administrator-Apostolic of the Western District, who was ordained in 1842 and consecrated in 1869, to the See of Glasgow. The death of the Pope, whose signature was required, delayed matters, but his successor, Leo XIII., some months after consummated the appointment and issued an allocutionary letter, a copy of which was burned on the Green on 13th April, 1878, in presence of several thousand protestors. This harmless proceeding was all that took place, and the authorities were relieved the necessity of interfering.

## THE CATHEDRAL.

### Foundation.—

In 1124 Bishop John Achaius began to build the Cathedral on the site of St. Mungo's wooden church. The edifice was partly of stone and wood, and was consecrated in presence of King David and his Court, on 7th July, 1136. On this occasion the King presented lands to the Bishop with which to endow the Cathedral; the gift included the lands of Partick, and the churches of Govan, Renfrew, Cadzow, etc.

### Burned and Restored.—

The above edifice was destroyed by fire in 1192; it could not have happened at a better time. Joceline, previously Abbot of Melrose, had been consecrated Bishop of Glasgow on 1st June, 1175; he was the man to grapple with the calamity, being brimful of energy and perseverance. He immediately obtained a charter from the king authorising him to receive subscriptions, whereby he was enabled to rebuild and open the new Cathedral on 6th July, 1197. He also erected a tomb to St. Mungo. The present Crypt is called Joceline's Crypt in honour of the founder, who died on 17th March, 1199, and was buried on the right side of the Choir. Had it not been for the biography of St. Kentigern which he wrote, Glasgow would practically have known nothing of her patron saint.

### Choir.—

The Choir was finished by public subscription between 1233 and 1258.

### Steeple and Vestry.—

In 1425 Bishop Lauder built the present steeple as far up as the battlements; he also laid the foundation of the vestry. Bishop Cameron, who succeeded him, finished what his

**Addition and Lands.**—Archbishop Blackadder continued to improve the Cathedral. He began the great aisle to the south, which is still known as Blackadder's Crypt. The organ screen is supposed to have been erected by him. The following lands belonged to the Cathedral, and were rented to various parties, *viz*, Auchenairn, Balshagray, Carniyle, Dalbeth, Gairbraid, Kenmuir, Shettleston, Woodside, etc., etc.

**Consistory House and Tower.**—The Consistory House and Tower, which stood at the western extremity of the Cathedral, was erected shortly before the Reformation. The Commissary Courts were held in it for more than 200 years.

**Records Removed.**—At the beginning of the Reformation troubles, Archbishop Beaton removed all the archives and valuables from the Cathedral to his own palace, where they had to be guarded by the loyal citizens from the fury of the people. But the clamour became so great, he had to fly to Paris in 1560, taking the following valuables with him which he deposited in the Scots College in the Carthusian monastery, *viz.*, image of Christ in gold, the Twelve Apostles in silver, two silver crosses adorned with precious stones, several portions of the Cross of Christ, a silver-gilt casket containing the hair of the Virgin Mary, several other silver caskets and phials containing the scourges of St. Kentigern and St. Thomas of Canterbury, part of the skin of Bartholomew the Apostle, a bone of St. Ninian, part of the girdle of the Virgin Mary, a bone of St. Magdalene, the milk of the Virgin, part of the manger in which Jesus was born, the fluid which flowed from the tomb of St. Mungo, bones of St. Kentigern, St. Thomas, St. Eugene, and St. Blaze, part of the tomb of St. Catherine the Virgin, a portion of the cloak of St. Martin, portions of the bodies of St. Kentigern and St. Thomas of Canterbury, a portion of the hair garment worn by St. Kentigern, and many other bones and relics of saints.

**Restored.** — The Cathedral received great injury at the Reformation in 1560, but on 21st August, 1574, the citizens voluntarily subscribed for its repair.

**Three Parish Churches.** — The Cathedral after the Reformation was used for three separate parish churches, *viz.*, the Inner High, occupying the Choir, the Outer High (now St. Paul's), the Nave, and the Laigh, (or Barony, the Crypt.

**Leaden Roof.**—Archbishop Spottis woode began to build the leaden roof of the Cathedral in 1600; it was finished by Archbishop Law about the year 1630.

**Damaged by Storm.**—The Cathedra was so much damaged by a storm on 13th and 14th January, 1740, that the magistrate applied to Parliament for £400 to assist in its repair.

**Renovation.**—After the Reformation the grand old building was going from bad to worse. Glasgow's mother-church wa Crown property, under the charge of the Commissioners of Woods and Forests, or whom pressure was brought to bear with the result that, in 1854, cleaning operation began, and the crypts cleared of rubbish The Consistory House and Tower at the western gable were removed, and the large west window and doorway opened up Since then, the magnificent stained glas windows—which are one of the chief sight: of the city—have been gradually added The four great windows were gifted respec tively by the Government, the Duke o Hamilton, the Bairds of Gartsherrie, and Miss Douglas of Orbiston. The Cathe dral—as it now stands—gives a fair idea o the improved artistic taste of the city dur ing the past fifty years.

**Organ.**—Dr. Burns, the late minister presented the Cathedral, in 1880, with the present magnificent organ, made by Willis of London. A tablet to the memory of the donor—erected at the entrance to the choi in the north transept—was unveiled by Professor Story on 25th January, 1899.

---

## "GLASGOW."

**First Mentioned.** — Many theorie are put forward regarding the origin of the name "Glasgow." As presently spelled it occurs, for the first time, in the charter granted by Prince (afterwards King) Davic in 1115.

**Its Origin.**—The names Cathures and Deschu belonged to two villages which stood on the present site of the city. It transcribing old manuscripts, it was no unusual to mistake the letters "cl" for "d" and it is possible the transcribers wrote "Cleschu" instead of "Deschu": from the former word Mr. Andrew Macgeorg thinks it probably became transformed into "Gleschu" or "Glaschu."

**Its Meaning.**—The following mean ings are given of the word "Glasgow,' *viz.* :—"Grayhound or Graysmith," the latter after some celebrated smith; "Darl glen," from the dark ravine, in the vicinity of the Cathedral, through which the Molendinar flowed ; *Glas* (Brit.), signifying "green," and *coed* "wood"—thus *Glas-coed*—conjectured on the existence of a forest around where the Necropolis now stands (called at one time "the Bishop's Forest"), *glas* meaning "green" and *cu* or *ghu* "beloved" or "dear," thus "beloved green spot."

## MONASTERIES.

**Black Friars.**—A monastery was founded in 1240 by Pope Gregory for the accommodation of Dominican or Black Friars on the east side of High Street, where the Midland Railway offices are now situated.

**Grey Friars.**—The Order of the Grey Friars or Franciscans in Glasgow was founded in 1476 in a monastery which stood between High Street and North Albion Street, immediately to the north of College Street. Certain feu duties were set apart for their maintenance by Bishop Laing. The building was destroyed at the Reformation, and the feu duties of both monasteries given to the University.

## BISHOP'S CASTLE.

**First mention.**—The Bishop's Castle (a *fac-simile* of which was shown in the International Exhibition of 1888) stood in front of the site of the Royal Infirmary. It was triangular in form. Behind were the stables; and on the north, the Stable Green Port ; while in close vicinity, and also in the Drygate, which was joined by Limmerfield Lane, were the manses of the rectors of Balernock, Monkland, Teviotdale, Cambuslang, Cardross, Eaglesham, Peebles, etc. There are no records to show when the "Castle of Glasgow"—for such it really was—was founded. The first time it is mentioned is in 1258, in the Chartulary of Glasgow, where it refers to the Bishop, William de Bondington, and states—"His Palace is without the Castle of Glasgow." Its name appears again the same century in the Registers of the Episcopate in 1268 and 1290, when it says, it had a garden.

**English Garrison.**—At the time John Baliol was King of Scotland, Edward I. of England had a small garrison of soldiers quartered in the Castle, which he honoured with a three days' visit in 1301. During his stay he resided with the Black Friars. Regarding this same garrison, Blind Harry refers to Sir William Wallace's attempt to

dislodge it, which resulted in the "Battle of the Bell o' the Brae."

**Great Tower Built.**—Bishop Cameron, who completed the present Cathedral steeple, added the *Great Tower*, and otherwise ornamented the Castle in 1438.

**Fortified.**—About 1510 Archbishop Beaton fortified the Castle with an embattled wall fifteen feet high, a bastion, ditch, and tower.

**Captured.**—During the minority of James V. the Castle was stormed and taken by Mure of Caldwell, but it was recaptured by the Regent, the Duke of Albany.

**Treachery.**—The Earl of Lennox garrisoned the Castle in 1544, and retired to his stronghold at Dumbarton Rock. The Earl of Arran, who was acting as Regent during the minority of Queen Mary, came from Stirling and demanded the Glasgow garrison to surrender, which they refused. He then invested the fortress, and for nine days kept up a continuous bombardment with brass cannon throwing shot weighing from ten to twelve pounds. On the tenth day the brave defenders offered to capitulate provided they were granted quarter. The offer was accepted, but no sooner had they laid down their arms than the Regent put them all to death except two who escaped. This treacherous act led to the "Battle of the Butts."

**Besieged.**—The Castle was besieged by the Hamiltons and other adherents of Queen Mary in 1570, and although Glasgow's stronghold had only a garrison of twenty-four they gallantly repelled the assault. For this, and the murder of Regent Murray, Hamilton Palace and other Clydesdale mansions were destroyed by the Earl of Lennox.

**Restoration.**—The Castle with nearly all other public edifices suffered greatly at the time of the Reformation, but about 1600 Archbishop Spottiswoode restored it to all its former splendour.

**Decay and Demolition.**—Previous to the Reformation the Town Council held their meetings in the Castle, but about 1576 they removed to the Old Tolbooth at the Cross, and from this time the ancient pile slowly began to decay. It latterly was used as a prison. Three hundred Jacobite prisoners were incarcerated in it. By the year 1720 it was reduced to a sort of quarry. In 1755 the Town Council granted permission for stones to be taken from it to build the Saracen's Head Inn. Two of the stones of Dunbar's Gateway, after being built in the wall of a tenement in 22 High Street, now adorn the mansion of Sir William Dunbar of Mochrum in Wigtownshire, while a stone bearing the arms of Archbishop Beaton has found a resting-place in the vestibule of St. Joseph's Roman Catholic Church in North Woodside Road. Prior to the interesting remains being removed accurate drawings were made of them. The ruins of the Castle were cleared away in 1792, when the building of the Royal Infirmary was commenced, under the surgical wards of which a portion of the old Castle wall may still be seen.

## GLASGOW UNIVERSITY.

**Origin and Early Days.**—The University of Glasgow was founded on 7th January, 1450, by a Bull granted by Pope Nicholas to Bishop Turnbull during the reign of King James II., who took an active interest in its institution, and granted a charter confirming great benefits and privileges on the seat of learning. The University was opened for teaching in 1451, the staff consisting of the Chancellor (Bishop Turnbull), a rector, masters, and doctors in four faculties :—*Natio Glottiana, Natio Transforthiana, Natio Rothesiana*, and *Natio Loudoniana*. Within two years more than 200 students were enrolled. At first the crypt of the Cathedral was allowed by the Bishop for the Classes, but ultimately a house was secured on the south side of the Rottenrow, near High Street, which was called the Pedagogium. In 1458 a new house was built for the accommodation of the students on the east side of High Street. In 1459 Lord Hamilton presented the University with four acres of ground between the house of the Black Friars on the south, and the lands of Sir Thomas Arthurlie on the north, and extending to the Molendinar burn on the east. In 1465 the University was transferred to the new site, and in 1466 Sir Thomas Arthurlie bequeathed his adjacent houses and lands, amounting to two acres, to the College. The new addition extended from the High Street along the New Vennel to the Molendinar. The buildings were annexed to the University property in 1475. In front of them, houses were built to accommodate the professors. The students were first lodged in the College buildings, the gates of which were shut at 9 o'clock in winter and an hour later in summer, the regents of the four faculties requiring to see that all their students had gone to bed

before they themselves retired for the night. The number attending the University exceeded the accommodation, and lodgings had to be found outside. Disputes regarding rents, however, arose, until Bishop Turnbull decided that the charges should be fixed by an equal number of members of the University and of the citizens ; these acted as arbiters. No student could be removed from his lodging so long as he paid his rent, and conducted himself properly. Bishop Turnbull died on 3rd September, 1454.

**First Chapter, Lord Rector, etc.**— The first meeting of the University Chapter was held in the adjoining Black Friars Monastery on 14th October, 1453. Master David Cadzow, the first Lord Rector, who was elected by the procurators of the four nations and other officials, gave his rectorial address in the same place on 29th July, 1460, reading the rubric of the Third Book of Gregory's Decretals on the life and uprightness of the clergy.

The students had the same professor during their three years' course of study.

**Charter.**—King James IV. granted a Charter, which is termed the *Magna Charta* of Glasgow University, giving it a *nova erectio* in 1577.

**Enlargement.**— In 1632 the University buildings were begun to be remodelled and enlarged. About £2,000 was collected for this purpose. The Town Council gave 1,000 merks (£55 11s. 1½d. sterling) for the building, and a similar sum to purchase books for the library. It is interesting to record that King Charles I. promised £200, which he failed to pay. Cromwell, however, became good for this in 1654. The Carved Gateway in High Street—now re-erected at Gilmorehill—was built in 1658, which date it bears, also the arms and initials of King Charles II. To give the names of the subscribers would take up too much space, but to show how much interest was taken in the matter it is only necessary to say that Scotsmen in London subscribed about £250.

**Gilmorehill.**—The old College buildings and grounds in High Street were disposed of to the City Union Railway Company in 1864 for £100,000. In the same year the University Senate purchased the lands of Gilmorehill for £65,000, Donaldshill for £16,000, and Clayslap for £17,400, for the purpose of providing adequate accommodation for the present University. To carry through their great undertaking, the University authorities had originally £138,900 at their disposal, £21,400 of which was promised by the Government, conditional on £24,000 being raised by public subscription. Sir G. Gilbert Scott was appointed architect, and on 2nd June, 1866, Professor Allen Thomson cut the first sod of the new seat of learning, which is rectangular in form, 540 feet long by 300 feet broad, divided by the Bute and Randolph Halls — which are connected fabrics — called in honour of the Marquis of Bute and Charles Randolph, the donors, who built them at a combined cost of £100,000. On 8th October, 1868, the Prince of Wales accompanied by the Princess laid the foundation stone amid scenes of great rejoicing. The Royal party arrived at Queen Street Station, where they were met by Lord Provost Lumsden and many other men of light and leading. After visiting the old College, the Prince received the freedom of the city in the City Hall. On arriving at the University, his Royal Highness and Prince John of Glücksburg were made LL.D.'s. After the stone was laid, the Royal party were entertained to luncheon in the Lord Provost's house in Bath Street, and they left the city at six o'clock. In the evening the Provost entertained the University authorities to a banquet in the Corporation Galleries. The city was gaily illuminated. The Lord Provost was afterwards knighted. The last meeting was held in the old College on 20th July, 1870, and on 7th November of the same year the opening ceremony, presided over by the Chancellor, the Duke of Montrose, was held in the new University.

**Tower.**—The Tower, at first only built to the battlements, was finished in 1887.

**Old College Gateway.**—The Lodge and Gateway is part of the entrance to the old College, and was removed and presented to the University by the late Sir William Pearce, Bart.

## CHURCHES.

**St. Thenna, St. Mungo, and St. Roche.**—About the year 1500 a small chapel with a graveyard was erected outside the West Port; this is the original of the present St. Enoch's Church. Another chapel called "St. Mungo-in-the-Fields" was planted in what is now Saracen Lane in 1500. It was built and endowed by David Cunningham, Provost of the Collegiate Church of Hamilton. A chapel named St. Roche or Rollox was erected in 1508 to the north of the Stable Green Port.

Historians state that a "St. Mungo's" Chapel stood in the Dovehill, and that a chapel dedicated to the mother of St. Mungo, called "St. Thenna's," was erected on the east side of High Street, a little to the north of the Cross; while Denholm refers to a "St. John the Baptist" Chapel at the head of the Drygate.

**Old Episcopal Chapel.**—The Episcopal chapel at the corner of Greendyke and James Morrison Streets at the Green was built on the banks of the then pellucid Molendinar in 1750, when prejudices ran high against the Church Episcopal. This was the first church to have an organ in the city, and so much offence did it give that the chapel was known as "the whistling kirk." It was attended by the Dukes of Hamilton, the Lords of Douglas, the Cathcart family, the Pollocs, and the *elité* of Glasgow and vicinity.

**Tron Church.**—In 1540 a Collegiate church, dedicated to St. Mary and St. Michael, was built on the south side of the Trongate; this is the original of the present Tron Church. In 1592, the church, which had been in a dilapidated condition, was repaired, and John Bell appointed its first minister. The present steeple, which is 126 feet high, was built in 1637. In the winter of 1821 the clock dials were illuminated with gas reflectors, the invention of John Hart, pastry baker in the city; this was the first clock so lighted in the Kingdom. The Session House in connection with the church was used for Presbytery meetings and as a guard-house for the burgess night guard. While the city watchers were out on their rounds, some youths who belonged to what they called the "Hell-Fire Club," entered the Session House and began some horse-play which consisted of tearing up the woodwork and throwing it into the fire which soon became a furnace, and, getting beyond control, it ignited the hall, and soon the church was ablaze. Fortunately the steeple was saved. The present church was erected the following year, 1793, at a cost of £4,000, and is still the meeting-place of the Glasgow Presbytery.

**Ramshorn Kirk.**—The name Ramshorn is said to have originated from a miracle St. Mungo performed on the spot in turning a ram's head that had been stolen into stone. Other theories are given, viz.:—(1) That it is the site of Sheep Bughts or Fanks; (2) that when digging the foundations for the church a huge ram's horn was found ; (3) that it has reference to the instruments that occasioned the fall of Jericho.  The lands of Rams-horn and Meadowflat (George Square) were purchased by the Town Council of Glasgow from Ninian Hill of Lambhill on 12th May, 1694, for £1,127 15s. 6⅜d. sterling.  Wm. Stewart & Son, gardeners, Candleriggs, were paid £9 1s. 4½d. sterling in January, 1719, as compensation for damage done to their fruit trees by the preparations for the erection of the Ramshorn Kirk (St. David's) and Churchyard, which was com-menced in 1721, and opened in 1724.  This church, having become insufficient, was taken down in 1824, and the present edifice erected in its place.  The ground to the north of the Trongate, which was used for gardens, and known as the Ramshorn Crofts, was feued by the city in 1775.                          \

**Secession Church.**—The Secession Church was formed by Ebenezer Erskine, in 1733, in Camphill, but subsequently a chapel was built in Inkle Factory Lane, which now forms part of College Street. While this was being erected they assembled in a tent on the north side of the Rottenrow. In 1742 a more commodious place of wor-ship was built in Shuttle Street.  The Rev. James Fisher, the first minister, was appointed the year previous.  The congregation built a new church, at a cost of £8,300, with a fine portico in front, in North Albion Street, in 1821, and it is now known as Greyfriars U.P. Church.

**Blackfriars Church.** — The Black Friars, who came to Glasgow in 1240, had a large monastery to the south of the Old College, in connection with which they nad a handsome chapel, with a steeple similar to that of the Cathedral.  The church, which survived the Reformation, was gifted by the Crown to the University, but between 1660 and 1668 it was so much shattered by lightning that it had to be taken down, and what was called the New Church erected in its stead at a cost of £2,000.  This was the Old College Church that was taken down when the University removed to Gilmorehill.

**St. Andrew's Church;**— St. Andrew's Church, St. Andrew Square, was completed in 1756, at a cost of over £20,000.  It is a copy of St. Martin's-in-the-Fields, London, with the exception of the spire, 160 feet high, which is built on five separate flat arches, with a keystone in the centre of each.  They are placed between the columns, and make a stronger

support than if the architrave carried the weight of the steeple by one arch formed from a single stone.  This explains the so-called mystery.  Mungo Naismith, a mason and self-taught architect, was the builder.  He was grandfather of David Naismith, founder of the City Missions. The Rev. Dr. Ritchie, minister of the church, purchased an organ from John Steven, musicseller, 35 Wilson Street, which had been built by the famous James Watt in his house in High Street, and placed it in St. Andrew's Church.  It was utilised one Sunday, but the Presbytery forbade its further use.  The interdict caused great excitement in the city.  The organ lay for years in the church unused, and was at length taken back to the shop of Mr. Steven, from whom it was pur-chased for about £400 by Bailie Archibald M'Lellan, who removed it to his house in Miller Street, formerly occupied by Colonel Graham.  After the Bailie's death the "Kist o' Whistles" was sent to the auction rooms of Hutchison & Dixon, in the Old Black Bull Buildings, in Virginia Street, where it was "knocked down" to Adam Sim of Coulter Mains, Lanarkshire, for £50. Mr. Peter M'Kenzie, in his *Reminiscences*, says :—"This interesting memento of the great inventor of the steam-engine should be rescued from oblivion and placed in one of the city's treasure-houses."

**Glassites.**—A Glassite Meeting House was opened in 1761.

**Baptist Church.**—The first Baptist congregation was formed in Glasgow in 1769.  They met in a house in High Street, Neil Stewart, wright, and George Begg, weaver, being the founders.  The first person baptised was the wife of the former, who was immersed in the Clyde at the Fleshers' Haugh.

**Independents.**—In 1770 an Indepen-dent congregation was formed in a house in High Street.

**Buchanites.**—Elspeth Buchan, the founder of this sect, was born in 1738. Her father was an innkeeper near Banff. Coming to Glasgow as a servant in her 22nd year, she married a Robert Buchan. Originally an Episcopalian, she became a Burgh seceder on her marriage.  About 1779 she began to interpret certain passages in the Bible in a strictly literal sense. She deserted her husband, and gathered some people around her, who all lived as one family, with one purse.  Hugh White, a relief minister in Irvine, became one of her converts, and the party all went to live in that town, but the natives stormed them out, and they eventually settled in the outhouse of a farm near Thornhill, which they purchased. Elspeth died in May, 1791, declaring she was the Virgin Mary, and would return and conduct her followers to the New Jerusalem. Failing, however, to carry out her good intention, her followers dispersed.

**Roman Catholics.**—In 1778 there were only 30 known Roman Catholics in Glasgow, their only place of worship being an obscure house in High Street. In 1785 Bishop Hay came from Edinburgh, and celebrated Mass in the back room of a house in Blackstock's Close, at the foot of Saltmarket. The Tennis Court in Mitchell Street was transformed into a temporary chapel in 1792. Five years afterwards a small chapel was built in Marshall Street, off the Gallowgate, where it still stands. On 22nd December, 1817, the handsome Gothic structure in Great Clyde Street, known as St. Andrew's Cathedral, was opened, having cost over £13,000 sterling. Some of the finest architecture in the city is to be seen in several of the chapels belonging to the Roman Catholic denomination. In 1898 there were 27 churches and 97 clergymen connected with the body.

**St. Enoch's.**—It is stated that Kentigern's mother followed her son from Culross to Glasgow, where she died, and that she was canonised. Her name was given to a church built outside the West Port or in High Street, St. Thenaw's, now corrupted to St. Enoch's. This is said to be the original of the well-known landmark in St. Enoch Square, the foundation stone of which was laid in 1780 by Provost William French. It was opened two years later having cost £4,000, but in 1827 it was taken down and rebuilt. The present steeple, which is about 150 feet high, was however, not disturbed, and it is consequently 119 years old. It was struck by lightning last year (1898), but fortunately the damage was not very serious.

**Barony.**—The Old Barony Church was built in Infirmary Square on the east side of Castle Street in 1798 at a cost of £2,800. From 1595 the congregation worshipped in the crypt of the Cathedral underneath the choir. The Old Barony will always have a warm corner in the hearts of Glasgow people on account of its association with Dr. Norman Macleod. The old kirk was taken down in 1889, and the present edifice

erected at a cost of about £20,000 at the corner of the Rottenrow and Old Kirk Street on the opposite side of the Square. It was opened on 27th April, 1889.

**Gorbals.**—The old Gorbals Kirk, instituted in 1600, was built in 1732. It was situated in Buchan Street. It was afterwards used by a Gaelic congregation. The present well-known church, which cost £9,000, was built in 1810 on the site of ancient granaries or barns, from which Gorbals takes its name. Owing to a dispute regarding the feu-charter the present kirk fell into the hands of the Free Church body, which necessitated the original possessors meeting in a schoolroom in the vicinity, but the legal difficulty was overcome, and they regained possession of their "own vine and fig tree." Its well-known spire is 174 feet high.

**St. George's.**—St. George's Church was erected (from the designs of William Stark) in Buchanan Street, in 1809, at a cost of £9,000. The original of this place of worship was the Old Wynd Church, built in 1687 by a party of privileged Presbyterians, when Episcopacy prevailed in the city. The church was originally covered with thatch. St. George's steeple is 162½ feet high. It has a bell which bears the following inscription:—" I to the Church the people call, and to the grave I summon all."

**Wellington U.P.** — The original of Wellington U.P. Church was the Relief Kirk, in Cheapside Street, Anderston, founded in 1770. The congregation built a new edifice at the corner of Wellington and Waterloo Streets, in 1827, with a crypt or sepulchral vaults, which entered from West Campbell Street, beneath the church. When the congregation removed to their present handsome edifice at the corner of University Avenue and Ann Street, Hillhead, the bones were removed from beneath the old place of worship—which is now the Waterloo Rooms—and buried in the Necropolis and elsewhere.

**St. Paul's.** — St. Paul's Established Church, in High John Street, was erected by the Town Council in 1836. The congregation had previously worshipped in the nave of the Cathedral from 1648.

**Congregationalists.**—At the close of last century, during the time the brothers Haldane were trying to institute the Congregational movement in the country, the Rev. Greville Ewing, who had his tabernacle in Jamaica Street, became attached to the new cause. In 1803 he was followed by the Rev. Ralph Wardlaw, D.D., who opened a church in North Albion Street. In 1811 a Congregational Theological Training College for Students was opened in the city, Messrs. Ewing and Wardlaw acting as professors. This was transferred to Edinburgh about 1860. Dr. Wardlaw removed to a new church in West George Street. He died on 17th December, 1853, and is buried in the Necropolis. Shortly after his death the Edinburgh and Glasgow Railway Company bought his church for £14,000, and they still use the premises for their offices. This money enabled the congregation to erect their present handsome church—known as Elgin Place—at the corner of Bath and Pitt Streets, where Messrs. Alexander Raleigh, Henry Batchelor, and Albert Goodrich have since acted as pastors. The Congregational body had a bright ornament in the late Rev. Wm. Pulsford, LL.D., who is so ably succeeded at Trinity Church, Claremont Street, by the Rev. John Hunter, D.D. The Congregationalists recently amalgamated with the Evangelical Union, which was founded in 1843 by Dr. James Morison, of Dundas Street E.U. Church, who had been suspended by the Secession Synod from Clark's Lane Church, Kilmarnock.

**Other Churches.**—St. John's Parish Church, in Græme Street, was opened on the 20th September, 1819, at a cost of over £9,000. Its tower is 138 feet high. This church will always be famous for its associations with Dr. Chalmers, who had formerly been minister of the Tron Church from July, 1815, until June, 1819, when he was transferred by the magistrates to St. John's. The name of Edward Irving also casts a romance over this church. St. James's Parish Church, in Great Hamilton Street, was built by the Methodists in 1817, but the Parish of St. James's was constituted by the city in 1820, when the church was bought by the Town Council. Other old churches, with date of erection, are :—Shettleston, 1752; Canon Street, 1766; Anderston Relief, 1770; Greyfriars Wynd Peculiar Independent, 1773; Dovehill, 1774; Ingram Street Gaelic, 1777; George Street Baptist, 1788; South Woodside, 1790; Campbell Street (Original Burgess), 1791; Campbell Street, 1791; Anderston, 1792; Calton, 1793; Campbell Street, 1794; Duke Street Gaelic, 1798; Anderston Chapel, 1799; John Street, 1799; Hutchesontown Relief, 1799.

**Church Statistics, 1899.** — The following is a list of the churches in Glasgow, divided into their various denominations :—Established, 100; Free, 95; United Presbyterian, 96; Episcopal Church of Scotland, 23; Episcopal Church of England, 1; Roman Catholic, 27; Congregational, 25; Baptist, 12; Wesleyan Methodist, 8; Christadelphian, 2; Children of Zion, 1; Primitive Methodist, 4; Church of Christ, 4; Catholic Apostolic, 2; Old Scots Independent, 1; United Original Secession, 3; Unitarian, 2; New Jerusalem, 2; Friends' Meeting-House, 1; Reformed Presbyterian, 1; John Knox Tabernacle, 1; German Protestant, 1; Free English Episcopal, 2; Hebrew, 2; Spiritualists, 1.

## THE CLYDE.

The Clyde rises from the same range of hills, on the borders of Lanarkshire and Dumfriesshire, as the Tweed and Annan, hence the doggerel—

> The Tweed, the Annan, and the Clyde,
> All rise from one hillside.

It is 98 miles long, and drains an area of 945 square miles; passing Lanark, Hamilton, and Rutherglen, ere it reaches Glasgow. In 1450 the Clyde was a pure and fordable stream, consequently useless for navigation, but famous for its fishing.

**Dumbuck Ford.** -- About the year 1556 the inhabitants of Glasgow, Renfrew, and Dumbarton, wrought for six weeks at a time removing a ford at Dumbuck, and some sand banks, which enabled small craft to reach the Broomielaw.

**No Harbour.**—In 1588 there was no harbour, and vessels were simply moored in mid-stream.

**"The Wee Key."**—In 1653 Glasgow had a shipping port at Cunningham in Ayrshire, but on account of its inconvenience, "ane litle Key and weigh-hous was builded ' in 1663, with oak taken from the Cathedral, at the Broomielaw, at a point between the present Custom House and Caledonian Railway Bridge. The erection boasted of a fountain and crane. This served the purpose until 1688, when a larger quay was built at a cost of £1,666 13s. 4d.

**Islands.**—In 1654 there were six small Islands on the Clyde between Stockwell Street and the mouth of the Cart at Renfrew, viz.: (1) opposite Carlton Place; (2) at the mouth of the Kelvin called Water Inch; (3) White Inch—whence the suburb takes its name; (4) Buck Inch, a little lower down; (5) King's Inch, at Elderslie, on which was a castle; (6) Sand Inch, at Renfrew.

**First Deepening.**—The first attempt to deepen the Clyde below the Broomielaw was made in 1740 by means of a "flatt-bottomed boat," which was employed to carry away sand and shingle from the banks in mid-stream, but the effort was futile, and only resulted in £100 being thrown away.

**Port-Glasgow Founded.**—In 1667 Dumbarton refused to give Glasgow ground to build a harbour for fear the influx of mariners would raise the price of provisions in the burgh. Troon also took a similar view. After some negotiation a piece of land was feued in 1668 from Sir Robert Maxwell of Newark, at an annual feu of 4s. 5½d. sterling, on which a pier, the first dry dock, and houses were built, called "Newport, Glasgow," now known as Port-Glasgow.

**1755.**—In 1755 Mr. Smeaton, the engineer, reported that the depth of the Clyde at Pointhouse was 1 foot 3 inches at low water, and 3 feet 8 inches at high tide. On his suggestion an Act was got from Parliament for the construction of a lock, 70 feet long by 18 feet wide, at Marlin Ford, four miles down the river, but the project fell through.

**1756.**—The sanction of Parliament was obtained in 1756 for the erection of a light-house on the "Little Cumray."

**Formation of Clyde Trust.**—Acting on the advice of John Golborne of Chester, an Act was obtained and the work of deepening the Clyde commenced in 1770. On the report of Golborne, confirmed by James Watt, Dr. Wilson, and James Barrie, it was shown that the average depth of water from Glasgow to Kilpatrick Sands was only two feet. Golborne's plan was to contract the channel for eight miles below the city by means of dykes, and dredge the waterway. The estimated cost was £8,640 sterling. The Magistrates and Town Council became Clyde Trustees, with liberty to charge one shilling a ton on all goods from Glasgow to Dumbuck.

**Made Navigable.**—In 1775 vessels drawing six feet of water were able for the first time to come up to the Broomielaw at high tide. Golborne, in deepening the river, erected 117 jetties, and so pleased were the Corporation with the way the work was accomplished—for he deepened the channel 10 inches more than he con-

tracted to do—that they presented him with £1,500 sterling and a silver cup, and also gave his son £100.

**1797.**—360 feet were added to the Broomielaw Quay in 1797.

**Towing Path.**—About 1806 a towing path, 20 feet wide, was constructed on the south bank of the river between Glasgow and Renfrew. This now forms a valuable right of way for the public.

**1809.**—In 1809 the Clyde was deepened to nine feet, at neap tide, between the City and Dumbarton. The Broomielaw Quay was further extended. Parallel dykes were built down the river. Telford, the engineer, suggested that a part of the centre of the river should be converted into a wet dock, but the suggestion was not acted upon.

**1822.**—Four hundred and eighty-two feet were added to the quay at Broomielaw in 1822.

**1825.**—An Act of Parliament in 1825 gave the Magistrates and Council power to add five trustees to the Clyde Trust, and to deepen the river to at least 13 feet between the Broomielaw and Port-Glasgow.

**1836.**—So keenly alive had the Clyde Trustees been to the necessity of continuing the dredging operations, that their engineer was able to report in 1836 that there were 7 to 8 feet of water at ebb tide and 12 feet at neap, and 15 feet at spring tides at the Broomielaw. Shipbuilding was also beginning to develop, and the number of Clyde steamers was "greatly on the increase."

**1840.**—An Act of Parliament was procured in 1840, granting permission to widen the Clyde to its present dimensions. Previous to this, the width of the river at Lancefield Quay was only 150 feet, and at the junction with the Cart 275 feet.

**Dredgings.**—Until the year 1862, the material dredged from the river was loaded on punts and discharged on the adjoining banks, and also below high water level on each side of the old channel below Dumbarton. On 28th August, 1862, the Clyde Trustees commenced depositing in Loch Long from hopper barges. This continued for 25 years, until—on complaint from the residents—it was interdicted by the Board of Trade; and all material, on and after 20th March, 1893, with the exception of the excavations from Princes Dock, had to be carried three mils S.S.W. seaward of Garroch Head. The total quantity dredged from harbour, docks, and river during the year ended 30th June, 1898, was 2,094,137 cubic yards, and the total quantity dredged from 1844 to 30th June, 1898, was 52,796,607 cubic yards. The work is performed by five dredging machines, one floating digger, two diving bells, and 21 steam hopper barges with carrying capacity ranging from 250 to 1,200 tons.

**Present Harbour.** — The present Harbour, nearly two miles in length, is formed by quays on each side of the river, the widths between averaging from 360 to ·620 feet. The following table shows the progress made during the past 100 years:—

1799.

| | |
|---|---|
| Length of quays and wharves | 382 lin. yds. |
| Area of water space - - | 4 acres. |
| Revenue - - - - | £3,319 16 1 |

1898.

| | |
|---|---|
| Length of quays and wharves | 14,568 lin. yds. |
| Area of water space - | 206 acres. |
| Revenue - - - - | £430,327 6 4 |

A large and increasing trade is carried on with all parts of the world. Regular steamship lines trade to Canada, United States, Mediterranean, India and China, and the Continent. Daily communication is kept up with Liverpool, Dublin, Belfast, etc.; and bi-weekly with the West Highlands, Southampton, Bristol, and the South. The Harbour is divided into two sections, called the Upper and Lower Harbours. The Upper Harbour, extending from Glasgow Bridge to Victoria Bridge, has a depth at low water of 10 feet, with the quayage all on the north side of the river, and is chiefly used by vessels in the mineral and coasting trades. Small lighters can also ascend the river for a further distance of two miles, to the numerous works on the banks. The Lower Harbour has a general depth of from 16 to 20 feet at low water, and extends from the mouth of the River Kelvin to Glasgow Bridge, the water area being 111 acres, with 5,116 lineal yards of quayage. From the River Kelvin outwards to Port-Glasgow, a distance of about 16 miles, a navigable channel, with a depth at low water of 20 feet, is maintained.

**Purification.** — The problem of the purification of the river was the subject of investigation in 1853-58-68-76-77-78-79-80-86. Irrigation was favourably thought of at one time. In 1868 a conduit of 28 miles, to the Ayrshire coast, at a cost of £1,250,000, was proposed. This idea was confirmed by a Royal Commission in 1876, but the cost was estimated at an additional million. By way of experiment sewage works were erected at Dalmarnock, on the site of the Old Waterworks, and were opened in May, 1894. The sewage of one-fourth of the city is here dealt with. Subsequently, as the result of the success of the experiment, Parliamentary sanction was obtained to treat the whole of the sewage on the north bank of the Clyde, including Partick, Clydebank, and neighbourhood, in the same way, at an estimated cost of £600,000. It is now proposed to construct a main sewer, nine miles in length, terminating at Dalmuir, on land acquired by the Corporation in 1877, where precipitation tanks and works will deal with the sewage. A new main sewer is also being made to purify the Kelvin, but until the vast area on the south side of the river is also undertaken the pollution of the Clyde will remain a disgrace to the city.

**Cluthas.** — The up-and-down harbour passenger steamers, named "Cluthas," were first introduced in 1884, when six boats were built. There are now, however, twelve plying between Victoria Bridge and Whiteinch Ferry. The full distance covered is about three miles, and the charge one penny. There are eleven landing stages on the route, alternately placed to suit both sides of the river. The time taken for the whole journey is 45 minutes. The number of passengers carried during the year ended 30th June, 1897, was 2,795,671, and the revenue £11,648 4s. 3d.

**Cross Ferries.** — Below Glasgow Bridge all cross-river communication is carried on by means of steam ferries, except at Finnieston, where there is also a tunnel, owned and worked by a private company. The first steam ferry was introduced in 1865. There are now ten of these boats. The landings, seven in number, are about a quarter of a mile apart. The ferries carry each about 100 passengers, and cost about £1,250. Service is maintained day and night. There are besides two special ferries—at Finnieston and Govan—which carry vehicles and passengers. That at Finnieston, opened in 1890, is an elevating deck ferry, built to obviate inclined roadways or slips, having the deck so constructed that it can be raised or lowered to suit the tide. It is propelled by twin screws at each end, and carries 300 passengers and eight loaded vehicles and horses. Govan Ferry is of an older type, the accesses being by inclined roadways or slips, and it propels itself along two chains stretched across the river.

**Harbour Tunnel.** — Parliamentary powers were obtained for this tunnel in 1889, and a company floated in August of the same year, with a share capital of £135,000, and borrowing powers to the extent of £45,000. The work was commenced in May, 1890, and it was opened for traffic in July, 1895. There are three separate tunnels devoted to north-going and south-going vehicular and foot-passenger traffic, the approaches to them being by hydraulic lifts for vehicles, and stairs for passengers.

**Cranes.**—Until 1883 the heaviest crane possessed by the Clyde Trustees had a lifting capacity of 75 tons. The increased size of boilers and engines rendered heavier lifting power necessary. A crane capable of negotiating a load of 130 tons was placed on Finnieston Quay at a cost of £16,000. It was officially tested on 3rd May, 1893. Another 130 ton crane was erected at the West Quay, Prince's Dock, at a similar cost. There are about 100 cranes in the Harbour, with lifts varying from 35 cwts. to 130 tons.

**Kingston Dock.**—The Kingston Dock, the first constructed on the Clyde, was opened on 10th December, 1867. It is made on what was formerly called Windmill Croft, 10 acres of which were purchased by the Clyde Trust for £40,000. The dock, costing £115,000 more, is a tidal basin with a water space of over five and a third acres, is 13 feet deep at low water, and has 830 lineal yards of quayage. A swing bridge worked by steam spans the entrance, which is 60 feet wide.

**Queen's Dock.**—In 1845 the Clyde Trustees bought 35 acres at Stobcross, and next year obtained Parliamentary sanction to construct a dock. Nothing was done until 1864, when the Edinburgh and Glasgow Railway Company got a bill to make a branch line from their Helensburgh line to a station to the north of the proposed dock. This new scheme was going to interfere with the undertaking, and, after considerable negotiation, which was ratified by Parliament in 1870, the proposed line was diverted further north, the trustees agreeing to extend their dock and give a loan of £150,000 to the Railway Company towards the making of the line. The dock was commenced in August, 1872, and completed, at a total cost of £1,500,000, on 20th March, 1880, when the copestone was laid by Lord Provost Collins. The great undertaking was, however, formally opened by Lord Provost Bain on 18th September, 1877, when the Anchor liner "Victoria" entered the tidal basin. It was named the Queen's Dock by special permission of Her Majesty. It is spanned at the entrance, which is 100 feet wide, by

a hydraulic swing bridge. The dock has a water area of 33¾ acres, and 3,334 yards of quayage, with a depth of 20 feet at low water.

**Prince's Dock.**—This tidal dock, the latest addition to the port, formerly known as Cessnock Dock by being constructed on the lands of Cessnock, is situated on the south side of the river, in the burgh of Govan. It was renamed the Prince's Dock by H.R.H. the Duchess of York on 10th September, 1897. It has a water area of 35 acres, including a canting basin of 15½ acres and three inner basins with a total length of quayage of 3,737 yards, or fully two miles; the entrance is 155 feet wide. There are commodious two-storey storing sheds, and a magnificent hydraulic installation for working cranes, capstans, etc. The south quay is solely devoted to mineral traffic. The depth of water ranges from 20 to 28 feet at low water and 31 to 39 feet at high water. The total cost, inclusive of land, equipment, and dredging, was £1,250,000.

**Graving Docks.**—In 1868 Parliamentary sanction was obtained to construct the first public graving dock in Govan. It was begun in 1869, and opened in 1875. It is 551 feet long and 72 feet wide at entrance, with 22 feet 10 inches of water at high tide. The development of the harbour necessitated the construction of a second dock, which was opened on 13th October, 1886. It is 575 feet long, 67 feet wide at entrance, and 22 feet 10 inches deep on sill at high water. The requirements of the port demanded still further accommodation, and accordingly dock No. 3 was commenced on 12th September, 1890. It is 880 feet long, and can be divided by steel gates, thus making two docks, the inner 420 feet long and the outer 460 feet. It is 83 feet at entrance, with a water depth of 26 feet 6 inches on sill at spring tides, and can accommodate the largest vessel afloat. The copestone was laid by H.R.H. the Duke of York on 10th September, 1897, and the dock was officially opened by Lord Provost Richmond on 27th April, 1898.

**Proposed New Docks.**—Bills are at present being promoted in Parliament for the construction of new tidal docks at Shieldhall and Clydebank, at a cost of about £1,800,000.

**Timber and Cattle Wharves.**—A depôt, situated at Yorkhill, is wholly devoted to the timber trade, which has so much increased that the old Cattle Wharf at Shieldhall and adjoining lands have been utilised for this growing business. The Cattle Lairage is now placed to the east of Yorkhill Wharf. It is under control of the local authorities.

### Revenue of the Clyde Trust.—The

following table shows at a glance the progress of Clyde Trust revenue :—

| Year. | | | | | £ | s. | d. |
|---|---|---|---|---|---|---|---|
| 1770 | . | . | . | . | 147 | 0 | 10 |
| 1780 | . | . | . | . | 1,515 | 8 | 4 |
| 1790 | . | . | . | . | 2,239 | 0 | 4 |
| 1800 | . | . | . | . | 3,319 | 16 | 1 |
| 1810 | . | . | . | . | 6,677 | 7 | 6 |
| 1820 | . | . | . | . | 6,328 | 18 | 10 |
| 1830 | . | . | . | . | 20,296 | 18 | 6 |
| 1840 | . | . | . | . | 46,536 | 14 | 0 |
| 1850 | . | . | . | . | 64,243 | 14 | 11 |
| 1860 | . | . | . | . | 97,983 | 18 | 1 |
| 1870 | . | . | . | . | 164,093 | 2 | 10 |
| 1875 | . | . | . | . | 196,326 | 18 | 10 |
| 1880 | . | . | . | . | 223,709 | 0 | 8 |
| 1885 | . | . | . | . | 291,658 | 4 | 11 |
| 1890 | . | . | . | . | 356,202 | 11 | 3 |
| 1895 | . | . | . | . | 353,813 | 6 | 2 |
| 1898 | . | . | . | . | 430,327 | 6 | 4 |

**Weirs**—The first weir on the river was constructed in the year 1772. It was situated a little below the new "Jamaica" Bridge, was composed of rough stones, and was built to preserve the bridge foundations against the scour of the river, these foundations not being made deep enough in the original construction of the bridge. The weir remained until 1842, when it was removed to the under side of the old "Stockwell" Bridge. But it was not destined to remain long in this position. In 1852 it was removed to its present position above the "Albert" Bridge. It was provided with a reach 74½ feet long by 25 feet wide, with a double pair of gates, and cost in all £6,000. The Clyde Trustees were exempted from maintaining the weir after the introduction of the Glasgow Corporation Waterworks Act, 1855. On 16th August, 1866, the Glasgow Water Commissioners obtained Parliamentary powers for the demolition of the weir and lock, and this was ultimately accomplished in 1884. The result was disastrous to the banks of the river. In consequence of the heavy expenditure entailed by the riparian proprietors, the Corporation were compelled to spend £50,000 in repairing and strengthening the foreshores along the entire extent of the municipal boundaries. Parliamentary sanction was obtained in 1894 to erect a new weir—the fourth—on the movable sluice principle, to cost £45,000. It resembles in appearance an ordinary arch bridge of three spans, with openings of about 80 feet, and headway 18 feet above ordinary high-water level at centre of arches. No lock will be provided, but the river traffic will be able to pass under the sluices.

### RIVERS.

**Kelvin.**—The Kelvin takes its rise in the Kilsyth Hills; it flows past Kirkintilloch and Maryhill, through the Botanic Gardens and West-end Park, and joins the Clyde at Partick. It is crossed by the following bridges within the city area, viz., Canniesburn Road, Bridge Street, Maryhill, Kelvindale Road, Ford Road (foot, opened July, 1886), Botanic Gardens (foot, opened 1895), Queen Margaret (1870), Belmont (1870), Great Western Road (29th September, 1891), Woodlands Road (1895), Prince of Wales (June, 1895), Kelvingrove Park (1881), Dumbarton Road (old bridge), Dumbarton Road (1877), Old Dumbarton Road (1896).

**Cart.**—The White Cart rises above Eaglesham, and passing Busby, it flows through Cathcart, Langside, Pollokshaws, and Paisley, and joining the Black Cart, which rises in Lochwinnoch, at Inchinnan, flows into the Clyde opposite Clydebank.

### BURNS.

**Molendinar Burn.**—In 1450 the Molendinar was a pellucid stream having its rise in Hogganfield Loch, and abounding in trout. It flows past the Cathedral, across the Gallowgate, past the Episcopal Chapel, and joins the Clyde opposite the Justiciary Buildings, where it can still be seen emerging in the form of a common sewer.

**St. Enoch's Burn.**—St. Enoch's Burn rose in the vicinity of St. Rollox, and meandered round by Cowcaddens, crossed Sauchiehall Street, ran down West Nile Street, and joined the Clyde opposite the Custom House.

**Kinning House Burn.**—The Kinning House Burn, which was also known as the "Mile" Burn and the "Shiels" Burn, flowed past Strathbungo, through Pollokshields, and acted as the county boundary on the south-west of the city until it lost itself in the Clyde beside the General Terminus.

**Camlachie Burn.**—The Camlachie Burn flowed from Carntyne, via Barrowfield Toll, through the Green to the north of Nelson's Monument. Its waters filled the dam used in connection with the washing-houses. It joined the Molendinar near the Episcopal Chapel in Greendyke Street.

**Blind Burn.**—The Blind Burn, which rose in Langside, flowed through Hutchesontown to the Clyde to the east of the Albert Bridge. It formed the eastern boundary of Gorbals.

**Mallsmire Burn.**—Mallsmire Burn, more commonly known as "Jenny's Burn," takes its rise in the lands of Aitkenhead, near Cathcart. It acts as the south-east city boundary, and runs through Mallsmire and Toryglen. It may be seen merging in the Clyde to the west of Rutherglen Bridge opposite the Flesher's Haugh.

**Pinkston Burn.**—The Pinkston Burn was a pellucid stream which flowed through the west of the city. Its waters were used by bleach-works in the Anderston district.

**Calton Burn.**—A burn flowed through Calton towards the east *via* Risk, Green, and Tobago Streets, and joined the Camlachie Burn. It is now doing duty as a common sewer.

**Poldrait Burn.**—The Poldrait Burn rose in the higher reaches of Parkhead; it flowed parallel with the Gallowgate, and joined the Molendinar between the Old and New Vennels.

---

## SHIPPING.

**Early Shipping.**—Before the Clyde was deepened ships loaded and discharged their cargoes at Port-Glasgow. Flat-bottomed boats conveyed the merchandise between that port and the Broomielaw.

**1735.**—The ships for the year 1735 numbered sixty-seven, with an aggregate tonnage of 5,600 tons. Fifteen of them were for Virginia, four for Jamaica, two for Antigua, two for St. Kitts, six for London, three for Boston, four for Straits Settlements, one for Gibraltar, one for Barbadoes, two for Holland, seven for Stockholm, and the remainder for the coasting and Irish trades.

**Henry Bell.**—The name of Henry Bell is synonymous with the first steamboat, although it must not be overlooked that ten years previous to Bell's invention, Symington constructed a steamboat named the "Charlotte Dundas," which plied on the Forth and Clyde Canal, at a speed of six miles an hour, and was only abandoned because the Canal directors feared it would damage the banks. Henry Bell was born in Torphichen on 7th April, 1767, and came to Glasgow in 1790, where he wrought as a house carpenter. He commenced business as a builder in Helensburgh in 1808, his wife keeping an inn and public baths. While there he applied himself to the

study of the steamboat, with the result he designed a boat to carry forty passengers, 40 feet long 12 feet broad, to draw 4 feet of water. It was built by John Wood and Co., carpenters, Port-Glasgow; the engine, of 4 horse-power, was made by John Robertson, and the boiler by David Napier, both of Glasgow, the total cost being £192. On 12th January, 1812, under the name of "The Comet," it commenced to ply between Glasgow, Greenock, and Helensburgh. This was followed within two years by the "Elizabeth," 30 tons, 10 h.p.; "Clyde," 65 tons, 14 h.p.; "Glasgow," 64 tons, 14 h.p. These were the pioneers of our war leviathans and ocean greyhounds. Bell, who latterly received an annuity from the Clyde Trust, died in Helensburgh in 1830. A monument is erected to his memory on the banks of the Clyde, at Dunglass Castle, west of Bowling, while his portrait hangs in the Clyde Trust Hall.

**First Ship to India.**—Messrs. Finlay and Co. (who still carry on business in West Nile Street) despatched "The Earl of Buckingham," a ship of 600 tons, with a cargo of Glasgow manufactures to India in 1816. The vessel returned the following year with a valuable load of Indian produce.

**Napier's Improved Steam Navigation.**—In November, 1817, the small steamer "Marion" was improved so much by David Napier, that it steamed through the Glasgow bridges against a strong current, a feat previously impossible.

**Shipbuilding and Engineering in 1850.**—The city was beginning to make great strides in shipping about 1850. The Clyde had been deepened to accommodate vessels drawing 18 feet of water, and steamships plied to London, Liverpool, and Ireland. David Napier was doing a thriving business in marine engineering and shipbuilding by this time. He had invented the tapering bows on vessels. Between 1846 and 1853, 14 wooden and 233 iron steamships were built on the Clyde. In 1854 the river was dredged to a depth of 19 feet. The first iron steamer was built on the Clyde in 1827 for Loch Eck, while the first to ply on the Clyde was the "Fairy Queen" in 1831.

**Pioneers of Shipbuilding.**—The principal shipbuilding firm in the fifties was Robert Napier, who built his first ironclad, the "Erebus," during the Crimean

War. He also supplied the engines for the "Terror." In 1859 he built the armoured steam frigate the "Black Prince," of 6,040 tons and 800 h.p.; while Messrs. Wood, Port - Glasgow, and Tod & M'Gregor, Meadowbank, Partick, also did a thriving business. Marine engineering had able representatives in Barclay, Curle & Co., Whiteinch, and Randolph, Elder & Co. John Elder served his apprenticeship with Robert Napier, and joined Charles Randolph in business in 1852.

**Emigration.**—During 1880 the Anchor Line alone carried 12,000 saloon and 50,000 second cabin and steerage passengers to the United States. Since then emigration has gradually declined.

**The "Livadia."** — Nothing in the history of shipbuilding caused more talk at the time than a yacht built by John Elder & Co. for the late Emperor of Russia, from the design of Admiral Popoff of the Russian Navy. The "Livadia" was a luxuriously fitted yacht, built on a turbot shaped foundation; she was 235 feet long, 153 feet broad, with a draught of 6 feet 6 inches, and 7,700 tonnage. The launch took place on 7th July, 1880, and was attended by the designer and the Grand Duke Alexis of Russia. Upon the death of the Czar this "yachting curio" was discarded.

**"America" Cup.**—In 1851 a cup was won in South of England waters by the yacht "America," an American-owned vessel, and between that date and 1886 the holders were challenged on seven occasions by British yachtsmen; the challengers in every instance were unsuccessful. In 1887 a syndicate, headed by ex-Lord Provost Sir James Bell, Bart., had a yacht built in Messrs. D. & W. Henderson's shipbuilding yard, Meadowside, Partick, designed by G. L. Watson, for the purpose of endeavouring to bring back the cup to the old country. After a gallant attempt the Clyde-built "Thistle" had to acknowledge the superiority of the Yankee "Volunteer." In 1893 the Earl of Dunraven made another bid for the trophy with "Valkyrie II.," built by Messrs. D. & W. Henderson, and designed by G. L. Watson; but the American yacht "Vigilant" was again successful in retaining the cup. "Valkyrie II." was unfortunately run into and sunk at Hunter's Quay, after her return home; she was lifted and taken to Finnieston Quay, Glasgow, and broken up. The next contest was in September, 1895, when "Valkyrie III.," also by the same builders and designer, was defeated by the American yacht "Defender."

**Liners.**—The following leading lines of ships have their headquarters in the city, viz. :—

STEAMSHIPS.

| | No. of Vessels. | Tonnage. |
|---|---|---|
| Clan Line............ | 41 | 79,863 |
| Anchor Line........ | 32 | 68,860 |
| Allan Line........... | 32 | 68 443 |
| Burrell & Son...... | 27 | 57,901 |
| Maclay & M'Intyre | 47 | 51,982 |
| City Line............ | 21 | 42,212 |
| Donaldson Line... | 9 | 21,102 |
| J. & P. Hutcheson | 11 | 4,310 |

SAILING VESSELS.

| | | |
|---|---|---|
| The Shire Line.... | 27 | 39,872 |
| The Loch Line.... | 16 | 24,305 |
| The Port Line...... | 10 | 16,489 |
| The County Line. | 9 | 16,210 |

In addition to the above, there is a large number of smaller firms trading within the United Kingdom.

**Tonnage from 1597 to 1898.**—The following is a list of the tonnage of shipping owned in, or on the register at, Glasgow at various periods from 1597 until 1898 :—

| Year. | Tons. | Year. | Tons. |
|---|---|---|---|
| 1597 ... | 296 | 1851 ... | 145,684 |
| 1656 ... | 957 | 1861 ... | 218,684 |
| 1692 ... | 1,182 | 1865 ... | 329,752 |
| 1811 ... | 2,620 | 1871 ... | 433,016 |
| 1820 ... | 6,131 | 1875 ... | 582,191 |
| 1825 ... | 31,089 | 1880 ... | 776,780 |
| 1830 ... | 39,432 | 1885 ... | 1,069,505 |
| 1835 ... | 59,151 | 1890 ... | 1,274,021 |
| 1840 ... | 87,707 | 1895 ... | 1,525,326 |
| 1846 ... | 134,603 | 1898 ... | 1,586,743 |

**Shipbuilding from 1852 to 1898.**—For the seven years closing with 1852, the total tonnage launched on the Clyde was 147,604 tons, giving an average of fully 21,000 tons a year.

| Year. | Tons. | Year. | Tons. |
|---|---|---|---|
| 1859 ... | 35,709 | 1879 ... | 157,605 |
| 1860 ... | 47,833 | 1880 ... | 241,114 |
| 1861 ... | 66,801 | 1881 ... | 341,032 |
| 1862 ... | 69,967 | 1882 ... | 301,934 |
| 1863 ... | 123,262 | 1883 ... | 419,664 |
| 1864 ... | 178,505 | 1884 ... | 296,854 |
| 1865 ... | 153,932 | 1885 ... | 193,453 |
| 1866 ... | 124,513 | 1886 ... | 172,440 |
| 1867 ... | 108,024 | 1887 ... | 185,362 |
| 1868 ... | 169,571 | 1888 ... | 280,037 |
| 1869 ... | 192,310 | 1889 ... | 335,201 |
| 1870 ... | 180,401 | 1890 ... | 349,995 |
| 1871 ... | 196,229 | 1891 ... | 326,475 |
| 1872 ... | 230,347 | 1892 ... | 336,414 |
| 1873 ... | 232,926 | 1893 ... | 280,160 |
| 1874 ... | 262,430 | 1894 ... | 340,885 |
| 1875 ... | 211,482 | 1895 ... | 360,152 |
| 1876 ... | 174,824 | 1896 ... | 410,841 |
| 1877 ... | 169,383 | 1897 ... | 340,037 |
| 1878 ... | 211,989 | 1898 ... | 466,832 |

**Launches.** — The following list is typical of the principal launches in their class since 1864:—

SHIPS.

| | | | |
|---|---|---|---|
| 1881—s.s. | "Servia" | ... ... | Clydebank. |
| 1881— | ,, "Alaska" | ... ... | Fairfield. |
| 1884— | ,, "America" | ... ... | ,, |
| 1884— | ,, "Etruria" | ... | ,, |
| 1888— | ,, "New York" | ... | Clydebank. |
| 1889— | ,, "Paris" | ... ... | ,, |
| 1892—H.M.S. | "Ramillies" | ... ... | |
| 1893—s.s. | "Campania" | ... | Fairfield. |
| 1893— | ,, "Lucania" | ... ... | ,, |
| 1894— | ,, "Tantallon Castle" | | ,, |
| 1895—H.M.S. | "Terrible" | ... | Clydebank. |
| 1895— | ,, "Jupiter" | | ,, |
| 1896— | ,, "Dido" | ... ... | Lon.'& Glasg. Ld. |
| 1897— | ,, "Europa" | ... | Clydebank. |
| 1898— | ,, "Argonaut" | ... | Fairfield. |
| 1898—s.s. | "Maplemore" | ... | C. Connell & Co. |
| 1898— | ,, "Pinemore" | ... ... | ,, |
| 1899—Japanese Govt., | "Asahi" | | Clydebank. |

PADDLE STEAMERS.

| | | | |
|---|---|---|---|
| 1864—"Iona" | ... ... ... | Clydebank. |
| 1878—"Columba" | ... | ,, |
| 1883—"Meg Merrilees" | ... | Barclay, Curle. |
| 1889—"Galatea" | ... ... | Caird & Co. |
| 1890—"Adder" | ... ... | Fairfield. |
| 1892—"Glen Sannox" | ... | Clydebank. |
| 1894—"La Marguerite" | ... | Fairfield. |
| 1895—"Redgauntlet" | ... ... | Barclay, Curle. |
| 1895—"Duchess of Rothesay" | | Clydebank. |
| 1896—"Jupiter" | ... ... | ,, |
| 1897—"Empress Queen" | ... | Fairfield. |

YACHTS.

| | | |
|---|---|---|
| 1883—"Capercailzie" (steam). |
| 1886—"Vanduara" (sailing). |
| 1890—"Iverna" (sailing). |
| 1891—"Thistle" (sailing) | ... | Henderson. |
| 1891—"Valkyrie I." (sailing)... | | ,, |
| 1893—"Valkyrie II." (sailing) | | ,, |
| 1895—"Valkyrie III."(sailing) | | ,, |
| 1896—"Nahama" (steam) | ... | Inglis. |
| 1899—"Gleniffer" (sailing) | ... | Henderson. |

## BRIDGES.

**Victoria or Stockwell**—*First Bridge.* — Bishop William Rae in 1350 caused the wooden bridge across the Clyde (which is twice referred to by Blind Harry as having been used by Sir William Wallace) to be pulled down, and at his own expense constructed a handsome stone erection of eight arches, 12 feet wide, which was called Glasgow Bridge for about 500 years. At the time it was considered one of the finest in the kingdom. Lady Lochow assisted the Bishop by bearing the expense of one arch.

*No Wheels.* — After 300 years' traffic it is not to be wondered that an order was passed on 18th September, 1658, preventing carts on wheels crossing the bridge, the wheels requiring to be taken off and the carts "harled" by the horse.

*Accident.* — During the Fair holidays on 7th July, 1671, the southmost arch fell. Fortunately no one was injured.

3.

*Widened.* — In 1777 the bridge was widened 10 feet on the eastern side, and the two north arches built up to prevent danger in times of spates on the river.

*Present Bridge.* — In 1821 the old bridge was overhauled; but in 1847, owing to the great increase of traffic, the grand old erection—which is to be seen in all the old maps of Glasgow—was removed, and the present bridge built. During the operations a wooden accommodation bridge was placed alongside at a cost of £3,149 5s. 6d. This temporary erection was opened in January, 1847.

**Jamaica**—*First Bridge.*—The foundation stone of the first Jamaica bridge was laid with masonic honours by Provost George Murdoch on 29th September, 1768. The architect was William Mylne. The new bridge was opened for traffic on 2nd January, 1772.

*Second Bridge.*—The growth of the City was so great during the next 65 years that the first bridge became quite inadequate. It was therefore resolved to take it down. The foundation stone of what is now designated the old Jamaica bridge was laid with masonic honours by James Ewing, the senior M.P. for the City, on 3rd September, 1833. It had seven arches, was 560 feet long, 60 feet wide, and cost £38,000, which included £4,000 for extra ground. It was opened in 1836. Telford was the engineer, his work being afterwards known as "Telford's masterpiece." During the building operations, a temporary wooden bridge was erected opposite South Portland Street.

*Present Bridge.*—The phenomenal increase of traffic again demanded increased accommodation. A temporary bridge was erected in 1895 immediately to the east of the old one, which was closed on 3rd June of that year and taken down, and the building of the new one begun. The memorial stone was laid by the Lord Provost, Sir James Bell, on 8th October, 1896. The new bridge, which is 80 feet wide, with seven arches, was opened by Lady Richmond on 24th May, 1899, in commemoration of the 80th birthday of Her Most Gracious Majesty Queen Victoria. The material of the old bridge was used in the new erection as far as possible. The estimated cost was £80,000.

**Rutherglen**—*First Bridge.*—Rutherglen Bridge was erected in 1776, at a cost of £1,800, towards which the ancient Royal Burgh contributed £1,000. The previous mode of communication was by means of a ford. Previous to the bridge being opened, the adjacent village was called Barrowfield, but in honour of the event, the name was changed to Bridgeton.

*Present Bridge.* — The old bridge having become antiquated, it was taken down, and a new bridge, 60 feet wide, with three granite arches, erected in its stead, at a cost of about £73,500, of which the city paid £58,145 9s. 1d., the balance being defrayed by the County Council and Burgh of Rutherglen. The new structure was opened on 7th August, 1896. During the building operations a temporary wooden bridge was erected alongside.

**Dalmarnock Road.** — The present bridge across the Clyde connecting Dalmarnock Road with Rutherglen was opened on 6th May, 1891.

**Hutchesontown or Albert—** *Swept Away.*—In 1792 the patrons of Hutcheson's Hospital agreed to subscribe £2,000 towards the expense of erecting a bridge to connect their new suburb with the city at the Green, the new structure to be 406 feet long, 26 feet wide, having five arches. Lord Provost Gilbert Hamilton laid the foundation stone on 18th June, 1794. When the Bridge was half finished, on 18th November, 1795, during a great flood on the river, two of the arches were swept away, and the rest of the structure left in ruins.

*Wooden Erection.* — There was no accommodation until 1803, when Hutcheson's Hospital erected a wooden foot-bridge, 340 feet long and 7 feet 4 inches broad, to temporarily substitute the one swept away. A pontage of one halfpenny was exacted from people crossing the temporary erection.

*Queen Caroline Demonstration.*—The introduction of the Pains and Penalties Bill in the House of Lords, at the request of George IV., against his unfortunate wife, Queen Caroline, caused a general revulsion throughout the country. At the instance of Mr. Peter Mackenzie, then a young lawyer's clerk, 35,000 inhabitants signed an address of sympathy to the persecuted Royal Consort, who returned a grateful letter of thanks. When the news arrived that the obnoxious bill was withdrawn, bonfires and illuminations became general. The magistrates called out the military, and read the Riot Act. The dragoons charged the crowd at the foot of the Saltmarket, and the people

rushing upon the temporary wooden bridge at Hutchesontown, it broke down, and the unfortunates fell into the river; luckily the tide was out and no one was drowned.

*First Stone Bridge.* — The wooden erection became crazy, and a new stone bridge was erected in 1830. The foundation stone was laid by Preceptor Robert Dalglish on 18th August, 1829.

*Present Bridge.* — The last bridge does not appear to have been a particularly substantial structure, for within forty years it was condemned, and closed on the 20th June, 1868. People were accommodated by a temporary wooden erection to the west of the doomed masonry. The foundation stone of the present bridge was laid with masonic honours by the Earl of Dalhousie on 3rd June, 1870, when the Earl was presented with the Freedom of the City. The bridge was called after the late Prince Consort, and was opened on 21st June, 1871, having cost about £50,000.

**Suspension.**—When the old Jamaica Bridge was being erected in 1833, a temporary wooden bridge was built at the foot of South Portland Street; after thirteen years it became unsafe, and was taken down. The heritors of Gorbals erected the present Suspension Bridge on the same site in 1853 at a cost of £6,000. For a few years passengers were required to pay a toll of one halfpenny when crossing.

**St. Andrew's.**—St. Andrew's Suspension Bridge was erected at the Green in 1855. Previous to this a ferry was the only means workers had to get to their employment. The new bridge was long known as "Harvey's," in memory of Bailie Harvey, who was the means of its erection.

**Proposed Bridges.** — It has been proposed to re-erect the present temporary bridge at Jamaica Street further up the Clyde, in a line with Govan Street. It is also proposed to put a footbridge at Oatlands or Polmadie Road. There is also talk of a bridge to the west of Jamaica Street.

---

## INCIDENTAL.

**Burgh of Barony.**—Bishop Joceline was a great favourite with King William the Lion, from whom he obtained a charter creating Glasgow a Burgh of Barony about 1180, fixing the weekly market day upon Thursday, and appointing a fair to be held for eight days, commencing on 6th July of each year. It was originally held at the Bell o' the Brae in High Street, and afterwards at the foot of the Saltmarket. The fair grounds are now situated at Vinegar Hill, Camlachie.

**Toll Exemption.**—About 1220 Bishop Walter obtained exemption for Glasgow from toll or custom, previously levied by the Royal Burghs of Rutherglen and Dumbarton.

**First Magistrates.**—In 1268 the first mention of the magistracy of the town is made, *viz.*, Richard de Dunidovis, Alex. Pathie, and Wm. Gleig.

**Mint.**—A mint house stood in the Drygate, immediately adjoining the old Bridewell, where some coins of King Robert III. were struck. On the obverse is the King's head, with a crown, and the words, *Robertus Dei Gratia Rex Scotorum*; and on the reverse outer circle, *Dominus Protector*; inner circle, *Villa di Glasgow*.

**Early Dress and Language.**—In the fifteenth century women wore coarse close-fitting gowns, with a handkerchief tied on their head. Men wore "hodden grey" short trousers, woollen bonnets, and covered their feet with undressed animals' skins. The educated spoke in Latin, and the vulgar used the vernacular.

**Trone (Gait).**—About the year 1500 a weighing machine or "trone" was erected under a Royal Charter in St. Thenaw's Gate, which ran from the Cross to the West Port. This led to the street being called the Tronegait.

**Provost = Deputes.** — The following were Provost-Deputes in Glasgow from 1430 until 1540, viz. :— Sir Thomas Stuart of Minto, Sir John Stuart of Minto, Sir Robert Stuart of Minto, Archibald Dunbar of Baldoon, Lord Belhaven, John Stuart of Minto, and Andrew Hamilton of Middop.

**Honorary Provost.** — The second Earl of Lennox was the Honorary Provost of Glasgow. About 1510 he resided in a house which he purchased in the Stable Green Port. The Earl and his depute in office, Sir John Stuart of Minto, and the Dean of Glasgow, were all killed at the Battle of Flodden, on 9th September, 1513.

**Early Feus.**—In 1518 Archbishop Beaton feued to Donald Sym, the new Walkmill in "Partik;" to Wat Stuart, the one-mark land of "Gwuan;" to Alan Heriot, "Ramys Horne" and Meadowflat (now George Square); to Jhone and Tome Gayne, land in "Kew Kadens."

**Martyrs.**—Jerom Russel and John Kennedy (of Ayr) were burned for reformation principles at the east of the Cathedral in 1538. James Risley had previously suffered a similar fate for the same cause in 1507.

**Burgesses.**—In 1576 strangers were required to pay £1 2s. 2⅔d. to become burgesses. The sons and sons-in-law of burgesses got the privilege for 8s. 4d. Next year, however, the strangers' fee was raised to £1 13s. 4d.

**Wappenschaw.**—In March, 1577, the Town Council passed a bye-law fining anyone 20s. Scots or 1s. 8d. sterling who absented himself from the wappenschaw, which was held on what is now the old barracks ground in the Gallowgate.

**Bye-laws in 1580.**—The following are a few of the bye-laws passed by the Town Council about 1580, *viz.* :—No salmon to be taken from the Clyde on Sundays. No one to have too large gatherings at their marriage, and the amount spent not to exceed 1s. 6d. a head. Shop doors to be closed and butchers to refrain from killing during time of church service on Wednesdays and Fridays. The holding of Christmas Day forbidden. Women were not allowed to occupy the same seats as the men in the Cathedral; they were either to sit "laigh" or bring stools with them, and were not allowed to wear shawls on their heads. The vicar of Inchinnan, near Renfrew, granted divorce by putting the husband and wife out by separate doors of his kirk; and before anyone could get married they required to have their parents' sanction, and had to learn and repeat the confession of faith, the ten commandments, and the Lord's prayer. On 26th December, 1591, a marriage was prevented owing to the intending Benedict failing in this task. Owing to inconvenience marriages were prohibited on Sunday forenoons, the afternoon being considered more suitable for the ceremony.

**Feus in 1588.**—Ground was feued in Stockwell and Greenhead in 1588 at 6⅔d. sterling an acre.

**First Poor Rates.**—The first poor rates were levied on 3rd July, 1595.

**City and Barony Parishes.**—On 21st July, 1599, the city was divided into two parishes—the City and the Barony. The former worshipped in the choir of the Cathedral and the latter in the crypt.

**Election of Magistrates.**—At the beginning of 1600 King James VI. gave the inhabitants liberty to elect their own magistrates, but owing to the jealousies that existed between the merchants and craftsmen the privilege had to be withdrawn in 1607.

**Hangman.**—A novel way was taken to secure a hangman. On 7th September, 1605, a certain John M'Clelland, who was under sentence of death, was offered his liberty if he accepted the post. The appointment was, however, very unpopular with the people, and an Enactment was passed penalising any one who annoyed him £5 Scots (or 8s. 4d. sterling).

**Frost.**—On 26th May, 1607, Ninian Anderson rented Glasgow (now Stockwell) Bridge as tollman for £17 10s. He, however, received an abatement of £3 6s. 8d. on account of the Clyde being frozen over for fifteen weeks.

**Archery.**—In April, 1611, archery was the only pastime apprentices and scholars were allowed to indulge in.

**Royal Burgh.**—By Act of the Scottish Parliament, on 17th November, 1641, Glasgow was made a Royal Burgh under a charter granted by King Charles I. on 16th October, 1636.

**Poor Rates Defaulters**—On 26th October, 1639, it was intimated by sound of drum that the poor rates defaulters would have their belongings confiscated for double the amount of their tax, and their names openly published in the kirks.

**First Map of Glasgow.**—James Colquhoun was paid £1 sterling for drawing the "first portrait of Glasgow," on 12th June, 1641.

**Irish Immigration.**—The early immigration of the Irish people to Glasgow is shown in a request from the magistrates to the citizens on 5th March, 1642, for contributions on behalf of the distressed people from the Green Isle.

**Trenches.**—On 9th May, 1646, the inhabitants were ordered to work at making trenches round the city every Monday.

**Psalms in Metre.**—The metrical version of the Psalms was used for the first time in Glasgow on 15th May, 1650.

**Cleansing.**—On 5th May, 1655, people were ordered to clear the gutters in front of their doors in the Trongate, owing to the necessity of placing stepping stones in the water and mud before their dwellings could be entered.

**Carters' Charges.**—On 17th October, 1655, a legal charge was fixed for carters, who had been extortionate.

**Coal Pits.**—The Council leased coal pits in Gorbals to Patrick Bryce and James Andersone in 1655. The lessees were, however, restricted from charging more than 4d. a hutch, and employing more than eight "hewars." In 1786 coals were sold by the weight instead of by the measure.

**A Good Turn.**—On the 26th March, 1656, the City Treasurer was repaid £10 sterling, which he had given to a friend in Edinburgh "for daing the toune ane guid turne."

**First Fire Engine.**—Glasgow became possessed of its first fire engine in May, 1657. It is referred to as an "ingyne for casting water on land that is on fyre."

**"Cock Stool."**—On 9th June, 1658, two men were appointed, at a weekly salary of 2s. 6d. sterling, to put importunate beggars on the "Cock Stool."

**Market Cross.**—The Market Cross stood, in 1440, at the junction of High Street with the Rottenrow and Drygate, at which place St. Mungo's Fair was held every January. On 22nd November, 1659, it was ordered to be taken down, and the ground on which it stood levelled with the street. This interesting old relic is lost. "Senex" says it is buried in St. Andrew Square, where an unsuccessful search was made.

**Circuit Court.**—The Circuit Court was established in 1672 for Lanark, Renfrew, and Dumbarton. In 1873 Dumbarton was detached and Bute took its place.

**Sunday Observance.**—On 1st February, 1690, a bye-law was passed prohibiting drinking in taverns after 10 p.m. on week nights, or during sermon time on Sundays, under a penalty of 3s. 4d. sterling, to be divided between the informer and the city poor. "Kail-herbs" not to be sold on the streets or water carried from the wells on Sundays. Marshals perambulated the streets during church hours to compel the people they met to go to church or return home, failing which they were apprehended. Peter Blackburn, grandfather of Mr. Blackburn, of Killearn, was imprisoned for walking on the Green on Sunday. He appealed to the Court of Session and won his case, and this was the death knell of the puritanical bye-law. Strangers were required to produce a certificate of good character from their previous residence before they could get a house. Magistrates were not allowed to hold public house licenses. In 1746 no one was allowed to walk the streets on Sunday, nor were lamps allowed to be lighted on that evening.

**Charter re Provost and Magistrates.**—On William and Mary ascending the throne Glasgow received a ratification of Charter, giving them power to elect their own Provost and Magistrates. This was previously in the hands of the Archbishop. The new Charter was dated, Kensington, 4th June, 1690. It was passed by the Scottish Parliament on 14th June of the same year.

**Assassination of Town Clerk.**—On 14th October, 1694, Mayor James Menzies stabbed Robert Park, the Town Clerk, in his own office. Menzies, who refused to surrender, was shot in Renfield Gardens.

**Second Burgh in Scotland.**—In 1695 Glasgow became the second burgh in Scotland, Edinburgh being the first.

**Dancing Master.**—John Smith received permission from the Town Council on 11th November, 1699, to teach dancing, provided he did so at reasonable hours, and allowed no balls or promiscuous dancing.

**Darien Scheme.**—The City of Glasgow and its citizens lost heavily through the Darien expedition in 1700, the Corporation alone losing about £4,000 sterling, an immense sum of money at that time.

**Parishes.**—The city was divided into six parishes on 13th September, 1701.

**Gipsies Transported.**—£13 was paid to the owner of the vessel "Greenock" for taking eight gipsies to Virginia. They were sent to the Tolbooth from Jedburgh, where they had been sentenced to transportation.

**Glasgow Plaids.**—On the suggestion of Provost Aird on 26th August, 1715, Glasgow presented the Princess of Wales with a swatch of plaids—for the manufacture of which Glasgow was famous. Her Royal Highness expressed herself delighted with the "fyne present."

**First Lamps.**—The first street lamps were erected and lighted in January, 1718. They were conical in form, and had tallow wicks.

**Lord Provost's Subsidy.**—On 31st March, 1720, the Lord Provost was voted a yearly allowance for wines used to entertain guests at his house.

**Houses and Customs in 1720.**—There were very few self-contained houses in the city in 1720, the better-class people living in flats entering from a common stair, principally in the vicinity of High Street, Bridgegate, Saltmarket, and Main Street, Gorbals. A dining-room was very seldom used, food being taken in bedrooms. The dinner hour was 10 a.m. and tea time at 4 p.m. Gentlemen did not go home to the latter repast. They usually adjourned to their clubs, which met in taverns, whence they generally returned to their domiciles about 9 p.m.

**Technical Education.**—In October, 1728, Susannah Smith, widow of the Rev. Archibald Wallace, of Cardross, was appointed, at a salary of £30 sterling per annum, mistress of a public school for teaching girls "to spin flax into fine yarn fit for making thread or cambric."

**Daniel Defoe.**—In 1727 Daniel Defoe, of "Robinson Crusoe" fame, published a book on a tour through Scotland, which contained a very flattering reference to Glasgow.

**Lands of Provan.**—The lands of Provan, which came into the possession of the city at the Reformation, were sold in 1729 for £5,374 12s. 8d. sterling, and an annual feu duty of £103 8s. The first Bailie of Provan was appointed in 1734.

**Charters.**—In 1739 the Town Council decided to obtain authentic copies of the City Charters, etc., which were carried to Paris and placed in the Scots College in the Carthusian Monastery by Archbishop Beaton at the Reformation in 1560.

**Triennial Parliaments.**—Neil Buchanan, M.P., was requested by the Magistrates in 1742 to move in support of a bill in favour of Triennial Parliaments.

**Municipal Elections.**—In 1748 the manner of municipal elections in the city was altered. Among other changes, heavy fines were passed on Councillors or Bailies who refused to accept office.

**First Carriage and Cabs.**—The first four-wheeled carriage made its appearance in the city in 1752. It was built for Allan Dreghorn (who was in the timber trade) by his own workmen. Henry Lawson was the first to introduce cabs to the city, at the beginning of this century. His office was in a grocer's shop in Queen Street, nearly opposite the present Royal Exchange, where a small board informed the public that it was a "one horse coach office." Previous to the cab era, sedan chairs were the aristocratic medium of locomotion. The last sedan chair office was in Drury Street, which, by the way, was originally called Drury Lane after the famous theatrical centre in London.

**Magistrates' Emblems.**—In 1766 it was decided that the Magistrates, etc., should wear gold chains when on duty. As far back as 1720 the Lord Provost was required to wear a velvet court dress in his official capacity in public.

**"Glasgow Magistrates."**—Fish merchants bringing herring to the Broomielaw for sale were obliged to send a specimen of their boat loads to the River-Bailie for inspection and approval. The samples were generally the best in the boat, hence the reason for picked or large herring being called "Glasgow Magistrates."

**First Lightning Conductor.**—The first lightning conductor was erected on the old University steeple in High Street in 1772, under the direction of Benjamin Franklin, the distinguished American philosopher and statesman.

**First Parochial Board.**—The first Parochial Board was formed in 1774. Walter Stirling, founder of Stirling's Library, was a member.

**First Pavements.**—The first pavement was laid in the city on the east side of Candleriggs, between Bell Street and the Trongate, in 1777. John Wilson, whose ironmongery shop was opposite Hutcheson's Hospital in the Trongate, shortly afterwards laid a pavement in front of his shop, and his praiseworthy example was soon copied by many other merchants. They were rewarded for their enterprise by the magistrates erecting nine lamps between the Laigh Kirk Steeple and Stockwell Street, and more were promised further west if the pavements were continued in that direction. The Police Act compelling pavements to be laid was passed in 1800.

**Severe Frosts.**—In 1780 a very severe frost greatly affected the city and caused great distress. The Clyde was frozen over for four months in 1785. Carnivals were held on the ice. A very severe frost also visited the city the following year.

**"Glasgow Punch."**—This was the favourite tipple in the city in the days of old, the proper manufacture of the concoction being considered of great importance. The "blender" would divest himself of his coat and proceed to mix in a china bowl the ingredients, which were composed of rum and sugar seasoned with limes or the juice of lemon.

"'Twas here they'd mix the genuine stuff,
    As they mixed it long ago,
With limes that on their property
    In Trinidad did grow."

The drink was very palatable; the sugar and acid hid the potency of the alcohol, but on reaching the open air the effect was instantaneous.

**Dues on Eggs.**—The dues on eggs brought to the city to be sold were one out of each basket.

**Sunday Schools Instituted.**—The year 1787 is memorable for being the one when Sunday schools were first started in the city. In 1775, however, the Rev. Dr. Burns of the Barony personally taught a Sunday school which he formed in the Calton.

**First Umbrella.**—John Jamieson, surgeon, brought the first umbrella to Glasgow from Paris in 1782. John Gardner, father of the well-known optician, attempted to manufacture umbrellas about 1786, but they were so clumsy the enterprise was abandoned.

**Sewers.**—There were no public sewers in the city before 1790.

**First Steam Power.**—Steam power was first used in Glasgow in 1792, by Mr. Todd, to work an engine in Springfield Cotton Works. To show the progress this new factor made in a few years, it may be mentioned that in 1814 an Act of Parliament was obtained for the regulation of steam engines, chimneys, etc., in the city and suburbs.

**Chamber of Commerce.**—In 1793 Patrick Colquhoun, a city merchant, formed the Chamber of Commerce, and was elected its first president.

**Ballooning.**—In 1795 Vincent Lunardie made the first balloon ascent in the city from St. Andrew's Square—before the church was built—landing at Hawick. He went up on a second occasion from the Merchants' House Garden in the Bridgegate, now the Guildry Court, and alighted at Campsie. In 1817 a balloon was sent up from the Old Barracks in Gallowgate, with a cat and a dog in the basket; strange to say, history repeated itself, the quadrupeds coming to *terra firma* near Hawick.

**Master of Works.**—In 1814 the office of Master of Works, which was held by a town councillor, was made honorary, with a professional man under him taking charge.

**New Issue of Silver Coins.**—The new silver coinage of sixpences, shillings, and half-crowns, was first issued in Glasgow on 13th February, 1817. There are a good number bearing this date still in circulation.

**First Watering Cart.**—A watering cart to hold 180 gallons, drawn by one horse, was purchased by the Police Board in April, 1817. Previous to this, the streets were watered in summer with watering cans.

**Last Execution for Forgery.**—An Irishman was executed on 28th May, 1817, for forging and endeavouring to pass Greenock Bank guinea notes.

**Statistics about 1817-1819.**—In the above years the annual statistics show:—Police department—20 officers, 80 watchmen, 20 patrol, 16 scavengers, and 1,472 street lamps; annual expenditure, £11,617 8s.; rates from 4d. to 1s. a £; fire brigade —48 men, 6 fire engines; road money, £2,511 2s.; poor rates, £11,864 16s. 6d.; Town Council income, £15,111 18s. 5d.; expenditure, £14,818 16s.; house-window and servants' taxes, £29,384 19s.; rental, £270,646 on a valuation of £6,779,900; 712 public houses; 6 miles of sewers; 1,064 shops, with rents from £20 to £150, in the eight principal streets; 1,440 prisoners; 109,803 cattle slaughtered, value £400,000; 52 cotton mills, containing 511,200 spindles, representing £1,000,000 capital; 100,000,000 yards cotton produced, value £5,000,000; 64,803 packages cotton, containing 18,198,500 lbs., imported; 46,565 packages exported, leaving 18,238 on hand; 18 steam weaving factories, containing 2,800 looms, producing 8,400 pieces of cloth a week. Including those in the surrounding country, there were 32,000 steam and hand looms, 18 calico printing works, 17 calenders, 9 iron works, several distilleries, several engine works, 45 steam engines manufactured, and 73 employed in the various works.

**Hall-mark.**—In 1819 Glasgow was made an assay town, the silver hall-mark being a lion rampant, city arms, makers' initials, date letter, and Sovereign's head.

**King George IV.**—On 15th August, 1822, Lord Provost Alston and a deputation from the Town Council, the Merchants' and Trades' Houses, were received by King George IV. in Holyrood Palace.

**Municipal Reform.**—One of the first acts of the first Reform Parliament was to pass a bill instituting municipal reform. Previously the Councillors were elected by their predecessors, the people having no voice in the matter. On 28th August, 1833, Parliament decided that all who had a parliamentary vote in royal burghs should

also have a municipal one. The city was divided into five wards, each having six representatives, and these, with a representative from the Merchants' and Trades' Houses, made the Council number thirty-two, the first election taking place in November, 1833.

**Failures.**—Owing to the fast growth of the city and the consequent speculation, several large mill owners failed for heavy amounts in 1840.

**Ten Minutes Lost.**—Glasgow lost ten minutes in 1848 by the adoption of Greenwich time, which was ten minutes in advance of the time formerly used in the city.

**Forbes Mackenzie Act.**—Forbes Mackenzie, then M.P. for Peebles-shire, had his Act for the better regulation of public houses in Scotland, passed in the House of Commons on 15th August, 1853, during which year it came into force in Glasgow. It is not generally known that the author of the Bill was the late Lord Kinnaird.

**Marriage of the Prince of Wales.**—When the Prince of Wales was married to Princess Alexandra of Denmark, on 10th March, 1863, Glasgow showed its loyalty by illuminating the city in a thorough manner in honour of the auspicious event.

**First Municipal Election by Ballot.**—In November, 1872, the Municipal elections were first conducted under the ballot system.

**Music in Public Parks.**—Brass band music was introduced into the public parks and Glasgow Green during the summer months of 1873.

**Bankruptcy Bill.**—Dr. Cameron, one of the Members of Parliament for the city, succeeded in getting his Bankruptcy Bill passed into law in 1880. This new Act did away with imprisonment for debt.

**Franklin Expedition.**—In December, 1880, the remains of Lieutenant Irving, who was a member of the ill-fated Franklin expedition, were brought to the Clyde in the "Circassia."

**City and Barony Parishes.**—The City and Barony Parishes joined in June, 1881, for poorhouse purposes. They became amalgamated entirely in 1898. The first meeting of what is now known as the Glasgow Parish Council was held on 1st December of the same year.

**Police Band.**—The police band was started in 1881 by permission of the Town Council.

**Crofters' Eviction.**—Fifty police were sent to Skye under Captain Donald on 17th April, 1882, to assist the local authorities in evicting crofters. This gave rise to much indignation among the citizens.

**Bells in Blackfriars Church.**—A chime of bells costing £230 was placed in the spire of Blackfriars Church in 1885.

**County of Glasgow.**—On 30th November, 1893, the City of Glasgow was made a County, which raised the Lord Provost to the dignity of Lord-Lieutenant, and transferred the licensing from the Lanarkshire to the City Magistrates.

**Indian Famine.**—£58,000 was collected in Glasgow and the West of Scotland in 1897 to help to augment the national subscription which was raised to assist the natives of India during the terrible famine which devastated their country at that time.

**Minimum Wage.**—In 1898 the Corporation decided to pay no able-bodied man in their employment less than 21s. a week.

**Memorial Tablets.**—The Pen and Pencil Club have placed memorial tablets on the following sites in the city commemorative of (1) Thomas de Quincey, at 79 Renfield Street, on the site of which stood the house where De Quincey resided, 1841-43; (2) Edward Irving and Thomas Carlyle, on tenement 34 Kent Street, in which Irving resided, and where Carlyle visited him in 1820; (3) Sir John Moore, on the building 90 Trongate, standing on the site of tenement formerly 88, in which Moore was born; (4) William Motherwell, birthplace, tenement in High Street, at south corner of College Street; and (5) site of the old Glasgow College, in High Street, now a North British Railway Station. Others will be proceeded with in due time, and as the means at the disposal of the club permit.

**Children's Day.**—The Children's Day, which had been instituted in the Diamond Jubilee year, was again held on Saturday, 27th May, 1899. About 89,000 of the rising generation were gathered together in the seven public parks and Yorkhill grounds. Music, buns, and play formed the entertainment. It is estimated that 117,000 spectators witnessed the interesting spectacle.

---

## EVENTS.

**Royal Visits.**—King David I. visited Glasgow on 7th July, 1136, on the occasion of the consecration of the Cathedral. Edward I. stayed in the city three days in 1301 when visiting his garrison in the Bishop's Palace, and resided in the Blackfriars Monastery. James IV. honoured St. Mungo in person in 1510, while his greatgrandson, James VI., followed his ancestor's example in 1601, and on 22nd July, 1617. James II. (VII. of Scotland), when Duke of York, was made a burgess on 3rd October, 1681, and accorded a royal reception. While in the city he stayed in the Bridgegate with Provost John Bell, who received the honour of knighthood. Queen Victoria paid her first visit to the city, in company with Prince Albert, on 13th August, 1849. Her Most Gracious Majesty again visited the western capital of Scotland on 22nd and 24th August, 1888, when she opened the new Municipal Buildings and visited the International Exhibition.

**Darnley.**—Darnley, the husband of Mary Queen of Scots, had a very close connection with Glasgow, his father having been honorary provost in 1510 when James IV. visited the town. The Earl of Lennox owned a house in the Stable Green Port, to the north of the Cathedral. While visiting his father in this house—or, as is asserted, in a new residence the Earl of Lennox had acquired in Limmerfield Lane, off the Drygate—Darnley was seized with an attack of small-pox. When he became convalescent, the Queen visited him and remained a few days with her consort, afterwards returning to Holyrood. Darnley soon afterwards went to Kirk-of-Field, where he met his mysterious and tragic death.

**General Assemblies**—*1610.*—The General Assembly of the Church met in Glasgow in June, 1610.

*1638.*—The General Assembly met in the Cathedral on 21st November, 1638, under most exciting conditions. Alexander Henderson (Leuchars) was elected Moderator. The Bishops objected to be under the authority of the Church Courts, but it was decided otherwise, the Covenanters outvoting the Episcopalians. The Marquis of Hamilton, the Lord High Commissioner, declared the meeting at an end, and caused a proclamation to be read at the Cross declaring all who remained to be guilty of high treason. The Assembly, however, continued its labours. It renounced Episcopacy, deposed and excommunicated the Bishops, and restored

Presbyterianism, finishing its work on the 20th December, 1638.

**Marquis of Montrose.**—After James Graham, Marquis of Montrose, had defeated the Covenanters under General Baillie at the Battle of Kilsyth on the 15th August, 1645, the Magistrates of Glasgow, whose active sympathy had been on the side of the Presbyterians, considering discretion the better part of valour, apologised for their want of loyalty, congratulated the victorious Marquis, and invited him to come to the town and partake of their hospitality. He accepted the invitation, and, after being fêted for two days, borrowed £50,000 Scots (£4,166 sterling), which, by the way, he forgot to repay.

**General David Leslie.**—After General David Leslie had vanquished Montrose at Philiphaugh, near Selkirk, exactly a month after the Kilsyth disaster, he likewise came to Glasgow, and borrowed £20,000 Scots (£1,166 13s. 4d. sterling), remarking that this would pay for the interest of the money Montrose had got.

**Oliver Cromwell.**—Oliver Cromwell, after defeating General Leslie at Dunbar, marched on Glasgow *via* Kilsyth. Hearing a rumour that a vault in the Bishop's Palace, in the Stable Green Port, was filled with gunpowder to blow up his army, he entered the city on 24th October, 1650, by way of Cowcaddens and Cowloan (Queen Street) to Silvercraigs House, which stood at the north corner of Steel Street and Saltmarket, the magistrates and leading inhabitants having previously fled. The Protector sent for, and entertained Patrick Campbell to such a sumptuous refreshment and long and earnest prayer that the minister of the Outer High Kirk became favourably impressed with the Ironside leader. On the Sunday, Cromwell and his staff marched in procession to the Cathedral. Zachary Boyd, the Barony Church minister, was the preacher. Nothing daunted, he gave the Protector a terrible cutting up to his face. Cromwell returned the compliment by inviting the intrepid divine to spend the evening with him. So well did the Roundhead general debate on theology, and pray for three hours, that the Barony pastor did not get away until three o'clock in the morning, thinking his host was not so black as he was painted. Cromwell visited the University, paid the £200 which King Charles I. had promised for the building fund, and also gave a donation of £500 himself. Glasgow was again favoured with a visit from the great man in the following

April. Nothing happened of importance. He attended the Inner High Church in the forenoon, Robert Ramsay preaching a suitable discourse. In the afternoon he surprised the community by going to the Outer High Church, where John Carstairs lectured and James Durham preached.

**Claverhouse.**—1660 saw Charles II. on the throne, and immediately thereafter Episcopacy was re-established. Andrew Fairfoul was appointed Archbishop of Glasgow on 14th November, 1661. In consequence of a complaint by him, a meeting of the Privy Council was held in Glasgow, which is now known as the "drunken meeting," all being "flustered with drink except Sir James Lockhart of Lee," at which an order was passed commanding the ministers and the people to become Episcopalians, under heavy pains and penalties. This was the beginning of the persecution. After two years of office, Fairfoul died, and was succeeded by Alexander Burnet, Bishop of Aberdeen—a most zealous Episcopalian. "For conscience' sake" citizens were put in the stocks; fourteen ministers in the city were compelled to give up their churches; heavy fines were levied. Among those who were mulcted were James Hamilton, of Aitkenhead, near Cathcart, John Spence (Town Clerk), while George Porterfield and John Graham, ex-Provosts, were banished from the country. Inhabitants were fined and persecuted for keeping conventicles, the City fined for countenancing them, and several county magnates suffered in a similar manner. Soldiers guarded the city gates on Sabbath mornings to prevent the citizens going to conventicles in the suburbs. The Highland host of 5,000 men was billeted upon the inhabitants, who were plundered and cast into prison. To such an extent were the people robbed, that the students and youths blocked the bridge and compelled the Highlanders to disgorge a large portion of the goods and chattels they had stolen. Claverhouse made sorties from the city in pursuance of his cruel work. After his defeat at Drumclog on 1st June, 1679, he again retired to Glasgow. The Covenanters endeavoured to beard the lion in his den, and entered the city by the Gallowgate and the College Vennel; but the soldiers poured deadly volleys among them from the shelter of the houses and closes and hastily erected barricades, so that half a dozen of the assailants were killed and several wounded. Claverhouse gave orders that the dead bodies were not to be buried, but left to be eaten by the butchers' dogs. The Covenanters retired to Tollcross Muir. This fight is known as the battle of the Gallowgate. After the fatal battle of Bothwell Bridge, Claverhouse wanted to burn and sack the city for favouring the rebels, but the humane Duke of Monmouth would not sanction it. The persecution went steadily on. Many of the citizens, including the Rev. Donald Cargill, minister of the Barony Parish, were executed in Edinburgh and at the Cross of Glasgow. Martyrs' heads were stuck on pikes at the Tolbooth Steeple. Their bodies were buried on the north side of the Cathedral, where a stone with the following inscription perpetuates their memory, *viz.*:

"These nine with others in this yard,
Whose heads and bodies were not spared,
Their testimonies foes to bury,
Caus'd beat the drums, then in great fury,
They'll know at Resurrection Day
To murder saints was no sweet play."

**1715 Rebellion.** — Glasgow, while always loyal, was not Jacobite. When the rising—in which the Union was an important factor—took place in 1715, the City offered King George I. to raise and sustain 500 men for sixty days. This was not considered necessary at the time, but on 18th September, 1715, 500 men were raised under Provost Aird, and sent to Stirling to defend the Castle, at the request of the Duke of Argyle, while he fought at Sheriffmuir. £500 stg. was borrowed to dig entrenchments round the city; 300 stands of arms from Edinburgh Castle were given to volunteers; the streets were barricaded, and cannons from Port-Glasgow placed in suitable positions; martial law was declared, and 353 prisoners from Sheriffmuir were lodged in the Castle prison. The Government in 1718 reimbursed the town £735 13s. 5d. towards these expenses. The Duke of Argyle reviewed two regiments of dragoons and examined the entrenchments in the Cowloan (Queen Street) on 5th December. Colonel Wm. Maxwell of Cardonald, who was in command of the city, was presented by the grateful community with a silver tankard, a set of sugar boxes, and a "server wing," which cost £35 1s. 9d. stg.

**Prince Charlie.** — When Prince Charlie began operations in July, 1745, Glasgow became greatly alarmed. Valuables were removed to Edinburgh and Dumbarton Castles. After Prestonpans, the "Prince Regent" (as he styled himself) took up his residence in Holyrood, and caused Glasgow to give him £5,000 stg. in money and £500 worth of goods. On his return from England, he arrived in Glasgow, with his hungry and ragged army, on Christmas Day, and took up his residence in Shawfield House, which stood exactly at the foot of Glassford Street. (The east wing of the house is still at the corner of Glassford Street and Trongate.) The Highlanders paraded the town, and at the Cross proclaimed the Pretender Regent of Scotland. Glasgow was compelled to cover its guests' nakedness with 12,000 linen shirts, 6,000 cloth coats, 6,000 pairs of shoes, 6,000 pairs of hose, 6,000 waistcoats, and 6,000 bonnets, which cost the town £3,556 10s. 9½d. stg. The Provost was also fined £500 for assisting the Government. Business was completely at a standstill, and all shops were shut. The Prince took two meals a day in front of his house, always being very fashionably dressed and particularly agreeable to the ladies, one of whom (Miss Walkinshaw, youngest daughter of John Walkinshaw of Barrowfield) followed him to France and became his mistress. In a week the Chevalier's army were decked in their "borrowed plumes," and a grand review was held in the Green on the Flesher's Haugh. The Prince took his stand under a thorn tree, which was afterwards known as "Prince Charlie's Tree," and was protected with a wooden railing until it disappeared, nearly a hundred years afterwards. After a stay of ten days the Prince retreated North, taking with him Bailies Cameron and Coats, as hostages for the balance of his goods; a printing press, types, paper, and three printers, and all the arms and ammunition that could be found. So unpopular was the Pretender that he only secured one recruit in the person of a drunken tailor. Dougald Graham, the City Bellman, followed the Prince's army and immortalised the "History of the Rebellion" in verse after the manner of Blind Harry's "Wallace." Shortly before his arrival in St. Mungo, the Prince published the following list showing his strength—Lochiel (Cameron of Lochiel), 740; Appin (Stuart of Ardshiel), 360; Athol (Lord George Murray), 1,000; Clanronald (Clanronald of Clanronald, junior), 200; Keppoch (Macdonald of Keppoch), 400; Glencoe (Macdonald of Glencoe), 200; Ogilvie (Lord Ogilvie), 500; Glenbucket (Gordon of Glenbucket), 427; Perth (Duke of Perth), 750; Robertson (Robertson of Strowan), 200; Maclachlan (Maclachlan of Maclachlan), 2,620; Glencarnick (Macgregor), 300; Glengarry (Macdonald of Glengarry, junior), 300; Nairn (Lord Nairn), 200; Edinburgh (John Roy Stuart), 450; several small corps, 1,000; Lord Elcho and Lord Kilmarnock's horse, 160; Lord Pitsligo's horse, 140; total, 9,947. When the news of Culloden reached the city, the bells were rung, bonfires lighted, and the town was illuminated. The "hostage" bailies received £13 15s. 8d. for expenses when in the custody of the Prince. Parliament gave Glasgow £10,000 stg. to help to repay their loss, and Provost Andrew Cochrane and Bailie George Murdoch also got £472 11s. 8¼d. stg. Even with this *solatium*, the "Royal visit" left Glasgow about £4,000 stg. out of pocket.

**General Wolfe.** — Major-General James Wolfe, the conqueror of Quebec, was stationed in Glasgow from March to October, 1749. He resided in Camlachie Mansion House, and was a frequent visitor at M'Dowall's of Shawfield House, Glassford's of Whitehill, Orr's of Barrowfield, Barclay's of Chapelrig, and Provost Cochrane's, etc. He engaged a tutor two hours a day to help to perfect him in Latin and mathematics. There being no Episcopalian place of worship, he regularly attended the Cathedral. In a letter to a friend a fortnight after his arrival he described the men—"civil, designing, and treacherous;" and the women—"coarse, cold, and cunning."

**Resurrectionists.** — Nothing created greater excitement in the city than the doings of the Resurrectionists. In 1749 the University windows were broken, and other riotous acts done by an enraged mob, who blamed the students for violating some graves in the Cathedral burying-ground. At the beginning of this century, graves in the Cathedral, Ramshorn, and Gorbals burying-grounds were opened, and bodies removed in sacks to the professors' and students' quarters at the College. A number of bags, supposed to be full of rags, but filled instead with dead bodies, which had been brought over from Ireland, were seized at the Broomielaw. This, in addition to the Burke and Hare scare in Edinburgh, nearly drove the inhabitants of our city frantic. The magistrates issued edicts calling for the citizens to act as guards, patrol the streets, and watch the burying-grounds. High railings, which are yet standing, were erected round the graves in the old burying-grounds to prevent the body-snatchers continuing their gruesome work. Ultimately, on 13th December, 1813, the body of a Mrs. M'Allister, which had been lifted from the Ramshorn Churchyard, was traced to the lecture rooms of Granville Sharp Pattison, which entered by a back door in College Street. A warrant was got, and, after being nearly baffled, a number of partially dissected bodies were found in and under a macerating tub filled with water standing on the middle of the floor. Pattison and three others were apprehended, and on 6th June, 1814, were arraigned before the Lords in Edinburgh. The case turned principally on the body of Mrs. M'Allister, but, owing to a technical flaw, the prisoners were acquitted. They had, however, to leave the country, public feeling being so incensed against them. The case served the purpose of frightening the students, and ended the Resurrectionist reign of terror in Glasgow.

**Rev. George Whitefield.** — The Rev. George Whitefield, the famous revival preacher, used to visit Glasgow. He preached in a field in Gorbals in 1748, and in the Cathedral Yard in 1753. He incensed the crowd so much against the theatre that they immediately demolished a temporary wooden building erected against the wall of the Bishop's Castle. In 1757, he preached a sermon in the Cathedral burying-ground at the request of the magistrates, when £58 sterling was collected on behalf of the poor, while the following year, under similar conditions, the Highland Society benefited to the extent of £60 sterling, with which they erected the Black Bull Inn, which stood at the corner of Argyle and Virginia Streets.

**Edmund Burke.** — Edmund Burke, who had been defeated by Adam Smith in 1752 for the Chair of Moral Philosophy, was elected Lord Rector of Glasgow University in 1783. He was installed on 10th April, 1784, and, after speaking for five minutes, broke down in his Rectorial address, stating that so learned an audience had unnerved him.

**Sensational Experiment.** — Dr. James Jeffrey, Professor of Anatomy in the University, received, with the object of being publicly dissected and anatomised, the body of a murderer named Matthew Clydesdale, who was hung on 4th November, 1818. The corpse was placed in a sitting position in a chair in the anatomical theatre, and an air-tube, connected with a newly-invented galvanic battery, was placed in one of the murderer's nostrils. When the bellows began to blow into the nostril, the chest began to heave. Another tube was immediately placed in the next nostril, and further similar operations caused the tongue and lips to move; then the eyes opened, and, after staring around for a second or two, the body rose upright on its feet. Dr. Jeffrey instantly rushed forward and severed the jugular vein with his lancet, and the culprit immediately fell bleeding to the floor. This event forms the reason why all murderers are buried in chloride of lime within the prison precincts.

**Francis Jeffrey.**—The illustrious advocate, Francis—afterwards Lord—Jeffrey, was installed Lord Rector of Glasgow University on 20th December, 1820. Jeffrey had a close connection with the city, receiving the earliest and by far the most valuable part of his education in its college. He was engaged in every case of note which went from the western to the eastern capital.

**Harvey's Dyke.**—A carter named Thomas Harvey, who had risen to be a wealthy publican and distiller, bought the mansion-house and lands of Westhorn, on the banks of the Clyde. He endeavoured to stop a right-of-way along the banks by building what became historically known as Harvey's Dyke. The people resented this interference with their rights, and on Saturday, 21st July, 1822, a large armed crowd marched to the obnoxious barrier and knocked it down. The Enniskillen Dragoons arrived on the scene of the disturbance and charged the people, none of whom were seriously hurt, although many were compelled to take a cold bath in the Clyde. The case was taken to the Court of Session, and in 1826 the people had their right-of-way confirmed. Harvey, who was a purse-proud ignorant parvenu, latterly died a ruined and broken man.

**Sir Walter Scott Rejected.**—After Francis Jeffrey's term of Lord Rectorship of the University expired in 1822, Sir Walter Scott and Sir James Mackintosh became candidates for the honour, and the novelist was defeated. Three years later he again tried to secure the post, but Henry Brougham tied with him, and the retiring Rector gave his casting vote against the "Wizard of the North."

**The Peel Banquet.**—Sir Robert Peel was elected Lord Rector of Glasgow University in 1836. A proposal to make him a burgess was defeated in the Town Council on account of the future "hero of the Corn Laws" being a Tory. The Conservative operatives, however, purchased the honour for him. He visited the city on 11th January, 1837, and delivered his rectorial address. On the 14th of the same month he attended a banquet, which was held in a specially erected building, 127 feet long by 126 feet broad, in the garden of John Gordon of Aitkenhead's town house, where Princes Square now is, at which over 3,000 persons were present, when he received his burgess ticket in a silver casket.

**British Association.**—That scientific body, the British Association, met for the first time in Glasgow in 1840. In 1855 it again visited the city under the presidency of the Duke of Argyle. It met for a third time in 1876, when Dr. Thomas Andrews was elected president. The meetings, which lasted from the 6th to the 13th September, were held in the University. £6,608 10s. was raised for a guarantee fund.

**Chartists.**—About 1840 the Chartist agitation was very strong in the city. In 1842 they held a convention, which was attended by the famous Feargus O'Conner. So great did the distress become that the working classes gathered on the Green and demanded bread. It was in this year that the Corn Exchange was founded.

**The Disruption.**—When the Assembly of the National Church met in Edinburgh in May, 1843, before beginning the proceedings the retiring Moderator, the Rev. Dr. David Welsh, rose and read the famous protest, after which the Moderator together with those adhering to it withdrew to the Tanfield Hall, Canonmills, and there constituted the Free Church. Dr. Chalmers was elected Moderator. 474 ministers and professors signed the deed of demission. When the news reached Glasgow the excitement became intense. The following Sunday every Established Church in the city was crowded to hear what those who remained in the "Auld Kirk" had to say, and those who were in favour of the Free Kirk preaching their farewell sermons. The outcome of the movement, so far as Glasgow was concerned, was the doubling of all the city churches, every parish having its "Free" counterpart. On the 17th of October following the new body made a very politic movement by holding their General Assembly in the City Hall. Dr. Chalmers retired from the Moderator's chair after preaching a sermon, and Dr. Thomas Brown of St. James's succeeded him. The proceedings lasted for seven days, and during the whole time the Assembly was attended by about 600 enthusiastic members, and the city was very busy with strangers from the country, who were interested in the new movement. A college was instituted in George Street, and a great amount of very important business and mission work transacted.

**Evangelical Union.**—Dr. James Morison, minister of Clerk's Lane Secession Church, Kilmarnock, was suspended by that body for heresy, and in 1843 founded the Evangelical Union denomination with its headquarters in the city. The body, which was popularly known as the "Morisonians," is now amalgamated with the Congregationalists.

**First Visit of Queen Victoria.**— The last Sovereign who had visited Glasgow was James VI. in 1617. After an interval of 232 years, word was received that the young Queen, her Royal Consort, and Princess Alice and Prince Alfred would visit the city. Great preparations were made for the occasion. The landing stage at the foot of West Street was made brilliant with bunting, a battery of artillery was placed where Kingston Dock now is—then called Windmill Croft—a triumphal arch was erected on the north end of Jamaica Bridge, and the Royal route was decorated with flags, etc. The Queen's yacht "Fairy" arrived in the Clyde on Monday, 13th August, 1849, and next morning, at 11.45 a.m., the Royal party were met by Lord Provost Anderson and all the local dignitaries. The chief magistrate was knighted before the Queen left her yacht. The Royal procession passed through the principal streets to the Cathedral, and to the University in High Street, from where they drove to Queen Street Station and took the train to Balmoral.

**Madeline Smith.**—Madeline Smith was arraigned before the High Court of Justiciary on 30th June, 1857, for poisoning her lover, Pierre Emile L'Angelier, a French clerk. Miss Smith's family were in a good position in the city. They lived in 7 Blythswood Square, at the corner of Douglas Street. Miss Smith, having become engaged to W. H. Minnoch, wanted to cast off L'Angelier, who objected. It was said she handed him a cup of coffee through the iron stanchions of her bedroom window, which is level with the pavement. At any rate, after drinking the coffee, he returned to his lodgings at 11 Franklin Place, Great Western Road, and was found by his landlady at the door at 2 a.m. Shortly after, he died in great agony. He is buried in the Ramshorn Churchyard. A *post-mortem* examination showed death had resulted from poisoning. During the trial—which lasted for ten days —the letters which had passed between the lovers were read in Court, and created a great sensation. John Inglis, Dean of Faculty (afterwards Lord President Inglis, when he took the title of Lord Glencorse), defended Miss Smith; and so skilfully did he handle the case that he was able to procure a verdict of "Not Proven," and at the same time lay the foundation of his future greatness.

**Sandyford Place Murder.**—Jessie M'Pherson was a servant in the employment of the Flemings in Sandyford Place. All the family were at the coast, with the exception of the father, who was an old, doted man. An acquaintance of Jessie M'Pherson, named Jessie M'Intosh or M'Laughlin, went to the house on Saturday, 4th July, 1862. Nothing further was heard until young Mr. Fleming returned to the house on Monday and found his father in bed as usual, who complained that the servant had never come to attend him since the Saturday. When the son proceeded downstairs to the kitchen he found everything in order, but could not get into the servant's bedroom. He burst the door open, and there found the mutilated body of Jessie M'Pherson. The matter was placed in the hands of the police, who discovered Jessie M'Laughlin had been drinking with the murdered woman on the Saturday night. After a search, M'Laughlin was apprehended, and the bloody clothes found hid on the farm of Eddlewood, near Hamilton. Jessie M'Laughlin made a very ingenious defence, stating that the two women and old Fleming were all drinking together, when the old man, in a drunken passion, committed the murder; and out of fear and threats, Jessie M'Laughlin only acted as she had done. This was believed by a large portion of the public, and great excitement prevailed; but the jury acquitted Fleming, and Jessie M'Laughlin was sentenced to be hanged. She was, however, reprieved, and was confined in Perth Penitentiary for about 20 years, when she was released.

**Dr. Pritchard.**—Dr. Edward William Pritchard was a medical practitioner in

Clarence Place, Sauchiehall Street, holding a good position in his profession. On 3rd July, 1865, he was tried for the murder of his wife and mother-in-law by a systematic poisoning. After a trial lasting five days, in which the medical evidence greatly differed, Pritchard was found guilty and sentenced to death. He was publicly executed at the South Prison at the Green on 28th July, 1865, this being the last public execution in the city.

### Freedom of the City to W. E. Gladstone.

The Right Hon. W. E. Gladstone (then Chancellor of the Exchequer under Lord Russell) received the Freedom of the City, in the City Hall, on 1st November, 1865. Mrs. Gladstone accompanied her husband. They visited the Cathedral and Royal Exchange ; received an address from the Reform Union in the Trades Hall ; attended a Corporation dinner in the Art Gallery in Sauchiehall Street, and received an address from the working men in the evening in the Scotia Music Hall, when the coming man of the day made a great speech on industrial progress.

### Industrial Exhibition.

An industrial exhibition was opened in 99 Argyle Street (where the Royal Polytechnic Ltd. now carries on business) on 12th December, 1865. The Duke of Argyle delivered the inaugural address in the City Hall. The exhibition lasted for four months.

### Fenianism.

Glasgow was not exempt from the " Fenian scare" that was passing over the country. The police became very active and special constables were enrolled. In January, 1868, Michael Barrett and James O'Neil were arrested by the police on a charge of recklessly discharging firearms in the Green. It was afterwards discovered that Barrett was implicated in the Clerkenwell explosion, which took place on 13th December, 1867, for which he was executed on 26th May, 1868.

### Benjamin Disraeli.

The late Lord Beaconsfield, then Benjamin Disraeli, defeated Mr. Ruskin in the contest for the Lord Rectorship of Glasgow University in 1871. On 19th November, 1873, the Conservative leader was installed in his office in the Kibble Conservatory in the Botanic Gardens, when he was made an LL.D. and delivered his rectorial address. He attended a banquet on the same evening in the City Hall, and received the Freedom of the City there next day. He also visited the Royal Exchange and the Cathedral, and was entertained to luncheon in the Corporation Galleries by the Town Council.

### Social Science Association.

The first Social Science Congress was held in the city in 1860, presided over by Lord Brougham. The Congress met again in Glasgow on 30th September, 1874, when the Earl of Rosebery took the chair.

### Visit of the Prince of Wales.

On 17th October, 1876, the Prince of Wales, accompanied by the Princess and Princes Albert Victor and George, and Prince John of Glücksburg, laid the foundation stone of the post-office buildings in George Square. The Royal party, who had been staying with Lord (then Colonel) Campbell, of Blythswood, arrived at St. Enoch Station, which was scarcely finished, and was fitted up for the occasion, about 11 a.m. They drove to the Green and witnessed a grand review of 6,000 Volunteers, after which they had lunch at Lord Provost Bain's residence at Park Terrace. About 5 o'clock they left his Lordship's house, accompanied by a great procession, including about 8,000 Freemasons, and proceeded to the "Square," where the Prince laid the stone with full masonic honours, after which the heir-apparent and his company left the city about 6 p.m. and returned to Renfrew. After this event the Lord Provost was knighted.

### U.P. Synod.

The United Presbyterian Synod met in John Street U.P. Church in May, 1877, when the Rev. Mr. France of Paisley was elected Moderator.

### Free Church Assembly.

The Free Church held their second Assembly out of Edinburgh in May, 1878, when they met in St. Andrew's Hall. The Rev. Dr. Andrew A. Bonar of Finnieston Free Church was elected Moderator.

### Visit of Mr. Gladstone in 1879.

Mr. Gladstone, accompanied by Mrs. Gladstone, arrived—from the seat of the Earl of Breadalbane—in Glasgow on Thursday evening, 4th December, 1879, and was met at Buchanan Street Station by the students, who gave them a torchlight procession to the house of Sir James Watson whose guest he was. Next day the "Grand Old Man" was installed as Lord Rector, had the honorary degree of Doctor of Laws conferred on him, and delivered his rectorial address. Later in the afternoon he delivered a political address in the St. Andrew's Hall, and in the evening Lord Provost Collins presented him with a congratulatory address on behalf of the Corporation in the City Hall, when he again made a speech. Next morning he left for Motherwell.

**Naval and Marine Engineering Exhibition.**—In the winter of 1880 an exhibition of Naval and Marine Engineering was opened in the Corporation Galleries, and proved a great success.

**Convention of Burghs.**—The Convention of Burghs met in what was formerly John Street Wesleyan Chapel— the site of which is now occupied by the new Municipal Buildings—on 3rd and 4th April, 1883. They were entertained to a banquet in the City Hall on the evening of the 3rd April, when every burgh in Scotland was represented.

**Channel Fleet.**—Six ships of the Channel Fleet visited the Clyde from 27th September to 2nd October, 1885, *viz.*, Minotaur (flag), Agincourt, Sultan, Iron Duke, Leander, Rifleman.

**Foreign Dignitaries.**—One hundred and fifty ladies and gentlemen, consisting of native Indian and African dignitaries, and others of British extraction from all parts of Her Majesty's foreign dominions, who had been visiting the Indian Exhibition in London in 1886, were entertained by the Corporation from 26th to 28th August, 1886.——His Excellency Count Saigo, of Japan, accompanied by a suite of military and naval officers, received the attention and hospitality of the Corporation from 23rd to 28th September, 1886.—— The Rajah of Narsinghgarh and suite were received on 29th July, 1886; while the Maharajah Gaekwar of Baroda and suite visited the city on 22nd December, 1887. ——Marquis Tzeng, Chinese Minister Plenipotentiary to Great Britain arrived in the city on 24th May, 1886, and after an exhaustive inspection of the principal industries, and being entertained to luncheon in the Council Chambers, he left on 27th May.——The late Shah of Persia visited the city on 18th July, 1889. The Eastern potentate resided at Buchanan Castle, the seat of the Duke of Montrose. He visited the Municipal Buildings, where he received an address; Royal Exchange; Clydebank Shipbuilding Yard, and was entertained to luncheon in the Corporation Galleries.—— In June, 1895, the Shahzada, the second son of the Ameer of Afghanistan, visited the city.——In October of the same year, three Bechuana Chiefs came to Glasgow to endeavour to interest the people against the Chartered Company of South Africa, who, they were afraid, threatened to take away some of their royal possessions.——

Li Hung Chang, the celebrated Chinese statesman and soldier, visited the city on 17th and 18th August, 1896. He was royally entertained, and shown the enterprise of the Clyde.

**Queen's Jubilee.**—On Thursday, 16th June, 1887, the Jubilee of Her Most Gracious Majesty Queen Victoria was celebrated in the city. Glasgow has always been a most loyal city, and it did not belie its reputation in showing love and respect for our exemplary Sovereign. A solemn and imposing service was held in the Cathedral; a review of the Regulars and Volunteers took place on the Green; 6,000 poor persons were entertained to a substantial dinner; a banquet and ball were held in St. Andrew's Halls; illuminations and music in the public parks closed a busy day. £7,404 was subscribed to the Imperial Institute Fund, and a jubilee memorial sculpture was placed on the pediment of the municipal buildings. The children were not forgotten, for on the 10th of the following September a fête was held on the Green attended by 37,000 of the rising generation.

**International Exhibition, 1888.** —The first sod of the International Exhibition of Science and Art was cut by the then Lord Provost, Sir James King, on 2nd May, 1887. The buildings were erected at Overnewton. A bridge was built across the Kelvin, and a large portion of the West End Park and University Grounds was utilised for the Exhibition, and the Kelvingrove Museum was used for the Queen's Jubilee presents, which her Majesty graciously placed at the disposal of the executive. The Exhibition was opened on 8th May, 1888, by the Prince and Princess of Wales, when, in addition to the police, there were 10,452 persons under arms from the Regular Army, the Volunteers, and the Boys' Brigade. The Exhibition was visited by Her Majesty Queen Victoria in State, on 22nd August, and again on 24th August Her Majesty honoured it with a more prolonged private visit. The Exhibition was admitted to be the finest ever held out of London. When it closed in November the returns showed that the total drawings amounted to £225,928 15s. 2d., which left a surplus of slightly over £54,000. No fewer than 5,746,000 persons were admitted during the six months.

**Important Meetings.**—The annual meetings of the British Medical Association, The British Archæological Association, The Literary Association, and Institute of Naval Architects were held in the city in 1888.

This was probably owing to the International Exhibition being in progress.

**Highland and Agricultural Society Show.**—The Highland and Agricultural Society held their annual show on Glasgow Green in July, 1888.

**East End Exhibition.**—An industrial exhibition was held in 1890 in the old Reformatory in Duke Street, It was opened by the Marquis of Lothian, the Secretary for Scotland. About £3,000 of a surplus was shown at the close of the Exhibition.

**Old Glasgow Exhibition.**—An exhibition illustrative of Old Glasgow and the history and progress of the city was held in the Institute of the Fine Arts, 175 Sauchiehall Street. It was opened on 11th July, and closed in October, 1894.

**Burns Exhibition.**—A Burns exhibition to commemorate the centenary year of the poet's death was held in the Fine Art Galleries, 175 Sauchiehall Street. The exhibits included portraits, pictures, relics, editions of works, manuscripts, and books relating to Burns and his times. The unique and interesting exhibition was opened on 15th July, and closed on 31st October, 1896.

**Diamond Jubilee.**—On Tuesday, 22nd June, 1897, the Diamond Jubilee of Her Most Gracious Majesty Queen Victoria was celebrated in Glasgow. The streets were gaily decked, the Volunteers assembled in George Square and marched through the city, a banquet was held in the Municipal Buildings, and displays of fireworks and illuminations took place in the evening. On the Saturday 90,000 children were entertained in the public parks in different parts of the city, and each presented with a small bronze diamond-shaped medal as a souvenir of the occasion.

**Missionary Exhibition.** — A missionary loan exhibition promoted by the Christian Institute was held in the St. Andrew's Halls from 5th to 14th March, 1899.

---

## CASUALTIES, RIOTS, etc.

**Plague in 1588.**—In 1588, Glasgow citizens were forbidden to trade in Paisley or Kilmalcolm, to prevent the plague—which was raging in these towns—spreading to Glasgow, and no stranger was allowed to enter the town without permission.

**Fire in 1600.**—A great part of Glasgow was burned in 1600.

**Plague in 1647.**—The plague was so bad in Glasgow in 1647, that the masters and students of the University retired to Irvine. Meal was selling at the time at 1s. 9d. stg. a peck.

**Fire in 1652.**—On 17th June, 1652, the great fire of Glasgow took place, one-third of the town being burned. The houses were nearly all thatched and built of wood. Over 1,000 families were rendered homeless, and the churches were opened to shelter them.

**Fire in 1677.**—On 3rd November, 1677, another great fire occurred in Glasgow. The Tolbooth was full of Covenanters at the time, and the people burst the doors open and allowed the prisoners to escape. The heat spoiled the clock in the Cross Steeple.

**Sectarian Quarrel.**—A dispute took place between the Presbyterians and Episcopalians at the Cathedral on 14th February, 1689. Several men and women were severely injured with sticks and stones.

**Union Riots.**—Previous to the Union taking place, Glasgow continued in a riotous state for about a month, the general feeling being very much against the Union. On account of Provost Aird declining to forward a petition to Parliament against it, the Council Chamber and the Provost's house were stoned. The chief magistrate himself coming in for a share of the missiles, fled to Edinburgh for shelter. A man named Findlay led the rioters with much success. The Act of Security was suspended ; but not until a detachment of Dragoons and Grenadiers, under Colonel Campbell, came from Edinburgh and arrested the ringleaders, including Findlay, was the reign of terror brought to an end. All were, however, liberated without further punishment after the Union was passed.

**Flood in 1712.**—The Bridgegate and Saltmarket and the lower parts of the city were submerged—by the Clyde overflowing its banks to eighteen and a half feet above high water mark—in 1712.

**Shawfield Riots.** — The Shawfield Riots occurred in June, 1725. Daniel Campbell, of Shawfield House, which was erected in 1711, and stood at what is now the foot of Glassford Street, was the member of Parliament. He voted in favour of a tax of 3d. on each barrel of beer. The citizens were enraged, and while he was staying at his country residence of Woodhall they attacked Shawfield Mansion and completely wrecked it. The following day they returned to renew their vengeance, but the military, under Captain Bushell, had arrived in the interval, and were stoned by the citizens, who were fired upon, and before Provost Miller could get peace restored nine persons were killed and seventeen wounded. Under a Government warrant nineteen people were apprehended and taken to Edinburgh. Eight were liberated, a man and woman banished, and the others publicly whipped through the streets of Glasgow. The Provost and Magistrates were also arrested, placed in the Tolbooth, and taken to Edinburgh Castle for favouring the rioters. Next day they were admitted out on bail, and two who immediately returned to Glasgow were received with ringing of bells and great manifestations of joy. Parliament voted Campbell £6,080 sterling for damages. He shortly afterwards purchased the Island of Islay, and founded the family of that ilk. The unfortunate affair, including the above sum, cost the City £10,000 sterling, which was raised by a tax on the ale and beer sold in the town.

On 26th April, 1727, Daniel Campbell sold Shawfield House to Col. William M'Dowall of Castle Semple, whose son added the east and west wings about 1760. The former is still standing. He disposed of the mansion proper and garden to John Glassford of Dougalston, in 1760, for £1,785. The west wing was sold to the Ship Bank in 1776. Glassford's son sold the mansion to William Horn in 1792 for £9,850, who removed it to allow Glassford Street to be opened up. Two sphinxes which stood on each side of the entrance to the famous mansion are to be seen at Woodend House, near Cathcart. Part of the stone balustrade, and a couple of globes of the same material are at Slatefield, off the Gallowgate.

**Fires in 1748-49.**—Two persons were burned to death by a fire which occurred in the Saltmarket on 25th July, 1748. Through a fire which happened on 5th June, in the following year, in Main Street, Gorbals, 150 families lost their homes, a public subscription being raised in their behalf.

**Roman Catholic Riots.**—The introduction of a Parliamentary Bill, in 1779, to repeal the Penal Statutes against the Catholics was the occasion of two riots in the city. The Catholic meeting-house in High Street was demolished with stones and the altars destroyed; while Robert Bagnall's dwelling-house in Gallowgate was burned, and his pottery warehouse in King Street destroyed. He afterwards received compensation for his loss. The streets were patrolled by the magistrates, deacons, and military until the Bill was abandoned, when the people became pacified.

**Weavers' Riots.**—In 1779, the weavers had their ire roused by the introduction of a Bill to remit the duties on French cambrics. An effigy of the minister who introduced the Bill, with a piece of French cambric in one hand and a copy of the Bill in the other, was marched through the streets, and hung up and blown to pieces with an explosive. This Bill was also withdrawn and peace was restored. At this time the price of oatmeal was 3s. 6d. a peck, and so great was the distress that the Meal Market, at the foot of Montrose Street, was robbed. A subscription was raised to alleviate the suffering.

**Flood and Famine in 1782.**—On Thursday, 11th March, 1782, the Clyde rose 20 feet above its level and inundated the Green, Bridgegate, Stockwell Street, Jamaica Street, Gorbals, and Saltmarket. The inhabitants in the last-named district had not time to leave their houses and had to be supplied with food by means of boats. One woman was drowned in Gorbals. Over £500 was raised by public subscriptions to alleviate the distress, which was increased by a famine in the country. The magistrates offered the farmers a bonus of 6d. a boll to bring all their meal to the Glasgow market. The following is engraved on a brass plate on the Jail in East Clyde Street, viz., "The upper edge of this represents the height of the great flood in Clyde, 12th March, 1782."

**Fire and Earthquake in 1786.**—Nine families were burned out in Gorbals in 1786. In the same year a slight earthquake was felt in the city.

**Weavers' Riots in 1787.**—The Calton weavers in 1787, unable to obtain an increase of wages, became riotous and wrecked the looms, and stoned the magistrates and the town officers. On the weavers attacking the military, where Tennant's Brewery now stands in Duke Street, the Riot Act was read. The soldiers fired, killing three men and wounding several others, after which the disturbance slowly subsided.

**Riot in 1794.**—A riot occurred in the city in December, 1794. A soldier who deserted, on being recaptured was assisted by his comrades, who were arrested, taken to Edinburgh, and four sentenced to be shot; three were, however, respited. On the return of the escort from the Capital the citizens stoned the men and officers. The magistrates and town officers ultimately pacified the disturbers.

**Stone Battles.**—It used to be a very common occurrence at the close of last century for stone battles to take place in the vicinity of the old Stockwell Bridge, between the Glasgow and Gorbals youths, for the possession of an island on the river —situated opposite where Carlton Place now stands—on which Bailie Craig, of the Waterport, piled his timber. The death of a boy caused the objectionable sport to be put down. Stone fights also took place between the students and the citizens, and the High School and Wilson's Charity Institution.

**Flood in 1795.**—A great flood occurred in November, 1795. The Clyde overflowed its banks, and for five days the Bridgegate, Saltmarket, Gorbals, Stockwell, and Jamaica Streets were inundated, and Hutchesontown Bridge, in course of erection, was swept away, and one little boy was drowned.

**Distress in 1800.**—Terrible distress, owing to the failure of the crops for two years, occurred in the city in 1799 and 1800, and public subscriptions had to be raised by the magistrates to supply the starving poor with grain under cost price. A supply to the value of £117,000 was required, but owing to the loss of several cargoes of grain, and the failure of the underwriters, a deficit of £4,000 occurred. An attempt to raise this sum by taxation on the rents was abandoned because of the hostile attitude of the ratepayers. In 1801 the bread assize was temporarily abandoned, the bakers being allowed a free hand in prices.

**Disturbance and Flood in 1815.**—In 1815 a slight disturbance occurred in the lower parts of the city over the passing of a Bill regulating the corn market. The Clyde rose seventeen feet above high-water on 30th December of this year, in consequence of which the low-lying parts of the town were under water, but fortunately the duration was short.

**Typhus Epidemic in 1818.**—A severe epidemic of typhus fever broke out in the city in 1818. All the fever wards in the Infirmary were filled, and a temporary hospital was built beside it. 1,929 patients were received in sixteen

months, 171 of whom died. Subscriptions were raised to help to alleviate the distress. Several parts of the town were disinfected.

**Storm in 1818.**—A very severe storm struck the city in 1818. Several houses were blown down, and great damage was done.

**Riot in 1822.**—The last case of a man being publicly whipped through the streets occurred in 1822, the reason of the punishment being the wrecking of John Provan's colour establishment in Great Clyde Street, which was formerly the residence of Robert Dreghorn of Ruchill. On 17th February of the same year a mob somehow got it into their heads that Provan was a resurrectionist; so serious did matters become that the military were called out and the Riot Act read, five rioters being transported for their share in the affair.

**Weavers' Strike in 1823.**—The power-loom tenters and dressers having struck work in 1823, new workers were engaged in their places. The strikers endeavoured to intimidate the new hands, and the presence of the military was necessary before things quietened down.

**Fall of House in Saltmarket.**—Provost Gibson erected a tenement at the corner of Saltmarket and Gibson's Wynd, which was designed by Sir William Bruce, and stood upon eighteen pillars or arches. Part of one of the walls fell on 3rd March, 1814, killing a woman and injuring several other persons. On 16th February, 1823, the greater part of the tenement fell, but luckily only one man was killed, the inhabitants having been warned out the previous day. This rung the death-knell of the old houses with wooden fronts.

**Fire in 1829.**—The premises of James Donaldson, cotton broker in Mitchell Street, were burned on 20th November, 1829, over £40,000 of damage being done. The fire smouldered for weeks after it broke out.

**Cotton Spinners' Riots in 1837.**—The Cotton Spinners came out on strike in 1837. They resented outsiders coming to work in their stead. Riots ensued and mills were wrecked and one man was shot in Anderston. Several of the ringleaders were transported for five years at the High Court of Justiciary.

**Bread Riots in 1848.**—It seems strange to think that only fifty years ago, on 6th March, 1848, a large mob collected on the Green on the pretence that they were starving, and owing to the incompetence of Major Pearce, the chief constable, they were allowed to march through the principal streets crying *Vive la République*, following this up by plundering jewellers' and other shops and damaging the mills. The arrival of the 3rd Dragoons and 71st Regiment caused the rioters to make their presence scarce. They, however, gathered again next day in the East End, but the militia and police dispersed them—not, unfortunately, before the militia had fired into the crowd, six of whom were killed and several injured, the innocent, sad to relate, suffering with the guilty. Several were afterwards arrested, and received sentences varying from one to eighteen years' imprisonment. The damage amounted to over £7 000, for which the ratepayers were assessed.

**Fire in 1848.**—On 30th October, 1848, fourteen lives were lost and damage done to the amount of £15,000 by the burning of Wilson & Son's sugar house in Alston Street, which is now part of the site of the Central Railway Station.

**Fatal Panic in Dunlop Street Theatre.** — On Saturday night, 17th February, 1849, during the second act of the "Surrender of Calais," in the Dunlop Street Theatre, some person in the gallery raised a false cry of fire. A frightful scene ensued. Everybody rushed to the doors, with the result that sixty-five persons were trampled to death, and many more injured.

**Cholera.**—After a lapse of two centuries, cholera visited this country in 1832. It began in Russia, and travelled through the Continent until it reached Sunderland in November, 1831. Every effort was put forth to prevent the terrible scourge spreading, but it reached Tranent on 15th January, 1832. It then touched Musselburgh, and on 22nd January appeared in Kirkintilloch. On 12th February cases were reported in the Goosedubs and Partick. Soon the plague became general. The hospitals became filled, and by May forty people died, while only 24 recovered. After the great demonstration in connection with the first Reform Bill on 4th June, when about 100 000 people were crowded on the streets, the disease assumed terrible dimensions, and by the time it had run its course in November, 6,203 persons had been afflicted, of whom 3,000 died, and 3,203 recovered. The cholera again visited the city in November, 1848, and continued until March, 1849, during which short time no

fewer than 3,777 deaths took place. On the first occasion the scourge principally attacked the poorer people, but this time the wealthier classes suffered most.

For a third time cholera returned in December, 1853, and by the time it disappeared in December, 1854, it claimed no less than 3,885 victims, the month of August alone being responsible for 1,023 deaths. In 1866 it came back to the country, but probably on account of the Loch Katrine water supply, and the improved sanitary arrangements, only fifty-three deaths took place in the city. A few years ago two cases were reported in the city, but the parties both recovered, and nothing further was heard of the matter.

**Traction Engine Explosion.**—Early in the sixties a traction engine exploded while taking in water at the junction of Morrison Street and Paisley Road. A number of children were killed.

**Fatal Ferry Accidents.**—The Govan ferryboat was overturned at Partick on 6th April, 1861, and seven lives lost. The accident was caused by overcrowding. This accident caused the pier at Partick to be shortly afterwards erected. About three and a-half years after this sad affair another similar accident occurred at Clyde Street. About 6 p.m. on 30th November, 1864, no fewer than twenty-seven men, mostly workmen, packed themselves into the Clyde Street boat. The water was rough, and the "Invernray Castle" passing at the time, bad steering caused the swell to come over the broadside of the rowing boat. The occupants crushed to the lee side, with the result that the boat upset. All were thrown into the water, and only eight were saved, nineteen being drowned. This calamity was responsible for the introduction of steam ferries.

**Dunlop Street Theatre Burned.**—The old theatre in Dunlop Street, where all the great lights of the stage shone in the fifties, was burned in January, 1863.

**Tradeston Flour Mills Explosion.**—Tradeston Flour Mills was the scene of a dreadful explosion on 9th July, 1872, fourteen persons being killed and many others injured. The calamity was supposed to be caused by the accumulation of explosive dust generated in the process of grinding.

**Partick Riots.** - A disturbance which really assumed the dimensions of a riot occurred at Partick on 5th August, 1875. A procession in honour of the O'Connell celebration passing through the burgh was attacked, and a fierce fight ensued, which spread to such an alarming extent, that the Riot Act had to be read, and the assistance of the Glasgow Police procured. No one was actually killed, but many were very seriously injured. By the following Monday, however, peace was restored, but the Police Court was kept busy for some days afterwards.

**Ice Floods.**—On 3rd January, 1875, ice floes came down the Clyde, the strong down flood forcing a passage for itself under the ice block, undermining the foundations of a portion of Custom-House Quay Wall, and causing it to bulge forward. The river was again blocked with ice from Stockwell Street Bridge to York Street Ferry in February, 1881, the Cunarder "Gallia" being carried from her moorings at Finnieston to Fairfield Shipbuilding Yard. Another serious ice block took place on 1st March, 1895. The "Clutha" steamers, berthed at Stockwell Bridge, were carried away from their moorings, and one of them, colliding with a lighter, was sunk. A small digger employed at the Upper Harbour also sunk at the General Terminus. The ferry traffic was suspended nearly the whole day, and the tug "Clyde" was kept moving about breaking up the ice.

**Shipbuilding Strike and Lock-out.**—In the summer of 1877 a great strike and lock-out occurred in the shipbuilding yards on the Clyde. The men demanded an increase of wages, which they failed to get, and after remaining out till the approach of winter, they returned upon the old terms, after suffering great want and causing much destitution.

**Blantyre Explosion.**—An explosion of fire-damp occurred on 22nd October, 1877, in one of Dixon's (William Dixon, Ltd.) High Blantyre Collieries. Over 230 miners lost their lives. The citizens showed their sympathy in a tangible manner by raising a relief fund for the widows and orphans amounting to £48,246 19s. 3d.

**Burning of Theatre Royal.**—The Theatre Royal in Cowcaddens, opened as the Colosseum Music Hall in 1867, was totally destroyed by a fire which broke out on Sunday morning, 2nd February, 1879, Happily no one was injured. The damages amounted to over £35,000. The theatre was again burned on 1st March, 1895, when £25,000 damage was done.

**Distress in 1879.**—During the winter following the failure of the City of Glasgow

Bank scarcely a day happened without a failure. The consequence was almost complete stagnation of trade, followed by great distress. A relief fund amounting to £29,225 16s. 1d. was raised. Work was instituted for the unemployed, and 419 skilled and 1,065 unskilled workers were provided with jobs. Out of 13,960 applicants, 12,666 were granted relief, and in all £27,208 10s. 4d. was disbursed.

**Relief Works.**—Owing to the distress in the city in consequence of bad trade, relief works were opened in the following years, viz.:—25th November, 1878, to 29th March, 1879; 17th September, 1879, to 31st January, 1880; winter of 1884 to spring of 1885; 1st December, 1885, to 1st May, 1886; 16th December, 1886, to 16th April, 1887; (2,801 men) 8th December, 1892, to 4th March, 1893; 4th November, 1895, to 16th March, 1896.

**Gas Explosion.**—On 1st January, 1881, a gas explosion occurred in Henderson Street, and five persons were killed and nine injured.

**Explosion.**—On 8th September, 1882, three men were killed by an explosion in a foundry at Port-Eglinton.

**Railway Collisions.**—Within three weeks two railway collisions occurred in the city. On 16th December, 1882, twenty-eight persons were injured at Cowlairs, and on 4th January, 1883, nine persons were injured at Sighthill. On 19th March, 1883, four persons were killed and many injured by two trains colliding at Eglinton Street Station.

**Dynamitards.**—On Saturday, 20th January, 1883, an endeavour was made to blow up Tradeston Gasworks and Ruchill Canal Bridge with dynamite. Happily the dastardly attempts were practically failures, although nine men were injured at the Gasworks. The perpetrators were sentenced to a term of penal servitude.

**"Daphne" Disaster.**—On 3rd July, 1883, while the steamer "Daphne" was being launched from Linthouse Shipbuilding Yard, the vessel capsized and over 200 workmen who were on board were immersed in the Clyde. The sight was one of the most appalling ever seen in the city, and despite every effort 146 lives were lost. Three weeks elapsed before the vessel was raised and the bodies recovered. A relief fund, amounting to £30,722 12s. 7d., was raised to assist the widows and orphans.

**Great Fires.**—The following is a list of the fires, with damage over £20,000, since 1875:—

| DATE. | LOCATION, ETC. | | LOSS. |
|---|---|---|---|
| 1875— | | | |
| July 28 ... ... | Broad Street, Mile-end ... | ... Cotton Spinners | £45,500 |
| August 4 ... | 23 West Street, South Side | ... Grain Mill ... | 26,000 |
| November 12 ... | Greenhead Street ... ... | ... Spinning Mill | 134,500 |
| 1878— | | | |
| June 8 ... | 34 Virginia Street ... | ... Apothecaries' Hall ... | £24,000 |
| 1879— | | | |
| February 2 ... | Cowcaddens | Theatre Royal | £35,000 |
| 1880— | | | |
| March 6 | 472 Garscube Road | ... Cotton Spinners ... | £28,500 |
| 1881— | | | |
| December 3 ... | Kelvinhaugh Street | Spinning Mill | £40,000 |
| 1882— | | | |
| January 18 ... | 30 Lancefield Quay | Engineers ... | £32,000 |
| October 14 ... | 21 Garngad Road ... | Spinning Mill | 22,000 |
| 1883— | | | |
| November 3 ... | Mitchell and Buchanan Streets | Furniture Warehouse | £128,500 |
| December 23 ... | St. Vincent at Renfield Street ... | Offices and Shops ... | 27,000 |
| 1886— | | | |
| January 28 ... | Crownpoint Road ... ... | Carpet Factory | £31,500 |
| April 3 ... ... | 5 South Hanover Street | Soft Goods ... | 27,000 |
| 1887— | | | |
| March 16 ... | 75 Buchanan Street | Silversmiths, etc. | £31,500 |
| 1888— | | | |
| October 14 ... | 20-24 Buchanan Street | Warehouses ... | £72,000 |
| October 31 | M'Neil Street ... | Spinning Mill ... | 61,000 |
| 1889— | | | |
| October 27 | Greendyke Street ... | Hides, Skin, and Wools | £36,500 |
| 1891— | | | |
| May 26 ... ... | 847 Duke Street ... | Tannery ... | £21,000 |
| June 8 ... ... | 20-28 Miller Street | Glass, etc. ... | 37,500 |
| 1892— | | | |
| August 17 ... | 66 Mitchell Street ... | Umbrellas, etc. ... | £27,500 |
| November 27 ... | 108 Boden Street ... | Curriers ... ... | 22,500 |
| 1895— | | | |
| March 1 ... | Cowcaddens | ... Theatre Royal ... | £25,000 |
| 1896— | | | |
| October 13 | 20-22 Clyde Place ... | ... Ship Chandlers, etc. | £20,500 |
| 1897— | | | |
| January 16 | 45 Anderston Quay | General Stores ... | £22,500 |
| October 26 | 23 York Street ... | Bonded Stores ... | 45,000 |
| 1898— | | | |
| April 25 ... | 27-39 East Howard Street | ... Printers, etc. ... ... | £122,000 |

**Star Music Hall Disaster.**—A very sad event happened on 1st November, 1884, in the Star Music Hall. Some evil-disposed persons raised a cry of fire, when a general panic took place, and in the stampede no fewer than fourteen persons were trampled to death and eighteen injured. This was the means of very stringent bye-laws being introduced to prevent similar occurrences being possible in places of public entertainment in the future.

**Gas Explosion.**—On 9th January, 1887, a gas explosion took place in a house in Barrowfield Street; ten persons were injured and four houses wrecked.

**Flood.**—On 31st August, 1887, an exceptionally heavy rainfall caused a drain to burst in the vicinity of Queen Street Underground Station, which was submerged to the depth of two feet

**Earthquake.**—An earthquake shock was felt in Crosshill, Mount Florida, Kelvinside, and in other suburban districts in 1888.

**Lightning.**—Three persons were killed in the city in May, 1888, by lightning.

**Mill Disaster.**—On 1st November, 1889, during a heavy gale, the gable of Messrs. Templeton's mill, on Glasgow Green, fell. Twenty-nine girls were killed and twenty-two were injured.

**Cyclone.**—A cyclonic storm, beginning in the south-east and ending in the south-west, visited the city on 13th October, 1891. It reached a velocity of 52 miles an hour, several gusts showing over 70 miles.

**Subsidences.** — Owing to the operations of the Subway and Glasgow Central Railway, several subsidences took place in 1892. In the following year the bridge across the Kelvin suffered from the Subway workings.

**High Death-rate.**—On the last week of February and the first week of March, 1895, the death-rate was 51 and 54 per thousand respectively.

**Students' Disturbance.**—In November, 1896, the students, who were holding a torchlight procession through the streets, endeavoured to enter the Skating Palace in Sauchiehall Street. On being refused admission they attacked the building, but were ultimately dispersed by the police and several arrested, who were fined at the Northern Police Court.

**Loss of Life at Fires** — In 1895 three lives were lost when Messrs. Higginbotham's Mills were burned. On 21st January, 1897, two persons were burned to death at a fire in an oil works in Kinning Park. On 7th January, 1898, four firemen lost their lives and two were injured during a fire in a chemical warehouse in Renfield Street. This was the first occasion on which firemen had been killed at a fire in the city. Two -persons were burned to death by a fire in a dwelling-house in Kinning Park on 27th March, 1899.

## BATTLES.

**The Bell o' the Brae.**—The Battle of the Bell o' the Brae, which is immortalised by Blind Harry was fought in High Street, where College Station now stands, between the Scots under Sir William Wallace and King Edward's English soldiers. The result was disastrous to the Sassenachs.

**The Butts.**—The Battle of the Butts took place on the site of the Old Barracks in the Gallowgate, during the minority of Mary Queen of Scots, between the Regent the Earl of Arran and the Earl of Glencairn. The Earl of Lennox had previously garrisoned the Bishop's Palace and retired to Dumbarton, when Arran came and

besieged it. After holding out for ten days, it surrendered under promise of quarter; but the promise was broken, and all the defenders were massacred except two, who made their escape. Glencairn came with about 800 men to avenge the slaughter, and the armies met at "The Butts," where the wappenschaws were held. After a very fierce and sanguinary encounter, Glencairn was defeated through his opponent being reinforced by Robert Boyd of Kilmarnock with a party of horse; about 300 were killed on both sides. After the fight the Regent gave the town up to plunder on account of the sympathy shown by the Provost and the citizens to his opponents. The town was completely wrecked, the very windows and the doors of the houses being carried away.

**Langside.**—After her escape from Loch Leven, Queen Mary went to Hamilton Palace, whence she endeavoured to reach Dumbarton Castle; her army was, however, intercepted at Langside by her half-brother, the Earl of Moray. The royal army was drawn up on the spot where the Deaf and Dumb Institution stands beside Mount Florida Station. The Regent Moray crossed the Clyde and marched by way of Main Street, Gorbals, to Langside. Part of the route is now taken away by the Caledonian Railway Company. It ran from the head of Main Street to the Butterbiggins Road, where a small portion of the old road may still be seen, to Camphill, where the Regent made his camp. He drew up his army where the curator's house stands in the Queen's or South Side Park. The night before the battle, it is said the Queen slept in Castlemilk at the foot of the Cathkin Braes. At any rate, she viewed the battle from the knowe overlooking Cathcart Castle. An upright, plain stone slab with a crown and the letters "M. R., 1568," now marks the spot, which is called the "Queen's Knowe." The Royalists endeavoured to force their way up Battlefield Road, the fighting taking place between where Queen's Park School and Langside Established Church are now situated, but the Regent's hag-butters were placed in the gardens and houses in the then narrow road and poured deadly volleys amongst the Royalists. The main body of Moray's army coming down the hill from where Queen Mary's Monument now stands Mary's troops broke and fled, leaving, it is said, 300 dead on the field, against one slain amongst the victors. The fight only lasted three quarters of an hour. When the Queen saw her army defeated, she still insisted on proceeding to Dumbarton Castle; but her followers insisted otherwise. The Queen becoming angry, she passionately exclaimed—" By the Cross on my loof I will be there to-night in spite of yon traitors;" hence the name Crossmyloof. Another legend is handed down which says that in flying from the battle by way of Rutherglen her horse stuck in the mire, the incident causing the district to be called " Mallsmire." Nearer Rutherglen a place called " Pants " is named after the panting her steed made in hurrying past ; while further on, at a spot called Dins Dykes, tradition states two haymakers waved their scythes and threatened to take " the fairest earth has seen " captive. She is lost sight of in the locality after crossing the Clyde at the " King's Ford " below Carmyle.

### " Battle of Garscube."—Dr. Strang

gives a reminiscence of a member of the Grog Club who took " part " in the " battle " of which the following is an epitome :—

At the beginning of this century the French Revolution caused a feeling of discontent amongst the working classes in this country, and rioting was not an unfrequent occurrence. One day intelligence was received in the city that the rioters were threatening to set fire to the house of Lord President Campbell at Garscube. In answer to the *Assembly* Rattle the Glasgow Volunteers soon gathered in George Square to the number of 300, and marched towards Garscube. On arriving at the bridge over the Kelvin (which was taken down in 1881 after an existence of 130 years) a halt was called, and a detachment sent forward to reconnoitre. They immediately took possession of the opposite bank, but no enemy was to be seen, only a few idle women and children who began to "chaff" the warriors. The day was particularly warm, and the Volunteers, unaccustomed to the tight lacing of their scarlet jackets, and laden with heavy muskets and well-filled cartouche-boxes, were in a sore plight with heat, hunger, and thirst. A council of war was summoned, the outcome of which was a unanimous resolution that a small party should keep the bridge, and the remainder go and forage for themselves. The result was that every farmhouse in the locality had to capitulate. Churns were emptied, and all the cheese and bannocks confiscated. The writer states his party, which included a Frenchman, consisted of three. They espied the smoke of a cottage, and made a bee-line for it. After some

chaff with the good-humoured matron, they were soon busy with the cake and cheese and " Mountain Dew." The Frenchman could not partake of the latter, and seeing a churn with butter-milk he put his head in it and began to lap the contents. The hostess objected to such a proceeding, and dealt the drinker a smart blow on the back, which caused him to lose his balance and pop head foremost into the gaping vessel ; his heels, which were in the air, were immediately seized by his companions-in-arms, and he was dragged forth like a cork from a bottle, and decorated with the *Order of the Bath.* The rest can be imagined. After presenting their bounty, the sound of the drum summoned the recruited soldiers to the Kelvin Bridge, when they learned that the Glasgow Volunteer Cavalry had, previous to the arrival of the infantry, dispersed the malcontents, who, after burning the Kilpatrick Parish Records, had taken up a position on a neighbouring hill. The only opposition they met with was from a vicious farm dog, which was turned by the point of a bayonet after a crack shot had failed to stop its progress. The dog, however, got the better of the encounter. The wielder of the bayonet determined to follow up his advantage by pinning his canine foe to the ground ; his second thrust, however, missed the mark, the steel piercing the earth instead, and, snapping under the weight of the quarterless volunteer, he went head foremost into the ditch. The only other incident of note was a rider being thrown from his runaway horse, happily without any bad effects. On reaching the rendezvous the army disbanded, and the battle was refought at a later hour in the taverns of the city.

## MILITARY.

### Cameronians.—When William of

Orange contemplated invading this country King James II. got ten companies of 120 men each raised on his behalf in Glasgow; but refusing to obey the magistrates they were disbanded on 23rd January, 1689. On the Prince of Orange arriving here, and while the Convention of Estates was deciding regarding the succession to the throne in Edinburgh, Glasgow raised a regiment 500 strong, which was sent to Edinburgh, under the command of the Earl of Argyle, to guard the Covenanters. Some authorities say they are the original of what is now known as the Cameronians, who have done great service to their country, even so lately as in the Soudan war at Atbara.

**Battle of Falkirk.**—Glasgow raised two regiments of Volunteers in 1745 to assist in putting down the Rebellion. They took part in the Battle of Falkirk, on 17th January, 1746, where they suffered rough handling and great loss by the Pretender's Highlanders. They were stationed in Edinburgh when Prince Charlie was in Glasgow.

**83rd.**—In 1778, during the American war, the City raised a regiment which was called the 83rd Foot, or Royal Glasgow Volunteers. Every encouragement was given to young men to join, over £30 being given as bounty money in some cases to strapping youths, and all were offered a burgess ticket free of expense. Those newly enrolled displayed their ticket behind their cockade when parading the streets. Taken all over, the regiment cost the citizens over £20,000. It was reduced in the Green at the Peace in 1783.

**Barracks.**—*Gallowgate*—The Gallowgate Barracks were erected on the site of the old Wappenschaw ground in the Gallowgate in 1795. They accommodated 1,000 men, and cost £15,000. Previous to their erection soldiers were billeted on the inhabitants. *Maryhill*—The site of Maryhill Barracks was bought from Davidson of Ruchill in 1868. The buildings, to accommodate over 1,000, were begun the following year, and completed in 1877. *Horse Barracks*—The cavalry were originally kept at Hamilton, but owing to the distance from the city horse barracks were erected at the head of Eglinton Street. Subsequently these were vacated, and when Maryhill Barracks were constructed accommodation was provided there. The Eglinton Street buildings were acquired by the Govan Parochial Board for their Poorhouse, from whence they had to remove to Merryflats, to make way for the construction of the Caledonian Railway. Eglinton Street Station now occupies the site.

**Guard-House.**—The Guard-House was first situated in the "Well Close," now St. Andrew Street, from whence it was removed in 1756 to the corner of Trongate and Candleriggs. It had a portico with four pillars in front, which extended about ten feet on the Trongate. Under this the sentry paced. This can be seen on many of the old prints of Glasgow. The Guard-House was removed in 1789 to the site of the old weigh-house in Candleriggs. In 1810 it was taken to the east side of Montrose Street

**Volunteers** —*Past*—Napoleon I. gave Glasgow great trouble. So serious had events become on the Continent at the end of last and beginning of this century that all loyal subjects were trying to strengthen the hands of the Government. Glasgow as usual was again to the front. In 1794 the first Volunteer regiment of five companies was raised under Act of Parliament. Three additional regiments were now added. The second regiment of Royal Glasgow Volunteers numbered ten companies. The Royal Glasgow Volunteer Light Horse consisted of sixty men, while the Armed Association had two companies. The sum of £13,938 14s. 6d. was sent to the Government for war purposes. Some French prisoners passed through Glasgow on their way to Edinburgh. While in the city the officers were lodged in the Tontine, and the privates quartered in the old Correction House in College Street near Shuttle Street. The Frenchmen's love for butcher meat greatly surprised the citizens.

*Great Review.*—At the Peace of Amiens, in 1802, the Glasgow Volunteer regiments were disbanded ; but upon the renewal of Napoleon's aggression in the following year, the undernoted new Volunteer Companies were formed in the city, viz. :—The 1st Regiment of Glasgow Volunteers, 900 ; 2nd or Trades Battalion, 600 ; 3rd or Highland Battalion (in Highland costume), 700 ; 4th or Sharpshooters' Battalion, 700 ; 5th or Grocers' Battalion, 600 ; 6th Anderston Battalion, 900 ; the Armed Association or Ancients, 300 ; Canal Volunteers, 300—the two latter were a kind of artillery, having two guns. In all, 5,000 men, or one to every seventeen inhabitants. The City Volunteers, in conjunction with regulars from Hamilton, and other Volunteer Companies from Greenock, Port-Glasgow, Dumbarton, Kilsyth, Cumbernauld, Airdrie, and Hamilton, were reviewed on Glasgow Green in 1804 by the Earl of Moira, afterwards Marquis of Hastings, Commander-in-Chief of the Forces in Scotland. This event created a great *furore* in the city. Apart from the brilliance of the display, the fact of each "warrior" firing off ten rounds of ammunition completely took the citizens' breath away.

*Present.*—From the inception of the Volunteer movement in 1859 Glasgow has always taken a very prominent and enthusiastic part in it, and has still the largest proportion of Volunteers to population of any town in the kingdom. The first formed and sworn-in companies in the city were known as the University and Western (now 1st Lanark) and the Southern (now 3rd Lanark), who were sworn in on 6th and 8th October, and 17th September, 1859, respectively. The Southern, University, Northern, and Eastern Companies were the first Volunteers ever seen in uniform by Her Majesty and Prince Consort, these companies acting as bodyguard at the opening of Loch Katrine Water Works. All branches of the service are represented in the City Volunteers—Yeomanry, Artillery, Engineers, Rifles, and Medical Staff Corps. The total establishment is about 12,000, and generally speaking the numbers are well kept up. In rifle shooting the reputation of Glasgow stands high, and besides innumerable minor successes, the Queen's Prize has three times been brought to the city—by Sergeant D. Reid of the Engineers, 1889; Private M. S. Rennie of 3rd Lanark, 1894; and Lieut. D. Yates, 3rd Lanark, 1898; while Private Boyd of 3rd Lanark also tied for it in 1895. This latter regiment has also performed the unique feat of winning the Belgian Cup for volley-firing seven times at the National Rifle Association's meetings at Wimbledon and Bisley.

The following are the Glasgow Regiments, with commanding officers:—Queen's Own Yeomanry Cavalry, Colonel James Neilson; 1st Lanarkshire Artillery Volunteers, Colonel A. B. Grant, V.D.; 1st Lanarkshire Royal Engineers, Lieut.-Col. Ewing R. Crawford; 1st Lanarkshire Rifle Volunteers, Colonel James Reid, V.D.; 3rd Lanarkshire Rifle Volunteers, Lieut.-Col. H. Morton, V.D.; 4th Lanarkshire Rifle Volunteers, Lieut.-Col. J. F. Newlands; 1st V.B. Highland Light Infantry (5th L.R.V.), Colonel R. C. Mackenzie, V.D.; 2nd V.B. Highland Light Infantry (6th L.R.V.), Colonel J. D. Young, V.D.; 3rd V.B Highland Light Infantry (8th L.R.V.), Colonel W. Clark, V.D.; 5th V.B. Highland Light Infantry (Glasgow Highlanders), Colonel C. M. Williamson, V.D.

**Boys' Brigade.**—The Boys' Brigade movement was originated in October, 1883, in the Woodside District Mission in connection with the Free Church College. The organisation, which is conducted on military lines, is presently composed of eighty-five companies, with a numerical strength of 4,831 boys and officers; while forty-three companies have bands. The headquarters are at 162 Buchanan Street. On the occasion of the opening of the International Exhibition by the Prince and Princess of Wales on 8th May, 1888, no fewer than 3,649 officers and boys acted as

one of the guards of honour; and when the Duke and Duchess of York visited the city on 10th September, 1897, the Brigade lined part of the route.

**Sir Archibald Allison, Bart.**—On 18th October, 1883, a sword of honour was presented in the City Hall to Sir Archibald Allison, Bart., K.C.B., together with a tiara of diamonds to Lady Allison. The sword and tiara, which cost £721 16s 5d., were publicly subscribed for by 12,000 persons. They were exhibited in the Corporation Galleries and other places in the city during November, a charge of 1d. being made, and £230 was raised for distribution on New Year's Day to the city charities.

**Memorials.**—In 1883 a mural tablet was erected on the south side of the nave of the Cathedral to the memory of William West Watson, jun., Lieutenant-Colonel 1st L.A.V., who was mortally wounded by the accidental bursting of a shell while on duty at Irvine on 6th March, 1880. A similar memorial was also erected on the south side of the nave of the Cathedral to the memory of the officers and men of the 74th Regiment who were killed at the Battle of Tel-el-Kebir on 13th September, 1882.

The colours of the 74th Regiment were placed in the Cathedral on 20th December, 1884; while on 9th July, 1885, the colours of the "Cameronians" found a last resting-place within the walls of Glasgow's mother church.

**Colonel Hector Macdonald.** — Colonel Hector Macdonald, who distinguished himself at the Battle of Omdurman, visited the city on 9th and 10th May, 1899. The Corporation gave him a banquet in the Council Chambers on the Monday. The following day he was presented with a sword of honour and an address, and entertained to a banquet by the Clan Macdonald in the St. Andrew's Halls.

_____

## COMMERCIAL.

**First Shippers.**—To William Elphinstone, who was connected with the Elphinstones of Gorbals and Blythswood, belongs the honour of being the pioneer of Glasgow's foreign trade. About 1450 he did a large business in curing salmon and herrings, which he exported to France, bringing in return brandy and salt. About the year 1500 Archibald Sym, son of Lord Glammis, began to trade between Glasgow, France, Holland and Poland.

**First Clockmaker and Surgeon.—** In 1576 the first clockmaker, David Kay, settled in Glasgow. In the following year the first surgeon, Alexander Hay, came to reside in the town.

**First Printers.—** The first printer— George Anderson—came to Glasgow in 1638. He came from Edinburgh, and was given £100 Scots, or £8 6s. 8d. stg., to bring his goods and chattels to the west Glasgow was without a printer from 1648 until 1658, George Anderson having died in the former year; but on his son, who was in business in Edinburgh, being offered the same subsidy as his father, he came to the west in the latter year. He was succeeded by Robert Sanders in 1661, who died in 1696, the business being carried on by his son, Robert Sanders, of Auldhouse.

**Soap and Sugar in 1667.—** In 1667 a Whale-fishing Company and Soap Manufactory, with blubber works at Greenock, was started with a capital of £12,000 stg. The Wester Sugar Work Company began business in the same year, occupying the ground now known as Stockwell Place. This was followed in two years afterwards by the Easter Sugar Works Company in the Gallowgate.

**Tobacco, Soap, and Sugar in 1700.** —The tobacco trade assumed large proportions at the beginning of 1700. Merchants sent their finished goods to Virginia and Maryland, and received tobacco leaf in return. Soap was also a staple industry, and soap and candle works were situated in Candleriggs, which derived its name from a field which was let out to the manufacturers in "rigs." Curing of herrings and sugar refining were also prosperous industries.

**Printers.—** In 1713 the University arranged with Thomas Harvie to become their printer; he does not seem to have been a success, for two years afterwards we find them making a seven years' engagement with Donald Govane. James Duncan began business in 1718 at the foot of the Saltmarket, and introduced the art of typemaking. He printed "M'Ure's History of Glasgow" in 1736. Robert Urie & Co. were printers in the Gallowgate in 1740; they executed several works for Robert Foulis. The *Glasgow Journal*, which first appeared on 20th July, 1741, was printed by Urie.

**White Linen.—** The manufacture of white linen was begun in 1725, the workers being brought from Holland and Ireland.

**Glass-Bottle Work.—** In 1730 the first glass-bottle work was built on the Old Green, where the Custom-House now stands in Great Clyde Street, near the corner of Jamaica Street. This is a prominent landmark in the maps of old Glasgow.

**Bleachfield and Thread Manufacture.—** In 1730 the first bleachfield was built at Wellhouse, and the manufacture of thread was commenced in a small way.

**Tobacco.—** Parliament interfered to the detriment of the tobacco trade, but it again revived in 1735, and agencies were established in the tobacco colonies.

**Cambric and Printfield.—** In 1742 the manufacture of cambric was begun, and the first printfield was erected by Ingram & Co. in Pollokshaws.

**Inkle Factory, Ironmongery, and West India Trade.—** In 1743 the Inkle Factory Company feued three roods of land in Ramshorn Yard, from Hutcheson's Hospital, at £2 16s. 3d., stg., per annum, for the extension of their business. An ironmongery manufactory was built "of ashlar work, on an eminency near the north side of the great key or harbour at the Broomielaw." A trade in sugar and rum was begun about this time with the West Indies.

**Copper, Tin, and White Iron.—** Copper, tin, and white iron for export were first manufactured in 1747, while a factory for the making of delf started in the Broomielaw the following year.

**First Shoe, Draper's, and Silversmith's Shops.—** The first shoe shop was opened in the city to the west of the Tron Church by William Colquhoun in 1749. Next year Andrew Lockhart opened the first draper's shop in the Saltmarket. In 1754 R. Luke began business as a silversmith.

**French Cambric.—** Cambric manufacture from French yarn started in 1752.

**Brush and Carpetmaking. —** In 1755 brushmaking was commenced.—Carpet weaving was begun two years later.

**First Hat Shops. —** The first hat shops were opened in the Saltmarket and Bridgegate in 1756. J. Blair has the honour of being the first hatter.

**Woollen Drapery.—** A woollen drapery business was started by Patrick Ewing in 1761.

**Tobacco, Shoemaking, and Weaving.—** In 1773 there were 38 firms of tobacco merchants in the city.—George

M'Intosh, King Street, employed over 300 shoemakers, while a similar number wrought with the Glasgow Tanwork Co.— Power-loom weaving was also introduced in 1773.

**Tobacco and West Indian Trade.** —The outbreak of the American war in 1775 was the death-knell of the tobacco trade. The tobacco lords, whose pride was a byword, and who strutted about in wigs and scarlet cloaks on the "plain stanes" (pavement) in front of the Exchange in the Trongate like peacocks, determined not to give up without a struggle. They even went the length of acting as recruiting sergeants, and raised and equipped a regiment of 1,000 men at an expense of £20,000, stg. This afterwards became the 83rd Foot. Ships were given for the transport of troops, and fourteen privateers, carrying from 12 to 22 guns, and about 1,000 men, were also fitted out. It was a vain effort. Attention was then turned to the West Indian trade of sugar, rum, and cotton, which soon became so important that the tobacco business was not missed.

**Flint-glass and Cudbear.** — The manufacture of flint-glass and that important dyeing requisite, cudbear, was introduced in 1777.

**Turkey-red Dyeing.** — The first Turkey-red dyeworks in Great Britain were erected at Dalmarnock by David Dale and George Macintosh in 1785, and a practical manager was brought from Rouen.

**First Distillery.**—The first distillery in the city was built in Kirk Street, Calton, in 1786.

**First Shipment of Tea.** — Messrs. James Finlay & Co., and John Fleming of Claremont brought the first consignment of tea direct from India to the Clyde, in the ship "Mountstewart," on 9th October, 1834. It consisted of 33 chests and 402 boxes.

**Dixon's Iron Works.**—The Govan Iron Works, better known as "Dixon's Blazes," at the head of Crown Street, were commenced in 1837.

**Tennant's Works.**—The chemical works of Messrs. Tennant, Knox & Co. in St. Rollox, were erected in 1800. In 1843 the firm erected their famous stalk, which is 500 feet above the level of the Clyde. It cost £12,000.

**Custom-House.**—The first Custom-House was situated in High Street, near the Old Vennel, from whence it removed to the Broomielaw, opposite the foot of

Oswald Street. In 1757 it was located at the foot of Stockwell Street, where it remained until after 1780, when new premises were secured on the west side of St. Enoch Square. All the business continued to be transacted here, until the present Custom-House was erected in Great Clyde Street in 1837. Customs revenue:—

| | | | | £ | s. | d. |
|---|---|---|---|---|---|---|
| 1801 | ... | ... | ... | 427 | 17 | 7¾ |
| 1811 | ... | ... | ... | 3,124 | 2 | 4½ |
| 1821 | ... | ... | ... | 16,147 | 17 | 7 |
| 1831 | ... | ... | ... | 68,741 | 5 | 9 |
| 1841 | ... | ... | ... | 526,100 | 0 | 11 |
| 1851 | ... | ... | ... | 675,044 | 15 | 10 |
| 1861 | ... | ... | ... | 924,445 | 10 | 0 |
| 1871 | ... | ... | ... | 999,572 | 9 | 7 |
| 1880 | ... | ... | ... | 969,339 | 7 | 4 |
| 1890 | ... | ... | ... | 1,341,435 | 4 | 7 |
| 1898 | ... | ... | ... | 1,748,822 | 11 | 9 |

**Introduction of Guano.**—Alex. and John Downie brought the first cargo of guano to the Clyde from the island of Ichaboe in 1844, and ever since Glasgow has been a large and increasing importing centre of this article.

**Cooking Depots.**—In 1860, Thomas Corbett (father of the M.P. for Tradeston) founded Cooking Depôts in the city for the benefit of the working classes. He used the profits wholly for the improvement of the food.

**Steel Company of Scotland.**—The Steel Company of Scotland was formed in 1871, and built their great works at Newton, near Cambuslang, for the manufacture of steel according to the Siemens process.

**Co-operation.**—The first co-operative society began business in Govan in 1777. The movement gradually grew in favour, and spread all over the country, being especially favoured in industrial districts. In 1868 the Scottish Co-operative Wholesale Society began business in Madeira Court. They employed six persons, their capital amounted to £1.795, and the sales for the first quarter totalled £9,697 7s. 1d. For the year ended 1869 their report shows :—Capital, £5,174 17s. 4d.; sales, £81,094 2s. 6d.; net profit, £1,303 15s.; depreciation on buildings and fixtures, £138 19s. 2d. In 1874 they removed to their own property at the corner of Morrison Street and Paisley Road, and in the following year added a drapery branch to their business. In 1880 the Society began to purchase ground and build in Clarence Street. Since then their progress has been one triumphal march. St. James's Street followed in 1883, Clarence Street again in 1886, Crookston Street in 1891, until the whole square was acquired to Morrison Street in 1892, where the magnificent pile of masonry now raises its head as one of the "lions" of the city. A huge factory was erected at Shieldhall, and branches were opened at Leith, 1877 ; Kilmarnock, 1878 ; Dundee, 1882. Mills have been erected in Edinburgh and Selkirk, a depôt established in Enniskillen, a creamery at Bladnoch, in Wigtownshire, and soap works at Grangemouth, the buildings alone being valued at £310,792, while the sites represent £47,220 more. The Society for the year ended 1898 shows:—Shares subscribed, 439,396; capital, £2,611,086 1s. 5d.; net sales, £4,692,330 9s. 9d.; net profit, £165,580 11s. 10d.; depreciation on buildings, etc., £558,723 13s. 9d.; people employed, 4,796, whose wage bill for 1897 amounted to £222,418 0s. 1d.

## MARKETS.

*Produce.*—In 1626 a Meal Market was erected opposite the Old College in High Street, whence it removed in 1796 to the foot of Montrose Street, and was incorporated with the butter, cheese, and poultry branches.

*Flesh.*—A Flesh Market is referred to in the Trongate in 1661. It stood on the north side, between Candleriggs and Hutcheson Streets.

*Beef, etc.*—In 1754 markets were built in King and Bell Streets. In the former the Beef Market was on one side of the street, and the Mutton, Fish, and Cheese Market on the other.

*Vegetable.*—The gardens which stood on the site of Charlotte Street served for the first Vegetable Market. When the ground was feued the Market found a resting-place in the Trongate, whence it removed in 1755 to the west side of Candleriggs. Subsequently a change was made to the site of the Old Wynd Church, with the principal entry from King Street.

*Bird.*—About 1800 the Bird Market was held alongside a dead wall at the corner of Montrose and Cochrane Streets, whence it removed to the front of the Ramshorn Church in Ingram Street. It was afterwards accommodated beside the Bazaar. Previous to finding its resting-place in its present quarters in Jail Square, it was temporarily located within a wooden barricade on the Green, at the corner of Jail Square and Greendyke Street. The Market is open for wholesale and retail business on Mondays, Wednesdays, and Saturdays

*Fruit.*—The first Fruit Market was held beside the Great Dovehill, from where it removed to the yard of an inn in Kent Street, previous to reaching its present headquarters in the Bazaar.

*Fish.*—The first Fish Market was at the Broomielaw. It removed to the west side of Candleriggs, next the old Guard House, whence it went to King Street. It was subsequently located in Great Clyde Street, between Dunlop Street and Ropework Lane. It is now situated in East Clyde Street, and occupies a space of 2,000 square yards.

*The Bazaar.*—The Bazaar buildings were erected in the Candleriggs in 1817, from plans drawn by James Cleland, Master of Works, who laid the foundation stone. The ground was formerly occupied as the old Glasgow Bowling Green. The Bazaar was rebuilt in 1886. It covers 7,879 square yards, and has cost £60,000. There are fifty-eight stances, and the income amounts to over £3,300. The Bazaar, Bird, and Old Clothes Markets form part of the Common Good.

*New "Toun" Market.*—What was called the New "Toun" Market stood on the site of the present *Herald* Buildings in Buchanan Street about 1830.

*Cheese.*—The Cheese Market at one time was situated in Montrose Street, but it is now situated beside the Bazaar, with an entrance from South Albion Street. It is open on Tuesdays, Wednesdays, and Fridays, when only a wholesale business is carried on.

*Old Clothes.*—The Old Clothes Market, which used to be popularly known as "Paddy's Market," was originally held in an uncovered space on the site of the present Bird Market; afterwards it was accommodated in the adjoining Old Slaughter-House, entering from the Bridgegate. In July, 1875, it removed to the present commodious building in Greendyke Street.

*Fruit and Vegetable.*—The Clyde Fruit-growers' Company erected a market at the corner of South Albion and Bell Streets. It was opened on 15th July, 1884.

**Cattle Market.**—*Trongate*—In 1739 the Cattle Market was held between what is now King and Stockwell Streets. Beef was 2d. per lb. Fifty head of cattle were bought for £100 stg. A cattle market stood in Argyle Street, opposite Virginia Street, from which the Black Bull Inn derived its name. *Great Clyde Street.*—At the beginning of this century the Cattle

Market and Horse Fair was held on the banks of the Clyde between what is now Jail Square and Jamaica Street. The horses were trotted out for inspection in Stockwell, Glassford, and Argyle Streets, and along the Trongate. *Graham Square.*—The Cattle Market between Duke Street and the Gallowgate was laid out in 1818. A stone wall was built enclosing 9,281 yards of ground, inside of which 150 sheep pens, sheds for cattle, and stabling accommodation were erected, also an inn. The site was originally intended for a residential one, under the name of Graham Square. At frequent intervals it has been enlarged, and now covers an area of 35,000 square yards, accommodates 2,000 cattle and 15,000 sheep in pens ; 1,000 cattle can be loose in sheds, and 160 milch cows can be fed in byres. Attached to the Cattle Market is a Horse Bazaar, which covers 980 square yards, and has stabling accommodation for 112 horses. The slaughter-houses extend over 12,500 square yards. The Dead Meat Market covers 3.700 square yards. In addition to these there is an hotel, several banks, and other offices. The principal market day is Wednesday, but business can be transacted any other day.

**Dead Meat Market.** — The Dead Meat Market, which covers 3,700 square yards of ground, and has 45 stances, was opened in Moore Street in September, 1879, for the sale of foreign cattle, which are slaughtered immediately they land at Pointhouse, Yorkhill, or Shieldhall, after which they are transferred to Moore Street. Pointhouse and Yorkhill erections were completed in 1894, at a cost of about £50,000. The market days at Yorkhill are Monday and Tuesday.

**Slaughter-Houses.**—The first public Slaughter-House or Shambles was erected in 1744 at the mouth of the Molendinar Burn, beside where the Justiciary Buildings stand at the corner of East Clyde Street. When the Cattle Market was built in Graham Square in 1818 the Slaughter-House, which had become a public nuisance, was removed to Moore Street, which is contiguous to the market. It covers 12,500 square yards of ground. There are two subsidiary Slaughter-Houses at Scott and Victoria Streets, but these will shortly be abolished and all the business transacted at Moore Street.

---

## BIBLIOGRAPHY.

**First Glasgow Printing.**—The first book printed in Glasgow was entitled "The Protestation of the Generall Assemblie of the Church of Scotland, and of the Noblemen, Barons, Gentlemen, Burrowes, Ministers, and Commons, Subscribers of the Covenant, lately renewed, made in the High Kirk, and at the Mercate Crosse of Glasgow, the 28 and 29 November, 1638. Printed at Glasgow by George Anderson, in the Yeare of Grace 1638."

**Black-Letter Edition of the New Testament.** — Robert Sanders, printer, published a black-letter edition of the New Testament in 1672.

**"The Jacobite Curse."**—Hugh Brown, printer, published an octavo volume in 1714, entitled, "The Jacobite Curse ; or Excommunication of King George." The University authorities were very much annoyed, Brown having called himself the University printer, a distinction he did not possess. The College printing had to be sent to Edinburgh to get even one page correctly done.

**"History of the Rebellion."**—In 1746 Dugald Graham, the city bellman, published a metrical "History of the Rebellion of 1745." It was sold by James Duncan, printer, Saltmarket, price fourpence, and passed through more than eight editions.

**"The Spectator."**—The Glasgow edition of *The Spectator* was printed by R. Urie & Co. in 1750, and the same firm also published the New Testament in Greek.

**Early Directories.** — The first "Glasgow Directory" was published by John Tait in 1783. The second directory, called "Jones' Directory," was published by Joseph Galbraith. Another, called "The Glasgow Directory," containing about 4,000 names, was published in 1807 by Wm. M'Feat & Co., stationers, Trongate, and printed by Thos. Duncan, 159 Saltmarket.

**Histories of Glasgow.**— *M'Ure's*— The first "History of Glasgow" was published by John M'Ure, clerk to the Register of Sasines, in 1736, being printed by James Duncan in the Saltmarket, near Gibson's Wynd (now Parnie Street). The following is a short summary of some of the principal items :—Length of city, one mile and a third from north to south, and three-quarters of a mile from east to west—Rottenrow to Drygate. Molendinar Burn bordered the north-east, crossed the

Gallowgate, ran alongside the east of Salt-market, and flowed into the Clyde to the south of the Bridgegate. St. Enoch's Burn ran to the west of the city, was crossed by three stone bridges, and joined the Clyde to the west of Stockwell Bridge. There were three parks—Craig or Fir Park (now the Necropolis); the "New Green" (now Glasgow Green), where the women washed their clothes in the Clyde; and the Old Green, which extended from what is now Jamaica Street to Stockwell Street; in this was situated a rope work and glass work. There were four malt mills and about a dozen coal pits within two miles of the city, and sixteen public and several private wells; freestone quarries, twelve stone bridges inside and eight outside the burgh, eight gates, ten principal streets, and seventeen lanes or wynds. High Street and High Kirk Street were about three-quarters of a mile long. The Duke of Montrose resided in the Drygate, which measured about half a mile; Rotten Row about 600 yards long, and the Gallowgate (where the best shops and lawyers were to be found) three-quarters of a mile. Salt-market, which contained a tenement built upon eighteen pillars, was a quarter of a mile in length. Gibson's Lane (now Parnie Street), was occupied by the Post Office and the *elite* of the city. Bridge Street or Bridgegate housed Colin Campbell of Blythswood, and many important merchants and tradesmen. Stockwell Street, recently formed, was where the landed gentry lived. St. Enoch Street, or Trongate, was a fashionable thoroughfare. In it was situated Shawfield House, belonging to Colonel William M'Dowall of Castle Semple. the Guard-House, Flesh Market, Tron Kirk, and Tolbooth. The seventeen wynds referred to were:—Limmerfield, Greyfriars, New Vennel, Grammar School, Blackfriars, Bell's, Old Vennel, King Street, Spoutmouth, Baker's, or St. Andrew's Street, Armour's, Main's, or Back, New, Old, Aird's, or Goosedubs, Moodie's, and St. Enoch's Wynds. Public works:—Wester Sugar Work in Stockwell Street; Easter Sugar Work in Gallowgate; South Sugar Work, foot of Stockwell Street; King Street Sugar Work; Rope Work on Old Green; three tanyards and a brewery on the Molendinar; an iron work at the Broomielaw; tobacco-spinning factory in King Street, a linen manufactory, and "the little sugar house in King Street."

*Denholm's.* — Denholm's "History of Glasgow" was published in 1797, and was followed by a second and third edition within the next few years. In Macgregor's "Exhaustive History of Glasgow" an interesting summary is taken from the old book. The following are a few items, *viz.*:—Beginning at the Old Gallowgate Toll-Bar, near Tureen Street (called after the tureens made in the adjoining potteries), between which and the Cross the Gallowgate extended, Sydney, Barrack, Claythorn, Gibson, Campbell, Kent, Suffolk, and Charlotte Streets were all formed and built up. Houses extended to the village of Calton. A one-arched bridge crossed the Molendinar in Gallowgate, which was here called the Gallowgate Burn. The Cross Steeple and Tolbooth had a very majestic appearance alongside the small houses of these days. Some splendid houses adorned the Trongate and Argyle Street, the Piazzas, King William's Statue, Tontine, and Tron Church and Steeple being prominent features. The houses in High Street for some distance up were built upon arches. Branching off this street were Bell Street, Buns or Greyfriars Wynd, Havannah, and George Streets. Historical reference is made to the Drygate, Limmerfield Lane, and Rottenrow. From the last-named, Taylor and Weaver Streets, which were being formed, branched off. At the head of High Street stood the Almshouse or Old Trades Hall, the bell of which tolled when a funeral passed to the churchyard. A slit beneath one of the windows gave the passing mourners an opportunity of slipping a coin in for the poor. The Royal Infirmary and St. Nicholas' Hospital were prominent buildings in their district. St. Andrew's Street led from the Saltmarket to St. Andrew's Square, where the church. surrounded by splendid houses, made a sight of which any city would feel proud. Arcades under the houses in the Saltmarket were utilised for shops. The slums of the city were where the Justiciary Buildings now stand in Jail Square. The streets connected with the Trongate were:—Candleriggs, Nelson, Wilson, Brunswick, North and South Albion, King, Hutcheson, Stockwell, Ingram, and Great Glassford Streets, the new Trades Hall being situated in the latter. Argyle, Virginia, Miller, and Dunlop were all prominent streets; the old theatre stood in the last-named. The new theatre, which was the largest out of London, stood in Queen Street. Hutcheson's New Hospital was being built in Ingram Street, and the Assembly Rooms were also in this street. Some elegant buildings adorned George

Square, around which were Hanover, Frederick, Cochran, George, and John Streets, and in the latter was the hall of Anderson's Institution, while the Grammar School was on the north side of George Street. Mention is made of Duke, Queen, and Maxwell Streets, and St. Enoch's Square is referred to as containing the Church, Surgeons' Hall, and fine, self-contained houses. Buchanan Street extended from Argyle Street "to the road leading from George Square to Port-Dundas." Elegant houses were in the street; the residence of Mr. Gordon stood in it, opposite Gordon Street, which was then being opened up. Jamaica Street, in which was situated the Riding School or Circus, used as a "Tabernacle," led to the new bridge at the Broomielaw, where a great number of vessels were daily loading and unloading. Clyde Street, which ran in line, contained a few houses from whose windows a good view of the shipping could be had. Union Place (now Union Street), was only partially built, and was intended to join Gordon Street. Alston, Madeira, and York Streets were in the west. Eulogistic reference is made to the Green, where the cows grazed, their owners paying the city a rent of 40s. for each cow for five months' grass. £300 to £400 revenue was obtained in the year in small fees for the use of a Public Washing-House. The suburbs were:—Eastern—Calton (a burgh of barony, with a prison and baron bailie), Bridgeton, and Camlachie. Southern—Gorbals, Lauries-ton, and Tradeston. Western—Anderston (in which were a fish market and shambles), Finnieston (with a crystal manufactory), Grahamston, and Brownfield. Northern—Cowcaddens and Port-Dundas. The following banks were in the city, viz.: the Old Ship Bank, the Thistle Bank, the Royal Bank, the Bank of Scotland, the British Linen Bank, the Paisley Bank, the Paisley Union Bank, the Leith Bank, the Stirling Merchant Bank, the Greenock Bank, the Falkirk Bank, the Perth Bank, the Renfrewshire Bank, and the Ayr Bank; and also several insurance offices.

**Histories of Glasgow.**—The following "Histories of Glasgow" have been published, viz.: John M'Ure, 1736; John Gibson, 1777; Andrew Brown, 1795; James Denholm, 1797; James Clelland, 1816; Rev. W. M. Wade, 1821; "Glasgow Delineated," 1821; Robert Chapman, 1822; "Chronicles of St. Mungo," 1843; James Pagan, 1847; "Glasgow Past and Present," 1849; Dr. Strang, 1856; "Senex," Robert Reid, 1864; Pe'er M'Kenzie, 1865; Andrew Macgeorge, 1866; Dr. Gordon, 1872; G. Macgregor, 1881; A. .Wallace, 1882. In addition to the foregoing, there are some valuable histories and reminiscences on special subjects, such as Crawford's "Sketch of the Trades House," M'Lellan's "History of the Cathedral," "Histories of the different Incorporations," "Nestor's Recollections," "Stuart's Views," and "Swan's Views," while Sir James Bell, James Paton, Sir James Marwick, A. Aird, and others have all contributed valuable works on the city.

**First Newspaper.**—The first Glasgow newspaper, *The Glasgow Courant*, a small quarto twelve-page paper, was published on 14th November, 1715, It was "printed by Donald Govan, for R. T.," appeared on Tuesdays, Thursdays, and Saturdays, price three half-pence, regular customers one penny, and was sold at the printing-house in the College, and at the Post Office. Gentlemen in the principal towns were requested to send news, especially from seaport towns, regarding shipping. After the fourth number the title was changed to the *West Country Intelligence*. Only sixty-seven numbers appeared.

**Newspaper Extracts, 1745.**—The second *Glasgow Courant* was published on 14th October, 1745. Macgregor, in his excellent "History of Glasgow," gives a few extracts from the paper, which I here cull, viz.:—"Mr. Graham, younger, of Dougalston, married Miss Campbell of Skirving, *a beautiful and virtuous young lady.*" "Dr. Robert Hamilton, married Miss Mally Baird, *a beautiful young lady with a handsome fortune.*" "Mr. James Johnstone, married Miss Peggy Newall, *a young lady of great merit and a fortune of £4,000.*" "James Hodge *sells burying crapes ready-made, and that his wife's neice, who lives with him, dresses dead corpses at as cheap a rate as was formerly done by her aunt, having been educated by her and perfected at Edinburgh, from whence she is lately arrived, and has all the newest and best fashions.*" "A barber, *having found his affairs going back, and having discovered the cause to be that he was underpaid for shaving and wig-dressing, decided to charge one halfpenny for dressing a wig and a penny for each shave; he hoped they would consider his reasonable and modest request.*" "William Murdoch, wright, in Gorbals, *at the sign of the Drum and Little Wheel, make: drums (conform'd to the method of*

*Herbert Heggins, Drum-maker to His Majesty's Office of Ordinance) either big or small, coarse or fine, for sea or land, at very reasonable rates, and as good as any in Scotland.*"

**"The Glasgow Herald."**—A newspaper called *The Advertiser* was published by John Mennons in 1783. Its name was changed in 1801 to *The Herald and Advertiser*, and during the same year it was renamed *The Herald*. It was owned by Samuel Hunter & Co., who also published for the following five years a paper called the *Clyde Commercial Advertiser*. Samuel Hunter was born in Stoneykirk Manse, Wigtownshire, on 19th March, 1769, and educated at Glasgow University. He continued editor of *The Herald* till 1837. His residence was in Madeira Court. George Outram and James Pagan, who subsequently became connected with *The Herald*, are well known in connection with Glasgow journalism. In 1859 *The Herald* became a daily paper. The *Herald* Office previous to 1800 was in 22 Salt-market. Subsequently it was situated as under, viz.:—44 Bell Street (1813-25), 90 Bell Street (1826-36), Old Post Court, Trongate (1837), Spreull's Court, Trongate (1841), St. Vincent Place (1859), Buchanan Street (1868).

**"Citizen" and "North British Daily Mail."**—In 1842 Dr. James Hedderwick instituted the *Glasgow Citizen*. In 1864 it was named the *Weekly Citizen*, when the *Evening Citizen* was first published. This was the first halfpenny evening newspaper in Glasgow. To the *North British Daily Mail* belongs the honour of publishing the first daily newspaper in Scotland, on 14th April, 1847. During an Industrial Exhibition, held in the City Hall in 1847, under the auspices of the Philosophical Society, Messrs. W. G. Blackie & Co. printed an eight-page daily paper dealing with the Exhibition, called the *Daily Exhibitor*. It had the additional novelty of being printed in one of the Exhibition stalls; eleven numbers were issued.

The following newspapers have been published in Glasgow. Only daily and weekly papers are given:—

| Name of Paper | From.To. | | Name of Paper | From.To. | |
| --- | --- | --- | --- | --- | --- |
| Advertiser ... | 1783 1801 | Thrice a-w'k | Evening Mail | 1865 1865 | Daily |
| Argus | 1833 1847 | Twice a-w'k | Evening Post | 1866 1868 | Do. |
| Argus Weekly | 1857 1857 | Do. | Evening Post | 1827 — | Do. |
| Advertiser ... | 1834 1864 | Weekly | Evening Journal ... | 1869 1869 | Do. |
| Advertiser, Forsyth's ... | — — | Do. | *Evening Times ... | 1876 — | Do. |
| Advertiser, Railway and Shipping... | 1850 1864 | Do. | Evening Star | 1870 1875 | Do. |
| Bulletin ... | 1855 1861 | Daily | Evening News and Star | 1875 — | Do. |
| *Bailie | 1872 — | Weekly | Echo, The Glasgow ... | 1893 1895 | Do. |
| Bee ... | 1873 1874 | Do. | Engineering and Iron Trades Advertiser ... | 1872 — | Weekly |
| Chronicle ... | 1775 1779 | Do. | Farming World ... | — | Do. |
| Caledonia ... | 1807 1807 | Do. | Free Press... | 1823 1834 | Twice a-w'k |
| Courant ... | 1715 1715 | Thrice a-w'k | Free Press... | 1851 1867 | Weekly |
| Courier ... | 1791 1865 | Do. | Freemason, The ... | 1868 1883 | Do. |
| Chronicle ... | 1811 1857 | Do. | Gazette ... | 1855 1864 | Do. |
| Courant ... | 1745 — | | Guardian, Weekly | 1858 1860 | Do. |
| Chronicle, Weekly ... | 1858 1859 | Weekly | General Advertiser | 1857 1859 | Do. |
| Constitutional ... | 1836 1855 | Twice a-w'k | Gentle's Advertiser | 1859 1859 | Do. |
| *Citizen, Weekly... | 1842 — | Weekly | Govan Chronicle... | 1878 1880 | Do. |
| *Citizen, Evening | 1864 — | Daily | *Govan Press ... | 1880 — | Do. |
| Commonwealth ... | 1854 1860 | Weekly | Hedderwick's Miscellany | 1862 1863 | Do. |
| Commerce... | — | Do. | *Herald, The Glasgow ... | 1801 1859 | Thrice a-w'k Daily since 1859 |
| *Christian News ... | 1846 — | Do. | | | |
| Christian Times ... | — | | Herald and Advertiser ... | 1801 1801 | Thrice a-w'k |
| Clyde Commercial Advertiser ... | 1805 1810 | Do. | Herald, Evening ... | 1865 1865 | Do. |
| Chiel ... | 1883 1889 | Do. | *Herald, Weekly... | 1864 — | Weekly |
| *Christian Leader ... | 1882 — | Do. | Illustrated Glasgow Family Times .. | 1859 1859 | Do. |
| Christian Herald... | 1876 — | Do. | Journal, Glasgow ... | 1729 1845 | Do. |
| Christian Scotsman | — — | Do. | Ironmonger, The... | — — | Do. |
| Daily Exhibitor ... | 1846 1847 | Daily | Journal, Weekly ... | 1869 1869 | Do. |
| Daily Mail ... | 1849 1851 | Do. | Judy, Illustrated ... | 1857 1857 | Do. |
| Daily Express ... | 1866 1870 | Do. | Liberator ... | 1833 1838 | Do. |
| Day ... | 1832 1833 | Do. | *League Journal ... | 1857 — | Do. |
| *Examiner, Glasgow | 1897 — | Weekly | *Labour Leader ... | 1889 — | Do. |
| Examiner ... | 1844 1864 | Do. | Lombard Daily Telegraphic News ... | 1870 1870 | Daily |
| Edinburgh, Leith, and Glasgow Advertiser ... | 1833 1838 | Do. | | | |

| NAME OF PAPER. | FROM. | TO. |  | NAME OF PAPER. | FROM. | TO. |  |
|---|---|---|---|---|---|---|---|
| Mail, The ... ... ... | 1842 | 1844 | Weekly | Scots Times ... ... | 1829 | 1841 | Twice a-w'k |
| Mercantile Advertiser and Shipping Gazette ... | 1849 | — | Do. | Scotch Reformers'Gazette | 1837 | 1855 | Weekly |
| Morning Journal... ... | 1858 | 1869 | Daily | *Scots Pictorial, The ... | 1897 | — | Do. |
| *Mail, Weekly ... ... | 1863 | — | Weekly | Scottish Guardian ... | 1832 | 1861 | Twice a-w'k |
| Military Record and Volunteer News ... | 1877 | 1883 | Do. | Scottish Railway Gazette | 1845 | 1848 | Weekly |
| Mercury ... ... ... | 1778 | 1786 | Twice a-w'k | Scottish Times ... ... | 1850 | 1850 | Do. |
| Mace, The... ... | 1879 | 1883 | Weekly | Scotchman ... ... | 1812 | 1813 |  |
| North British Advertiser | 1839 | 1874 | Do. | Scottish Journal ... ... | 1865 | 1868 | Do. |
| N. British Railway and Shipping Journal ... | 1846 | 1860 | Do. | Scottish Banner ... ... | 1859 | 1864 | Do. |
| N. British Telegraph and Advertiser ... ... | 1850 | 1851 | Do. | Scottish Standard ... | 1869 | 1881 | Do. |
| *N. British Daily Mail ... | 1847 | — | Daily | Sentinel ... ... ... | 1821 | — |  |
| News, Weekly ... ... | 1856 | 1857 | Weekly | Sentinel ... ... ... | 1851 | 1877 | Do. |
| News, Daily ... ... | 1855 | 1857 | Daily | Sentinel ... ... ... | 1809 | 1811 | Thrice a-w'k |
| News, The Glasgow ... | 1873 | 1888 | Do. | Saturday Post & Paisley & Renfrewshire Reformer | 1827 | 1875 | Weekly |
| *News, Evening ... ... | 1875 | — | Do. | *Saint Andrew ... ... | 1899 | — | Do. |
| National Liberator ... | 1842 | 1842 | Weekly | St. Mungo ... ... ... | 1897 | 1897 | Do. |
| National ... ... ... | 1844 | 1845 | Do. | Signs of our Times ... | 1870 | 1875 | Do. |
| National Advertiser ... | 1847 | 1848 | Do. | Scottish Reformer and Weekly Review ... | 1882 | 1886 | Do. |
| Now ... ... ... | — | — | Do. | *Scottish Nights ... ... | 1883 | — | Do. |
| Northern Times ... ... | 1856 | 1856 | Do. | Sphinx ... ... ... | 1883 | 1883 | Do. |
| National Penny Press ... | 1858 | 1858 | Do. | Scottish Reader ... ... | 1884 | 1885 | Do |
| National Advertising List | 1869 | — | Do. | *Scottish Farmer, The ... | 1893 | — | Do. |
| News of the Week ... | 1875 | 1877 | Do. | Scottish Athletic Journal | 1882 | 1888 | Do. |
| *National Guardian ... | 1881 | — | Do. | *Scottish Cyclist, The ... | 1888 | — | Do. |
| *Observer ... ... ... | 1885 | — | Do. | Scottish People ... ... | 1886 | 1887 | Do. |
| Packet, Glasgow ... | 1813 | 1815 | Do. | *St. Rollox & Springburn Express ... ... ... | — | — | Do. |
| Penny Post ... ... | 1856 | 1877 | Do. | Scottish Umpire ... ... | 1884 | 1888 | Do. |
| *Pollokshaws News ... | — | — | Do. | *South Suburban Press | 1887 | — | Do. |
| *Property Circular ... | 1856 | — | Do. | Scottish Fancier, The ... | — | — | Do. |
| *Partick & Maryhill Press | — | — | Do. | *Scottish Referee ... | 1888 | — | Twice a-w'k |
| Punch Bowl (Illustrated) | 1849 | 1850 | Do. | *Scottish Sport ... ... | 1888 | — | Do. |
| Protestant Layman ... | — | — | Do. | Telegraphic News ... | — | — | Weekly |
| Quiz... ... ... ... | 1882 | 1898 | Do. | Tattler, The ... ... | 1882 | 1882 | Do. |
| Radical Reformer ... | 1857 | 1857 | Do. | Times, Glasgow ... ... | 1856 | 1869 | Do. |
| *Reformer, The Scottish | 1887 | — | Do. | Tickler, The ... ... | 1883 | 1883 | Do. |
| Reformers' Gazette ... | 1831 | 1837 | Do. | Trade Advocate ... ... | 1829 | — | Do. |
| *Record, Daily ... ... | 1895 | — | Daily | To-Day ... ... ... | — | — | Do. |
| *Record, The Scots Commercial ... ... | 1898 | — |  | Volunteer News ... ... | 1869 | 1876 | Do. |
| Reporter, Weekly ... | 1834 | — | Weekly | Workman, The ... ... | 1856 | 1858 | Do. |
| Register, Weekly... ... | — | — | Do. | West Country Intelligence | 1715 | 1716 | Thrice a-w'k |
|  |  |  |  | Western Star ... ... | 1813 | 1815 | Thrice a-w'k |
|  |  |  |  | *Weekly Record... ... | 1899 | — | Weekly |

An asterisk (*) denotes the papers still being published.

## Mitchell, Stirling, and Baillie Libraries.

—Mitchell—Mr. Stephen Mitchell, who amassed a large fortune in the city, bequeathed £66,998 10s. 6d. for the institution of a public library in 1874. The Town Council accepted the gift, and secured premises in East Ingram Street, which were opened on 1st November, 1877, by Lord Provost Bain. During the three years interest had raised the original sum to £70,000. After being temporarily housed from May, 1890, to October, 1891, in the vacated City Chambers in Ingram Street, the library was removed to more commodious and central premises in Miller Street, which had been built in 1860 for the Corporation Water Offices. The reopening ceremony was performed by the Marquis of Bute on 7th October, 1891. In 1877 there were 13,000 volumes, now there are over 100,000.—Stirling's—Mr. Walter Stirling gave £1,000, some heritable property, and his private collection of 804 books for a public library in 1791. The institution was housed in a room in the Surgeons' Hall in St. Enoch Square, and afterwards in Hutcheson's Hospital in Ingram Street, but is now located in 48 Miller Street. It was confined to subscribers until 1848, when it was thrown open to the public during certain hours every day. In 1871 the Glasgow Public Library was amalgamated, and the name was changed to Stirling's and Glasgow Public Library.—Baillie's—Mr. George Baillie in 1863 left £18,000 for the endowment and maintenance of an institution to be called after his name. The donor was senior member of the Faculty of Procurators, whose Dean and Council were left to see his wishes carried

5

out. The money was, however, not to be available until 1884, and it was to be applied, in the first instance, to "aid the self-culture of the operative classes, from youth to manhood and old age, by furnishing them with warm, well-lighted, and every way comfortable accommodation at all seasons for reading useful and interesting books in apartments of proper size, attached to one or more free libraries provided for them," which were to be open on Sundays; and, secondly, "for providing the education and industrial training of children of the same class gratuitously or on the payment of small fees." In the event of the money being insufficient for both purposes, the schools to be deferred in favour of a library, which was opened in 48 Miller Street on 29th September, 1887.

**Old Lending Libraries.**—In 1783 John Smith, at the George Buchanan's Head, facing the Laigh Kirk, Trongate, placed 5,000 volumes at the public service, catalogues 6d. each, yearly subscriptions 10s.; and Archd. Cobrough, High Street, offered 4,500 volumes for public reading.

**Public Libraries Act.**—Several attempts have been made to have the Public Libraries Act adopted in Glasgow, with the following result, viz. :—A public meeting of the citizens was held in the City Hall on 17th April, 1876, when the proposal was rejected by 1,779 votes to 993. In 1884 an influential committee was appointed at a public meeting with a view to securing the adoption of the Act. A plebiscite was taken on 9th May, 1885, when 29,946 voted against, and 22,755 for. Another trial was made on 27th April, 1888, with the same result; 22,987 voted against, and 13,550 for. An Act was passed in 1894 giving the Town Council power to adopt the Act. An endeavour was again made in 1897 with a negative result.

## CITY AND SUBURBS.

**Old Boundaries.**—The boundaries of Glasgow about 1450 were—North, the Cathedral; South, Blackfriars Monastery; East, the Drygate; West, the Rottenrow. About this time the town began to spread. High Street was continued to the Cross, the Gallowgate was formed and buildings erected. Houses were also built to where the Tron Steeple now stands, and also continued towards the Clyde. At the time of the Union the population was about 14,000. The boundaries were — East, Gallowgate Port, at Great Dovehill Street;

West, West Port (originally near the foot of Brunswick Street, but in 1588 it was removed to the corner of Argyle and Stockwell Streets); South, Water Port, at foot of Stockwell Street; North, Stable Green Port, in Castle Street; North-West, Rottenrow Port. At this time Bell Street, Candleriggs, King Street, and Princes Street were all green fields. Wade states there were seven gates in the city at one time, situated at the following places, viz. : — Stable Green Port, West Port, Gallowgate Port, Water Port, corner of Bell Street and Candleriggs, junction of Drygate and Rottenrow, and Trongate, at Cross. Saltmarket used to be called Waulker or Fuller's Gate, from which one would infer a gate stood in it.

**Rottenrow.**—The meaning of the word Rottenrow is explained by the Glasgow historian Wade to be derived from the French words *routine* (usual) and *route* (way), the road being the usual way from the west to the Cathedral, hence Routine-route, which in time became transformed to the present unsavoury appellation. In the year 1440 a tenement in the Rottenrow, with a garden and as much land as a team could plough during a season, was sold by Donald Taylyburn to John de Dalgles for five merks Scots (5s. 6⅜d. sterling). In 1780 the following advertisement appeared in the local papers :—"Summer quarters to be let at the west end of Rottenrow, in the Common Gardens."

**Gorbals.**—The lands of St. Ninian's Croft belonged to Lady Campbell of Lochow, who built the hospital of that name in 1350. From her they appear to have descended to Duncan Campbell of Lochow, the first of the race who bore the title of "Argyll." He was married to Marjory Stewart, daughter of Robert, Duke of Albany, who was the third son of King Robert II. The lands afterwards fell into the hands of the Church, from whom they were acquired by a branch of the Elphinston family about 1578. About this time the name was changed to "Gorbals." Sir George Elphinston of Blythswood was the last of the family in possession. He built the old baronial hall which stood at the corner of Main Street and Rutherglen Road. At his death the lands were bought by Lord Belhaven, who dying without issue they descended to his nephew, Sir Robert Douglas of Blackerston, from whom they were bought by the Town Council, Trades House, and Hutcheson's Hospital in 1648. They were annexed to the city on 26th October, 1661. The Trades House and Hutcheson's Hospital decided to feu their ground in 1790, and laid out Eglinton and Bridge Streets—the district to the west being called Tradeston, and that to the east Hutchesontown. The charges were £10 a Scotch acre, and from 1s. 6d. to 8s. a square yard. The last-named institution subscribed £2,000 towards erecting Hutchesontown Bridge to connect the new suburb. Gorbals was called Bridgend at one time.

**Stobcross.**—In 1725 Anderson of Stobcross prepared plans for the feuing of his ground.

**Ford of Gorbals.**—In 1730 the Merchants' Lane, which ran from the Bridgegate to the Clyde, was a horse road that led to a ford in the river, which came out on the Gorbals side near where the Glasgow and South-Western Railway bridge is built. There was an island on the Clyde at the Green fully an acre in size. A bank near Rutherglen Bridge was the situation of the principal salmon shoots in the river.

**Duke Street.**—In 1765 Duke Street was laid out through the agency of the Carron Company, for the accommodation of their works at Cumbernauld.

**Finnieston.**—Mr. Anderson of Stobcross began to feu Finnieston in 1770. It was called after his chaplain, the Rev. Mr. Finnie. It became a favourite summer retreat.

**St. Andrew's Square.**—In 1771 the making of St. Andrew's Square and the enlarging and completing of the churchyard was decided upon, also the opening of a street from St. Andrew's Church to the Saltmarket. Eight years afterwards the work was begun.

**Dunlop and Miller Streets.**—Dunlop Street, named after the house of Dunlops of Garnkirk, which stood at the head of it, and which afterwards became the Buck's Head Inn, was opened in 1773; while Miller Street, named after Miller of Westerton, was formed the same year.

**St. Enoch Square.**—St. Enoch Square was laid out in 1778. It had a grassy enclosure in the centre where sheep grazed and volunteers paraded. The Surgeons' Hall was on the east side, and the Custom House on the west. Several handsome mansions also adorned the aristocratic quadrangle.

**George Square.**—George Square was planned for feuing in 1782. It was previously a piece of marshy land called Meadowflats. The square was laid out in 1787, the locality being called the New Town. At the beginning of this century the centre was a green where sheep grazed, surrounded by a four-feet railing, with a gate facing Miller Street.

**Buchanan Street**—Buchanan Street was laid out for feuing in 1786. It was originally intended to be the villadom of the city. It was called after the proprietor of the land, Andrew Buchanan, a " tobacco lord," whose house stood at what is now the corner of Buchanan and Argyle Streets.

**Carlton Place.**—In the early part of the century Carlton Place was one of the most aristocratic quarters in the city. The eastern portion was built in 1804 by James Laurie. The western part had vaults underneath the pavement ready for the erection of the western mansions which were erected in 1818. All behind was used as fields and gardens. The street front was private, enclosed, at what is now Bridge Street, with a large white padlocked gate. A row of trees adorned the river banks. James Laurie and his brother, after whom Laurieston is named, lived in the centre houses with the portico, one of which is occupied by the Govan Parochial Board.

**Calton.**—Walkinshaw of Barrowfield purchased the pasture lands of Blackfauld from the Corporation of Glasgow in 1705. The ground was feued, and a village soon sprang up, which was named Calton. On 30th August, 1817, the villages of Old and New Calton were by a Crown charter created a burgh of barony, with a provost, three bailies, a treasurer, and eleven councillors.

**Monteith Row.**—The plans for Monteith Row were drawn out in 1819. It was called after Lord Provost Henry Monteith of Carstairs, who had rendered valuable services to the city both in his official and private capacity.

**Anderston.**—The village of Anderston, which was famous for being the pioneer of linen and cotton manufacture, was created by Crown charter into a burgh of barony in November, 1824, with a provost, three bailies, a treasurer, and eleven councillors.

**Island of Shuna.**—James Yates, a native of Glasgow, who died in Devonshire, bequeathed in 1829 to his native city the Island of Shuna, which lies about twenty miles from Oban. It is two and a half miles long, and one and a half broad, and embraces about 1,400 acres. The donor stipulated that the revenue, which is presently £240 a year, should be devoted to scientific and charitable purposes.

**Blythswood.**—The lands of Blythswood were added to the city in 1830, when a Police Act was obtained dividing the new addition and the surrounding district into nine wards, each to return one general and two resident commissioners.

**Suburbs in 1830.**—In 1830 building operations nearly connected the villages of Cowcaddens, Calton, Anderston, and Bridgeton with the city, while Tradeston and Gorbals were busy with many new erections.

**Grahamston.**—The village of Grahamston, the site of which is almost entirely occupied by the Central Station, extended from Argyle Street to Gordon Street, and from Union Street to Hope Street. It only boasted of one street, called Alston Street, which ran north and south. No fewer than six market gardeners carried on a thriving business in this small suburb, which could also boast of granaries and stores, and a large sugar-house, which fell on 2nd November, 1848, when twelve men were killed. The first permanent theatre in the west of Scotland was built in Grahamston. Between Grahamston and Anderston travellers passed the villages of Smithfield (Oswald Street to York Street), Brownfield (Brown Street to M'Alpine Street), while Delftfield was situated at the Broomielaw.

**Argyle Arcade.**—The Argyle Arcade was built about 1827 by Robertson Reid, and Brother, progenitors of the Reids of Gallowflat. It is the oldest covered way the city possesses. Previous to building, Mr. Reid made a tour of inspection to London and elsewhere, to enable him to make the new arcade perfect in every way. In addition to the shops there was a small public hall at the corner of Argyle Street, which was used for a Fine Art Exhibition in 1829.

**First Great Annexation.**—The first great annexation scheme was brought forward in 1842, when a bill was introduced into Parliament for liberty to annex the burghs of Gorbals, Calton, and Anderston, together with the villages of Milton and Port-Dundas, for police purposes. After a great deal of worry—during which the Government introduced and ultimately withdrew a Police Bill dealing with the whole parliamentary area—the measure promoted by the City became law in 1844. Complications ensued. Anderston made an attempt to annex its aristocratic neigh-

bour Woodside, which Glasgow wished to claim. Bridgeton wanted to commence business on its own account, but Calton was anxious to swallow it up. When this "kettle of fish" came before Parliament the committee stated that if the parties failed to come to an amicable agreement the Government would introduce a bill on the subject themselves. This caused a conference to be held, the outcome of which was a new bill abolishing the old Police Board which had held sway since 1800. The parliamentary became the municipal area, which included all the above-mentioned burghs, villages, and lands. This received parliamentary sanction on 27th July, 1846. When the new Act came into operation on 3rd November, the city was divided into sixteen wards, each returning three representatives, who, with the Dean of Guild and Deacon-Convenor, made the Council consist of fifty members.

**No Man's Land.**—Partick became a burgh on 17th June, 1852 ; Maryhill on 15th May, 1856; Govan in June, 1864 ; Hillhead in 1869; Crosshill on 6th September, 1871 ; and Kinning Park on 21st September, 1871. Glasgow annexed Gilmorehill and other small portions of territory in 1872. A small strip of land lying between the city and Crosshill remained outwith the jurisdiction of either, and on account of the unique position it occupied it was called "No Man's Land." In 1875 Crosshill promoted a bill in Parliament seeking to take the "derelict" under its wing. This was too much for the City, who immediately made a counter-move, and asked Parliament to give them the custody of this adjoining ground. Crosshill triumphed in the Commons, but the preamble was rejected by the Lords, so a great deal of money went for nothing. "No Man's Land" naturally thought it was time it was looking after itself, and on 4th July, 1877, it became an independent burgh under the name of Govanhill. Pollokshields West and Pollokshields East also protected themselves by forming governments of their own in 1876 and January, 1890, respectively.

**Greater Glasgow.**—On 1st November, 1891, all the suburbs became annexed to the city, except the burghs of Govan, Partick, and Kinning Park, which had a population of 113,525. The new "territory" annexed consisted of—Govanhill (14,339), Crosshill (3,798), Pollokshields East (6,681) and West (3,028), Hillhead (7,738), Maryhill (18,313), Polmadie (2,675), Mount Florida, Langside, and Crossmyloof (8,161), Shawlands (2,660), Strathbungo (2,951), Bellahouston (144), Kelvinside (5,526), Possilpark (7,853), Springburn and Barnhill (7,350), and Westhorn (15). Total population, 91,232; acreage, 5,750; rental, £596,645. This raised the population of the city from 565,714 to 656,946, acreage to 11,861, and rental to £4,052,155. This necessitated the alteration of the representation on the Town Council, and in November, 1896, the city was divided into twenty-five wards, each of which was allowed three representatives.

**Streets.**—The after-mentioned streets, etc., were opened on the following dates, viz.:—

| | | | |
|---|---|---|---|
| Albion St., N. & S. | 1808 | Havannah Street | 1763 |
| Back Wynd* | 1690 | High* | 1100 |
| Balmano Street | 1792 | Hutcheson | 1790 |
| Barrack | 1795 | Ingram | 1781 |
| Bath | 1802 | Jamaica | 1763 |
| Bell* | 1710 | John | 1783 |
| Blackfriars Wynd* | 1400 | Kent | 1802 |
| Bridgegate Street* | 1100 | King | 1724 |
| Brown | 1800 | Kirk* | 1100 |
| Brunswick | 1790 | M'Farlane | 1815 |
| " Place | 1805 | M'Alpine | 18co |
| Buchanan Street | 1780 | Miller | 1773 |
| " N. | 1804 | Montrose | 1787 |
| Buns Wynd* | 1560 | Nelson | 1798 |
| Campbell Street | 1784 | New Wynd* | 1690 |
| Candleriggs | 1724 | Old Wynd* | 1690 |
| Canon* | 1360 | Portland Street | 1802 |
| Carrick | 1800 | Princes | 1724 |
| Castle | 1100 | Queen | 1777 |
| Charlotte | 1779 | Richmond | 1804 |
| Cathcart | 1798 | Rottenrow* | 1100 |
| Clyde W. | 1773 | Saltmarket* | 1100 |
| " E. | 1812 | St. Andrew's Sq. | 1787 |
| Cochrane | 1787 | " St. | 1771 |
| Dempster | 1792 | St. Enoch Square. | 1782 |
| Drygate* | 1100 | St. George's Place | 1810 |
| Duke | 1794 | St. Vincent St., E. | 1804 |
| Dundas | 1812 | " W. | 1809 |
| Dunlop | 1772 | Stirling Street | 1797 |
| Frederick | 1787 | " Place | 1805 |
| Gallowgate* | 1100 | Stockwell Street* | 1345 |
| Garthland Street | 1793 | Suffolk | 1802 |
| George Square | 1787 | Taylor | 1794 |
| " Street | 1792 | Trongate* | 1100 |
| Glassford Street | 1793 | Virginia Street | 1756 |
| Gordon | 1802 | " N. | 1796 |
| Great Hamilton St. | 1813 | Weaver | 1792 |
| Hamilton Street | 1791 | Wilson | 1790 |

Those marked with an asterisk (*) were opened prior to date.

**Old Castles.** — Cathcart — Cathcart Castle is one of the old keeps of Scotland whose origin is lost in the mists of antiquity. During the time of Wallace and Bruce it was in possession of Alan de Cathcart, who was a staunch supporter of "Scotia's ancient heroes." He gave 20s. stg. out of the lands of Bogton to the Blackfriars Monastery, on 14th August, 1336. About the middle of the sixteenth century the castle and lands passed out of the possession of the Cathcarts; but in 1801 the late Earl of Cathcart, a lineal descendant of the original owners, purchased the old pile and surrounding lands. The mansion-house stands on the banks of the Cart in a park immediately to the south of the old castle.

*Haggs.*—The ruins of Haggs Castle are situated near Maxwell Park. The old building has all that is necessary in the way of walls, vaults, etc., to show that it was a power in days of old. The only reliable history regarding it shows that it was erected in 1585 by Sir John Maxwell and his spouse, Margaret Conignham. It was used by their descendant, Sir John Maxwell, in Covenanting times to shelter the persecuted Presbyterians, for which Sir John was fined £8,000 sterling, on 2nd December, 1684. On refusing to pay, the baronet was imprisoned for sixteen months. He died shortly after being released. *Partick.*—What was supposed to be the ruins of Partick Castle stood at the junction of the Kelvin and Clyde; but it was latterly found to be the remains of a house built by Mr. George Hutcheson, the founder of Hutcheson's Hospital. Of course it is possible the house is erected on the ruins of an old castle; but there is nothing to show that such is the case.

## INSTITUTIONS.

**Municipal Buildings.**—*First Council Chamber*—Previous to the Reformation the Town Council met in the Bishop's Castle, whence they removed to the Cross.

*Tolbooth and Town Hall.*—A Tolbooth at the Cross is mentioned as early as 1454. It is referred to in old documents as the "Pretorium," and seems to have combined both Town Hall or Court-House and Prison. This, which appears to have really been the first municipal building, became unsuitable. It was taken down, and the "grund stane," of what we now refer to as the Old Tolbooth, was laid on 15th May, 1626. The building and steeple were finished in 1627. The Town Hall adjoining was commenced in 1736 and finished in 1740. The building contained a council hall and assembly rooms, which were used for dances until the new Assembly Rooms were built in Ingram Street in 1796. The council chamber also served for a picture gallery. The building was originally surrounded with a piazza, but an outside stair and porch was afterwards placed in the Trongate.

*Spikes.* — The Tolbooth Steeple until 1790 was surrounded with spikes, on which were stuck the heads of those whose fate the authorities wished proclaimed to all the city.

*Musical Chimes.* — The musical bells on the steeple were completed in 1736 at a cost of £316 1s. 9d.   They played the following tunes, *viz.* :—Sunday, "Easter Hymn;" Monday, "Gilderoy;" Tuesday, "Nancy's to the Green Wood Gane;" Wednesday, "Tweedside;" Thursday, "The Lass o' Patie's Mill;" Friday, "The Last Time I Cam' o'er the Muir;" Saturday, "Roslin Castle." A new carillon of 16 bells was erected in place of the above at a cost of £1,165. The inauguration ceremony was performed on 26th December, 1881, when the following tunes were played, viz. :—"The Queen's Anthem," "Mariners," "Innocent," "Caller Herrin'," "Scots Wha Hae," "Christmas Chimes," "Christmas Hymn," "Hark! the Herald Angels Sing," "Chime Again, Beautiful Bells," "Duncan Grey," "Rule Britannia," "British Grenadiers," "Marseillaise," "A Highland Lad," "March of the Cameron Men," "God Save the Queen." On the "Bourdon" or big bell was inscribed —"This carillon of 16 bells, erected A.D., 1881. The Hon. John Ure, Lord Provost; John Carrick, Master of Works; J. C. Wilson & Co., founders, Glasgow." The weight of the bells was exactly 4½ tons.

*Jailer.* — Gawan Naythsmyth was appointed first jailer in the Tolbooth at an annual salary of £2 4s. 5¾d. sterling.

*First Encroachment.* — The first encroachment on the Cross building was made on 3rd January, 1801, when £5 per square yard was paid to the Council for ground under the piazza to be converted into shops.

*Sold.* — On 14th May, 1814, the Council agreed to sell the Cross building, but it was decided to retain, support, preserve, and repair the steeple.

*Jail Square.* — From the Cross the Town's Chambers were removed to Jail Square; and what is now known as the Justiciary Buildings were erected at a cost of £34,811 on what was then a part of the Green. They were opened in February, 1814. William Stark, of Edinburgh, was the architect.

*Wilson Street.* — On 18th November, 1842, the foundation stone of the City and County Buildings in Wilson Street was laid. They were completed two years later at a cost of £54,000, which included

£17,000 for the ground, nearly half of which was paid by the County of Lanark. The immigration of the officials to their new home enabled the Court halls and general accommodation in the old Jail buildings to be greatly improved.

*Ingram Street.* — The accommodation in Wilson Street having become too small, new Council Chambers were erected at the other end of the quadrangle facing Ingram Street at a cost of £50,812, the opening ceremony being performed on 24th February, 1874.

*George Square.* — The foundation stone of the new Municipal Buildings in George Square was laid with masonic honours by Lord Provost Ure on 6th October, 1883. The day was observed as a public holiday, and great rejoicings were indulged in. In the evening a public dinner and conversazione was held, and displays of fireworks took place in the public parks. The new Hotel de Ville, which cost about £520,000, including site and furnishing, was built from the plans of William Young, architect, London, who is a native of Paisley. The style is Italian Renaissance. It is a square 230 feet long by 245 feet deep, covering 6,000 square yards. The total floorage measures 210,000 square feet. The principal tower is 237 feet high. In addition to the council chamber, banqueting hall, and state apartments, the building contains the offices of the following departments of the city, viz. :—Town clerk, chamberlain, and finance sections; gas, water, police, and other rate-collecting suites; also public works, police clerk, cleansing, and lands valuation offices; dean of guild court and rooms; library, sub-committee rooms, etc., etc. This concentration of the above departments is an inestimable boon to all concerned. The marble and alabaster staircase and corridors are unsurpassed in any similar building. This monument of Glasgow's enterprise was formally opened on 22nd August, 1888, by Her Majesty Queen Victoria. 400,000 persons passed through the buildings between 2nd and 11th September, 1889, when they were thrown open for public inspection. The first meeting was held in the buildings on 10th October, 1889.

## Trades House. — *Alms House* — The Trades House is composed of representatives from each of the fourteen incorporated trades, along with the president, who is called the deacon-convener. The original Trades House was known as the Alms

House. It had formerly been the prebendal manse of the rector of Morebattle, and was adapted by the Trades House after the Reformation. It was situated in Old Kirk Street at Cathedral Square, and was erected during the seventeenth century, being used as a retreat for reduced members of the incorporations. There was a small hall in connection with the building, which was used for meetings by all the incorporations. When funerals passed to the Cathedral a small bell in the turret of the building was tolled, and the mourners showed their appreciation of the respect by depositing a small donation in a box which was placed in one of the windows of the house, above which the following words were cut in stone —"Give to the puir and thou sal have treasur in Heavin.—Matt. xix. chap."

*Trades Hall.*—Owing to the Alms House becoming unsuitable, it was decided to erect new premises. Ground was secured in Glassford Street, and in 1791 the present Trades Hall was commenced. It was completed three years afterwards at a cost of nearly £8,000, which included £952 15s. 6d. for the site. Two years later a bell, made by Mears, of London, was placed in the dome.

**St. Ninian's Hospital.**—Lady Lochow erected a lepers' hospital about 1350, which was known as St. Ninian's Hospital, to meet the ravages of a plague of leprosy which visited Glasgow and decimated the population. The building stood on the Gorbals side of the river between Main Street and Crown Street.

**St. Nicholas' Hospital.**—A hospital, built and endowed in 1471 by Bishop Muirhead, stood on the west side of High Kirk Street, beside where the present Barony Church stands. The building was called St. Nicholas' Hospital. It accommodated twelve indigent old men and a chaplain.

**Merchants' House.** — *Bridgegate* — The Merchants' House had its origin in 1605 in consequence of disputes between the craftsmen and their fellow-townsmen, the questions of rank and precedence giving rise to a good deal of feeling, while disagreements were frequent regarding trading privileges. An agreement was made and ratified by Parliament in 1612 whereby a "Letter of Guildry" defined the position of each party. The new body soon became affluent, and they decided to have a habitation in addition to a name. The Merchants' Hospital, designed by Sir William Bruce, of Kinross, was built in the Bridgegate about 1659. The building fronted the street, and the

steeple, which is 164 feet high, was erected behind. What is now the Guildry Court was then used as a flower garden. The building was sold in 1817 for £7,500, and it was shortly afterwards taken down. The steeple was, however, preserved, and presented to the city, who still retain it as a grand monument of old Glasgow. *Wilson Street*—When the Town Council erected their new Municipal Buildings in Wilson Street the Merchants' House added a splendid hall for themselves in connection therewith, at a cost of £10,300. It now forms part of the County Buildings *George Square*—The handsome display of architecture at the north-west corner of George Square was built by the Merchants' House in 1877. It cost about £99,000, including £31,998 for the site.

**Hutcheson's Hospital.**—*Founded*— Hutcheson's Hospital was founded on 16th December, 1639, by George Hutcheson of Lambhill, writer and notary public. The lands of Lambhill were bought on 21st January, 1557, by his father, who was previously the farmer of Gairbraid. George Hutcheson bequeathed a house to the west of the West Port for the shelter of as many poor men as the interest of 20,000 merks, or £1,111 2s. 2⅜d. stg., would provide for at the rate of 4s. Scots each daily. His brother Thomas, also a writer and register of sasines, a few years afterwards left 68,700 merks, or £3,816 13s. 4d. stg., for the maintenance and education of twelve orphan boys—sons of burgesses—those of the name Hutcheson or Herbertson to have the preference.

*First Hospital.*—The first hospital was built in the Trongate, near the foot of Hutcheson Street, in 1641. It had a leaded spire, 100 feet high, with a clock. The school was in connection with the building, and a square at the back was used for a playground.

*Thomas Hutcheson's Statue.*—A statue to Thomas Hutcheson was placed in the hospital in the Trongate on 29th November, 1655, at a cost of £27 15s. 6⅜d. stg.

*Present Hospital.*—The old hospital was removed to allow of Hutcheson Street being opened to the Trongate. The present hospital was built in Ingram Street in 1805, at a cost of £5,260. Two statues of the founders, which occupy recesses in front of the building, were previously placed in two niches on the north wall of the old hospital on each side of the steeple. The hospital has two schools—one for girls in Elgin Street, and one for boys in Crown Street.

**Post Office.**—*Past*—The General Post Office was first located in Gibson's Wynd, Princes Street (now called Parnie Street); rent £6. In 1800 it was removed to St. Andrew's Street; rent £12. Three years afterwards it was situated in the back land of a court in 114 Trongate, beside the old Lyceum Rooms; rent £20. In 1810 it found a habitation on the east side of Nelson Street, which was built by Dugald Ballantyne, the postmaster, who received £30 for rent. In 1840 it was removed to Glassford Street, on the site of Wilson, Mathieson & Co.'s warehouse, and in 1856 it reached the corner of South Hanover Street and George Square.

*Present.*—The first portion of the present post office, from Frederick Street to the west side of the posting lobby, was commenced in May, 1876. The foundation stone was laid, with full masonic honours, by H.R.H. the Prince of Wales on 17th October of the same year. The building was completed in 1879 at a cost of about £28,000. The second portion, from the west side of the posting lobby to Hanover Street, was begun in 1880, and completed in 1883, having cost about £15,000. The Athenæum portion, in Ingram Street, was commenced in May, 1890, and finished in 1896. The building cost about £22,000, and the site about £30,000 more. The basement is utilised for the engine room, etc., and telegraph delivery room; the first floor is used for parcels (¾) and letters (¼); the second floor is the postmen's office; and the third flat is utilised for the instrument room. In 1889 177,630,544 letters and 2,482,168 parcels were dealt with, while in 1899 the letters had increased to 267,850,024, and the parcels to 5,235,568. The trunk system of the telephone, which was first publicly used by Messrs. Denny, of Dumbarton, in 1879, was taken over by the Government in 1896, and is now worked from the post office.

**Inland Revenue.**—Previous to 1860 the stamp-tax and Excise offices were conducted in different parts of the city, but in that year the old Clydesdale Bank in 13 Queen Street was secured, and the different branches were consolidated under one roof. In 1885 new premises were built at the north-east corner of George Square, where the business is now carried on. The building cost about £18,000, and the site £23,000 more.

**Royal Exchange.**—Wm. Cunningham, of Lainshaw, a Virginia merchant, made a great fortune through buying all the tobacco he could secure at 6d. per lb. When the American War broke out, the "Narcotic Weed" afterwards rose to 3s. 6d. per lb. In 1779 he built the most magnificent mansion-house in the city in the Cowloan or Queen Street. At his death the house was purchased by William Stirling & Sons, who used one of the wings for their office, while the remainder of the building was occupied by the family for twenty-eight years. The Royal Bank of Scotland, who previously had their office in the south-east corner of St. Andrew's Square, bought the property in 1817. They erected a handsome double stair in front of the house which reached to the drawing-room window, and planted a shrubbery in the space in front. It was used as the Royal Bank for ten years. In 1827 it was purchased by the New Exchange Company, who transformed the dwelling-house into offices, constructed the portico in front of the mansion, and erected the large room or hall at the back on the ground formerly used as the garden. It was opened as the Royal Exchange in 1829 at a total cost of about £50,000.

**Corn Exchange.**—The Corn Exchange was built in 1840 at the corner of Hope and Waterloo Streets. It was partially rebuilt with new façade in 1896. Previous to the Exchange being erected the grain merchants transacted their business in front of the Tontine at the Cross. The farmers and others who used to congregate in St. Enoch Square on Wednesdays, previous to the Subway operations, now meet in the Corn Exchange.

**Stock Exchange.**—The Stock Exchange was formed through the exertions of the late Sir James Watson in June, 1844, when the formation of railways was at its height; it started with twenty-eight members. The first premises were in the National Bank Buildings in Queen Street, but the handsome building at the corner of Buchanan Street and George Place was built at a cost of over £50,000, and opened in April, 1878.

**Lyceum.**—The Lyceum Institution stood on the east side of Nelson Street. It had a saloon 54 feet by 53 feet, and a library 33 feet by 32 feet. Members paid a subscription of two guineas a year, for which they were supplied with a large stock of newspapers and periodicals. The place was also let for property sales, creditors' meetings, etc.

**Anderson's College.**—Anderson's College for arts, medicine, law, and theology—the two latter were never formed—was founded in 1796 by John Anderson, Professor of Oriental Languages and Natural Philosophy in Glasgow University, his *Alma Mater*. Two rooms in the Grammar (High) School in George Street were first secured for class purposes, and a house in Duke Street was taken for a museum and library. Dr. Thomas Garnet was the first professor; he gave lectures daily in the class-rooms, and delivered a popular course twice a week in the Trades Hall. Leaving for London, he was succeeded by Dr. George Birkbeck, who started a special class for mechanics in 1800, and from this the Mechanics' Institution sprung in 1823. In 1798 the Flesh Market on the west side of John Street was purchased and transformed into a college, but it was sold to the Bank of Scotland in 1827 for £4,700, and the old Grammar (High) School in George Street purchased for £3,000. This historic building has been gradually altered, embellished, and enlarged to its present condition. Dr. David Livingstone obtained his medical training within its walls. When the Technical College was formed in 1886 it took over the college, and the medical school was given £5,000, which enabled it to become a separate body. In 1887 it was incorporated as an association, called Anderson's College Medical School, and handsome new buildings were erected in 1889 on Dumbarton Road, beside the gate of the Western Infirmary.

**Mechanics' Institute.** — The Mechanics' Institute sprang from a class taught by Dr. Ure on Saturday nights in the Andersonian Institution in John Street in 1823. Its object was to assist the working men in literary and scientific knowledge. Their first meetings were held in the gallery of an old Secession meeting-house in Inkle Factory Lane, which was afterwards fitted up as an institution. James Watson, latterly Sir James and Lord Provost of Glasgow, then a clerk in the Ship Bank, was its president in 1824. Lord Brougham and Dr. Birkbeck took an active part in the foundation of the institution. About 1826 a handsome building was erected for its use in North Hanover Street, but, latterly, an elegant structure was built by the institution itself on the north side of Bath Street, between Renfield and West Nile Streets. Shortly after the institution was formed, several similar organisations sprang into existence in Anderston, Calton, Mile-End, and Bridgeton districts. When the Technical College was formed in 1886, the Mechanics' Institute amalgamated with it.

**Athenæum.**—The Athenæum sprang from the Glasgow Commercial College, which met in the Andersonian University in 1845. At a meeting held in Steele's Coffee-House on 18th January, 1847, it was decided to form an Athenæum; and on 11th February a further meeting took place in the Wellington Hotel, when office-bearers were appointed. So successful did the new society become that it was agreed to lease the Assembly Rooms in Ingram Street, which were opened on 13th October, 1847, when Charles Dickens occupied the chair, and made a racy, characteristic speech. The Assembly Rooms were built in 1796 on the Tontine principle of 274 shares of £25 each. The wings, which harmonised with the main building, were added in 1807. The Athenæum managed to secure a share for £70 on 8th October, 1850. By 1882 they had become interested in the property to the extent of one-fourth, and when the Government bought the edifice, their share of the institution amounted to £6,500. It became advisable to look out for permanent premises; and to secure that, the constitution was altered, and the institution formed into a limited company, with a capital of £15,000. The assets, which amounted to £7,500, were handed over to the new formation, who bought a site in St. George's Place for £10,000; and the memorial stone of the new Athenæum was laid by J. A. Campbell, M.P., on 7th January, 1887. The building, which cost £26,000, was opened by the Marquis of Bute on 25th January, 1888. A large addition, with a handsome frontage to Buchanan Street, was made in 1893, the total sum expended on the new home amounting to no less than £80,000. The façade of the old Athenæum was purchased from the Government, and re-erected as an archway at the London Street entrance to Glasgow Green, at the expense of the late ex-Bailie M'Lennan.

**Free Church College.**—The handsome building and tower at the head of Lynedoch Street was erected by the Free Church as a college in 1862.

**St. Mungo's College.**—When the University removed from High Street to Gilmorehill in 1870, the students who attended the Royal Infirmary for their practical and clinical instruction and demonstrations were placed at a great disadvantage. To meet this difficulty the Infirmary obtained powers and opened a medical school in 1876, for which a handsome erection was built opposite the

Infirmary in Castle Street in 1882. Under the affiliation clause of the Scottish Universities Bill of 1899, the medical school was incorporated by special license of the Board of Trade and with the approval of Dover House as St. Mungo's College.

**Queen Margaret College.**—Queen Margaret College sprang from the Glasgow Association for the Higher Education of Women, which was instituted in 1877, and to whom the college professors delivered a course of lectures in one of the class-rooms of the University. Mrs. Elder acquired the building and ground of North Park, Kelvinside, which she fitted out and gifted to the college. The building was opened in November, 1884. A medical branch was added in 1889. Queen Victoria visited the college on 24th August, 1888, when Her Majesty was presented with an address.

**Christian Institute.**—In 1873 a movement was started, and a committee formed, for the purpose of providing an institute which would be the headquarters of the Young Men's Christian Association, and a central meeting-place for all bodies of a religious character. The subscription list was headed by five gentlemen giving £1,000 each, and in a short time £28,000 was collected. Ground was purchased outright for £13,963, the site chosen being in Bothwell Street, midway between West Campbell and Mains Streets. The total cost, including site, building, and furnishing came to £30,000; and on 10th October, 1879, when the building was opened by Lord Shaftesbury, the additional £2,000 was subscribed, certain city merchants responding to an appeal and donating £50 apiece.

**Young Men's Christian Association Club, Limited.**—On the west side of the Christian Institute stands a handsome building known as the Young Men's Club. The building was commenced in 1895, Lord Overtoun laying the foundation stone; and the same nobleman opened the premises on 7th September, 1897. The club is to provide residential apartments for young men. The cost of building and furnishing was about £35,000, and in the building there are 195 bedrooms, and drawing, music, writing, and smoke rooms.

**Bible Training Institute.**—On the east side of the Christian Institute is the Bible Training Institute, the erection of which was due to the Glasgow United Evangelistic Association. The site and building cost £50,000, all of which, except

£6,680, was given by Lord Overtoun and his sister, the late Mrs. J. E. Somerville. The building, which was opened by Lord Overtoun on 17th October, 1898, contains 100 bedrooms for male students and 50 for female students, while there are separate dining, writing, and sitting rooms and libraries for each sex. Steam is used for heating, and electricity for lighting

**Royal Infirmary.**—The foundation stone of the Royal Infirmary was laid with masonic honours on 18th May, 1792. R. and J. Adam were the architects, and Messrs. Morrison & Burns contractors. The Infirmary is erected on the site of the Bishop's Castle, sanction of the Treasury being received to remove the ancient ruin. Many of the stones of the old palace were used in the new building, which was completed and opened in December, 1794. Sir David Richmond, Lord Provost of the city, to celebrate Her Majesty's Diamond Jubilee inaugurated a fund to rebuild the Infirmary. Building operations are expected to begin in a few months. The plans and elevations are now prepared. The ultimate cost of the undertaking will probably be from £150,000 to £200,000.

**Western Infirmary.** — When the University removed to Gilmorehill in 1870 an infirmary in close proximity became a necessity. The property of Clayslaps was purchased for a site, but this was exchanged to the Corporation for a portion of the land of Donaldshill, to which was subsequently added ground to the north and west, about ten acres in all. The total cost of the site was £23,136 11s. The University contributed £30,000, ...d about 1871 public subscriptions were invited, and a general committee formed to carry out the undertaking. Building operations were begun in March, 1871, the foundation stone being laid in August of the same year; and the first portion of the Infirmary, containing two hundred beds, was opened in 1874. The late Mr. Freeland contributed £40,000 in 1879, which enabled the Freeland wing to be opened on 1st June, 1881. An erysipelas ward was added in 1883. The total cost of the Infirmary including site amounted to £135,141 4s. 11d.

**Victoria Infirmary.**—The idea of an infirmary on the south side of Glasgow began to be seriously talked about in 1878, but nothing was done until 1881, when, at a meeting held in the Religious Institution Rooms, a provisional committee was appointed, who set about obtaining subscriptions, and feued four acres of ground from the City on the south-west corner of the Queen's Park Recreation Grounds. The sum of £38,987 9s. 8d was ultimately handed over to the proposed institution by the Trustees of the late Robert Couper of Cathcart. With this valuable backing, and other handsome subscriptions (Mr. and Mrs. W. S. Dixon, £8,500 ; Wm. Stirling, £5,000; Charles Kidston, £3,000), Parliamentary sanction was got, and the first sod cut by Mr. Renny Watson on 4th July, 1888. The first portion of the new Infirmary was opened by the Duke of Argyle on 14th February, 1890. Several new wings have been added since. The cost of the entire building amounted to £59,521 16s. 6d., while furnishings and feu, etc., have cost an extra £12,557 5s. 8d.

### Belvidere Hospital.—

In 1870 relapsing fever invaded the city, and the accommodation of the Parliamentary Road Hospital—the first hospital erected by the Corporation, opened on 25th April, 1865, containing 136 beds, and increased in 1869 to 250 l eds—was speedily exhausted. After the usual trouble in obtaining a site, the estate of Belvidere, extending to about thirty-two acres, was purchased by the Corporation for £17,000, converted into a ground annual of £680. The smallpox hospital was the first permanent erection. Operations were begun on November, 1874, and the hospital was completed and formally opened on 5th December, 1877. It contains 150 beds in ten wards, arranged in five isolated pavilions. The total cost, exclusive of site, was £30,235. The fever hospital has grown up from year to year by substitution, addition, and reconstruction into its present form. It began with temporary wooden pavilions, and large sums were spent in maintaining these for some years. The total amount of money expended on hospital and grounds is about £90,000. The wards are distributed in pairs, in thirteen isolated pavilions, containing 390 beds.

### Ruchill Fever Hospital.—

Operations were started at Ruchill in April, 1895, the ground having been purchased for £21,373. Accommodation is provided for 408 patients. There are twelve large pavilions, each with thirty beds, and four small pavilions, each with twelve beds. Each pavilion has two acute and two convalescent wards. The hospital, a magnificent pile of buildings, has been constructed on the latest and most improved principles of hospital construction, its administrative block being a special feature. The area of ground covered is thirty-four acres, which, at the highest point, is 265 feet above sea level. Including the price of ground, contracts have been entered into amounting to £230,265, which is equal to £564 per bed, but this does not take into account the cost of furniture and the laying out of the grounds.

### Knightswood.—

Knightswood Hospital, at Anniesland, for infectious diseases in Maryhill, Hillhead, and Partick, was opened in 1887. It became a joint hospital between Partick and Glasgow when the annexation of the two first-named burghs took place in 1891.

### Glasgow Royal Asylum.—

The late Mr. Robert M'Nair, of Belvidere, collected £7,000, and securing a representative committee, they began in 1810 building the Lunatic Asylum in Parliamentary Road, which was opened in 1815. This was taken over as the City Poorhouse when Gartnavel Asylum was built in 1843.

### Museums.—Hunterian.—

The Hunterian Museum was founded in 1804. Dr. Hunter, the donor, was born at East Kilbride in 1718, and educated in Glasgow University, Edinburgh, and London. He was Physician-in-Ordinary to the Queen, and President of the Royal College of Physicians. He died in 1783, and by his will he bequeathed his museum, valued at £130,000, and endowed it with £8,000, to the Principal and Professors of Glasgow University The collection contained pictures by Murillo, Guido, Rembrandt, Rubens, Correggio, Salvator, Sir Joshua Reynolds, etc The Museum, which was erected to the rear of the Old College buildings, was opened to the public on 26th August, 1808. The building was taken down when the Old College was swept away, and the collection is now housed at Gilmorehill.

*Kelvingrove.* — The old Kelvingrove Mansion - house, situated alongside the Kelvin, in the West End Park, was turned into a Museum by the Corporation in 1870, and so much was this appreciated, and so fast did the curios accumulate, that in 1874 an addition, costing £10,000, was made to the building.

*People's Palace.*—The People's Palace, combining an art gallery, museum, recreation and reading rooms, and winter garden, was built on Glasgow Green from £18,000 received from the Caledonian Railway Company as compensation for allowing them to run their line under the Green. The building was opened by Lord Rosebery in January, 1898.

**Observatories.**—*First*—The first observatory in the city was built on the east of the Old College garden through the agency of Professor Wilson, the instruments being given by Alexander Macfarlane, a Jamaica merchant, formerly a College graduate.

*Garnethill and Dowanhill.*—An observatory was erected on the south side of Garnethill in 1808. Dr. Ure, Andersonian Professor of Natural Philosophy, was its first observer and superintendent. The institution was visited on several occasions by Dr. Herschell. It was afterwards removed to Dowanhill.

**Corporation Galleries.**—The late Bailie Archibald M'Lellan, a coachbuilder in the city, erected a block of buildings, with galleries behind, in Sauchiehall Street, where he exhibited his collection of pictures and sculpture, which were known as the M'Lellan Galleries. The owner intended to bequeath them to the City, but he died within a year of executing his deed, when it was found his affairs were embarrassed, and the Corporation were therefore under the necessity of purchasing the buildings, saloons, and pictures in 1856. They gave £29,500 for the stone and lime, and £15,060 for the collection. William Ewing presented the City with thirty works of art in June, 1856, and in 1874 he bequeathed the remainder of his collection. Mrs. Gilbert Graham of Yorkhill presented her husband's collection of pictures to Glasgow in April, 1877, and in 1896 Messrs. Reid of Hydepark gave ten pictures, value £23,000, which are all safely housed in the Galleries. In 1867 the upper floor of the building was transformed into galleries and exhibition halls at a cost of £4,000. The eastern section was appropriated by the School of Art, and the western portion of the block was occupied by the Philosophical Society and the Institution of Engineers and Shipbuilders. In 1862 the Galleries were let to the Institute of the Fine Arts for their annual exhibition. A series of loan exhibitions was instituted in the Galleries in December, 1879, by the exhibition of the Prince of Wales's Indian presents. These have been continued with much success. The first Corporation picture gallery was situated in the Town Buildings at the Cross.

**Art Gallery and Museum.**—The Sauchiehall Street Galleries having become unsuitable, it was decided to build galleries worthy of the name and enterprise of the City. A surplus of £46,000 from the International Exhibition of 1888, £15,000 from Sir John Muir, and £60,000 from a few prominent citizens, together with a free site in Kelvingrove Park, to which the Corporation added a sum equal to the Exhibition surplus, enabled the work to begin. The memorial stone was laid by the Duke of York on 10th September, 1897. The new galleries, which will cost about £180,000, will be ready for the Exhibition of 1901, of which they will form a very imposing portion.

**Fine Arts Institute.**—The Institute of Fine Arts which is built in Sauchiehall Street was opened in the spring of 1880. In addition to the art exhibitions which are annually held, the building is greatly used for church bazaars.

**City Hall.**—The City Hall was erected in the Candleriggs in 1840. The organ was added in 1855 at a cost of £1,600. A new frontage was added in Candleriggs in 1886; while extensive alterations were made on the South Albion Street entrance in 1891-92. There is accommodation for 3,950 persons.

**St. Andrew's Hall.**—The foundation stone of the handsome building situated in Kent Road, Granville and Berkeley Streets, was laid on 22nd May, 1875, with masonic honours. The square pile was completed two years afterwards at a cost of about £101,000. It was built by a syndicate, and called St. Andrew's Halls. The City purchased the halls in 1890 for £37,500, and have since spent over £6,000 in improvements. One of the finest organs in the kingdom stands in the main hall of the building. There is accommodation for 4,500 persons.

**Public Halls.**—The following Halls have been acquired or built by the Corporation, *viz.*, Maryhill, holding 800 people, acquired in 1891 at the annexation; Dixon Hall (1,000), taken over for £7,000 after Govanhill and Crosshill were annexed in 1891; Pollokshields (360), originally cost that burgh £5,000, taken over in 1891 under the annexation statute; Hillhead (360), taken over at annexation in 1891; Eastern (400), in Police Office Buildings in Tobago Street; Western (400), in Police Office Buildings in Cranston Street. The following additional halls are to be built, *viz.*, St. Rollox and Springburn (1,200), to cost £12,000; Langside and District (550), to cost £6,000. It is also proposed to build halls for St. George's Road and Paisley Road districts.

**Incorporations.**—The following trades were incorporated in the after-mentioned years, and their numbers in 1604 were as shown, *viz.* :—Hammermen, 11th October, 1536—27 ; tailors, 1546—65 ; cordiners and barkers, 1460—50; weavers, 1528—30; bakers, 1556—27; skinners and furriers, 28th May, 1516—21 ; coopers, 1567—23 ; wrights, 3rd May, 1600—21 ; fleshers, 26th September, 1580—17; masons, by King Malcolm III., 5th October, 1057 —11 ; barbers, 30th November, 1559 ; surgeons, 1656—2 ; dyers and bonnet-makers, 29th October, 1597—12; maltmen, 1604 ; gardeners, 1690.

**Bakers.**—The bakers of Glasgow, in return for supplying the Regent Murray's victorious troops with bread after the Battle of Langside in 1568, were given a charter of incorporation by him, and granted the lands of Bunhouse on the Kelvin to erect mills thereon.

**Faculty of Physicians and Surgeons.**—The Faculty was founded in 1599 by a royal charter from King James VI. Early in its career a bye-law was passed for a kind of modified admission of barbers. In 1656 the surgeons and barbers were incorporated into a City Guild. The bodies became separated in 1719. The first Faculty Hall was erected in 1697 in the Trongate immediately to the west of the Tron steeple. This was succeeded in 1790 by the hall in St. Enoch's Square, where the Faculty remained till they acquired their present building at 242 St. Vincent Street about 1860.

**Wrights.**—In 1600 the wrights, who were formerly incorporated with the masons, were granted a separate Letter of Deaconry.

**Buchanan and Highland Societies.**—The Buchanan Society was formed in 1725, and the Highland Society in 1727.

**Literary and Philosophical Society.**—In 1747 the first Literary and Philosophical Society was formed in the city. Dr. Hutcheson, Adam Smith, Dr. Reid, Dr. Moor, Professor Richardson, and Robert Foulis were amongst its membership.

**The Faculty of Procurators.**—It may be said that the Faculty of Procurators has been in existence since the time of the old ecclesiastical courts. In 1668 the procurators in the Commissary Courts of Glasgow, Hamilton, and Campsie formed a society, and exercised several of the powers of a corporate body. On 6th June, 1796, a charter was granted by George III., creating the Faculty into a body politic and corporate for ever. With the aid of the late Mr. George Baillie (the donor of Baillie's Library), and others, a library was established in 1817 ; it now contains 20,000 volumes. At first the library formed part of the Lyceum Rooms in Nelson Street. In 1873 it was transferred to Sproul's Land, Trongate ; in 1831 it was transferred to the Bank of Scotland buildings on the south side of John Street ; and in 1856 it was removed to the Faculty's own building in St. George's Place, where it still is. While the membership in 1668 only numbered 29, it is now over 300 ; and the capital stock has increased since then from about £60 stg. to over £50,000. In olden times the Faculty possessed the ancient court room and record room in the old Consistory House, which used to stand on the south side of the west front of the cathedral; and the members were exempted by the municipal authorities from watching and warding within the burgh, and from having soldiers billeted upon them. For many years the once-famed Lyceum Rooms were the chief place patronised by the Faculty for the sales of heritable property, which now take place in the Hall of Faculty, erected by the Faculty in 1856.

**First Friendly Society.**—The first friendly society was instituted in 1746 under the cognomen of " Bell's Wynd Society."

**Philosophical Society.**—The Glasgow Philosophical Society was formed in 1802. It met in a room in the Surgeon's Hall in St. Enoch Square.

**Scottish Temperance League.**—In 1848 the Scottish Temperance League was established, having for its first president Mr. Robert Kettles.

**Choral Union and First Musical Festival.**—The Choral Union was founded in 1843. In January, 1860, they promoted the first musical festival ever held in Glasgow. It took place in the City Hall, and continued for four nights, *viz.* :—Tuesday, " Elijah." Wednesday, " Miscellaneous Concert." Thursday, " Gideon." Friday, " Messiah." Sims Reeves was a soloist ; Henry Smart, organist ; and H. A. Lambeth, conductor ; the proceeds being given to the Royal Infirmary and Blind Asylum.

**I. O. G. T.**—The Independent Order of Good Templars, a temperance organisation founded at Syracuse, New York State, America, in July, 1852, was introduced into Scotland by Thomas Roberts, who instituted " Scotland's First " Lodge, No. 1, in the Cross Hall, Glasgow, on 13th August, 1869. The Grand Lodge (the national governing body) was instituted in the hall of the Great Western Cooking Depot, Trongate, on 7th May, 1870, with forty-three lodges, twenty-eight of them being in Glasgow. The present strength of the Order in Scotland is :—Lodges, 1,165 ; membership, 79,025.

**House of Refuge.**—A House of Refuge was erected on the lands of Whitehill, on the north side of Duke Street, for the accommodation of juvenile thieves and outcasts, with the object of educating them and teaching them a trade. The citizens raised £13,000 to build and maintain the institution, but it was afterwards kept up by public assessment.

**Foundry Boys.**—The Foundry Boys' Society was instituted in 1867. The first general meeting of the new organisation was held in the City Hall on 14th January, 1867, when Sir John Burns of Castle Wemyss presided.

**G.P.D.A.**—The Glasgow Parliamentary Debating Association was established in October, 1876, for the purpose of discussing political and social topics according to the forms of the House of Commons. Weekly meetings have been held every winter since. Several similar bodies have also sprung into existence, but they have all gone to the wall.

**Charities.**—There are over 300 charitable and beneficent institutions in Glasgow outside the three infirmaries, of which the following are types.

*The Charity Organisation Society, 115 Bath Street.*—Instituted 1874. Objects: (1.) The discovery of the deserving poor, and the procuring for them such relief as shall effect permanent benefit in their condition. (2.) The organisation of charitable efforts in the city and the prevention of overlapping, the repression of mendicity, the exposure of imposture, and the collection and distribution of subscriptions for all *bona fide* charitable and benevolent institutions in the city. (3.) The promotion of thrift and of well-advised methods for improving the conditions of the poor.

*Mission to the Out-door Blind, 4 Bath Street.*—Instituted 1859. Has upwards of 1,300 blind persons under its care.

*Seamen's Friend Society.* — Instituted 1822. For religious and social work among sailors.

*Society for the Prevention of Cruelty to Children, 87 Montrose Street.*—Instituted

1884. For the prevention of the public and private wrongs of children, etc.

*Glasgow Magdalene Institution.*—Established 1859. For the repression of vice and the reformation of penitent females, etc.

*Association for the Relief of Incurables.*—Instituted 1875. For the establishment and maintenance of one or more hospitals for the relief of persons suffering from chronic or incurable diseases. The Association has a Home at Kirkintilloch, known as "Broomhill Home."

*Royal Hospital for Sick Children, Scott Street.*—Opened in 1882. For the medical treatment of poor children suffering from non-infectious diseases or accidents.

*Dunoon Seaside Homes.*—Opened, 1869. Since then upwards of 70,000 patients have been restored to health.

*Eastpark Home for Infirm Children, Gairbraid Street.*—Opened in 1874 for relief of infirm children. There are about 80 inmates.

*Orphan Homes of Scotland, Bridge of Weir.*—Established 34 years ago by Mr. Quarrier. There are 52 buildings, which accommodate 1,300 children and young people.

*Institution for Orphan and Destitute Girls, Whiteinch.*—Established 1825 as a home for orphan and destitute girls, to educate them and train them for domestic service, etc.

*Sailors' Orphan Society of Scotland.*—Founded, 1889, to provide for the destitute children of seafaring men throughout Scotland. Upwards of 500 children are under the care of the Society.

*Lying-in Hospital.*—The Lying-in Hospital was originally founded in 1792, but was interdicted by the magistrates. It was resuscitated in 1834, when the top storey of the Old Grammar School, in what is now Nicholas Street, was secured for an hospital. A change was made to St. Andrew's Square, but in January, 1860, a house at the corner of North Portland Street and Rottenrow was bought, and the staff and patients were removed thither. On this becoming unsuitable it was taken down, and the present hospital built on the same site at a cost of £8,000. It was begun in November, 1879, and opened in January, 1881, during which interval the work was carried on in the old fever hospital, off Parliamentary Road. A branch was opened over ten years ago at 491 St. Vincent Street.

*Blind Asylum.*—The Blind Asylum in Castle Street was erected by public subscription in 1828. John Leith, a wealthy citizen, partially blind himself, had previously left £5,000 for its maintenance. It provides for the education and technical and industrial training of the blind, and secures employment for them in the institution. About 250 blind persons are educated, maintained, and employed.

*Deaf and Dumb Institution.* — The Glasgow Society for the education of the Deaf and Dumb was formed in 1819. A sum of £2,000 was subscribed, and buildings were provided in the Barony Glebe. In 1866 it was decided to secure more suitable premises, the outcome of which was the erection of the handsome institution at Prospect Bank, Queen's Park.

*Samaritan Hospital,* Coplawhill Street, instituted 1885, is exclusively for the treatment of diseases peculiar to the female sex, and for the training of nurses.

*Eye Infirmary.* — The Eye Infirmary was founded in 1824 in North Albion Street. In 1835 it was removed to College Street, and in 1852 more commodious premises were secured in Charlotte Street, in the house once occupied by David Dale. In 1874 a new infirmary was built in Berkeley Street at a cost of about £14,000.

*Glasgow United Evangelistic Association.* —This body was formed in 1874 to carry on evangelistic work among the masses. It has places of meeting all over the city, the principal being the Tent Hall, Saltmarket (which cost £17,000), the Bethany Hall, London Road, and the Mizpah Band Hall, Pitt Street. The halls belonging to this body are used by the Corporation as soup-kitchens when necessary. The Association has charge of the Children's Fresh-Air Fortnight Scheme, and controls and manages nine homes of various dimensions at coast or country resorts to which the children are yearly sent. The Association is upheld solely by voluntary subscriptions, the income in 1897 amounting to £33,816 11s. 10d.

*Humane Society.*—James Coulter left £200 towards the formation of the Humane Society. The present house on the Green, beside the Suspension Bridge, was built in 1795. About 100 years ago, when golf was played on the Green, the players had the use of the house for their golf sticks. The Geddes family, who still occupy the house, have done noble service in their day for the institution.

**Societies.**—The following table gives an approximate number of the Societies in the city in 1899, *viz* :—

| | |
|---|---:|
| Religious and Moral ... ... ... | 43 |
| Charitable and Beneficent ... ... | 300 |
| Artistic, Literary, Scientific, Medical, and Musical ... ... ... ... | 47 |
| Political ... ... ... ... | 25 |
| Educational ... ... ... ... | 35 |
| Commercial ... ... ... ... | 18 |
| Miscellaneous ... ... ... ... | 250 |

**Poorhouses. — City —** The Town's Hospital or Poorhouse was built by the Town Council, General Session, Trades' House, and Merchants' House in 1733, on the old Green in Great Clyde Street, at what is now the corner of Ropework Lane. The Poorhouse was in front, the Infirmary behind, below which was the Lunatic Asylum, the windows of which faced Ropework Lane. When the Royal Lunatic Asylum removed to Gartnaval in 1843, the building in Parliamentary Road was taken over as the City Poorhouse.

**Gartloch Asylum.**—Situated about a mile from Garnkirk Station, was opened in November, 1896, and has accommodation for 530 lunatic patients. The cost of erection and furnishing, including the price of land, was about £200,000, and recently an elegant Nurses' Home has been erected in connection therewith.

**Barony— Barnhill.**—Was opened in 1853. The cost of erection was about £34,000, but there have been considerable alterations and additions made to the building since. It has now accommodation for upwards of 1,420 inmates, including complete hospital accommodation for about 350 sick poor, who are attended by qualified sick nurses.

**Woodilee Asylum.** — This asylum, situated near Lenzie Junction, was opened in 1875. The original cost, including price of land, was £201,202, but the asylum has been considerably enlarged since, and the total cost will be not less than £350,000. The present accommodation is for about 900 patients.

**Union of City and Barony Parishes.**—These parishes were united for poor law purposes, under an order from Lord Balfour of Burleigh, Secretary for Scotland, on the 18th October, 1898, and a new Parish Council was constituted in December, 1898; this council has the control of both the City and Barony poorhouses, and of the Woodilee and Gartloch Asylums.

**Govan — Merryflatts.** — The first poorhouses occupied by the Govan Parochial

Board were small premises situated in Coburg Lane and Dale Street, from whence they removed about 1850 to the Old Horse Barracks in Eglinton Street, which they were compelled to quit to make way for the Caledonian Railway Company, when they built their handsome poorhouse and asylum at Merryflatts, which was opened in 1872. The cost of erection and furnishing, including the price of land, was £120,000, but it has been considerably added to since then. There is at present accommodation for 814 ordinary inmates, including hospital accommodation, under trained nurses, for 200 sick poor, and in addition there is asylum accommodation for 200 lunatic poor. At present there is in course of erection a new hospital with accommodation for 160 sick poor, which is expected to meet the wants of the parish for a good many years to come.

**Hawkhead Asylum.** — Situated on the River Cart, about two miles from Paisley, was opened in 1896 ; has accommodation for 510 patients. The cost of erection and furnishing, including price of land, was about £190,000.

## BANKS.

**Bank of Scotland.** — After an unsuccessful attempt in 1697 a branch of the Bank of Scotland was opened in 1731 through the exertions of Paterson, founder of the Bank of England, and originator of the Darien Expedition. It was abandoned in 1733. A branch was again opened in Queen Street about 1793. The office was located in Miller Street in 1820. In 1840 it was in 66 Ingram Street. It is now situated in St. Vincent Place, at the corner of George Square.

**Ship.** — The Ship Bank figures prominently in all the old histories of Glasgow. Dunlop, Houston & Company founded the bank in 1749. The other partners were W. M'Dowall of Castle Semple, Andrew Buchanan of the Drumpellier family, Robert Dunlop, Allan Dreghorn, and G. Oswald. Dunlop, Houston & Company were succeeded in 1776 by Moore, Carrick and Company, and latterly the firm became Carrick, Brown & Company. The bank offices were originally in the Bridgegate. In 1776 they removed to the west wing of Shawfield House, at the foot of Glassford Street. "Robin" Carrick, the principal, was born in Houston Parish Church Manse; he lived in the rooms above the bank, and was well known for his caution and frugality, and many stories are told regarding

him. He was a Bailie in the city in 1796, and Dean of Guild in 1802 and 1803. The Ship joined the Glasgow Bank. They had their offices in 1840 at 12 Ingram Street and 31 Trongate. Latterly they became merged in the Union Bank of Scotland, whose office was at 24 Virginia Street.

**Glasgow Arms.** — The Glasgow Arms Bank was opened in the Bridgegate in 1750. This was the second bank belonging to the city established within four years. In 1755 the bank removed to 55 King Street, from where it migrated in 1778 to the foot of Miller Street. This bank failed in 1793, but paid all its liabilities in full.

**Thistle.** — The Thistle Bank was established in Virginia Street in 1761. This was the third Glasgow bank.

**Merchants.** — A concern called the Merchants Bank began business at the west corner of Maxwell and Argyle Streets about 1765, while a fifth local bank was started in Virginia Street about the same time by Messrs. George & Thomson. Both banks failed in 1793, but paid their debts in full.

**Royal.** — In 1783 the Royal Bank established a branch in Glasgow. David Dale acted as agent in his yarn shop in Hopkirk's Land in High Street, near the Cross, the rent being £5 a year ; but Mr. Dale considered this too extravagant, and let half of his premises to a watchmaker for 50s. The bank office was afterwards removed to the south-east corner of St. Andrew's Square. In 1817 the bank bought the mansion which is now embodied in the present Royal Exchange, from where it removed to the present premises behind the Exchange in 1827.

**Old Paisley.** — The Old Paisley Bank, founded in 1783, opened a branch opposite the Tontine in 1784.

**Paisley Union.** — The Paisley Union Bank, instituted in 1788, opened an office at 17 High Street in 1789, from where it removed (1) to the south-east corner of South Frederick and Ingram Streets; (2) to the corner of Hutcheson and Ingram Streets.

**Greenock.** — The Greenock Bank opened an office in the old mansion at the head of Queen Street (now embodied in the Union Bank) about 1793. The bank removed to King Street, afterwards to the Tontine, from thence to Nelson Street, and finally reached 64 Buchanan Street, where it was amalgamated with the Western Bank.

**British Linen.** — About 1793 the British Linen Bank transacted its business in Stirling, Gordon & Co.'s counting-house. In 1840 the office was at 71 Queen Street. The directors purchased the Gaelic Church (now St. Columba, of which Dr. Norman Macleod was minister) for £10,000, which stood at the corner of Ingram and Queen Streets, on the site of which they erected their present bank, at a cost of £30,000.

**Leith.** — The Leith Bank, about 1793, had an agency on the east side of Brunswick Street, in Brown, Smith & M'Nab's office.

**Falkirk.** — About 1793 the Falkirk Bank began business in the shop of Charles Walker, in the Gallowgate.

**County.** — Messrs. Watsons were agents for a number of county banks about 1795. Their original office was in Leitch's Court, from where they removed to the Old Post Office Court, and finally they carried on business at the foot of Virginia Street, on the west side.

**Renfrewshire.** — The Renfrewshire Bank opened an office in 1803 at the head of Miller Street, on the east side. In 1840 it was situated in No. 94 of the same street.

**Glasgow Banking Company.** — The Glasgow Banking Company, under the management of James Dennistoun of Golfhill, began business in May, 1809, in an old house in North Albion Street, but they soon transferred their headquarters to an old mansion at the south-west corner of Montrose and Ingram Streets, which formerly belonged to Mr. Buchanan of Ardenconnell. The premises were afterwards occupied by the Sanitary Department before they were installed in their present offices at corner of Montrose and Cochrane Streets.

**Commercial.** — The Commercial Bank opened an office in 1810 in Ingram Street, opposite the head of Brunswick Street. In 1840 it was situated in 66 Virginia Street, removing from there to the handsome building in Gordon Street, which has since been improved by the addition of the grand front in Buchanan Street.

**National.** — In 1840 the head office of the National Bank was situated in Virginia Buildings, 43 Virginia Street. In 1842 the address is given as 13 Virginia Street. Subsequently the house of Kirkman Finlay in Queen Street was acquired, and when it was reconstructed it became the head office of the bank.

b

**Union.** — The Union Bank was the first bank in the city formed on the joint-stock principle, in 1830, under the name of the Glasgow Union Bank, but subsequently changed to the Union Bank of Scotland. The first office was in the Old Post Office Court off Trongate, from whence it was removed to 15 Virginia Street. The Union Bank subsequently acquired the business and property of the Old Thistle Bank, to whose premises the business was transferred, ultimately removing to the present site in Ingram Street. The following banks became amalgamated with the Union, viz., 1st, The Thistle; 2nd, Paisley Union; 3rd, William Forbes & Co., of Edinburgh; 4th, Hunter & Co., of Ayr; 5th, the Ship and Glasgow Banks (which had previously joined); 6th, the Old Bank of Aberdeen.

**Western.** — The Western Bank became a joint-stock company in 1832, and had its office at 4 Miller Street. The following banks became incorporated with it, viz., 1st, the Old Greenock Bank ; 2nd, the Dundee Union Bank ; 3rd, the Paisley Commercial Joint-Stock Bank; 4th, the New Glasgow Bank; and 5th, the Ayrshire Bank.

*Western Bank Failure.* — On 9th November, 1857, the Western Bank, which had an authorised capital of £4,000,000, in 200,000 shares of £200 each, closed its doors on account of an American commercial panic bringing down four leading firms, who were in debt to the bank to the extent of £1,603,728. This caused about £1,000,000 of deposits to be withdrawn in a few days The Western had 101 branches throughout the country. At the annual meeting in June, the report showed profits £145,826 5s. 6d. They paid 9 per cent., and carried forward £10,826 5s. 6d, which left £226,777 3s. 3d. of assets. The panic was great ; the magistrates advised people to accept the bank notes. Two calls, equal to £125 per share, yielding £2,054,566 4s. 10d., were made by the liquidators, who found the whole taken-up capital to be only £1,500,000. The total liabilities ultimately came to £6,360,170 18s. 6d. When the affairs were wound up in 1877, those who paid up received £72 15s. per share back; but besides their capital the shareholders lost £1,167,393 12s. 8d., or, in capital and calls combined, £2,667,393 12s. 8d. The City of Glasgow Bank also closed its doors for a few days during the panic, but afterwards resumed business as usual.

**Glasgow Provident.** — In 1840 the Glasgow Provident Bank had an office at 86 Miller Street.

**Savings Banks.**—In 1840 the Anderston Savings Bank transacted its business in Anderston Church Session House in Clyde Street; while the Gorbals Savings Bank had its office at 23 Nicholson Street.

**National Security Savings.**—The National Security Savings Bank was established in 1836 by the amalgamation of a number of smaller savings banks. The first office was in Hutcheson's Hospital buildings in John Street, and afterwards in Hutcheson Street, and, later, at the corner of Virginia and Wilson Streets. It was then removed to Glassford Street, and is now situated in a handsome erection in Ingram Street.

**Aberdeen Town and County and Ayr.**—The business of the Aberdeen Town and County and Ayr Banks was transacted by their agents, the Royal Bank, in 1840.

**Clydesdale.**—The Clydesdale Bank began business as a joint-stock company at 101 Miller Street in 1838, but it shortly removed to 13 Queen Street, where business was carried on until the handsome property in St. Vincent Place was erected. The Greenock Union Bank became incorporated with the Clydesdale.

**City of Glasgow.**—The City of Glasgow Bank began business at the north corner of Wilson and Virginia Streets in 1839, but shortly removed to 58 Virginia Street, where it remained till the end. The Eastern Bank of Scotland and the Isle of Man Commercial both became merged in the City of Glasgow Bank.

*City of Glasgow Bank Failure.*—The City of Glasgow Bank was very popular with the moneyed and working classes alike. When the Western Bank failed in 1857 the "City" Bank stopped payment for a few days during the panic, but when quiet was restored it resumed business again, and was apparently flourishing like the proverbial "green bay tree." In 1878 it had 133 branches over the length and breadth of the land, and in June of the same year declared a dividend of 12 per cent., carrying forward £13,222. Words fail to express the chagrin and astonishment that were felt when it was announced on 2nd October, 1878, that the bank had closed its doors, the first intimation the public received being in the morning news-papers or news-bills at the shop doors. Fortunately several of the other banks agreed to accept the "City" Bank's notes. The panic was, however, not lessened by the failure, within a few days, of the follow-

ing firms, *viz*:—Smith, Fleming & Co., Potter, Wilson & Co., Hugh Balfour & Co., T. D. Finlay & Co., etc., etc. William Anderson and Dr. A. B. M'Grigor made an investigation of the bank's affairs, and found that the loss amounted to £5,190,983 11s. 3d., to which fell to be added the capital of £1,000,000. Notes had been issued on 28th September for £604,196, whereas the bullion against them only amounted to £366,464. The shareholders had been led to believe that £1,126,764, more than was actually the case, had been lent on credit, and that £926,764, more than was a fact, was held in security for same. The gold reserve was found short by £200,000, and a chimerical sum of £7,345,359 was treated as available assets on the balance sheet. The following were arrested, *viz*:—Henry Inglis, Lewis Potter, Robert Salmond, John Stewart, William Taylor, John Innes Wright, directors; Robert Summers Stronach, manager; and C. S. Leresche, secretary. The charge against the latter was withdrawn. The trial of the others was begun in Edinburgh, on 20th January, 1879, and lasted for eleven days; Potter and Stronach got eighteen months' imprisonment, while the remaining five were sent to durance vile for eight months. The bank went into voluntary liquidation, and on Messrs. William Anderson, George Auldjo Jamieson, James Haldane, and John Cameron being appointed liquidators, they immediately made a call of £500 on every £100 of stock held by the shareholders, payable in two instalments, which represented about £4,000,000. The community showed their sympathy by raising nearly £400,000 as a relief fund for those who had suffered through the gigantic fraud. The fund was wound-up in November, 1888.

**Glasgow Joint-Stock.**—The Glasgow Joint-Stock Bank opened an office at 101 Miller Street. It removed in 1843 to 37 St. Vincent Place, and became amalgamated with the Edinburgh and Leith Bank on 1st January, 1844, when the titles of both banks were changed to the Edinburgh and Glasgow Banks.

**North British.**—The North British Bank was instituted as a joint-stock concern in 1846.

**Present Banks.**—The following is a list of the banks in the city, with the situation of their head offices, and the number of their branch offices, *viz*:—Clydesdale, St. Vincent Pl., 18 branches; Commercial, Buchanan Street, 14 branches; Bank of

Scotland, St. Vincent Place, 19 branches; British Linen, Queen Street, 24 branches; National, Queen Street, 17 branches; Royal, Royal Exchange Square, 20 branches; Union, Ingram Street, 15 branches.

## POLICE, Etc.

**First Police.**—Previous to 1800 the citizens themselves did duty in watching the city at night. The first Glasgow Police Force was instituted in 1778, by the appointment of an inspector (with a number of men under him), at an annual salary of £100. The citizens would not be assessed for the upkeep of the " guardians," and after three years' trial they were disbanded.

**Gallows and Pillory**—The gallows originally stood on the site of the Old Barracks in the Gallowgate, whence they were removed to the Howgate, where the Monkland Canal Basin is situated. They stood here from 1765 to 1781. From 1784 to 1787 they were erected in the yard of the Bishop's Castle, and from 1788 to 1813 they stood at the Cross, where the pillory was placed. In 1813 they were removed to the Jail, in Jail Square, where the last public execution took place in 1865. Executions are now carried out in Duke Street Prison.

**Bridewell.**—The Old Prison in Duke Street was erected in 1798. Previous to this prisoners were incarcerated in Bridewell, in the Drygate, which was purchased by the City from the Earl of Glencairn in 1635, and in a temporary building in College Street, near the corner of Shuttle Street. The Tolbooth was also used for prisoners.

**Duke Street Prison.**—The magistrates handed over their old Bridewell and grounds in Duke Street to the Commissioners, who built a prison, which was opened for inmates in 1826. This prison is now mainly set apart for female prisoners. The Drygate wing is only appropriated for male prisoners awaiting their trial, after which they are removed to Barlinnie, which was opened in 1872.

**Institution of Present System.**— The present police system was established by Act of Parliament in 1800. An attempt to do this the year previous was thwarted by the citizens objecting to the taxation. John Stenhouse, chief constable, had a salary of £200 per annum ; a clerk, £85 ; a treasurer, £80 ; three sergeants, £40 each ; nine officers, £30 each ; and sixty-eight watchmen, 10s. each a week, for

whom sentry-boxes were put up. New lamps were also erected, and sanitary arrangements received attention. The following taxes were levied, *viz.* :—4d. per £ on £4 and £6 rents ; £6 to £10, 9d. ; £10 to £15 and upwards, 1s. This and other sources brought in £5,000 of revenue, and the outlay amounted to only £4,600 during the first year.

**Central Police Office.**—Ground was purchased in South Albion Street in 1822 at a cost of £4,659 6s. 2d., on which the present Central Police Office was erected. The building was finished three years later. The Police Board had previously been authorised by Act of Parliament to appoint two resident Commissioners for each Ward. The first Police Office was in the Tron Kirk Session House, from which it was removed to the north-west corner of Bell Street and Candleriggs, in the *Herald* Office close, one stair up. Its next change was to premises above the Guard-House at the west side of Candleriggs, and, after remaining there ten years, was ultimately located on the present site in South Albion Street, where the Meat Market used to stand. It has been reconstructed twice, the final being in 1877. The building has cost £13,000. The following Offices have since been erected, or acquired, *viz.*:— Divisions—A, East Clyde Street (Office and Barracks, opened 1893, cost £10,000). B, Western, originally in an old Methodist Chapel, now in Cranston Street (opened 1860, cost £14,000). C, Eastern, Tobago Street ; *Camlachie*, Great Eastern Road ; *Bridgeton*, Dalmarnock Road. D, Southern, originally in the old Baronial Hall in Main Street, afterwards in South Portland Street (this building cost £8,000), from where it was removed to Oxford Street in 1896 (the new building cost £27,000) ; *Paisley Road; South Wellington Street.* E, Northern, Maitland Street (opened 1891, cost £12,000); *Camperdown Street.* F, St. Rollox, Tennant Street (opened 1877, cost £10,000) ; *Springburn*, New Keppochhill Road. G, Queen's Park, Craigie Street (opened 1898, cost £18,000, including Fire Station). H, Maryhill, Gairbraid Avenue ; *Hillhead*, Byars Road. Marine, M'Alpine Street.

**Fire Brigade.**—The Fire Brigade used to be in connection with the Police Office, but the growth of the city rendered it necessary to have premises specially for fire purposes. These were erected in College Street ; but new and more modern buildings are being built in Ingram Street, where this important branch of the Corporation will soon be housed. The brigade is fully equipped with over twenty powerful steam and manual engines, and over 50,000 feet of hose, and has the following stations situated as under, *viz*.:—Sub-station, St. Enoch Square ; Northern, 509 St. George's Road; Hillhead, Burgh Buildings, Byars Rd. ; Maryhill, Gairbraid Avenue; Southern; 26 Warwick Street ; Queen's Park, 52 Allison Street; Western, 59 Cranston Street, Eastern, 27 Soho Street; Springburn, Keppochhill Road.

**Cleansing.**—The cleansing of the city was taken under the direct control of the Corporation in 1868. Previously it had been let out on the contract system. At first the refuse of the city was collected and stored in depots at different parts of the city, from whence it was despatched to farmers and others. This primitive method is now superseded. Refuse despatch works have been erected at Port-Eglinton, Kelvinhaugh, and St. Rollox, where all the city's garbage, about 1,261 tons a day, is treated on the latest scientific and sanitary principles. Some is cremated, and the product sold, over 50 per cent. being sold to farmers for manure, and the unsaleable portion is sent to tips. The Cleansing Department manages the municipal farms, *viz*.:—Fulwood Moss, near Houston, 142 acres, lease expires in 1910 ; Ryding, at New Monkland, 565 acres, purchased in 1891 for £12,575; Maryburgh, 31 acres, near Glenboig, purchased in 1895 for £1,000 ; Hallbrae, 45 acres, adjoining Maryburgh, leased in 1895 for 19 years.

**City Improvement Trust.** — The rapid growth of the city caused overcrowding and the utilisation of houses quite unfit for human habitation. This source of danger gave great anxiety to the authorities, who succeeded, after much trouble, in receiving Parliamentary sanction, on 11th June, 1866, for a City Improvement Act, with power to levy a tax of 6d. in the £1 for five years and 3d. in the £1 for the succeeding ten years, and liberty of compulsory purchase of property in defined areas. Lord Provost Blackie was at the head of the Corporation at the time, and to him and ex-Bailie James Morrison and their far-seeing colleagues Glasgow owes much for its great sanitation fame. In 1871 the Trust received a further extension of time for the compulsory purchase of lands. In 1880 the Act was amended, and power given to levy an assessment of 2d. in the £1. Property was bought to the amount of £1,616,000 within the compulsory areas, and the sum

of £125,000 was spent outwith these bounds. £103,000 was expended in the formation of streets, squares, sewers, and covering in the Molendinar Burn, etc., and Alexandra Park was bought and laid out at a cost of £40,000. The first property was erected in the Drygate in 1870 at a cost of £3,426, and immediately after the first model lodging-house was built adjoining it, while one for women was erected in East Russell Street. These were soon followed by similar erections in Greendyke Street, Portugal Street, Clyde Street (Calton), North Woodside Road, and Hydepark Street, which cost, including sites (but not subsequent additions), £87,212. Since 1897 the Trust has been self-supporting. In 1888 the Trust again began to build dwelling-houses in Saltmarket and vicinity. The "Family Home" in St. Andrew's Street was commenced in July, 1894. The Trust, under the able convenership of ex-Bailie Chisholm, is still continuing its good work, and is serving as a model to all the great cities in the world.

**Revenue of City Improvement Trust.** · The Act was obtained in 1866, and a tax of 6d. per £1 was levied for the first financial year, ending in 1867 ; from then until 1872 the rate was 4d. per £1 ; from 1872 to 1874, 3d.; from 1874 to 1885, 2d.; 1885 to 1888, 1½d.; 1888 to 1893, 1d.; 1893 to 1896, ½d.; 1896 to 1897, ¾d. Since then the department has been self-supporting, and the tax was abolished.

| | | | | |
|---|---|---|---|---|
| 1867 | .. £37,891 | | 1875 | ... £19,098 |
| 1868 | ... 27,039 | | 1876 | ... 20,262 |
| 1869 | ... 27,991 | | 1877 | ... 21,472 |
| 1870 | ... 31,390 | | 1878 | ... 22,402 |
| 1871 | ... 30,867 | | 1879 | ... 22,287 |
| 1872 | ... 24,199 | | 1880 | ... 22,251 |
| 1873 | ... 25,382 | | 1890 | ... 58,336 |
| 1874 | ... 17,867 | | 1898 | ... 63,455 |

**Model Lodging-Houses.**—The Corporation have erected the following model lodging-houses, which are a great boon to the poorer classes of the community, *viz*. :—Hydepark Street (cost £15,000), Portugal Street (£22,000), North Woodside (£16,800), Drygate (£18,800), Calton (£14,700), Greenhead (£11,500), East Russell Street (for women, £9,000), and the Family Home in St. Andrew Street, opened in 1896, having cost £13,000. There are also several private model lodging-houses in different parts of the city. They are handsome buildings, and are conducted on similar lines to those belonging to the Corporation.

**Sanitary Department.**—In the beginning of the century people threw out all their refuse in the street, where it lay in heaps. When the Police Board was formed in 1800 the chief constable acted as sanitary inspector, and scavengers were employed to sweep the streets. Acts were passed in 1848-49 and 1856 for the removal of nuisances. Dr. W. T. Gairdner was appointed medical officer in 1863. The Public Health Act was passed in 1867, and on the initiative of Mr. John Ure (afterwards Lord Provost) the present Sanitary Department was established with Kenneth Macleod as sanitary inspector. Mr. Peter Fyfe now holds the post. Dr. J. B. Russell succeeded Dr. Gairdner in 1872, and on his retiral in 1898 Dr. A. K. Chalmers secured the appointment. The staff have elegant new offices at the corner of Montrose and Cochrane Streets, which cost £30,000.

### Baths and Wash-Houses.

The subject of Public Baths was first raised in the Town Council on 24th May, 1869, by the late Bailie William Wilson. No practical steps were taken until 8th February, 1875, when a special committee was appointed, which procured the site of the old washing-house on the Green for the erection of the Greenhead Baths and Wash-Houses. They were opened on 19th August, 1878, at a cost of about £12,000. Prior to this, washing-houses had been erected in London Road, on 1st July, 1876, at a cost of £2,250, and a similar establishment was opened the following year in Kennedy Street. Since then the following have been erected, viz. :—Woodside, opened September, 1882; Cranstonhill, May, 1883; Townhead, June, 1884; Gorbals, April, 1885 ; Springburn, 1898 (cost £13,680); Maryhill, 1898; Hutchesontown, 1897 ; Kennedy Street, 1899 ; Stobcross Street, and Bain Square. Another is in course of erection at Whitevale. They are being largely taken advantage of. The charges for bathing are moderate, and housewives using the wash-houses may either do their own washing or have it done by the attendants.

### Weigh-House.

A weigh-house stood in Candleriggs, but it was removed to the the corner of Ingram and Montrose Streets. The present passage in the Tron Steeple in Trongate was also used for a weigh-house. There are at present twenty-six public weighing machines in the city.

### Weights and Measures.

Previous to 1881 there was no systematic inspection of weights and measures. In 1890 the Act requiring weights to be stamped by the inspector came into force. It is now made compulsory that every place of business be visited by an inspector once a year.

### Labour Bureau.

A Labour Bureau was opened in Nelson Street, but the office is now situated at 158 George Street. The Corporation has voted £250 a year for its maintenance.

## WATER.

### Clyde and Public Wells.

During last century the water supply was obtained from the Clyde and public wells. The former was better adapted for washing purposes, but was used only by those who could afford to employ their own servants or others for this labour. The wells were used by all. The water-bearers "lined up" waiting their turn, as people do at present outside the theatre doors. History records the great " chaff and banter " that took place around the wells all day long. The large box well at the West Port was so much run upon that the crowds often interfered with the traffic. It was taken down, and a small iron pump substituted at the foot of Glassford Street. A few favoured citizens had private pumps in the gardens of their mansions in Buchanan, Queen, and Miller Streets. The following is a list of the public wells in the city in 1816, viz. :—

| Street. | Depth. | Situation. |
|---|---|---|
| Argyle | 13ft. oin. | near Union Street. |
| Argyle | 9ft. | near Shutt Wynd. |
| Argyle | 13ft. 6in. | near Turner's Court. |
| Argyle | 23ft. 6in. | near Stockwell Street. |
| South Albion | 30ft. | at Police Office. |
| Bridgegate | 16ft. 11in. | near Goosedubs. |
| Buchanan | 14ft. 1in. | at Argyle Street. |
| Campbell | 26ft. oin. | near Gallowgate. |
| Canon | 30ft. oin. | at Ramshorn Church. |
| Castle | 42ft. oin. | near Howgate. |
| Claythorn | 9ft. oin. | near Gallowgate. |
| Cochrane | 18ft. 11in. | at John Street. |
| Duke | 16ft. oin. | at Prison. |
| George | 11ft. oin. | at Andersonian College. |
| George | 35ft. oin. | at Balmano Brae. |
| George | 11ft. oin. | near High Street. |
| High | 29ft. oin. | at Old Vennel. |
| King | 12ft. 1in. | at Beef Market. |
| Kirk | —ft. —in. | at Old Trades House. |
| Ladywell | 5ft. oin. | — |
| Montrose | 12ft. oin. | opposite Guard-House. |
| Saltmarket | 12ft. oin. | south of Bridgegate. |
| Shutt Wynd | 9ft. oin. | near Howard Street. |
| Spoutmouth | 18ft. 10in. | near Gallowgate. |
| Stockwell | 9ft. 6in. | near Jackson Street. |
| S:. Andrew's Lane | 12ft. oin. | near Gallowgate. |
| St. Andrew's | 22ft. oin. | near Saltmarket. |
| Trongate | 24ft. oin. | near Back Wynd. |
| Trongate | —ft. —in. | west of Cross. |
| Wilson | 25ft. oin. | near Hutcheson Street. |

### First Attempt at Gravitation.

In 1785 an endeavour was made to bring water into the city from Whitehill, but after the ground had been surveyed the project fell through.

### Harley's Enterprise.

The water supply was so scarce in the city at the

beginning of 1800 that a William Harley, who was a manufacturer in South Frederick Street, laid pipes from springs in his property at Willowbank to a reservoir near the intersection of Bath and West Nile Streets. He sent out the *aqua pura* in specially-made tanks placed on four-wheeled vehicles, retailing it at a halfpenny a stoup. He also had byres situated in Sauchiehall Road, and to the foregoing added the sale of milk and bread. Harley built public baths in Bath Street, from whence the name is derived. He also leased Blythswood Hill, which became known as Harley's Hill; it was much higher then than now, and Ben Lomond and Tintock "tap" could easily be seen from its summit on a clear day. The top was lowered to make all the streets in the vicinity. The hill was enclosed and laid out as a garden, ornamented with a fountain, and tickets for admission found a large and ready sale in the town. This enterprising public caterer is said to have netted £4,000 a year from the sale of water alone.

**Waterworks.**—The first waterworks company in the city, with a capital of £100,000 in £50 shares, called the Glasgow Waterworks Company, was formed in 1806, under Act of Parliament. The water was taken from the Clyde to filtering works at Dalmarnock, and from there conveyed to reservoirs in the Rottenrow and Sydney Street. The engineer was Thomas Telford, C.E., of old Jamaica Bridge fame. The company possessed two steam engines, one of 36 horse-power, and in 1816 had seventeen miles of water main pipes. The Cranstonhill Waterworks Company was formed in May, 1808, with a capital of £30,000 in £50 shares, and borrowing powers to the extent of £10,000. The water was taken from the Clyde to their reservoirs in Cranstonhill, and in 1816 they had nine and a-half miles of water mains. Householders had to pay from 4s. to 42s. a year of water rates according to rent, and public works were charged on quantity of water used. Sheriff Barclay, under the *nom de plume* of "Nestor," gives a very interesting account of the early water supply in his "Recollections of Glasgow." In 1846 the Gorbals Gravitation Company, with a capital of £180,000, was formed to supply the south side of the river. Their reservoir was supplied from a stream near Barrhead. When Glasgow took over the private water companies, the Gorbals shareholders received £6 per cent. per annum on their capital. The Glasgow Water Company preference shareholders got 6 per cent.,

and the ordinary shareholders got 4½ per cent. per annum; while a mortgage debt of £75,000 was transferred to the Corporation.

**Loch Katrine.**—The rapid growth of the city made an increase of the water supply an urgent need. Glasgow was supplied with *aqua pura* from the reservoirs of the Glasgow and Gorbals Gravitation Companies, who, finding their quantity and quality not up to the requirements, in 1853 introduced a Bill into Parliament to bring "gravitation water" from Loch Lubnaig. This was defeated by the Town Council, who the following year endeavoured to get powers to buy the company and bring water themselves from Loch Katrine. They failed in their first attempt, but on 2nd July, 1855, Parliament gave its sanction. J. F. Bateman, C.E., drew the plans; and in four years the thirty-four miles of tunnelling were completed, a reservoir formed at Mugdock, near Milngavie, and everything completed, at a cost of £700,000. However, before landowners were bought out and all the water rights got, and connections made between Lochs Katrine, Vennacher, and Drunkie, the money spent amounted to £1,500,000. The new scheme supplied the city with fifty million gallons of water a day. The Queen, who was staying at Balmoral, received a deputation from the City, and agreed to perform the opening ceremony. She arrived at Holyrood, along with the Prince Consort, on the 14th October, 1859, and next day proceeded by rail to Callander, and thence by coach to Loch Katrine. The day was very wet and blowy, but this did not prevent a large number of Glaswegians taking advantage of the special railway facilities to witness the scene. The new Glasgow Volunteer regiment, and a detachment of the 42nd and 79th Highlanders, with eighty members of the Glasgow Celtic Society, acted as a guard of honour. Lord Provost Stewart met Her Majesty and the royal party with the screw steamer "Rob Roy," which steamed to the mouth of the tunnel. Her Majesty said, "Such a work is worthy of the enterprise and philanthropy of Glasgow, and I trust it will be blessed with complete success." After a blessing by the Rev. Dr. Craik, the Queen turned the handle, and the water rushed into the tunnel. After examining the works, the party returned as they came. A red marble slab at the entrance to the tunnel commemorates the event. The supply was introduced into the city in March, 1860. The memorial fountain in the West-End Park was erected on 14th August, 1871, to commemorate the event and the services rendered by Lord Provost Stewart. In 1882 it was decided to build a new aqueduct, and power was obtained to increase the capital to £3,370,000. The work was begun in 1886, and, there being no immediate hurry, it was leisurely and well done. The tunnel between Mugdock and Strathblane was opened on 24th July, 1889, and the water turned on on 31st October of the following year; and by the end of June, 1893, the Kelty and Duchray section of the new aqueduct was opened. A new reservoir was made at Craigmaddie, at a cost of £300,000. It has a water surface of eighty-six and a quarter acres, and a capacity of seven hundred million gallons, and was opened in June, 1896. There are five hundred miles of water pipes in the city, which supply daily fifty-one million gallons. The Corporation fitted up and opened on 30th May, 1895, a hydraulic power station at Cathedral Square, at a cost of about £60,000, for the use of lifts, hoists, etc. There are three 200 horse-power engines, which supply water at half a ton to the inch.

## GAS.

**First Gas Light.**—The Glasgow Gas Light Company was formed, under Act of Parliament, in June, 1817, with a capital of £40,000. Lord Provost Henry Monteith, of Carstairs, was chairman. On 5th September, 1818, James Hamilton, grocer, 128 Trongate, gave the first public exhibition of the new product with six "jetties" which he had fitted up in his shop. Previous to this the streets were lighted with a few oil lamps erected on wooden pedestals. The gas was immediately afterwards introduced into the old Theatre Royal, in Dunlop Street. On the 18th September every part of the house was filled with all the *élite* of the city, in evening dress; and when the large crystal lustre in the roof was turned on, the audience thought for a moment they had been ushered into another world.

**Corporation Gas.**—The Corporation bought out the two gas companies in the city in 1869, having previously acquired the Partick Gas Works. On 1st July, 1891, the Maryhill, Partick, and Hillhead Gas Works were bought for £202,500, and those belonging to Pollokshaws were acquired for £14,500. New works were constructed at Dawsholm, the Partick and Townhead works were discontinued, and extensive enlargements made at Tradeston and Dalmarnock works, costing in all

£160,000. The gas-holders erected at Temple works in 1893, and at Tradeston in 1896, each hold 6,000,000 cubic feet of gas, and are the third largest in the world. In 1898 it was decided to erect new gas works at Blochairn and Blackhill, to cost £1,000,000. The present price of gas is 2s. 2d. per 1,000 feet., as against 4s. 7d. in 1869. In 1877 the rat-tail burners were supplanted by Siemen's regenerative and Sugg's argand lights.

**Incandescent Light.**—The incandescent light was fitted on the lamps in the principal streets in July, 1894.

**Electric Lighting.**—In 1890 the Town Council obtained power to provide electric energy. On 1st March, 1892, the Corporation purchased the works of Mavor and Coulson, Limited, in John and Miller Streets, for £15,000. New works were built in Waterloo Street, and on 25th February, 1893, the current was switched on. During the first year there were 108 consumers, increased to 855 in 1896. 408,000 units were generated in the first twelve months; in 1896 it had increased to 1,279,687 units. The price was originally sevenpence, but was subsequently reduced to sixpence. In 1898 a new scheme was agreed upon, which will entail an additional cost of £400,000.

## EDUCATION.

**High School.**—*Founded*—The High School, originally called the "Grammar Scule," stood anciently in the Rottenrow, from where it was transferred to what is now called Nicholas Street, between High Street and Shuttle Street. The seminary was instituted before the University was founded. The house in Nicholas Street appears to have been knocked down about 1600, and during the building of the new school, which was finished in 1601, on the same site, the scholars were taught in the Cathedral. Nicholas Street was originally called "The Grammar School Wynd," and afterwards "Greyfriars Wynd."

*George Street.*—In 1789 a new school was erected on the north side of George Street at a cost of £1,950.

*John Street.*—The foundation stone of the High School of 1834 was laid by John Alston in 1820, on an elevated piece of ground on the north side of George Street. This commodious erection is now the present City Public School which stands in John Street.

*Elmbank Street.*—The School Board purchased the old Glasgow Academy in Elmbank Street, to which the High School was transferred in 1878. The building has since been considerably enlarged by the addition of two wings, in 1887 and 1897, to accommodate the great increase in scholars.

**Established Normal.** — An Industrial School was erected in 1827 by the philanthropic exertions of David Stow. It was so successful that it led to the institution of the Normal School, which was erected at Dundas Vale in 1837 at a cost of £15,000, toward which, £3,500 were subscribed publicly in Glasgow, and £4,500 obtained from the Government.

**Free Church Normal.**—So strong did the Free Church become in three years that they were enabled to build a Normal Seminary in Cowcaddens in 1846 at a cost of £8,000.

**Glasgow Academy.**—Glasgow Academy was instituted in 1846. The directors built the handsome school in Elmbank Street, which continued to be used until the present building was erected at Kelvin Bridge. The old school was bought by the School Board, and the High School transferred to it from John Street.

**Kelvinside Academy.** — Kelvinside Academy is situated in Kirklee Road, Kelvinside. Owing to the growth of the city it came desirable to have another first-class educational establishment in the West End, and the gentlemen in the district are to be congratulated on adding such a high-class beautiful school to meet the wants of the locality.

**Allan Glen's School** was instituted for practical and theoretical education ; it is situated at 68 North Hanover Street, and is now under the Technical College.

**Logan and Johnston's School of Domestic Economy** is built on the site of the original school in Greenhead Street. A certain number of girls, from twelve to sixteen years of age, are taught practical housekeeping, and are also fed and clothed free; while others are admitted on payment of fees.

**Highland Society's School** was situated in Montrose Street, and did valuable work in educating children of Highland descent. The school as such is abolished, but the building is used by the Glasgow School Board for their Pupil Teachers' Institute. The Highland Society continues

to grant scholarships and bursaries for higher education in schools, the Technical College, and University.

**General Educational Endowments Board.**—This Board applies the endowments of Muir's School Fund, Millar and Peadie's, Wilson's, Gardner's, M'Lachlan's, and Graham's schools, to provide free scholarships, bursaries, etc., to pupils in public and state-aided schools in Glasgow and vicinity.

**School of Art,** for drawing, painting, modelling, architecture, and decorative art, has this year entered into a splendid building situated at the corner of Renfrew and Dalhousie Streets. It previously occupied the eastern section of the Corporation Galleries in Sauchiehall Street.

**City Educational Endowments Board.**—The Board applies the following endowments :—Anderson's School, Dr. A. Bell's Bequest, Coulter's Mortification, Scotstarvit Mortification, Murdoch's School, Hood's School, Maxwell's School, Alexander's Endowment, M'Grigor's Bequest, Macfarlane's School, and M'Millan's Bequest. The Board's scheme provides for the maintenance of a school for boys, free scholarships, bursraies, etc., and the payment of a subsidy to the Technical College.

**Buchanan Institution.**—Established 1859. It is situated at 47 Greenhead Street. Three hundred boys receive an education and industrial training in various trades, in addition to which they are fed three times a day at the school.

**Technical College.**—The Glasgow and West of Scotland Technical College was founded by an order of the Queen in Council dated 26th November, 1886, according to which Anderson's College, the College of Science and Arts (formerly the Mechanics' Institution), and the Atkinson Institution were amalgamated and placed under one governing body. The curriculum of the day classes extends over three years, and special courses of study are arranged in every department of engineering, architecture, metallurgy, and agriculture. That of evening classes is arranged for in four sessions in which the foregoing studies and others are undertaken. Students are prepared for the Technical College in Allan Glen's School. A large number of scholarships and bursaries are given.

**School Board.**—When the Education Act was passed in 1872, Glasgow was in a most backward condition educationally.

The first election took place on 26th March, 1873, 39 candidates coming forward for 15 seats. Mr. Alex. Whitelaw was appointed chairman. The early proceedings were remarkable for the disputes that arose over opening the meetings with prayer. The new Board found 87,000 children, and they had accommodation for only 57,000, much of it of a very unsatisfactory kind, such as would not be tolerated at the present day. It was reported to the Board of Education, in December, 1873, that 30 schools with accommodation for 22,000 scholars would be necessary to supply the deficiency. Building operations were immediately commenced, and have been going on ever since, the accommodation now being regarded as complete, any further building being only required for the increase of the population. To meet the expenditure in providing and enlarging schools the Board has borrowed £1,296,000. Of that sum £342,000 have been repaid, leaving liabilities amounting to £954,000. To meet these there are assets consisting of school buildings and sites belonging to the ratepayers, which may be moderately valued at a million and a quarter sterling. In the schools of the Board there is accommodation for 81,000 scholars, and in denominational and other schools for 23,000, a total of 104,000 places, sufficient for all the children of school age. The denominational schools mostly belong to the Roman Catholics, who have school places for 18,000 scholars. With the exception of these, education in Glasgow is wholly under the control of the Board. The following statistics show what the Board has done since 1873:—Number of schools at start, 1; number of schools at present, 70. Number of teachers at start, 19; number of teachers at present, 1,792. Number of scholars at start, 680; number of scholars at present, 76,000. Amount of income at start, £35,800; amount of income at present, £326,000.

**Free Education.**—In 1889 the Government gave grants out of local taxation and customs, which were devoted in Scotland only for free education up to Standard V. In 1892 a second grant was given, so that no fees were charged to children between the ages of three and fourteen. Glasgow and Govan, however, still retain a few fee-paying schools.

———

## PARKS.

**Old Green.**—The Old Green of Glasgow, which was known as the Dowcot Green, extended from the Clyde to Argyle Street, and from Stockwell Street to Jamaica Street, and included a small island in the river. About the year 1700 it was a fashionable promenade shaded with trees, but latterly encroachments began to be made, and a ropework, bottle work, and the Town's Hospital were built upon it, and portions sold and feued, until it gradually disappeared.

**The Green.**—*Low Green*—The present Green of Glasgow was at one time part of the Bishop's Forest, which extended for several miles to the east. It is not known when the Green became the property of the community, but James II. made a grant of what is now known as the Low Green to Bishop Turnbull, on 20th April, 1450, who in turn would probably present it to the town. In 1662 and 1664 the City purchased the lands of Linningshaugh.

*High Green.*—The Green was greatly improved between 1630 and 1700, during which period the lands of Kinclaith, Daffiegreen, and Craignestock were purchased. These went to form what is known as the High Green. In 1773 an addition was made to it by the purchase of land from Colin Rae, of Little Govan, who received £2,103, while small portions were bought from Kinclaith and others. Monteith Row and the neighbouring properties were feued off the High Green from 1812 onwards.

*Provost's, or Flesher's, Haugh.*—The lands of Provost's Haugh were purchased from Patrick Bell, of Cowcaddens, in 1792, for £4,000. The Haugh was formerly what its name denotes, but between 1890 and 1896 it was raised to the level of the King's Park by the Caledonian Railway Company with the excavated material from the Central Railway and elsewhere.

*Feuing.*—In 1745 the Magistrates feued a quarter of an acre of land for a woollen manufactory; but, owing to the opposition of the citizens, the project had to be abandoned.

*Sawmill Dispute.*—A sawmill built on the Green, beside the Molendinar Burn, by William Fleming and William Murdoch, at a cost of £600 sterling, was objected to by the citizens. An order for its removal, as a nuisance, not being complied with, it was knocked down by order of the Magistrates on 23rd June, 1764. On appealing to the Court of Session, Fleming obtained damages to the extent of £610 1s. 4d. In commemoration of his success, Fleming changed the name of his estates of Young-field and Hamilton Hill to Sawmillfield. A street of this name, on the estate near Garscube Cross, now keeps this memory green.

*Serpentine Walks.*—In 1756 the formation of the Serpentine walks was commenced.

*Arns Well.*—Arns well, immortalised by Hugh Macdonald, who says it is named after a group of alder (*Scottice*, "arn") trees which stood on the spot, was opened in 1777. James Watt states he was passing the spot when his great invention flashed across his mind.

*Cows.*—In 1450 the cows of the citizens grazed on the Green, the Gallowmuir, and the Cowcaddens. In 1736 it is recorded that the cows were driven by the town's herd to the North-West Common—in the vicinity of Port-Dundas Road—by way of Cow Loan (Queen Street) and Cowcaddens, to be milked. In 1800 the cows which pastured on the Green were milked morning and evening at the south end of Charlotte Street and at the foot of Saltmarket. The charge for grazing was £3 3s. a head; but in 1816 the amount was raised to £4 4s. per annum, with 2s. 6d. extra for the herd. The town kept two bulls.

*Promenade.*—The fashionable promenade at the end of last century was from the Cross to the south corner of Queen Street; while the Green was also much frequented by the *crème de la crème* of society, who lounged beneath the widespreading branches of a double row of trees.

*Washing-Houses.*—At the beginning of the century the Green consisted of several sections. The west portion was called the Low Green, and the Justiciary Buildings were built on it. Where Nelson's Monument stands was a considerable hill, on which stood the herd's house. It was latterly utilised by the golfers. The High Green was separated from Calton by the Camlachie Burn, which filled a large dam for supplying the washing-houses, erected about 1730, on the High Green, for the use of which about 1s. 6d. a day was charged; water was also carried from the Clyde; the clothes were bleached on the Low Green, which was thickly covered with grass. An avenue of trees divided the King's Park from the High Green, and to the south of the former was the Flesher's Haugh. Great Hamilton Street and Monteith Row were taken off the Green in 1819.

*Coal.*—Boring operations took place in the Green in 1823 to find if coal could be found in paying quantities; nothing further, however, was done.

*Railway.*—The Glasgow and Airdrie Railway Company in 1847 endeavoured to connect a proposed terminus on the College grounds with their lines on the south side of the river by means of a viaduct across the Green to the east of Nelson's Monument, but the opposition of the citizens prevented it.

*Encroachment.*—A proposal to take 2,216 square yards off the Green into Greenhead Street was strenuously opposed by the citizens, who obtained, at an expense of £368 1s. 1d., a suspension and interim interdict against the Town Council, in 1868. After an eight months' fight the matter was compromised by an agreement that the roadway in Greenhead Street should be eighteen feet wide and the pavement eight feet wide; also that paths and rails be erected to mark the boundary of the people's park.

*Richmond Park.*—The Corporation purchased the land on the south side of the Clyde in 1897, opposite the Flesher's Haugh, from William Dixon's trustees for £45,000. They intend to lay it out and make it a valuable addition to the "people's park" under the name of Richmond Park.

**Kelvingrove.**—Twelve acres of ground on the left bank of the Kelvin passed from the hands of James Campbell of Blythswood, in 1754, to Alex. Wotherspoon, whose son sold them in 1782 to Patrick Colquhoun, who was Provost of Glasgow at the time. The last purchaser fenced and laid off the grounds, and added wings to each side of the mansion-house, and named his new possession Kelvingrove. Mr. Colquhoun went to London, and the estate was bought by John Pattison, who purchased an additional twelve acres alongside. In 1806 Richard Dennistoun became the proprietor, until Colin M'Naught invested in the estate in 1841. On his death in 1853 the Town Council purchased for £99,569 this and the adjoining ground lying on the left bank of the Kelvin between Woodside and Sandyford. Part of this land was feued, which nearly recouped the original cost, and the remaining portion, amounting to 45 acres, was formed into a public park. This was called Kelvingrove Park, and it is now popularly known as the West End Park. The park was formed to plans designed by Sir Joseph Paxton and others. The Corporation relieved the

University of the lands of Donaldshill and the unappropriated portion of Gilmorehill (20½ acres) for £19,000, and added these to the park. Donaldshill was subsequently exchanged with the University (who wanted it for the site of an Infirmary) for the lands of Clayslaps. Overnewton was afterwards purchased from the Improvement Trust. A portion of Kelvinbank was secured indirectly from the Trades House. Clayslaps Mill was got from the Bakers' Incorporation, who also sold the City the grounds of Bunhouse (6½ acres) in 1895 for £30,000. More purchases were made, bringing the total cost to £95,000. The whole area of the park is now 91½ acres, which have entailed an expenditure of £270,000. The park contains the Kelvingrove Museum; Russian cannon captured at the Crimean war; the Stewart Memorial Fountain; three early specimens of steam engines; a replica of a lioness and cubs, presented by J. S. Kennedy, of New York, in 1867, and an ornamental pond for waterfowl.

**Queen's.**—The lands of Pathhead and a portion of Pollok estate (143 acres), lying to the south of Crosshill, were purchased by the Corporation in 1857 from Neale Thomson of Camphill at the cost price of £30,000. In 1862 53 acres were set apart for feuing, 33 acres were allocated for a recreation ground, and 57 acres were laid out as a public park from plans prepared by Sir Joseph Paxton. Fifty-eight acres of ground, known as Camphill, lying immediately to the west of the Queen's Park, belonged to Hutchesons' Hospital, who purchased it from Neale Thomson's trustees in 1866 for £24,000, was transferred to the City in 1894 for £63,000, which is the original cost plus 4 per cent. per annum of compound interest, and it now makes a splendid addition to what is admitted to be the finest situated park belonging to the city. The total extent of the park and recreation ground is 148 acres. The old Camphill mansion-house, situated on the grounds, is being utilised for exhibition purposes.

**Alexandra.**—The City Improvement Trust purchased 80 acres of ground from Walter Stewart of Haghill for £25,664 in 1866. Alex. Dennistoun gifted an additional five acres. This was taken over by the City in 1870. £40,000 were spent in buying and laying out the park, which was named in honour of the Princess of Wales. In 1891 40 acres of the adjoining lands of East Kennyhill were bought for £8,000,

and added to the park, which is 90 acres in extent. A disused quarry in the north-east corner was formed into a bathing pond. The park has also a model yacht pond and a golf course.

**Cathkin.**—The portion of Cathkin Braes, extending to 49 acres to the south-west of Rutherglen, was presented to the City on 31st August, 1886, by Mr. James Dick, of guttapercha fame, who purchased the land from John Miller, of Fernhill. The donor stipulated that the park is to be kept in its natural state as far as possible, and that football and similar games are to be prohibited.

**Bellahouston.**—176 acres of land in Bellahouston were purchased in August, 1895, from the trustees of the Bellahouston Bequest Fund, for the nominal sum of £50,000, and this has been formed into a public park, which promises to be one of the prettiest spots belonging to the citizens.

**Ruchill.**—The estate of Ruchill, consisting of 91 acres, was purchased by the City in 1891 for £35,700. The eastern portion, consisting of 34 acres, has been appropriated for the Fever Hospital, while 53 acres lying to the west have been made into a public park. Putting the ground in order has raised the cost to £48,500.

**Maxwell.**—Sir John Maxwell presented the burgh of Pollokshields with a park of 21 acres in 1888, but when the City annexed the district in 1891 it became the property of Glasgow.

**Tollcross.**—82¾ acres of land in Tollcross were purchased on 19th June, 1897, for £29,000, and a park formed. It is beautifully wooded, and is considered by many our finest park.

**Springburn.**—53¼ acres of land were purchased by the City in Springburn in 1892 for £20,710 for a public park for the district. The ground, which rises to a height of 310 feet, commands an extensive view of the surrounding country.

**Suburban.**—The Victoria Park, Whiteinch (in which is the Fossil Grove), and the Elder Park, Govan, are situated in the suburbs before named, and are outside the city boundary, but they are well patronised by the citizens of Glasgow.

**Botanic Gardens.**—*Sandyford*—Nearly £6,000 in ten guinea shares was raised by some of the leading citizens in 1816, with which they purchased six acres of ground in what was then called Sauchiehall Road, beside Sandyford, on which they established Botanic Gardens. The University contributed £2,000, in return for which their Professor of Botany and students had the free use of the Gardens for botanical study, a right they still possess. A stone on the gable of Fitzroy Place, in Claremont Street, beside Trinity Congregational Church, keeps this memory green with the following inscription:—"Glasgow Botanic Garden, instituted 1817."

*Kelvinside.*—The growth of the city made it desirable for the company to secure new ground (22 acres), which was obtained in Kelvinside, extending from Great Western Road to the Kelvin. To this then rural spot the Gardens were transferred in 1842. They were largely taken advantage of by the subscribers. The public were also admitted on payment of 6d. The Gardens were, however, not a paying concern, and the City being a bond-holder to the extent of £59,531, was pressed to take them over in 1877, which they ultimately did on 1st November, 1891. In 1895 they added considerably to their size by taking in 8½ acres of land at a cost of £3,800 on both sides of the Kelvin. Access across the river is got by two neat bridges. The Gardens are now free to all. The Corporation received £12,660 from the Caledonian Railway Company for way-leave of the Gardens in connection with their Central Railway.

*Kibble Palace.*—The Winter Garden, which is known as the " Kibble Palace," was originally built by Mr. John Kibble at his residence at Coulport, and removed from there in 1871 to the Gardens, in which it is re-erected on an enlarged scale.

**Open Spaces.** - Maryhill Park, 5½ acres, 1892, £2,089. Govanhill, 4 acres, 1894, £12,200. Bunhouse, 6½ acres, 1895, £30,000. Phœnix, 2 acres 1 rood 24 poles, £25,000, and ground annual of £84. George Square, 2 acres. Oatlands Square, 2 roods 16 poles. Hutcheson Square, 3 roods 24 poles. Overnewton Square, 2 roods 16 poles. Maxwell Square, 3 roods 24 poles. Cathedral Square, 1 acre 1 rood 24 poles. Wishart Square, 2 roods 16 poles. Blythswood Drive, 1 rood 24 poles. Pollok Street, 1 rood. Titwood, 1 acre 3 roods (gift of Sir J. Maxwell). Nithsdale Road, 1 acre. Oatlands river-side ground, 3 roods 24 poles.

*Graveyards used as Open Spaces.*—Ramshorn, 1 acre 2 roods. Gorbals, 2 acres 1 rood 24 poles. North Street, 1 acre. Clyde Street, Calton, 1 acre 1 rood 8

poles. Cathedral, 4 acres. St. Mark's, 1 acre and 32 poles. John Street, Calton (closed to public), 1 acre and 32 poles.

**Glasgow Necropolis.**—The Necropolis was opened for interment in May, 1833. The site was originally called Craig's Park, but after being planted with fir trees at the beginning of 1700, the name was changed to the Fir Park; it was part of the estate of Wester Craigs, which had been purchased in 1650 by the Merchants' House from Stuart of Minto for £1,291 13s. 4d. The foundation-stone of the bridge, with a 60-feet span across the Molendinar Burn, to admit to the Necropolis, known as the " Bridge of Sighs," was laid on 18th October, 1833; it cost £1,240. Dr. Strang, author of "Glasgow Clubs," compares the Necropolis to the famous " Père la Chaise " of Paris. The Molendinar has now been transformed into a common sewer, and a handsome roadway now takes its place.

**Sighthill Cemetery and Southern Necropolis.**—The lands of Sighthill, consisting of 46 imperial acres, which belonged to Archibald Ewing, about 1750, were bequeathed by Jonathan Anderson to the Magistrates of Forres, from whom they were purchased by a company, which originally laid out 12 acres as the Sighthill Cemetery, the first interment taking place on 24th April, 1840. Ground on the estate of Little Govan was also bought by a joint-stock company about 1840, and formed into the Southern Necropolis.

**Eastern Necropolis.**—The Eastern Necropolis, popularly known as Janefield Cemetery, consists of about 27 acres. The lands formed part of the estate of Tollcross. At the beginning of 1700 the portion which was cultivated as a farm, under the name of " Little Hill of Tollcross," belonged to a Mr. Corbet, who, in September, 1751, feued his property to William Boutcher, who turned it into a nursery garden, and surrounded it with a dyke. Boutcher failed in 1754, and in 1756 the property was sold to Patrick Tod for £81 sterling, who, in 1758, sold it to Robert M'Nair for £100. M'Nair, who was a well-known fruiterer in King Street, called his new possession Jeanfield in honour of his wife; he built a house and resided on his new estate, where he died on 7th June, 1779. Two years later Jeanfield was purchased by John Mennons, of the *Glasgow Herald*, for £2,435. He sold it in about a year to a son-in-law of Robert M'Nair, named John Finlayson, who acquired seven additional acres of land adjoining, and began to sink coal pits, but, being unfortunate, in 1825 James Harvey became proprietor, and, continuing the working of coal, he likewise failed. In 1846 the Cemetery Joint-Stock Company purchased the estate. The house was pulled down in 1847, and the ground converted into a necropolis.

**Other Cemeteries.**—The following cemeteries are now used by those not possessing lairs in the older burying-grounds, *viz.*:—Craigton, Cathcart, Sandymount (Shettleston), Northern Necropolis (Lambhill), Western Necropolis (Maryhill) (a crematorium was erected in the latter in April, 1893, by the Scottish Burial Reform and Cremation Society, Limited), St. Kentigern's (Maryhill), and Dalbeth (Tollcross). The two latter are both Catholic.

**Burying-Grounds in 1826.**—The following places were used for interments in 1826:—

High Church Burying-Ground.
Blackfriars Burying-Ground.
Ramshorn Burying-Ground.
Episcopal Burying-Ground, Greendyke Street.
Calton Burying-Ground.
Bridgeton Burying-Ground.
Gorbals Burying-Ground.
Anderston Burying-Ground.
Anderston Burying-Ground, Cheapside Street.
Anderston Burying-Ground.
Anderston New Burying-Ground.
Partick Burying-Ground (Quakers).
High Church Vaulted Cemetery.
St. David's Vaulted Cemetery.
Wellington Street Vaulted Cemetrey.

## MONUMENTS.

**King William.**—The equestrian statue of King William III. was presented to the city by one of its sons, James Macrae, Governor of Madras, and erected opposite the old Tontine at the Cross in 1735. In 1898 it was removed to the middle of the Trongate to the west of the Caledonian Railway Station.

**Nelson.**—On the anniversary of the battle of Aboukir, 1st August, 1805, the foundation-stone of Lord Nelson's monument was laid by Sir John Stuart, P.G.M., on Glasgow Green. The obelisk is built of Possil freestone, 144 feet high. It cost £2,075, which was raised by public subscription. On 5th August, 1810, the upper part of the column was shattered by lightning, but the damage was repaired a few years afterwards by public subscription.

**William Pitt.**—The great financier and orator, who so successfully guided the State during the stormy period of the French Revolution, and carried through the Union between Great Britain and Ireland, is represented by a marble life-sized statue, by Flaxman, in the Corporation Galleries. It was subscribed for by the citizens of Glasgow. The pedestal bears the following inscription:—Gulielmo Pitt, Cives Glasguenses, Posuerunt, A.D., 1812.

**Sir John Moore.**—The hero of Corunna was born in Donald's Land, on the north side of the Trongate, opposite the Tron Steeple, on 13th November, 1761. His father was a doctor in the city, and his mother a daughter of Professor John Simson, of the University. After the death of their brave son on 15th January, 1809, a monument, which cost £4,000—the first in Glasgow's Valhalla—designed by Flaxman, was placed in George Square on 15th August, 1819, by his fellow-citizens, on the suggestion of John Douglas, writer, in a paper read before the Literary and Commercial Society of the city. Parliament erected another memorial to him in St. Paul's Cathedral; while Marshal Soult built a third over his grave in the citadel of Corunna.

**John Knox.**—The monument in the Necropolis to John Knox was erected on 22nd September, 1825, by public subscription, in what was then known as the Fir Park. The pillar was designed by Hamilton, of Edinburgh, and the statue by Forrest, the sculptor. On the occasion of the laying of the foundation-stone the Rev. Dr. Thomas Chalmers conducted the services in St. George's Church.

**Lord Clyde.**—Glasgow has no son of whom she should be more proud than Colin Campbell, born at 63 High John Street on 28th October, 1792. His father was a cabinetmaker, named John M'Liver, his mother's name being Campbell, and at the suggestion of a maternal uncle, an officer in the army, he adopted her name. By the assistance of his mother's relations the future hero was educated at the High School, and afterwards at Gosport Military Academy. From his first appointment, in 1808, under his fellow-townsman, Sir John Moore, in Spain, until he crushed the Indian Mutiny in 1858, he saw more fighting in his day than perhaps any general of modern times. After his brilliant and gallant achievements in the Crimean War he was loaded with honours, and the title of "Sir Colin." At the conclusion of the Mutiny he was raised to the peerage, with an allowance of £2,000 a year, his title—Lord Clyde—showing he had not forgotten the city of his birth. He died on 14th

August, 1863, and was buried in Westminster Abbey. The monument in George Square was erected to his memory by his admiring fellow-townsmen in 1866.

**James Watt.**—James Watt was born in Greenock on 19th January, 1736. In 1755 he went to London to learn the mathematical instrument trade. In 1757 he came to Glasgow and began business as a maker of mathematical instruments ; but, being molested by the burgesses, the University gave him a shop within their precincts and appointed him their mathematical instrument maker. He afterwards became a civil engineer in the city, and made several surveys of canals and harbours. The idea of a separate condenser occurred to him in 1765. In 1769 he took out the patent for the improvements of the steam engine to which his idea was applied. In 1774 he began business with Mr. Boulton, in Birmingham, for the manufacture of steam engines and draining pumps. He retired from business in 1800, when his patent, which had been renewed in 1775 for twenty-five years, expired. The great man died on 25th August, 1819, and was buried at Handsworth, near Birmingham. The monument in George Square was erected to his memory by public subscription in 1832, Chantrey being the sculptor.

**Sir Walter Scott.**—The monument to Sir Walter Scott in George Square was erected in 1837. It has the distinction of being the first memorial erected to our greatest novelist. The statue was designed by Ritchie, and the column by Rhind. It is interesting to record that the site in the centre of the Square, where the monument is built, was originally intended for a statue to King George III., after whom the Square is named.

**Duke of Wellington.**—The equestrian statue to the "Iron Duke" was erected by public subscription, amounting to nearly £10,000, in front of the Royal Exchange, in Queen Street. It is the work of Baron Marochetti. The handsome memorial was unveiled on 8th October, 1844, before an immense assemblage, including the Scots Greys, 92nd Highlanders, and a large number of Waterloo veterans. The Peninsular and Waterloo hero declared he "regarded this as one of the highest compliments he ever received, coming as it did, altogether unexpectedly, from a city of such rank and importance in connection with the western counties of Scotland."

**Queen Victoria.**—An equestrian statue of Queen Victoria, by Baron Marochetti,

was erected in St. Vincent Place in 1854 ; but on the occasion of the Prince Albert memorial being placed in George Square, in 1866, the Queen's monument was removed to the east side of Sir Walter Scott's column, to balance the symmetrical proportions of Glasgow's principal square.

**Prince Albert.**—The equestrian statue to Prince Albert in George Square was erected by public subscription, nearly £6,000 being raised. Baron Marochetti, who had previously produced the Duke of Wellington's equestrian statue, was the sculptor. The Duke of Edinburgh, on behalf of the Queen, unveiled his father's memorial on 19th October, 1866. Previous to the ceremony the Prince was presented with the freedom of the city in the City Hall.

**Burns.**—A committee, under the guiding hand of that most estimable citizen, the late Bailie William Wilson, succeeded in raising a handsome sum in one shilling subscriptions for the erection of a monument to our immortal poet, Robert Burns. The memorial was put into the hands of the late Mr. George Ewing, sculptor. A site was secured in George Square, and on the anniversary of the bard's birth, 25th January, 1877, a procession of trades and societies assembled on the Green at 11 a.m., and after marching through the principal streets, were welcomed by about 30,000 people in George Square. Lord Houghton delivered an eulogium on our national poet, and unveiled the statue, which was handed over to the City, through Lord Provost Bain, by Bailie Wilson. Lord Houghton presided at a banquet in the Crown Halls in the evening. Burns's connection with Glasgow remains to be written. He visited the city, and slept in the old Black Bull Hotel, now part of Mann, Byars & Co.'s warehouse. The "Jolly Beggars" was first published in Glasgow in pamphlet form by Stewart & Meikle in 1799.

**Thomas Graham.**—Thomas Graham, who was born in Glasgow on 20th December, 1805, was educated at the University, and became Lecturer on Chemistry in the Mechanics' Institution. He was appointed Professor of Chemistry in Anderson's College, from which he was translated in 1837 to the same post in the University College, London. He became Master of the Mint in 1855, as successor to Sir John Herschell, and published "The Elements of Chemistry," was a D.C.L., and a Fellow of the Royal Society. He died in September, 1869. The statue to his memory in George Square is the gift of Mr. Young of Kelly; Brodie was the sculptor.

**Thomas Campbell.**—The author of the "Pleasures of Hope" was born in High Street on 27th July, 1777, and was the youngest of ten children, his father being a respectable shopkeeper. He received his education at the Grammar (High) School and the University. His great poem was published when he was only twenty-two years of age. It went through four editions, on the profits of which he took a Continental tour, and witnessed the Battle of Hohenlinden, which he immortalised in verse. In 1823 he married his cousin, Miss Matilda Sinclair, of Greenock, and went to reside in Sydenham. He was elected Lord Rector of his *Alma Mater* in 1826. Through the interest of Mr. Fox he received a pension of £300. In 1809 he published two volumes of his poems, and in the same year he took up the editorship of the *New Monthly Magazine*. He also assisted in the foundation of London University. His other works included "Theodrie," "Life of Mrs. Siddons," etc. Telford, of Jamaica Bridge fame, left him a legacy of £500. He died at Boulogne, where he had gone for his health, on 15th June, 1844, and was buried in the Poet's Corner in Westminster Abbey. The monument in George Square was erected to his memory by public subscription.

**James Oswald.**—In 1856 a bronze statue, by Baron Marochetti, was erected to James Oswald at Charing Cross, where it stood for about twenty years, when it was removed to the north-east corner of George Square. James Oswald was at one time a ropemaker, and resided in Ropework Lane, and latterly represented the city in Parliament.

**Sir Robert Peel.**—The memorial to the hero of the Corn Laws was erected in George Square in 1858. Mossman was the sculptor.

**James Arthur.**—A monument was erected in Cathedral Square to the founder of the well-known firm of Arthur & Co., Limited, by his employees.

**James Lumsden.** — Sir James Lumsden was Lord Provost of the city from 1866 to 1869. He was knighted on the occasion of the Prince of Wales laying the foundation-stone of the University at Gilmorehill in 1868. A monument is erected to his memory in Cathedral Square.

**James White.**—James White of Overtoun, who was a well-known philanthropist, and gave large donations for the furtherance of church schemes, had a monument erected

to his memory in Cathedral Square on 21st August, 1891, when it was unveiled by Sir James King.

**Rev. Dr. Norman Macleod.**—Norman Macleod was born in Campbeltown on 3rd June, 1812, where his father, after whom he was named, was minister. Norman senior became minister of the Gaelic Church, called St. Columba Church, in Hope Street in 1836. After being educated in Glasgow University, young Norman became minister of Loudon Parish in Ayrshire, from whence he was transferred to Dalkeith in 1843. In 1851 he succeeded Dr. Black in the Barony Church, and three years afterwards the Queen, with whom he was a great favourite, made him one of her Scottish Chaplains and Dean of the Order of the Thistle, and 1860 saw him filling the editorial chair of *Good Words*, a post he held till his death. In 1869 he was appointed Moderator of the General Assembly of the Church of Scotland. During his long and brilliant career he contributed largely to *Good Words* and other magazines, and found time to publish some most popular works, including "The Starling," "The Old Lieutenant and his Son," etc., etc. The greatest Established Church divine of modern times passed away on 10th June, 1872, and was buried in Campsie Kirkyard. A monument was erected by public subscription to his memory on 26th October, 1881, beside the church where he enthralled his audiences for over twenty years.

**David Livingstone.**—David Livingstone, the great African explorer, was born at Blantyre in 1817. After a very elementary education, at ten years of age he entered a cotton factory as a "piecer," and by dint of hard work and still harder study, at the age of sixteen he had mastered Horace, Virgil, and other classical writers. After attending the University in High Street he passed for a doctor in 1838. The London Missionary Society sent him to South Africa in 1840. After a few years' residence he married a daughter of Robert Moffat, by whom he had a family. His great work on the Zambesi, which he followed to its estuary; his coming home in 1856; his return to Africa two years later; the death of his wife at Shupanga; his last visit to England in 1864; the return to find the source of the Nile in 1865; his subequent discoveries and reported death; being found by Stanley at Ujiji on 3rd November, 1871; the lonely death near Lake Bangweolo; the heroic act of his two faithful servants in bringing his body to England, and its burial in Westminster Abbey, on 18th April, 1874 — are all details in the life of one of the bravest and most unselfish men that ever lived.  His monument in George Square is a small token of the love and respect which the people of Glasgow feel towards one who was in early life so closely connected with the city.

**Langside Battlefield Memorial.** —This monument was erected by public subscription to commemorate the battle of Langside.  On account of the extension of the city, and the gradual disappearance of the rural village, it was approved that a monument to commemorate the site should be erected where the engagement took place.  The late J. Wyllie Guild, Esq., laid the foundation-stone, and on its completion it was unveiled by Sir James King, Bart., 1887.  In style and treatment the design is classical, being an ornate column on a "rusticated" pedestal 58 feet in height, surmounted by a lion in a sitting position represented as looking over the battlefield with its fore paw resting on a cannon ball.  The cost was about £1,000, and the whole work was designed and superintended gratuitously by Alexander Skirving, I.A.

**Fountains.** —The following public fountains have been gifted and erected throughout the City, *viz.* :—

Iron Canopy, in Great Clyde Street, by Francis Smith.
Iron Canopy, in East Clyde Street, by Francis Smith.
Iron Canopy in Bain Square.
Iron Canopy in Green.
Iron Canopy, in Great Eastern Road, by Bailie M'Lennan.
Iron Canopy in Paisley Road.
Iron Canopy, at Mount Florida, by public subscription.
Granite, in George Square, by James Crum.
Collins Memorial, in Jail Square, by public subscription.
Martin Memorial, in Green, by public subscription.
Macdonald Memorial, in Green, by public subscription.
Martyrs' Memorial, in Castle Street, by public subscription.
Sir Charles Cameron Memorial, at Charing Cross, by public subscription.
Torrens Memorial, in New City Road, by public subscription.
Iron, at Saracen Cross, by Walter Macfarlane.
Stone, at Crown and Cathcart Streets, by Bridgegate Free Church.
Iron, in Infirmary Square, by M'Dowall, Steven and Co.
Doulton, in Green, by Sir Henry Doulton.

There are 104 public drinking fountains and 27 water troughs in the city.

**Doulton Fountain.** —The Doulton Fountain, which stood in the 1888 Exhi-

bition, in Kelvingrove Park, was presented to the City by Sir Henry Doulton, and erected on the Green, opposite the entrance at Jail Square, on 27th August, 1890.  It is made of terra cotta, is forty-six feet high, and has a life-size statue of Queen Victoria on the top.

**Gladstone Memorial.** — A sum of £4,000 has been collected by public subscription for a statue of the late W. E. Gladstone, which is to be erected on the east side of George Square.  Mr. Hamo Thornycroft has been entrusted with the design.

---

## PARLIAMENTARY.

**M.P.'s Expenses.** —Hugh Montgomerie of Busby, Provost of Glasgow, was the last representative for the city in the Scottish Parliament in Edinburgh, where he was allowed 6s. 8d. stg. a day for his expenses, which amounted to £52 15s. stg. between 8th October, 1706, and 15th March, 1707.  He was appointed by Queen Anne one of the Commissioners to negotiate on the Union, his expenses in London being defrayed by the City.

**Parliamentary Representation after the Union.** —After the Union Glasgow, in conjunction with Dumbarton, Renfrew, and Rutherglen, had only one member—Sir John Johnston being the first.  This state of matters continued until after the passing of the Reform Bill in 1832.

**Reform Agitation.** —The agitation in favour of the Reform Bill was nowhere keener in the country than in Glasgow.  In October, 1816, about 40,000 persons held a demonstration in a field at Thrushgrove, near the city, and passed a resolution praying the Prince Regent (afterwards George IV.) to assist in amending the representation and Corn Laws.  The Government immediately became alarmed, soldiers were drafted into the city, and Kirkman Finlay, the local M.P., was instructed to keep the Secretary of State in touch with all that was going on.  Finlay employed a Pollokshaws weaver, named Richmond, to act as a spy.  This individual was capable of anything, and he managed to get a Calton weaver, named Andrew M'Kinlay, and others to sign a document known as the Treasonable Oath, which bore an endeavour to obtain by moral or physical strength free and equal representation and annual Parliaments.  This was forwarded to the Government, with the result that M'Kinlay and his fellow dupes were apprehended on a charge of high treason, and lodged in Edinburgh Castle on 28th February, 1817. They lay in durance vile for four months, when they were brought to trial for their lives. Campbell, a Crown witness, stated he had been promised a Government appointment if he would swear lies against M'Kinlay. The case immediately collapsed, which prevented the intended suspension of the Habeas Corpus Act. The Rev. Neil Douglas, a dissenting minister in 2 Upper John Street, of 70 years of age, was arrested and tried for sedition in Edinburgh on 26th May, 1817, for comparing George III. to Nebuchadnezzar, the Prince Regent to a drunken prodigal son, and denouncing the Government. The shorthand notes of three men sent to take down his words not agreeing, he was acquitted, but he afterwards ceased his tirades. For the next few years the Government spies were very busy trying to incite the poor reformers to deeds of violence. On 1st April, 1820, bills were posted in the streets calling upon the people to rise and assert their rights. The military were immediately drafted into the city, the local volunteers, called the sharpshooters, under the command of Samuel Hunter, of the *Herald*, were called out, people were ordered to leave the streets, shops had to shut at 7 p.m., and a reward of £500 was offered for the author or printer of the treasonable bill. All sorts of rumours, including that of a French invasion, filled the air. Seventy starving men, armed with muskets, pikes, and swords, met on where the Necropolis now stands, and elected a Glasgow weaver named Andrew Hardie, leader, and John Baird, a Condorret weaver, lieutenant, and under instructions from the spies marched on Falkirk. A troop of Hussars overtook them at Bonnymuir, near Carron, where the number had now dwindled down to thirty. They refused to surrender, were charged by the soldiers, and only when they were nearly all wounded did they surrender. They were taken to Stirling Castle, and tried for high treason, and eighteen sentenced to death. The extreme penalty was not carried out on sixteen of the number, but Hardie and Baird were executed in Stirling Castle on 8th September, 1820. Their bodies were privately removed to Sighthill Cemetery on 20th July, 1847, where a monument is erected to their memory. A poor Strathaven weaver, named James Wilson, aged 60, was condemned and executed at Glasgow nine days previous to the Stirling martyrdom for active sympathy with the revolutionary movement. Mr. Peter Mackenzie, in his valuable " Reminiscences of Glasgow," gives a very interesting account of all the events that happened at this period. The old "Loyal Reformer" succeeded in exposing the spy system and bringing Richmond's guilt home, and further, was the means of procuring a free pardon from William IV. for the Bonnymuir prisoners, who still survived their banishment to Botany Bay.

**First Reform Bill.**—For over thirty years Glasgow was one of the principal centres of the Reform Bill Agitation in the Kingdom. When the Bill, giving a vote to all male householders who paid an annual rent of £10, was introduced into the Commons on 1st March, 1831, by Lord John Russell, petitions were sent from the city in its favour. The citizens became greatly excited when the second reading was carried in the Commons on 21st March, 1831, by a majority of *one*. So great was the anxiety for news that Sir Daniel K. Sandford, Professor of Greek in the University, and other Glasgow gentlemen rode to Bothwell and Hamilton on horseback to meet the London mail coach, and, immediately they got the intelligence, came galloping back to the Exchange and Tontine, and declared the result to the anxious crowds. When the London papers arrived later with the coach, David Bell, in the Royal Exchange, Thomas Atkinson, bookseller, and Peter Mackenzie, in the Tontine, mounted the tables and read the Parliamentary reports aloud. Bells were rung, and the city illuminated. In front of Provost Dalglish's house in St. Vincent Street the words, "Let Glasgow Flourish," formed with lighted gas jets, with a variegated background, were the wonder and admiration of the people. Sir James Lumsden's house in Queen Street, and the mansions of other prominent citizens, were similarly decorated with gas designs. A dinner, attended by one hundred of the leading citizens, was held in the Royal Exchange Tavern.

The delay of the passage of the Bill in Committee caused feverish excitement to the community. A multitude, numbering about 150,000, assembled in Glasgow Green on 8th September, 1831—Coronation Day of King William IV. and Queen Adelaide—and demonstrated in favour of the Bill, their motto being "the Bill, the whole Bill, and nothing but the Bill." The Bill passed the Commons on 22nd September by a majority of 109, only to be rejected by the

Lords on 7th October. Glasgow became wild. At a public meeting of the citizens, held in the Trades Hall on 16th November, the Glasgow Political Union was formed for the promotion of the Bill, with Mr. Peter M'Kenzie secretary. In March, 1832, the Bill again passed the Lower House, only to be mutilated by the gilded chamber. A great demonstration was again held on the Green on 12th May, at which a protest was passed against the Lords' action. Ultimately, Earl Grey, with the reluctant assistance of William IV., carried the Bill on 4th June, 1832, and Glasgow became pacified, after being on the point of rebellion.

**First Election after Passing of First Reform Bill.**—Previous to the passing of the Reform Bill Glasgow, in conjunction with Rutherglen, Dumbarton, and Renfrew, returned one member to Parliament. When the Bill became law the new redistribution gave the city two representatives to itself. The new electoral roll showed 7,024 voters, this including the suburbs of Gorbals, Calton, and Anderston. Each "free and independent" had two votes. The election took place on 18th and 19th December, 1832, with the following result, the two highest being elected:—

| | |
|---|---|
| James Ewing, of Strathleven ... ... | 3,214 |
| James Oswald, of Shieldhall ... ... | 2,838 |
| D. K. Sandford ... ... ... ... | 2,168 |
| John Crawford ... ... ... ... | 1,850 |
| John Douglas ... ... ... ... | 1,340 |
| Joseph Dixon, of Little Govan... ... | 995 |

After the election a list was published in the local papers showing how each individual voted. Think of that, ye who now claim the protection of the ballot!

**Second Reform Bill Demonstration.**—On 17th October, 1866, after the defeat of Lord Russell's Government Reform Bill, a great demonstration in favour of the measure was held on the Green, when from six platforms the "Adullamites" and Conservatives were subjected to the usual political condemnation. After the oratory was exhausted the crowd marched in procession through the principal streets amidst scenes of the greatest enthusiasm. In the evening John Bright spoke in the City Hall, and next morning the great orator was publicly entertained to breakfast.

**First Election after Passing of Second Reform Bill.**—When the second Reform Bill, which gave a vote to all who were not exempted from the payment of poor-rates was passed in 1868, Glasgow was given three representatives instead of

two. The electors were, however, only allowed two votes, under what was known as a "three-cornered constituency system." The election took place on Tuesday, 17th November, 1868, with the following result, the first three being elected:—

| | |
|---|---|
| Robert Dalglish (Liberal) ... ... ... | 18,281 |
| William Graham (Liberal) ... ... ... | 18,090 |
| George Anderson (Liberal)... ... ... | 17,804 |
| Sir George Campbell of Succoth (Con.)... | 10,814 |

Under the new Bill Glasgow and Aberdeen Universities were given a Parliamentary representative, when Mr. James Moncrieff (Liberal), afterwards Lord-Justice Clerk, was elected by 2,067 votes against Mr. Edward Strathearn Gordon, Lord-Advocate (Conservative), who received 2,020 votes.

**The 1880 Parliamentary Election.**—When the Conservative Government dissolved in 1880, the representatives of the retiring party in the city determined to recover the seat they had lost in the bye-election through the death of the late Alex. Whitelaw. This was possible under ordinary conditions, Glasgow having three representatives, but the electors had only two votes. Charles Tennant decided to assist his side by trying to capture Peebles-shire for the Liberal party. R. T. Middleton came forward in his place, to run with Messrs. Cameron and Anderson, the old members, and William Pearce, of John Elder & Co., and Sir James Bain championed the cause of the Conservatives. The Liberals, alive to the danger they were in, adopted an ingenious alphabetical method of voting, which was faithfully carried out, as the following result of the poll, which took place on 2nd April, 1880, shows, viz.:—

| | |
|---|---|
| George Anderson (Liberal) ... ... | 24,016 |
| Dr. Charles Cameron (Liberal) ... | 23,658 |
| R. T. Middleton (Liberal) ... ... | 23,360 |
| William Pearce (Conservative) ... | 11,622 |
| Sir James Bain (Conservative) ... | 11,071 |

Out of 57,920 electors 47,512 voted.

**Franchise Demonstration.** — The greatest demonstration since the advent of the first Reform Bill was held in the Green on 6th September, 1884, to agitate in favour of the extension of the Franchise. It was attended by over 70,000 persons.

**Parliamentary Representation of Glasgow.**—Prior to the Union between England and Scotland the Burgh of Glasgow was represented in the Scottish Parliament and Conventions of Estates by a person elected by the Town Council of the city, who was always a member of that body, and who frequently held the position of Provost. The first time Glasgow is mentioned in the authentic records as being represented in the Scottish Parliament is under the date of 1546.

MEMBERS OF THE SCOTTISH PARLIAMENT.

| | |
|---|---|
| 1546 | Andrew Hamilton of Middop, Provost. |
| 1560 | Robert Lindsay of Dunrod, Provost. |
| 1567 | William Maxwell. |
| 1569 { | John Stewart of Minto, Provost. |
| | James Fleming. |
| 1571 { | Matthew Stewart, Younger of Minto. |
| | James Fleming. |
| 1572 | Matthew Stewart, Younger of Minto. |
| 1578 | Thomas Crawford of Jordanhill, ex-Provost. |
| 1579 | George Elphinston of Blythswood, Bailie. |
| 1581 | Matthew Stewart of Minto. |
| 1583 | John Grahame, Younger. |
| 1584 | George Elphinston. |
| 1585 | Robert Rowat. |
| 1586 | Archibald Hiegat. |
| 1592 | William Cunninghame. |
| 1593 { | Robert Chyrnside. |
| | James Stewart. |
| 1594 { | Robert Chyrnside. |
| | Sir Matthew Stewart of Minto, Provost. |
| | Robert Rowan. |
| 1596 | James Bell. |
| 1598 | John Ros. |
| 1600 | James Forrett. |
| 1604 | James Forrett. |
| 1605 | James Forrett. |
| 1607 | James Forrett. |
| 1608 | James Inglis, Provost. |
| 1612 { | James Inglis. |
| | James Bell. |
| 1617 { | James Inglis. |
| | James Hamilton, ex-Provost. |
| | James Stewart, Provost. |
| 1621 | James Inglis. |
| 1625 | Patrick Bell. |
| 1628 | Gabriel Cunningham, Provost. |
| 1630 | Gabriel Cunningham, Provost. |
| 1639 | Patrick Bell, Provost. |
| 1640 | Gabriel Cunningham, Provost. |
| 1643 | James Bell, Provost. |
| 1644 | James Bell, Provost. |
| 1645 | Colin Campbell. |
| 1646 | George Porterfield, Provost. |
| 1648 { | George Porterfield, Provost. |
| | John Graham. |
| 1661 | John Bell, ex-Provost. |
| 1665 | William Anderson of Newton, Provost. |
| 1667 | William Anderson of Newton, Provost. |
| 1669 | William Anderson of Newton, Provost. |
| 1678 | James Campbell, Provost. |
| 1681 | John Bell, Provost. |
| 1685 | John Johnston of Claughrie, Provost. |
| 1689 | John Anderson of Dowhill, Provost. |
| 1703 | Hugh Montgomerie of Busby, Provost. |

By the Union of England and Scotland, accomplished on the 7th May, 1707, Glasgow was deprived of its independent member of Parliament, and it was one of a group—Rutherglen, Renfrew, Dumbarton, and Glasgow—which returned one member.

MEMBERS OF THE BRITISH PARLIAMENT SINCE THE UNION.

| | |
|---|---|
| 1707 | Sir John Johnston, Knight. |
| 1708 | Robert Rodger, Lord Provost. |
| 1710 | Thomas Smith, Dean of Guild. |
| 1713 | Thomas Smith, Dean of Guild. |
| 1715 | Daniel Campbell of Shawfield. |
| 1722 | Daniel Campbell of Shawfield. |
| 1727 | Daniel Campbell of Shawfield. |
| 1734 | Colonel John Campbell of Croombank. |

| | |
|---|---|
| 1741 | Neil Buchanan, merchant. |
| 1747 | Lieut.-Colonel John Campbell of Mamore. |
| 1754 | Lieut.-Colonel John Campbell of Mamore. |
| 1761 | Lord Frederick Campbell, Keeper of the Privy Seal of Scotland. |
| 1768 | Lord Frederick Campbell, Lord Clerk Register. |
| 1774 | Lord Frederick Campbell, Lord Clerk Register. |
| 1780 | John Crauford of Auchenames. |
| 1784 | Ilay Campbell of Succoth, Lord-Advocate. |
| 1790 | John Crauford of Auchenames (in room of Ilay Campbell, who had become Lord-President of the Court of Session). |
| 1790 | William M'Dowall of Garthland. |
| 1796 | William M'Dowall of Garthland. |
| 1802 | Boyd Alexander of Southbar. |
| 1806 | Archibald Campbell of Blythswood. |
| 1807 | Archibald Campbell of Blythswood. |
| 1809 | Alexander Houston of Clerkington. |
| 1812 | Kirkman Finlay, Lord Provost of Glasgow. |
| 1818 | Alexander Houston of Clerkington. |
| 1820 | Archibald Campbell of Blythswood. |
| 1826 | Archibald Campbell of Blythswood. |
| 1830 | Archibald Campbell of Blythswood. |
| 1831 | John Dixon, advocate. |

By the passing of the Great Reform Bill of 1832, Glasgow was restored to its ancient right of independent representation, and, in consideration of its importance, it had the privilege granted it of returning two members.

MEMBERS OF THE IMPERIAL PARLIAMENT SINCE THE PASSING OF THE GREAT REFORM BILL.

| | |
|---|---|
| 1832 { | James Ewing, Lord Provost. |
| | James Oswald of Shieldhall. |
| 1835 { | James Oswald. |
| | Colin Dunlop of Tollcross. |
| 1836 | Lord William Bentinck (in room of Dunlop —Chiltern Hundreds). |
| 1837 | John Dennistoun of Golfhill (in room of Oswald—Chiltern Hundreds). |
| 1837 { | Lord William Bentinck. |
| | John Dennistoun. |
| 1839 | James Oswald (in room of Bentinck—Chiltern Hundreds). |
| 1841 { | James Oswald. |
| | John Dennistoun. |
| 1847 { | John M'Gregor |
| | Alexander Hastie. |
| 1852 { | Alexander Hastie. |
| | John M'Gregor. |
| 1857 | Walter Buchanan (in room of M'Gregor, Manor of Northstead). |
| 1857 { | Walter Buchanan. |
| | Robert Dalglish. |
| 1859 { | Walter Buchanan. |
| | Robert Dalglish. |
| 1865 { | William Graham. |
| | Robert Dalglish. |

Under the Reform Act of 1868, Glasgow was granted three Members of Parliament.

| | |
|---|---|
| 1858 { | Robert Dalglish. |
| | William Graham. |
| | George Anderson. |
| 1874 { | Charles Cameron. |
| | George Anderson. |
| | Alexander Whitelaw. |
| 1879 | Charles Tennant (in room of A. Whitelaw, deceased). |
| 1880 { | George Anderson. |
| | Charles Cameron, LL.D. |
| | Robert T. Middleton. |
| 1885 | T. Russell (in room of G. Anderson—Chiltern Hundreds). |

By the new Redistribution Act of 1885, the city was given seven members, to represent the seven divisions of the city, viz.:—Bridgeton, Camlachie, St. Rollox, Central, College, Tradeston, and Blackfriars and Hutchesontown.

1885 {
Sir E. R. Russell (Bridgeton).
Hugh Watt (Camlachie).
John M'Culloch (St. Rollox).
Gilbert Beith (Central).
Sir Charles Cameron (College).
A. Cameron Corbett (Tradeston).
Mitchell Henry (Blackfriars and Hutcheson-town).
}

1886 {
J. G. A. Baird.
Sir E. R. Russell.
Hugh Watt.
J. Caldwell.
A. D. Provand.
Sir Charles Cameron.
A. Cameron Corbett.
}

1887 Sir G. O. Trevelyan (in room of Sir E. R. Russell).

1892 {
A. D. Provand.
Sir G. O. Trevelyan.
Alexander Cross.
J. G. A. Baird.
Sir C. Cameron.
Sir J. M. Carmichael.
A. C. Corbett.
}

1895 {
A. D. Provand.
Sir G. O. Trevelyan.
Alexander Cross.
J. G. A. Baird.
Sir John Stirling-Maxwell.
F. F. Begg.
A. C. Corbett.
}

1897 Sir C. Cameron (in room of Sir G. O. Trevelyan—resigned).

Under the Reform Act of 1868, Glasgow and Aberdeen Universities were jointly given a representative in Parliament, viz:—

1868 James Moncrieff (Lord-Advocate).
1869 E. S. Gordon, LL.D.
1876 William Watson (Lord-Advocate).
1880 James A. Campbell, LL.D.
1885 James A. Campbell, LL.D.
1886 James A. Campbell, LL.D.
1892 James A. Campbell, LL.D.
1895 James A. Campbell, LL.D.

## TRAVELLING.

**Coaches.**—*First Coach to Edinburgh.*— The first stage coach began to run between Glasgow and Edinburgh in 1678. William Hoom, or Hume, of Edinburgh, the proprietor, received a grant of £22 4s. 5¾d. stg., and an annual subsidy of £11 2s. 2¾d. stg. for five and a half years, from the Magistrates of Glasgow, whose burgesses were to have the preference.

*Coach and Four.*—A mail coach drawn by four horses commenced to run between Glasgow and Edinburgh, with Falkirk as the half-way station, in 1758.

*Coaches in 1819.*—The mode of travelling at the beginning of this century was by coach, horse, or foot. In 1819, eight public coaches with four horses, and seven with two horses, left and returned to the city daily, viz.:—One to London, five for Edinburgh, three for Paisley, two for Greenock, and one each for Perth, Ayr, Hamilton, and Kilmarnock. One coach with four horses and one with three left and returned three times a week for Carlisle and Lanark. At that time Glasgow could boast of ten cabs.

**Carriages.**—In 1832 there were 402 public and private carriages in the city and suburbs.

**Omnibuses.**—The first omnibus started from Barrowfield Toll, Bridgeton, to the Gusset-House, Anderston, on 1st January, 1845. It was owned by Robert Frame, who acted as his own conductor, and charged twopence for the single journey. The success of the new venture induced four rivals to enter the field. The potato blight and famine in the spring of 1846, when corn rose from 16s. to 35s. a boll, brought Frame to bankruptcy and extinguished his rivals. His stock, which a few months before was valued at £2,000, only brought £400 when sold by auction in 1847. For about eighteen months there were no 'buses in the city. In the fall of 1848 Forsyth and Braig took up Frame's original route, and they were soon followed by Mitchell and Menzies. Four years after, *penny 'buses* were placed on the routes between the Cross and Anderston and Bridgeton and the Cross, by Hutchison and Craig respectively; but they had to succumb to Menzies, who had become sole partner of his firm. Duncan MacGregor took up the reins, and maintained a running fight; but Walker's and Menzies' 'buses ultimately secured the lion's share of the traffic. The stables of the former were in Cambridge, Buccleuch, and Blackfriars Streets; while the latter had the largest and most complete accommodation for horses in the kingdom, in North Street. MacGregor's headquarters were at the east end of London Street. All these establishments were taken over by the Tramway Company when the "car era" dawned.

**Toll Bars.**—The following toll bars were situated as shown, viz.:—Gallowgate and Carntyne, Gorbals and Muirhouses, Shawfield, Dalmarnock, and Barrowfield, Stockwell and Jamaica Bridges, Cowcaddens, Townhead or Inchbelly, Anderston or Clayslaps, Drygate or Whitevale, Paisley Road, Govan Road, Port-Dundas, Garngad.

**Canals.**—*Forth and Clyde.*—In 1767 Lord Frederick Campbell, the member for the Glasgow district of burghs, brought in a bill for a Forth and Clyde Canal, four feet deep and twenty-four feet wide. It was rejected; but, upon being amended to eight feet deep and fifty-six feet wide, it received the sanction of the House the following year. Sir Laurence Dundas, Bart., cut the first sod on 10th June, 1768, and it was opened from Kirkintilloch to Stockingfield on 10th November, 1775. On 29th July, 1790, the whole canal, thirty-five miles long, was completed, Archibald Speirs, of Elderslie, chairman of management, performing the opening ceremony by launching a hogshead of the Forth water into the Clyde at Bowling. The basin at Hamilton-hill being inconvenient, eight acres of land were purchased, and one made at Port-Dundas, which is called after Lord Dundas, the governor of the company. The Monk-land Canal, for the benefit of the Lanark-shire coalfields, was begun in 1769. It was twelve miles long, twenty-five feet wide, four feet six inches deep, and had four locks.

*Paisley and Johnstone Canal.* — The work of making the Glasgow, Paisley, Johnstone, and Ardrossan Canal was begun in 1805. It was never made to the latter place, Johnstone being the furthest point reached. In 1869 the Glasgow and South-Western Railway Company secured the canal, and in 1881 obtained powers to shut it up and transform it into a railway, which they made between Port-Eglinton and Paisley, at a cost of about £100,000. This is known as the Canal line, which joins the main line at Elderslie. It was opened on 1st July, 1885.

**Railways.**—*Berwick Railway.*—In 1803 Telford surveyed and proposed a railway between Glasgow and Berwick to cost £2,926 a mile, but the project came to nothing.

*First Railways.*—In 1808 the Duke of Portland constructed at a cost of £40,000 the first railway in Scotland, between Kilmarnock and Troon; it was ten miles long. In 1810 the Glasgow and Berwick Railway was again talked about, but it ended there. In 1824 the Monkland and Kirkintilloch Railway, with a capital of £25,000, was incorporated by Act of Parliament. 1825 saw the Glasgow and Garnkirk Railway set a-going with a capital of £169,195; it was eight miles long, St. Rollox being the Glasgow station. The Johnstone and Ard-rossan Railway, twenty-two miles long, with a capital of £106,666, followed in 1827, while the Wishaw and Coltness Railway for minerals, thirteen miles long, was instituted two years after, with a capital of £160,000. In 1830 the Pollok and

Govan Railway Company, capital £66,000, and Rutherglen Railway Company, capital £20,000, was formed, and in 1837 the Paisley and Renfrew Railway, 3¼ miles long, capital £33,000.

**Greenock and Ayr.**—The railway between Glasgow and Greenock was commenced in 1837. Trains began to run to Paisley on 14th July, 1840. On 31st March, 1841, the line was opened to Sugaropolis. The Ayr railroad was also begun in 1837, the joint expenses of £812,000 being borne by the Glasgow and Greenock and Glasgow and Ayr companies. Trains were started between Ayr and Irvine on 5th August, 1839; and on 12th August, 1840, amid a scene of great rejoicing in the "Auld Toon," the first train arrived in Ayr from Glasgow at new Bridge Street Station—which was formerly the Methodist chapel of the Rev. Valentine Wood.

**Edinburgh and Glasgow.**—In 1838 the Edinburgh and Glasgow Railway Company was formed, with a capital of £900,000 in shares and £300,000 on loan. The railway was 46 miles long, and cost a million and a quarter of money. The tunnel between Queen Street and Cowlairs, three-quarters of a mile long, cost about £40,000, and was the greatest engineering feat hitherto attempted in Scotland. Amid scenes of great rejoicing in both cities, on 18th February, 1842, communication was established. In spite of great opposition on the part of the people, trains were run on Sundays. The company built locomotive works at Cowlairs.

**Boat and Train Accommodation in 1840.**—In 1840 there was a service of trains nearly every hour to Ayr, nine in summer and six in winter went to Greenock, while the Garnkirk line boasted of five in summer and four in winter. Passenger boats plied regularly on the Forth and Clyde, Monkland, and Paisley and Johnstone Canals, and a large fleet of steamers sailed on the Clyde. So keen did the rivalry become that the fare to Rothesay was only 6d. for a long time; it actually came down to 3d., and racing of the most exciting character was a daily occurrence.

**North British Railway Company.** The North British Railway Company was formed on 19th July, 1844, when Parliamentary sanction was obtained for a line from Edinburgh to Berwick, with a branch to Haddington. In 1845 the N.B. Company purchased the Edinburgh and Dalkeith and Edinburgh and Hawick lines, and on 29th July, 1862, they added the Edinburgh,

Perth, and Dundee and the West of Fife and subsidiary lines.

*Helensburgh Railway.* — In 1855 the Glasgow, Dumbarton, and Helensburgh Railway Company, with a capital of £240,000, was authorised to construct a line from the junction of the Glasgow and Edinburgh main line, at Cowlairs, to Bowling, with a branch from there to Helensburgh. They thus became connected with the Caledonian and Dumbartonshire Railway, constructed in 1846, which ran from Bowling to Balloch. The Edinburgh and Glasgow Railway Company was interested to the extent of £50,000 in the new company.

*Edinburgh and Glasgow Railway.* — The Edinburgh and Glasgow Railway Company became amalgamated with the North British Railway Company by Act of Parliament on 5th July, 1865.

*Queen Street and College Street Stations.* — Queen Street Station used to be an antiquated, dingy terminus, and the North British Railway Company with commendable enterprise renovated the entire structure, and transformed it, about 1880, into the present modern station, the roof of which is 450 feet long and 250 feet wide. College Station, which also belongs to the same company, is nothing to boast about in appearance, but has a fair amount of accommodation, especially for goods and mineral traffic. It was opened in 1874.

*City and District.* — The City and District Railway, which belongs to the North British Railway Company, was opened on 15th March, 1886; it is a circular line, partly underground, from Queen Street *via* Alexandra Park, Springburn, Maryhill, and Partick.

*Fort-William.* — The North British Railway line, between Glasgow and Fort-William *via* Helensburgh, Arrochar, Ardlui, Crianlarich, and Rannoch Moor, was opened in August, 1894.

**Caledonian Railway Company.** — The Caledonian Railway Company was authorised by Act of Parliament in 1845. Powers were given for a line from Carlisle to Edinburgh and Garriongill, with a branch from near Gartsherrie to Castlecary to join the Scottish Central line at Greenhill. The Scottish Central Company was taken over by the Caledonian Company in 1865. The following is a copy of an early advertisement of the company, *viz.* :—"On and after 10th September, 1847, until further notice, mail coaches will run from Glasgow

and Edinburgh to Beattock, and connect there with trains for Lockerbie, Carlisle, Preston, Liverpool, Manchester, and London, the journey to the metropolis being performed in 21½ hours from Glasgow and 20 hours from Edinburgh. For hours of starting and fares see time-table. J. W. Coddington, Secretary."

*Buchanan Street Station.* — On 1st Nov., 1849, Buchanan Street Station was opened for passenger traffic. Previous to this the Caledonian Railway Company purchased the Garnkirk Railway and several small companies. It was intended to continue the Garnkirk Railway's terminus at St. Rollox to Buchanan Street, by means of a bridge over the Port-Dundas Canal, but the project was abandoned and a tunnel constructed below the canal. Goods traffic was not worked until the following January.

*Central Station.* — The Caledonian Railway Company had formerly carried on their traffic from Buchanan Street Station, and a station situated at the head of Main Street, at the junction of Cathcart Street and Pollokshaws Road, which in time became very inconvenient. They, therefore, brought their line from Gushetfaulds round by Eglinton Street, and built the bridge across the Clyde, over which they carried their line to the centre of the city at Gordon Street. Here they erected their handsome station, at a cost of about £700,000, which was opened on 31st July, 1879, to the mutual benefit of the public and Railway Company. Plans are now prepared to still further extend the station and line across the Clyde to Bridge Street.

*Cathcart District.* — On 1st March, 1886, the Cathcart District Railway from the Central Station was opened as a double line *via* East Pollokshields and Queen's Park to Crosshill, and from thence to beyond Mount Florida as a single line. The whole line to Cathcart was completed and opened on 25th May, 1886. The railway was subsequently made circular, *via* Langside, Pollokshaws, and Shawlands, the extension being opened on 2nd April, 1894.

*Central Railway.* — The Caledonian Railway Company began to construct an underground railway from Dalmarnock to Maryhill, 6½ miles long, with twelve stations, in June, 1890. In April, 1894, goods traffic was begun on a portion, and in November, 1895, it was opened from Dalmarnock to Glasgow Cross, and from Anderston Cross to Maryhill. The remaining portion, between the Cross and Anderston, was completed in August, 1896.

*Lanarkshire and Dumbartonshire.* — One loop of the Lanarkshire and Dumbartonshire Railway, which was begun in October, 1891, commences from the Central Railway at Stobcross Street, passing westward into Partick. Another loop starts from a junction with the Central Railway near Maryhill Barracks, and passes southward, crossing Great Western Road near Gartnavel, and joins the main line at Partick West. It was opened in October, 1896.

*Hamilton Hill.* — The Hamilton Hill line, a branch of the Caledonian Railway, commencing at the termination of the Central Railway at Gairbraid Street, Maryhill, and terminating near Provanmill, is meantime wholly used for goods and mineral traffic. It was begun in July, 1892, and opened in February, 1896.

*Tollcross Railway.*—The Tollcross Railway was commenced in October, 1893. From a junction with the Central Railway at Bridgeton Cross, it passes eastwards along London Road, and joins the main line at Carmyle. It was opened on 1st February, 1897.

## Glasgow and South-Western Railway Company.—On 28th October, 1850, when the Cumnock and Gretna line was opened, the Glasgow, Dumfries, and Carlisle Railway Company and the Glasgow, Paisley, Kilmarnock, and Ayr Railway Company amalgamated and became the present Glasgow and South-Western Railway Company.

*St. Enoch Station.*—In 1850 the station of the Glasgow and South-Western Railway Company was in Bridge Street. In conjunction with the City Union Railway Company, they constructed a new line from Pollokshields *via* Gorbals, bridging the Clyde to St. Enoch Square, a branch passing over the Bridgegate, Saltmarket, and Gallowgate, joining the North British Railway at Bellgrove, St. Enoch Station being only in course of erection. The new line was opened on 12th December, 1870, to Dunlop Street, which was dignified by the name of a station, which it continued to be until July, 1880, when St. Enoch Station and Hotel was completed. This imposing structure has no superior in the kingdom. The station roof spans 205 feet, is 84 feet high, and 525 feet long. Its formal opening took place on 17th October, 1876, by the Prince of Wales, on the occasion of his laying the foundation stone of the new Post Office. The Glasgow and South-Western Company took St. Enoch Station

over from the City Union Railway Company in 1883. The latter company was divided between the Glasgow and South-Western Company and the North British Company in August, 1896. The Glasgow and South-Western Company took the part from St. Enoch Station to Shields Road and the portion extending to near Bellgrove. The Glasgow and South-Western Company are presently doubling their line from St. Enoch Station to Port-Eglinton. The station is to be enlarged, and a handsome new iron bridge is being erected across the Clyde. The undertaking will cost about £500,000.

**Subway.**—The Subway Cable Railway Bill was promoted in Parliament in 1887, but owing to great opposition it was not approved of until 1890, and the year following the work was begun, Mr. Alexander Simpson undertaking the engineering difficulties. The line, which is underground, passes once under the Kelvin and twice under the Clyde, and in making the western tunnels the bed of the Clyde was blown up several times; on one occasion a 20-foot hole was made. Each line of rails has a separate tunnel. The railway, which was the first cable passenger line, is 6½ miles in circumference with 15 stations. The power station is situated in West Scotland Street, where two engines, each capable of developing 1,500 horse-power, propel two endless cables 36,300 feet long and 1½ inch in diameter, which draw the cars, which are fitted with grippers, at a rate of 12 miles an hour. The line, which cost about £1,500,000, was opened on 14th December, 1896, but had to be closed on account of the rush and an accident in which 19 were injured. The fare was, however, increased, and on 21st January, 1897, the working was again begun. The returns for the half-year ended 31st July, 1898, show that 5,779,119 passengers were carried, representing £27,882 7s. 10d. in money.

**Tramways.** — *Tramway Company.* — Parliamentary sanction was given on 10th August, 1870, for the construction of tramways in the city. The Corporation leased the tramways to the Glasgow Tramway and Omnibus Company, Limited (which was to have a capital of not less than £200,000) for twenty-three years from 1st July, 1871. The lines were laid by the Corporation, but the Company had to pay the interest on the cost, and all expenses connected with the undertaking, also 3 per cent. per annum on the gross sum expended on capital account, this interest to be set aside as a sinking fund for the reduction of the cost of the construction. The Company was also required to hand over the tramways and the roadway between the lines in good condition at the end of the lease, and to pay £150 a year for every mile of rail used for traffic. Between thirty and forty miles of tramway rails was laid, at a cost of about £345,000. The first route, between St. George's Cross and Eglinton Toll, was opened on 19th July, 1872. The other sections were opened in the following order, *viz.*:—(2) Cambridge Street to Royal Crescent; (3) Bridgeton Cross to Candleriggs; (4) Bridge Street to Paisley Road Toll; (5) Whiteinch to Royal Crescent; (6) Whiteinch to Bridgeton Cross; (7) St. Vincent Street to Dennistoun; (8) Great Hamilton Street to Camlachie Burn; (9) New City Road *via* Cowcaddens to Sauchiehall Street; (10) Bridgeton Cross to London Road; (11) Eglinton Toll to Crosshill.

*Vale of Clyde Tramways.*—The Vale of Clyde Tramway Company received the sanction of Parliament on 13th July, 1871, to run steam cars from Paisley Road Toll along Govan Road to Govan.

*Corporation Tramways.*—When the Company's lease expired they failed to come to terms with the City for a renewal, and the Corporation decided to carry on the business for the benefit of the city. Preparations were begun in June, 1893, and by 1st July, 1894, when the Company's term expired, the Corporation cars were ready to continue the service. The undertaking was a success from the beginning, and during the first four weeks no fewer than 6,114,789 passengers were carried. The first annual report, of eleven months, showed a balance of £24,204. £8,260 5s. 6d. was handed to the Common Good Fund, £6,750 was placed to reserve, and £9,294 was written off for depreciation. In 1896 the Govan and Ibrox tramways were leased and worked by the Corporation. In 1898 there were thirty-seven miles of rails belonging to the City, which, with four miles leased from Govan, makes forty-one miles at present being worked. Electric cars began to run between Springburn and Mitchell Street on 13th October, 1898. A service between Springburn and Glasgow Cross was opened on 23rd January, 1899, while an extension to Govanhill is in active preparation. Contracts have been placed to fit up the following routes with electric traction:—Whiteinch to Anderston Cross (cost, £25,739); Langside to Overnewton, *via* Eglinton Street, Bridge Street, Jamaica Street, Union Street, Renfield Street, and Sauchiehall Street (£32,610); Anderston Cross to Bridgeton Cross, and Bridgeton Cross to London Road (£20,754); Bridgeton Cross to Dalmarnock Road, Pollokshaws to Eglinton Toll, Pollokshields to Eglinton Toll, and Braehead Street, *via* Rutherglen Road, to Crown Street (£22,973); while extensions to the following places are proposed, *viz.*:—Shettleston, Tollcross, Rutherglen, Cathcart, Pollokshaws, Paisley, Dalmuir, etc. For the year ended 31st May, 1899, the gross revenue of the Corporation Tramways Department was £439,000, the expenditure being £318,000, leaving the handsome surplus of £121,000.

**Free Ferries.**—It is proposed to institute a system of free ferries, and the York Street and Clyde Street cross ferries will in future ply without a charge being made. Compensation will be given the Clyde Trust.

## CLUBS.

**Old Clubs.**—Dr. Strang, in his most readable book, "Glasgow and its Clubs," gives a very interesting and valuable account of the old clubs of the city, from which I cull the following:—At the beginning of the century the houses of the city did not possess drawing and smoking rooms. It was not the custom in those days to spend the evenings at friends' houses. People generally took their meals in their bedrooms. One o'clock was the dinner hour, and the women entertained their female acquaintances to tea at four o'clock. When the day's business was finished, the male population, instead of returning home, as is now the custom, went direct and met their companions at their club or in a favourite tavern, where wine and tobacco played a prominent part.

*The Anderston Club* met every Saturday at two o'clock, in John Sharpe's hostelry in Anderston. Dr. Robert Simson, the celebrated professor of mathematics, was its founder and president. The club was composed of the men of light and learning in the city. The president gave the company Hellenic poetry, Professor Adam Smith political economy and his Oxford career, Dr. Moir his experiences with Lord Kilmarnock, Professor Ross his views on Smollett, and Robert Foulis what he had seen on the Continent. On the death of Professor Simson the club ceased to exist.

*The Hodge Podge Club* was originally of the literary society order, but latterly degenerated to sixpenny whist. It met every fortnight, at seven o'clock, in Cruickshanks' Tavern. It was composed of the tobacco lords and other leading merchants of the city, and amongst the number was Dr. John Moore, the father of the immortal hero of Corunna. The club could boast of a poet-laureate, who wrote a "sonnet," hitting off the idiosyncrasies of the principal members.

*My Lord Ross's Club* held high revel every night of the week, Sunday excepted, in a public-house parlour in High Street. It partook of the "smoking concert" order. Bailie David Hendrie was its last president. Its proceedings might be aptly described in Sir Walter Scott's "Some drove the jolly bowl about."

*The Morning and Evening Club* met in a tavern in Currie's Close on the east side of High Street. Thither the members gathered before breakfast-time to see the papers, which arrived by the Edinburgh Mail Coach at five a.m. When the postal messenger appeared with the letters, a gun was fired at the Cross. This served as a signal to the members of the club to repair to the club-room. Around a blazing fire they supped their "morning," and discussed the latest news till eight o'clock, when they adjourned for breakfast and business. They returned again at seven in the evening, and continued their punch and politics until the "wee short hour ayont the twal'." Archibald Govane, writer, Dr. Whyte, Deacon Murray, James Stewart, spirit dealer, and Matthew Gilmour, writer, were leading lights in the club.

*The Gaelic Club* was formed in 1780, the membership qualification being a Highland connection by birth, parents, or property, its first president being George M'Intosh of Dunchattan, father of Charles M'Intosh, the inventor of the waterproof and chloride of lime. The secretary was Mr. M'Diarmid, first Gaelic minister in the city. The club met on the first Tuesday of every month from November till April, and only twice in the summer season, in Mrs. Scheid's tavern in the Trongate, "to converse in Gaelic according to their abilities from seven till nine." Gradually this was departed from and conviviality indulged in; a piper often appeared and sounded the pibroch. The club was located in different hostelries during its happy career. After leaving Mrs. Scheid's it remained in Mrs. M'Donald's until 1794, when it removed to Hemming's Hotel, from where it removed to the Star Hotel where the old club was formally dissolved and a new one organised, the members of which required to be connected with the Highland Society. The meeting place was changed to the Black Bull Inn. Several dinners and balls were given which were the talk of the city. The Black Watch got a complimentary dinner in 1792, and twenty-four years afterwards their officers were entertained by the club, when Kirkman Finlay presided. The club subscribed largely to all objects connected with Highlanders, and taken all in all was perhaps second to none compared with any similar organisation.

*The Accidental Club* met in the house of John Tait in the Gallowgate. Its leading member was John Taylor, who had a small school two stairs up in Buchanan's Land at the head of King Street. The appellation of the club aptly describes its character.

*The Face Club* met in Lucky Black's tavern, which was situated down a long "closs" at the head of the Gallowgate. Partaking of sheep's head dinners was its *pièce de résistance*.

*The Grog Club* owed its existence to the "Napoleon scare," its members all being connected with the local volunteers, who loyally enrolled themselves and drilled on the Green in the early morning, for the defence of their country against the threatened French invasion at the end of last century. The club members were nearly all bachelors and good sportsmen, golf being their great game. It was played on the Green until the improvements took away all the *hazards*, a particularly good one being a small pellucid stream that passed through the middle of the Green. The club's meeting place was in the Black Boy in Gallowgate, where the turf, the sod, and the ring were all eagerly discussed. The marriage of their hostess caused the club to become *non est*.

*The Camperdown Club* was formed in honour of Admiral Duncan's great victory over the Dutch on 11th October, 1797. Its first meeting place was in Jane Hunter's tavern in the Trongate, where punch and politics of a very decided Tory character were the chief features.

*The Meridian Club*, as its name signifies, met during the dinner hour between 1 and 2 p.m., when it was customary for business houses to shut their doors, in Lamont's at the head of Stockwell Street. Marshall, a drouthy clerk in the Ship Bank, was a never-failing member.

*The Pig Club*, which took its name from the figure of a pig that was attached to a silver chain worn by the chairman, was composed of the aristocrats of the city. John Gordon of Aitkenhead was its first president. The club much resembled our present-day whist clubs, with a supper attached, and betting on the European war. The subscription was 30s. a year. The session always began with a swell dinner.

*The Beefsteak or Tinkers' Club* met originally at 4 p.m., and latterly at 6 p.m., in Bryce Davidson's tavern in Stockwell Street. It somewhat resembled the Meridian Club.

*The Medical Club*, as its name denotes, was composed of the leading members of the faculty. It met once a month from 4 till 10 p.m., first in Mrs. Pollock's in Princes Street, and latterly in the "Prince of Wales" in Brunswick Street. It existed for fifteen years, and during that time spent many a merry evening of the "hail fellow, well met" order.

*The What you Please Club* met every evening at 8 p.m. in Mrs. Porteous's tavern on the west side of the Saltmarket, then in Mrs. Elmslie's in King Street, and latterly in Henderson's oyster-house at the south end of the Candleriggs, opposite the Guard-House. It was originated by its first president, Dr. Drumgold, inspecting medical recruiting officer of the district, and was composed originally of his brother officers. Its fame spread abroad, and soon well-known civilians and several of the theatrical profession were included in its ranks. On Dr. Drumgold being transferred elsewhere he was succeeded by Thos. Orr. Song and sentiment were the chief characteristics of the club, whose minutes show that they subscribed handsomely towards the erection of Lord Nelson's and Sir John Moore's monuments, and frequently gave donations to the Royal Infirmary.

*The Coul Club* was instituted on 12th January, 1796. It took its name from the ancient British King whom the old ballad thus describes :—

" Old King Coul
 Was a merry old soul,
 And a merry old soul was he,
 And he called for his pipe,
 And he called for his glass,
 And he called for his fiddlers three."

The club was composed of the better class of the citizens, who were all knighted on being admitted. For example, James Lumsden, afterwards Lord Provost of the City, was dubbed "Sir Christopher Copperplate." James Sheridan Knowles, dramatic author, then a teacher of elocution in the city, was known as " Sir Jeremy Jingle." The meetings were conducted on the Literary Debating Society principle. Amongst the many laudable acts performed by the club was the subscribing of £50 to the Royal Infirmary, £25 to Ayr Burns Monument, and a similar sum to Nelson's Monument on the Green.

*The Gegg Club* was composed of the harum-scarum better-class youths of the city. They had no particular place of meeting. Sometimes they congregated in a tavern, and at other times in a private house. After a few hours of song and sentiment, they generally wound up the evening with some practical joke, such as locking a night watchman in his box or overturning it on top of him.

*The Banditti Club* commenced its career in 1808 in Gardner's tavern in Gibson's Wynd (Princes Street). The description of the Gegg Club is also applicable to this one.

*The Packers' Club.*—It was the custom for exporters to send their goods to the calenderers for the purpose of being packed for the carriers to take to Greenock, etc. It being necessary for a representative of the consigner to be present to see that all was in order, these delegates formed themselves into the Packers' Club, which met in John Gregg's "Three Tuns" Tavern. The members were very musically inclined, and were the originators of subscription concerts. Their harmony evenings were generally very lively. Latterly the club changed its name to the *Every Night Club*, and became very enthusiastic in Freemasonry.

*The Post Office Club* met in John Neilson's tavern, in the Tontine Close, at eight p.m. It was composed of the Post Office employees, who met after the mails were made up, to talk over the latest news of the day, for which the club was specially famous. The Post Office at this time was in charge of Dugald Bannatyne.

*The French Club* was formed in 1816. The members consisted of the French Consul and Vice-Consul and the foreign clerks connected with James Finlay & Co. and other foreign merchants. Card-playing and anecdotes were its principal characteristics.

*The Anderston Social Club* was formed on 13th June, 1813. It was originally composed of thirty members, who chiefly resided in the villages of Anderston and Finnieston. It met in a tavern in Anderston, belonging to John Adam, every Monday night, from half-past eight till eleven o'clock. In addition to talking over the latest war news, poetry was a speciality with the members, among whom was William Glen, the author of "Wae's me for Prince Charlie." Many of the songs composed by the members are contained in the minute-books of the club.

*The Partick Duck Club* met in the Bunhouse Tavern, Partick, every Saturday afternoon, between three and four o'clock. The members belonged principally to Glasgow, and walked from there to their clubhouse every week for dinner, and rum and recollections, with unfailing regularity. Convener M'Tyre was the leading light. William Reid, the well-known bibliophile, was the club poet, and some of his effusions are particularly interesting. He hit off the worthy convener, who was a carnivorous gourmand, very aptly in the following couplet :—

The ducks at Partick quake for fear,
Crying, "Lord preserve us! there's M'Tear."

The club did not belie its name. When its season began, in June, the Kelvin was covered with the feathery tribe ; and when it closed, in October, nothing remained on the then pellucid stream but a few sorrowing parents.

*The Waterloo Club* was formed immediately after Wellington's greatest victory. The meeting very appropriately took place in a tavern bearing the name of Britain's most glorious encounter. One of the characteristics of the club was the giving of distinctions to the members—such as "Knights of the Grand Cross," who were composed of the original twenty-five members, while those who followed were made "Knight Commanders." This "honourable" company met nightly for years, taking an active interest in supporting the powers that be against the imaginary Radical risings.

*The Shuna Club.* — James Yates, a London merchant, who was a native of St. Mungo, gifted the Island of Shuna to the city of his birth. The donor died in 1829, but difficulties arose regarding the transference of the property, causing many meetings to be held. The outcome of these was the promotion of the Shuna Club, which originally met in a tavern in the Post Office Court in Trongate, and latterly in the restaurant under the then New Royal Exchange in Queen Street,

which was known by the soubriquet of the *Crypt.* The magistrates and prominent citizens composed this somewhat aristocratic organisation, which was conducted very much on the "pies and porter" principle.

*The Sma' Weft Club* met first in Mrs. Kerr's Shakespeare Tavern in Saltmarket, and latterly in a tavern at the entrance to Dunlop Street. The members were all loyal reformers, and anyone who knows the history of the twenties and thirties, when the club was in its zenith, can well imagine that politics rather than punch would be their *raison d' être.*

*The Crow Club* was of the political committee order. After the passing of the first Reform Bill, a committee met in the Eagle Inn in Maxwell Street for the furtherance of the candidature of Messrs. Oswald and Crawford, who were seeking the suffrages of St. Mungo's electors in 1832. Finding more suitable quarters, the members removed to Powell's Vine Tavern in the same street. Oswald was successful, and Crawford was defeated, but on the resignation of Sir John Maxwell from the representation of Paisley, Crawford stood for the vacancy, and again the "Crows" flew to his assistance, but Sir Daniel Sandford made him once more take a back seat. However, at the next Parliamentary election, three years afterwards, the club had the satisfaction of finding both their candidates successful in the persons of Messrs. Oswald and Dunlop. On the death of their landlord the headquarters were taken to Cossack Tavern in Jamaica Street, and afterwards to the Crow Hotel in George Square, where the club eventually went to roost, after a useful and busy life.

**Other Clubs.**—Dr. Strang summarises the remaining clubs, whose names are as follows, viz.:—*The Beggar's Benison*; *The Cape*; *Consistory*; *Dirty Shirt*; *Amateur*; *White Wine Club*, which met monthly in David Dreghorn's tavern in Long Govan ; *Town and Country*, which met in the Prince of Wales Tavern on Wednesday afternoons ; *Jumble* ; *Breeze* ; *Rumble Gumpy*, which met in Mrs. Anderson's tavern near where the head of Stockwell Street is now situated ; *Bridgegate*, which met for the first time in 1812 in the street of the same name ; *Union* ; *Badger* (from which sprung the present *Western Club* in Buchanan Street), which was formed by Major Monteath in 1825, and was originally housed in the old dwelling of Mr. M'Inroy. The present quarters were opened in 1841. During the building operations the club was temporally put up in 36 St. Vincent Place. Card clubs were represented by the *Board of the Green Cloth*; *Stallion*; *Oyster*; *Miss Thomson's Tea*, and the *Driddle*.

**Modern Clubs.**—It is impossible to give a list of the modern clubs in our limited space, but the following are the leading organisations which have a habitation in addition to a name:— *Western*, 147 Buchanan Street; *New*, 144 West George Street; *Liberal*, 169 Buchanan Street; *Conservative*, 33 Bothwell Street; *Junior Conservative*, 46 Renfield Street; *Imperial Union*, 82 St. Vincent Street; *Merchants*, 17 Cochrane Street.

**The Roberton Hunt.**—On 8th April, 1771, a club was formed called the Roberton Hunt. It was composed of twenty-three of the leading men in the city. They purchased a pack of hounds and built a kennel. The first meet took place on Hamilton Moor on 17th November, 1771, where a fox was found and killed. At a meet on 1st November, 1779, a fox was found at Tollcross, which crossed the Clyde three times, and was followed from 9 a.m. until 4.30 p.m., and at last got to ground in Hamilton Wood after a chase of about fifty miles. On another occasion the huntsman was drowned crossing the Clyde during a flood at Bothwell.

---

## THEATRES.

**First Theatre.**—The first theatrical entertainment held in Glasgow after the Reformation is said to have been in Burrell's Hall, where Burrell's Lane now adjoins High Street, in 1750. Two years afterwards the first theatre was erected in the city; it was of a temporary character, built of wood against the ruined wall of the Bishop's Palace. So much were the public against it that the patrons of the drama had to be protected by the military. In 1754 this temporary theatre was demolished by a congregation which had been hearing the Rev. George Whitefield preach in the High Churchyard.

**First Permanent Theatre.**—Owing to the opposition of the citizens, and the refusal of the authorities, the first permanent theatre was built in 1762 outwith the city boundary—which was marked by a pillar on the west side of Union Street. The building was erected in the suburb of Grahamston, where the Central Railway Station now stands. Mrs. Bellamy opened

it in 1764, when an unsuccessful attempt was made to set fire to it. Fire destroyed it on 5th May, 1780, when over £1,000 was lost in actors' properties alone. There was a strong suspicion that this was an act of incendiarism.

**Dunlop Street.**—Dunlop Street Theatre was opened in January, 1782. It afforded two separate places of amusement. At one time it was turned into a circus. In 1822 Mr. Alexander leased the lower part, and seven years afterwards he purchased the whole building for £6,000.

**Queen Street.**—Owing to the inadequacy of Dunlop Street Theatre, a new theatre was erected in 1803 at the corner of Queen Street and what is now Royal Exchange Square. This was the most handsome building of the kind Glasgow ever possessed, and cost £18,500. Unfortunately this city ornament met the fate which seems to attend Glasgow theatres, being burned in 1829.

**Old Theatres.**—The Adelphi and City Theatres, and Cook's Circus, used to stand on the Green, at Jail Square. Calvert, of the wooden Hibernian Theatre, erected a brick edifice immediately to the east of the Episcopal Chapel in Greendyke Street.

**Riding Schools.**—A riding school or circus was erected in Jamaica Street in 1797. The Glasgow Volunteers frequently drilled in it. Another riding school was erected at the top of York Street.

**Present Theatres, etc.**—The following theatres are presently in Glasgow, *viz.*:—Grand (Cowcaddens), Royal (Hope Street, Cowcaddens), Royalty (Sauchiehall Street), Royal Princess's (Main Street, Gorbals), Metropole (Stockwell Street), Queen's (Watson Street); Empire, Britannia, and Tivoli Music Halls; Hengler's and Zoo Circuses; and three waxworks.

---

## OLD HOTELS AND TAVERNS.

**Saracen's Head.**—The Saracen's Head Inn was erected in 1755, on the north side of the Gallowgate, between what is now the Great Dovehill and Saracen Lane. The site it still occupies was at one time the Auld Kirkyard of Little St. Mungo. The inn was partly built with stones taken from the ruins of the Bishop's Castle. The Saracen's Head was the principal hotel in the city at one time. It was the head-quarters of the Lords of Justiciary and the great sporting Duke of Hamilton when in

Glasgow. Dr. Samuel Johnson and his biographer, Boswell, slept one night under its roof, when they returned from their Hebridean tour, *en route* for Auchinleck, in Ayrshire. Sitting before the fire in one of the the rooms the great lexicographer is reported by his biographer to have said : " Here am I, an Englishman, sitting by a *coal* fire." The distinguished *litterateurs*, when in the city, had a meeting with the professors, nd supped with Professor Anderson. About 1751 the inn was sold, and converted into dwelling-houses and shops. During the alterations a great many human bones were found. The building is still standing, being let out for houses of one apartment, with small shops in front. A bill states it is for sale. *Sic transit gloria mundi!*

**Buck's Head.**—The Buck's Head was situated at the corner of Argyle and Dunl p Streets. It was formerly the mansion-house of Provost Murdoch and the Hopkins of Dalbeth. There was an outside stair entering from either side. C. M'Farlane, the lessee in 1788, advertised " an ordinary, every day at three o'clock ; charge, eightpence per head."

**Tontine.**—The Tontine, which was for many years the Exchange of the city, was erected next the Town's Buildings, at the Cross, in 1782, by the merchants of the city, who took shares in the concern, the subscription being fixed at twenty-five shillings a year. Mr. Smart leased the building as an hotel, and a coffee-house was opened in it in May, 1784, when the Lords of Justiciary were in the city. The old Assembly Hall was purchased by the new company, who built another, which formed part of the Tontine. The grandest ball that had ever been held in the town took place in the hall on the 13th of the same month. The hall came to be used exclusively for public assemblies, until the Assembly Rooms, in Ingram Street, were built, in 1796. The Tontine is redolent with exciting incidents of old Glasgow history, especially those in connection with the passing of the first Reform Bill. The "Plain Stanes" were in front of the Tontine. The arcade of the Town Hall was thrown into the piazzas. Each arch of the vestibule had grinning effigies. Two of the originals are now to be seen in Fraser, Sons & Co.'s building, in Buchanan Street. The Tontine is now converted into the warehouse of Moore, Taggart & Co.

**Black Bull.**—This well-known inn, which gave up business in 1851, was built by the Highland Society from the proceeds of a collection they gathered in the Cathedral Churchyard when the Rev. George Whitefield preached a sermon for their benefit. The Black Bull was situated at the corner of Argyle and Virginia Streets. It had a large hall in the latter street, which was afterwards used by Hutcheson & Dixon for their auction mart. The accommodation of the hotel consisted of dining-room, eleven parlours, eighteen bedrooms, and stabling for forty horses. It was the headquarters of the first Edinburgh coach. The building has now been transformed into Mann, Byars & Co.'s warehouse. Previous to the above well-known hostelry being built, another of the same name used to stand in Argyle Street, nearly opposite.

**Star Inn.**—The Star Inn was situated on the north side of Ingram Street, facing Glassford Street. The stables, which accommodated seventy horses, entered from Cochrane Street. The Lords patronised this hotel alternately with the Black Bull.

**Prince of Wales and Eagle.**—The Prince of Wales Tavern stood on the west side of Brunswick Street. The site is now occupied by the Sheriff Court buildings. The Eagle Inn was situated in Maxwell Street, the spot being now swallowed up in St. Enoch Station.

**Hotels in 1820.**—The following hotels were in existence in 1820 :—Commercial Bank Restaurant, 413 Gallowgate ; Black Bull, 640 Argyle Street ; Eagle, 30 Maxwell Street ; Saracen's Head, Gallowgate; George, 18 George Square ; Buck's Head, 30 Argyle Street; King's Arms, 164 Trongate; Cossack, 40 King Street ; Tontine, Cross; and Star, 57 Ingram Street.

**Taverns.**—In 1780 the most popular taverns in the city were in High Street, Saltmarket, and Gibson's Wynd—afterwards called Princes Street, and now renamed Parnie Street ; while other celebrated resorts were the *Black Boy*, in Gallowgate ; *Jane Hunter's*, in Trongate ; *Lamont's*, at head of Stockwell Street; and the *Bacchus*, in the Laigh Kirk Close. A famous oyster shop was kept by Mrs. M'Alpine, "Iron Ravel Closs," on north side of Trongate. There were two famous "tripe shops" in the Bridgegate.

## ATHLETICS.

**Bowling.**—Bowling is of a very old date in Glasgow. Where the Bazaar now stands was the site of a bowling green during last century. There are at present 29 clubs connected with the Glasgow district, *viz.*:—

| | | | | | |
|---|---|---|---|---|---|
| Albany | - | - | - | Instituted | 1833 |
| Wellcroft | - | - | - | ,, | 1835 |
| Willowbank | - | - | - | ,, | 1835 |
| Whitevale | - | - | - | ,, | 1836 |
| Partick | - | - | - | ,, | 1844 |
| Govan | - | - | - | ,, | 1849 |
| Hillhead | - | - | - | ,, | 1849 |
| Belvidere | - | - | - | ,, | 1853 |
| Pollokshaws | - | - | - | ,, | 1854 |
| St. Rollox | - | - | - | ,, | 1857 |
| Bellahouston | - | - | - | ,, | 1858 |
| Springburn | - | - | - | ,, | 1858 |
| Kingston | - | - | - | ,, | 1859 |
| St. Vincent | - | - | - | ,, | 1859 |
| Maryhill | - | - | - | ,, | 1862 |
| Shawlands | - | - | - | ,, | 1862 |
| Pollokshields | - | - | - | ,, | 1863 |
| Burnbank | - | - | - | ,, | 1866 |
| Hutchesontown | - | - | - | ,, | 1866 |
| Queen's Park | - | - | - | ,, | 1867 |
| Polmadie | - | - | - | ,, | 1876 |
| Tollcross | - | - | - | ,, | 1877 |
| Possilpark | - | - | - | ,, | 1878 |
| Broomhill | - | - | - | ,, | 1879 |
| Whiteinch | - | - | - | ,, | 1884 |
| Camphill | - | - | - | ,, | 1886 |
| Cathcart | - | - | - | ,, | 1889 |
| Titwood | - | - | - | , | 1890 |
| Parkhead | - | - | - | ,, | 1806 |

**Cricket.**—Cricket will probably never be a game for the public like football, although it has increased in popularity during the past few years. The chief ground in Glasgow originally was Holyrood Park, situated behind Burnbank Gardens and belonging to the Caledonian Club, from where they removed to the site of the present Glasgow Academy, at Kelvin Bridge. The principal clubs in the city at the present time are the West of Scotland (ground Hamilton Crescent, Partick), Clydesdale (originally in Kinning Park and now at Titwood, Crossmyloof), and Poloc (Shawholm policies).

**Curling** is indulged in during the winter time. There are several old - established clubs in the city, *viz.*:—Northern, Timber Trade, Hillhead, Kelvindock, North Woodside, Kingston, Willowbank, Sir Colin Campbell, Lilybank, Pollok, and Cathcart.

**Cycling.**—Previous to 1889 cyclists in Scotland were controlled by the National Cyclists' Union of England, whose headquarters are in London; but in the year mentioned a number of gentlemen interested in the pastime, being convinced that the time had arrived when Scotland should have an independent governing body, met and

founded the Scottish Cyclists' Union. The objects of the S.C.U. are generally to look after the welfare of cyclists, to oppose restrictive or harassing legislation, to endeavour to secure improved roads and the proper maintenance of milestones and direction posts, to erect warning notices on dangerous hills, to provide legal assistance to cyclists when considered advisable, to agitate for reasonable charges for the carriage of cycles by railway and steamer, and to control the sport of cycle racing. To this comprehensive constitution has recently been added the fostering of cycle touring, and in this connection the Union at the beginning of 1899 instituted a Pastime Board, and resolved to cater largely for individual members—its strength having hitherto been almost entirely drawn from the cycling clubs throughout the country. A monthly magazine is one of the products of the touring section, which has attracted in its first year close upon a thousand members. The Union is composed of five District Councils—Eastern, Western, Central, Northern, and Southern, covering all Scotland, each having complete control in its own territory—and a General Council. The District Councils consist of delegates from the clubs and from the individual members, while the General Council is composed of delegates from the District Councils. The District Councils usually hold monthly meetings; the General Council meets six times a year, in the headquarters of the various District Councils. The growth of the Union has been very rapid, the club strength increasing from 25 in 1889 to 216 in 1897. Since that time there has been a slight falling off, but the decrease has been more than counterbalanced by the development of the individual membership. At the present time there are about forty clubs in Glasgow. In 1897 the Union achieved great fame by its successful engineering of the Championships of the World. These were contested at Celtic Park, Glasgow, the racing extending over three days. They were witnessed by close on 40,000 persons, and the revenue from all sources amounted to £2,637 4s. 10d.

**Football.**—The origin of football is unknown. During the sixteenth century laws were passed prohibiting football, as it was interfering with the practice of archery. Football was played in Perthshire and the Border counties during last century and at the beginning of this. The game has now been codified under what is known as the Rugby and Association rules, and the latter has become practically the national game of the country. Association football originated in the public schools of England, notably Eton, Harrow, and Charterhouse. Mr. C. W. Alcock, the late secretary of the English Association, introduced the game into London about 1863.

The Queen's Park club began to play Association football in the South-Side Park, Glasgow, in 1867, and to it belongs the honour of bringing the game to Scotland. The Queen's Park club played the first international match against England, at Partick, in 1872, and succeeded in making a draw. Since then the rise of the game has been remarkably rapid. The Scottish Football Association was instituted in 1873, and did great work in introducing the game all over the country by means of the Scottish Challenge Cup. Glasgow has always remained the headquarters of the game. Its principal clubs are the Queen's Park (instituted 1867), Rangers (1872), Third Lanark (1872), Clyde (1874), Partick Thistle (1875), Linthouse (1881), and Celtic (1888). Since the institution of the Glasgow Charity Cup, in 1877, £19,560 have been allocated to the city charities. £3,309 17s. 11d. were drawn at an international match on Celtic Park on 4th April, 1896, when over 57,000 spectators were inside the enclosure. About £50,000 during the year are drawn by the clubs in the city.

The Rugby code is represented by the West of Scotland (ground Hamilton Crescent), Clydesdale (Titwood), Glasgow Academicals (Anniesland), Kelvinside Academicals (Great Western Road), Glasgow University (Gilmorehill), High School (Crow Road), and Partickhill (Yoker). The general public takes comparatively little interest in it, and the support accorded it comes pretty much from the better class school element, the Rugby code being greatly in favour at Glasgow and Kelvinside Academies and the High School.

**Golf.**—The ancient game of golf has a very old connection with the city. During last century the Green was the headquarters of the golfers. At present there are two public links in the city, viz.—Alexandra Park (18 holes) and Bellahouston Park (9 holes). There are thirty-three clubs in and around the city, and of this number the following have private courses, viz. :— Glasgow (Blackhill), Alexandra (Cumbernauld Road) Bearsden, Busby and Clarkston, Cambuslang, Campsie, Cathcart Castle, Cathkin Braes, Douglas Park (Bearsden), Eastwood (Giffnock), 1st L.R.V. (Yorkhill),

Kelvinside (Crossloan Road), Levern (Nitshill), Milngavie, North-Western (Maryhill), Pollok (Pollokshaws), Scotstounhill, and Toryglen (Crosshill).

**Harriers.**—There are several cross-country clubs in the city, the principal being the Clydesdale and West of Scotland Harriers.

**Quoiting.**—There are but twenty-two clubs affiliated to the Scottish Quoiting Association, whilst outwith their bounds quite 150 clubs flourish. Under the jurisdiction of the Scottish Quoiting Association all matches are played at 21 yards' distance. Some clubs in the suburbs of the city play at 18 yards, and this is the regulation distance in all outlying districts. The present champions of Scotland are the Springside, who defeated the famous Darvel club. The latter is, nevertheless, unquestionably the premier club, both in point of members and enthusiasm, and the frequency with which their members play in open tournaments and matches. It is passing strange that the Scottish single-handed champion, Kirkwood of Bannock, is a member of a non-association club, whilst the Lochgelly organisation, now outwith the bounds of the Scottish Quoiting Association, also contains the second-best Scottish individual player in the person of R. Waters.

**Rowing.**—*Clydesdale Amateur Club* is the oldest existing club in the city, being upwards of thirty years doing useful work. It has suffered decadence during the past few years, but doubtless will assume a renewed life and vigour with the reconstruction of the weir.

*Clyde Amateur Club* is nearly a quarter of a century old. It has had an intermittent but at times enthusiastic and victorious career. It has a good club-house and a splendid collection of boats—skiffs, jollies, and racing gigs.

*Police Athletic and Rowing Club* is, as the name implies, composed of the policemen of Glasgow, and is in a flourishing condition.

*Glasgow Trades Professional Club* is also a club of long standing. It has in its members some of the best professional oarsmen in Scotland. It has not been so fortunate these last few years, but previously it ran close and victorious races against Greenock Unity, Leven Lass, and other Dumbarton, Dunoon, Oban, Greenock, and Helensburgh crews. It has a nice club-house and good stock of craft.

*Glasgow Rowing Association.*—Organised for the purpose of holding regattas, and so encouraging emulation amongst the various clubs and crews. It has been in existence for two years, and has held two professional regattas.

*Glasgow Daily Press and Letterpress Printers.*—This is not a club properly so called, but is a committee in charge of the annual regatta, the races of which are in skiffs, pairs, and fours, and for the classes as indicated by the title of the organisation. It holds challenge cups, one for all printers in crews from offices, one for pair oars, one for apprentices, and one for rowers in newspaper offices.

There are several clubs in connection with different public works, but these confine their races to competition amongst themselves, and do not possess boats of their own.

**Shinty.**—The ancient Celtic pastime is played by the Glasgow Cowal Shinty Club. The club was formed in March, 1877, and was confined to natives of the district of Cowal Argyllshire, resident in the city; but after some years of exclusiveness the membership was thrown open to anyone, and the result was a large increase in numbers. Their first ground was on Glasgow Green, then Cessnock Park, and now they are located at Moray Park, Strathbungo.

**Swimming.**—Glasgow has always played the most prominent part in regard to swimming affairs in Scotland, and the present Scottish Amateur Swimming Association, instituted in 1888, had its origin from a body known as the Associated Swimming Clubs of Glasgow. There are close on thirty clubs in the city connected with the S.A.S.A., and these have an aggregate membership of something like 3,000. Besides these, several smaller clubs connected with churches, workshops, etc., practise regularly in the Corporation Baths. The oldest club in the city is the West of Scotland, instituted in 1867; and the most prominent within recent years have been those in connection with Western and Pollokshields Private Baths, which have produced not a few champions. There are five of these private bathing establishments in the city—Arlington, near St. George's Cross; Western, in Hillhead; Pollokshields and Victoria, on the South-Side; and Dennistoun, in the district after which it is named. They are all luxuriously fitted up, and, besides having swimming ponds, are each provided with Turkish and other baths, billiard and card rooms,

and a gymnasium. All the Scottish championships at present in existence were originally promoted by Glasgow clubs, and the competitions were held annually at their entertainments and under their management.

## PROMINENT MEN.

**Rev. Robert Woodrow.** — Robert Woodrow, the Church historian, was born in Glasgow in 1679, being the second son of the Professor of Divinity in the University, which he afterwards attended. He was given the charge of Eastwood by Sir John Maxwell of Nether Pollok, and there he wrote his invaluable "History of the Church of Scotland." He died on 21st March, 1734.

**Robert and Andrew Foulis.**—Robert and Andrew Foulis commenced business in the city in 1741 as printers and booksellers. They were appointed printers to the University in 1743, and in the same year proved their right to the title by printing the first Greek book from a Glasgow press, "Demetrius Phalereus de Elocutione." They published an edition of Horace in 1744, called the "immaculate edition," the proof sheets being hung up in the College and a reward offered to the discoverer of inaccuracies. Two editions of Homer followed in 1747; in 1749 Cicero's works in twenty volumes. The plays of Shakespeare (in 1756), "Hymns of Callimachus," an edition of the "Odyssey" (in 1758), Gray's works (in 1767), and Milton's poems were all the enterprise of this firm. Robert Foulis was a great lover and patron of art, and having travelled on the Continent, he was an authority on the "Old Masters." He established an academy of painting and sculpture, the students receiving permission to copy the classic pictures in Hamilton Palace; and through his instrumentality the first exhibition of fine arts in the city was held in the College quadrangle in 1760. Andrew died on 18th September, 1775, and the business broke up shortly afterwards, Robert going to London to sell his pictures to relieve his embarrassments. He died in Edinburgh on his way back to Glasgow, on 2nd June, 1776, a disappointed man, leaving heavy debts behind him. David Allen, painter, and James Tassie, modeller, were pupils of the "Elzevirs of Scotland."

**Famous Professors.**—Adam Smith, Professor of Logic and Moral Philosophy, author of the "Wealth of Nations;" Thomas Reid, Professor of Natural Philosophy; James Watt, improver of the steam engine; John Anderson, Professor of Oriental Languages and Natural Philosophy, and founder of Anderson's College; Principal Leechman, for fifteen years Professor of Theology; Joseph Black, Professor of Chemistry and Medicine; John Millar, Professor of Law; Professor Moor, Professor of Greek; William Richardson, Professor of Humanity, were all connected with the University in the latter half of the eighteenth century.

**David Dale.**—David Dale was born in Stewarton, and came to Glasgow when he was 24 years of age. He commenced business in a small shop in High Street, five doors from the Cross, and did an extensive trade importing French yarns. He was appointed agent for the Royal Bank in 1783, when he erected a splendid residence at the north-west corner of Charlotte Street. He was the pioneer of the cotton trade in Scotland, and erected cotton mills at Lanark and Catrine and in Sutherlandshire, while he was also one of the originators of turkey-red dyeing. He filled the office of Bailie in 1791 and 1794. Seceding from the Established Church with others, he formed a Congregational Church, which first met in a private house, and latterly they secured a "vine and fig tree" of their own in Greyfriars Wynd. This was known as the "Candle Kirk," and Mr. Dale continued to act as pastor, for which he suffered great persecution when he appeared in the streets. But his good life and great liberality gradually wore down this bitterness, and latterly a more popular and better respected citizen never lived. He died on 17th March, 1806, aged 68 years, and an inscription marks his resting-place in the Ramshorn Churchyard.

**Captain Patoun.**—Captain Patoun was a well-known old Glasgow worthy. His father was a physician in the city, who left his son a tenement called Paton's Land, on the south side of the Trongate, opposite the Cross. The Captain had held a commission in a Scottish regiment raised for the Dutch service, and when he returned to his native city he lived with his two maiden sisters in the property which had been bequeathed to him. His elegantly dressed spare figure was to be constantly seen parading the plainstanes at the Cross or in the Tontine Coffee Room, where he entertained his hearers with accounts of the Battles of Minden and Dettingen. He died on 30th July, 1807, aged 68 years, and was

laid in the family sepulchre in the Cathedral burial grounds. J. G. Lockhart published a serio-comic lament of twelve verses in "Blackwood's Magazine" in September, 1819, immortalising the eccentric Captain, each stanza closing with the words:—

"Oh we ne'er shall see the like of Captain Paton no mo'!"

**Alexander Gordon.**—Alexander Gordon, better known as "picture Gordon," of the firm of Stirling, Gordon & Company, built a house in 1805 on the site of the present Royal Bank in Royal Exchange Square. It faced Gordon Street (which is called after his name), and, in order to have an unobstructed outlook, he bought a portion of the ground for some space in front of his house. The stables stood on the site of the south arch in Royal Exchange Place. Mr. Gordon had a splendid collection of oil paintings valued at £30,000. He died in 1850 in Upper Canada, aged 95 years. The above must not be confused with his brother, John Gordon of Aitkenhead, whose house in Buchanan Street stood on the site of Princes Square.

**Robert Dreghorn.**—Robert Dreghorn of Ruchill was known as the ugliest man in Glasgow. His residence stood at what is now the corner of Ropework Lane and Great Clyde Street, presently altered and used as a warehouse. He was one of the "dandies" of the town and a great admirer of the fair sex. He was nick-named "Bob Dragon," and served the part of the "bogie man" when mothers wanted to quiet their children. He committed suicide in 1806.

**Major General Sir Thomas Munroe.**—Thomas Munroe was born in the city in 1761, his early life being spent between Stockwell Street and North Woodside House on the banks of the Kelvin. After being educated in his native town, he entered the East India Company's service, and rose to be Governor of Madras, with the rank of Major-General and title of knighthood. He visited his native city, and spent much of his time amidst the haunts of his early life, where he was well known as "Millie Munroe." He returned to India, and died of cholera on 5th July, 1827.

**Thomas Muir.**—During the latter half of the eighteenth century agitation in favour of the Reform Bill was beginning to raise its voice. Thomas Muir, advocate, who was born in High Street about 1764, became the leader of the movement in the city. He was brought before the High

8

Court of Justiciary in Edinburgh on 30th August, 1793, and, along with several other reformers, sentenced to transportation to Botany Bay. Mackenzie gives a most interesting history of this martyr in his " Reminiscences of Glasgow."

**Kirkman Finlay.**—Kirkman Finlay, one of the early merchant princes of the city, was the son of James Finlay, the founder of the present old-established firm of that name. He was the pioneer of the shipping connection between the Clyde and India, described in a previous paragraph, and did more, as an individual, than perhaps any other man in laying the foundation for Glasgow becoming the great city which it now is. Finlay was educated in the High School and University, after which he travelled on the Continent. He lived in a mansion-house in Queen Street, on the site of which the National Bank Buildings now stand. He was governor of the Forth and Clyde Canal, president of the Chamber of Commerce, Lord Provost, member of Parliament, Dean of Faculty, Lord Rector of the University, in addition to being connected with all the principal undertakings in the city. He built Castle Toward, where he died, on 4th March, 1842, in his seventieth year. A statue is erected to his memory in the vestibule of the Merchants' House.

**Henry Monteith.**—Monteith Row is called after Henry Monteith, who was a son of James Monteith, of Anderston, where Henry was born in 1765. He lived for some time in the third flat of Light-body's Land, south side of Bell's Wynd, and became the head of Monteith, Bogle and Co., who had large textile works in Bridgeton. He was Lord Provost of Glasgow on two occasions—1814 and 1818. In 1819 Carstairs estate was purchased by him, and he was elected M.P. for Lanark district of burghs in 1821. After a useful career he passed away on 14th December, 1848.

**Charles Tennant.**—The founder of the famous Glasgow firm was born at Ochiltree House, Ayrshire, in 1768. He learned the silk weaving at Kilbarchan, and afterwards wrought at the loom at Kilwinning. He became a bleacher at Darnley in company with Mr. Cochrane, of Paisley, and married the daughter of a neighbour—Miss Wilson, of Hurlet. Discovering the properties of applying chlorine gas to bleaching purposes, he established chemical works at St. Rollox in 1799, in partnership with Charles Macintosh, James Knox, Alex-ander Dunlop, and Dr. William Cooper. He was one of the most prominent men in the city, and was well known for his good works. He died suddenly at his residence in Abercrombie Place in 1838, aged 71 years. His son, John, carried on the business until he likewise passed away in 1878, aged 82 years. Sir Charles Tennant of the Glen is a grandson of the first named, and a worthy successor of worthy progenitors.

**Dr. James Cleland, LL.D.**, author of " The Rise and Progress of the City of Glasgow," was born within the sound of St. Mungo's bells in 1770. He became a partner with his father, who was a cabinet-maker, in 1791, and was appointed Superintendent of Public Works in 1814. His " Annals of Glasgow" appeared in 1816, followed the following year by an abridged edition, and 1820 saw the publication of his well-known " Rise and Progress." The Government appointed him Census-taker in 1821 and 1831, and he drew up the mortality returns from 1820 until 1834. As previously stated, he designed and laid the foundation of the Bazaar buildings in the Candleriggs. On several occasions he published valuable historical and statistical documents about Glasgow. He was an LL.D. of the University. After a long illness he passed away on 14th October, 1840. Lord Inverclyde and Mr. J. Cleland Burns are his grandsons.

**James Ewing.**—James Ewing, of Strathleven, was born in Glasgow on 7th December, 1774. His father was Walter Ewing M'Lae, of Cathkin, who was a large West Indian merchant, to which business the son succeeded in 1814, under the name of James Ewing & Co. James Ewing resided in a mansion at the head of what is now Queen Street, which he purchased from George Crawford—who built it—for £5,000. It had a famous rookery, on the site of which Queen Street Station is now situated. There was nothing of any note connected with the city that James Ewing was not actively interested in. He was one of the promoters of the Royal Exchange and Duke Street Prison. He suggested forming the Fir Park into the Necropolis, and was a Councillor, Dean of Guild, Lord Provost, and M.P. in connection with the city. After losing his seat in Parliament he purchased the estate of Levenside, to which he retired. He died on 29th November, 1853, leaving a fortune of £280,000, of which sum he bequeathed £70,000 to charitable and other institutions.

## Thomas Hamilton and James Grahame.

Thomas Hamilton, author of the novel "Cyril Thornton," "Annals of the Peninsular Campaign," and " Men and Manners in America," was a native of Glasgow, as was also James Grahame, author of the " Sabbath."

### Rev. Dr. Thomas Chalmers.

The history of the greatest divine of modern times has been so fully written that I shall merely touch upon the great preacher's association with the city. He came from Kilmany, in Fife, to succeed the Rev. Dr. M'Gill in the Tron Church, where he was inducted by the Rev. Sir Henry Moncrieff on Friday, 21st July, 1815. He lodged in the Rottenrow till he was joined by his household, when he took up house first in Charlotte Street, and latterly in Kensington Place. He removed to St. John's Parish in 1819, where he was assisted by Edward Irving, and continued there until 1823, when he went to Edinburgh. Dr. Chalmers' Glasgow life was a great triumphal march. Several things stand out prominently, such as his wonderful astronomical discourses in the Tron Church on Thursdays at midday, when standing room could not be got. The lectures were published, and in ten weeks six thousand copies had been sold, the sale eclipsing that of Scott's "Tales of my Grandfather," which were running at the same time. His great scheme for dealing with the poor is admitted to be the greatest ever attempted in this country, and had it been so ordered that he could have remained in Glasgow to carry out his ideas, it is certain we should not have the misery that presently exists in our midst. It is interesting to know that a brother of Dr. Chalmers was a bookseller in the city, his firm being Chalmers & Collins, in Wilson Street. The latter was the father of Sir William Collins.

### Edward Irving.

Edward Irving was born in Annan in 1792. While in Ulster, in the year 1819, Dr. Chalmers invited him to become his assistant in St. John's Parish Church. He was a splendid and popular preacher, but was considered heterodox. He went to London in 1822, where his fame spread abroad, but he was ultimately deposed from the ministry, when he returned to Glasgow, and died a disappointed and broken-hearted man at the early age of 42. A monument marks his resting place in the Necropolis.

### James and Archibald Smith.

James Smith was born on 15th August, 1782. He became a great scientist, and contributed largely to geographical and geological societies. Amongst other works, he published "The Voyage and Shipwreck of St. Paul," "The Ships and Navigation of the Ancients," etc. He died on 17th January, 1867. His son, Archibald Smith of Jordanhill, was born in 1814. He made a special study of engineering, mechanics, and the compass, and assisted in the perfecting of iron shipbuilding. He was an F.R.S. and an LL.D. of Glasgow University, and, unlike the general run, proved a worthy son of an able sire. He passed away on 26th December, 1872.

### John Donald Carrick.

J. D. Carrick was born in the city in April, 1787; after a sojourn in London and Birmingham he returned to the banks of the Clyde and began business as a china merchant in Hutcheson Street. In 1825 he wrote the " Life of Sir William Wallace" for "Constable's Miscellany," and some of his songs and poems appeared in Robertson's "Whistle Binkie." He was a sub-editor of the *Scots Times*, and afterwards editor of the *Perth Advertiser* and *Kilmarnock Journal*. In 1835 he projected and edited the "Laird of Logan." He died in 1837, and was buried in the High Kirkyard.

### J. B. Neilson.

Previous to 1827 cold air was forced into blast furnaces, which made smelting a slow and expensive process, but in that year it struck J. B. Neilson, a talented engineer in the employment of the Glasgow Gas Company, that if the air were heated before being injected it would be an improvement. The discovery was tried in 1829, in the Clyde Iron Works, and was a great success, the process being patented. The inventor realised a handsome fortune, thus laying the foundation of the well-known "iron kings" who so worthily uphold the family name.

### Sir James Campbell.

James Campbell was born in 1790. He founded the deservedly-popular and well-known firm of J. & W. Campbell & Company. He was elected Lord Provost in 1840, and was knighted in 1841 on the occasion of the birth of the Prince of Wales. He died on 10th September, 1876. Sir James was the father of Sir Henry Campbell-Bannerman, leader of the Liberal party in the House of Commons.

### Alexander Dennistoun.

Alex. Dennistoun was born in the city in 1790. He became the principal in the firm of J. & A. Dennistoun. In 1835 he was returned as the Parliamentary representative for Dumbartonshire. A year afterwards he succeeded to the Golfhill estate on the death of his father. He feued his new inheritance, which is now known as Dennistoun. He died on 15th July, 1874.

**Robert and David Napier.**—Robert Napier was born in Dumbarton on 18th June, 1791, his father being a blacksmith, with whom he served his apprenticeship. He afterwards wrought to the famous Robert Stephenson in Edinburgh, but returning to Glasgow, he began business in Greyfriars Wynd, from where he removed to Camlachie Foundry, and afterwards to the Vulcan Foundry, in Washington Street. He founded the famous shipbuilding firm of R. Napier & Sons, who have a world-wide reputation, and have done so much to make Clyde shipbuilding the power it now is. He built a magnificent mansion at Shandon, on the Gareloch, where he died on 23rd June, 1876. His pictures and curios realised about £50,000, and his residence is now the well-known Shandon Hydropathic. David Napier was a cousin of Robert. He was born in 1790, and established a flourishing engineering business in the city, rendering valuable assistance to Henry Bell in the construction of the "Comet." Through his exertions steam communication was established between Glasgow, Belfast, Dublin, and Holyhead. He died in 1869.

**Principal Barclay.**—Thomas Barclay, D.D., was born in Unst, in Shetland, in 1792, where his father was minister. Dr. Barclay was educated in King's College, Aberdeen. He acted as a Parliamentary reporter for the *Times* for four years. In 1822 he received his first call to a church in his native county, after which he gained experience for the higher honours which awaited him in the parishes of Lerwick, Peterculter, and Currie. When Principal Macfarlan died in 1858, Dr. Barclay succeeded him as Principal of the University of Glasgow, which post he held until his death in February, 1873. He was succeeded by the late Principal John Caird, the "prince of preachers." The position is now occupied by Principal Story.

**John Gibson Lockhart.**—What student of our greatest novelist has not read Lockhart's "Life of Scott"? The author of it was born in Glasgow in 1795, his father being minister of the College Church. Securing the Snell scholarship, he became an exhibitioner in Baliol College, Oxford; was called to the Scottish Bar in 1816; married Sir Walter Scott's daughter four

years later; acted as editor of the *Quarterly Review* for several years; and ultimately became the biographer of his father-in-law, by which work his name will be handed down to posterity.

**William Motherwell.**—William Motherwell, the poet, was born in Glasgow on 13th October, 1797. When twenty-one years of age, he became Sheriff-Clerk Depute at Paisley. and wrote an essay on the poets of Renfrewshire, which was prefixed to "The Harp of Renfrewshire," published at Paisley in 1819. He became editor of "Minstrelsy, Ancient and Modern," which appeared in 1827; and, after editing a Paisley Conservative paper for two years, he was appointed editor of the *Glasgow Courier*, and had a delicate task representing Tory opinions during the time of the Reform Bill. He published his "Poems, Narrative and Lyrical," in 1832. Two years afterwards, in conjunction with Hogg, the "Ettrick Shepherd," he edited an edition of Burns in five volumes. Motherwell died on 1st November, 1835, and was buried in the Necropolis, where a handsome tombstone marks his resting-place.

**Peter M'Kenzie.** — Peter M'Kenzie was born in Glasgow in 1799, his early life being spent in a lawyer's office. He became a great reform enthusiast, and wrought day and night on behalf of such a laudable and necessary object—in fact, so bent did he become in his purpose that he started *The Reformers' Gazette*, and so ably did he conduct it that it continued a power in the city for about thirty years, and even at this date old bound copies are much sought after in the book market. His exposure of what was known as the "spy system" was enough in itself to cause his name to be revered by the citizens of the town he so dearly loved. I strongly recommend all who have an interest in old Glasgow to read his valuable "Reminiscences of Glasgow," and they can then judge for themselves what the grand old loyal reformer did for the city of his birth. He died on 18th March, 1875, respected by all who knew him.

**Rev. Dr. William Anderson.**—The Rev. Dr. William Anderson was born in Kilsyth in 1800. He was educated in Glasgow University, and was called to John Street U.P. Church at the early age of 22, where he laboured with great success for fifty years, during which time he published several theological works. He died in September, 1872.

"**Senex**" **and** "**Caleb.**"—Reference has been made in preceding paragraphs to several early Glasgow historians. One that cannot be omitted is the principal contributor to "Glasgow: Past and Present," "Senex." The bearer of this *nom de plume* was Robert Reid, a successful Glasgow merchant, who was born in Candleriggs on 27th January, 1773. After a university course and fortunate business career, he retired when about sixty years of age, and devoted himself to old Glasgow lore. He contributed a series of very interesting articles on old Glasgow to the *Herald*, which were afterwards edited by James Pagan, of the *Herald*, and included in that excellent work, "Glasgow: Past and Present." He died in 1865, over ninety years of age, and to show how he maintained his faculties to the last, he published "Old Glasgow and its Environs" six months prior to his death. What lover of Nature who professes to know anything regarding the history of the West of Scotland has not read "Rambles Round Glasgow" and "Days at the Coast"? The author of these valuable local sketches was Hugh Macdonald, who was born in Bridgeton in 1817. Mr. James Hedderwick discovered the hidden talents possessed by the young East-ender, and took him into the staff of the *Citizen*, where he became a sub-editor. He contributed a column for three years under the *nom de plume* of "Caleb," and the articles met with so much acceptance that they were published in book form, in 1854, under the title of "Rambles Round Glasgow" and "Days at the Coast." It is to the reminiscences of men like Robert Reid, John Buchanan, Hugh Macdonald, Peter M'Kenzie, "Nestor," and a few others that lovers of Glasgow history are indebted for the little they know.

**John Buchanan.**—John Buchanan was born in Glasgow in 1802. Educated in Glasgow University, he became an advocate, and was appointed secretary of the Western Bank, which position he held until the bank's failure. He was a great antiquarian, and contributed valuable articles on the subject to the *Glasgow Herald*. They were afterwards collected, and included, under the *nom de plume* of "J. B.," in "Glasgow: Past and Present," along with the writings of "Senex." As a Glasgow historian, Buchanan deserves to be remembered by his fellow-townsmen.

**Rev. Robert Buchanan, D.D.**—Dr. Buchanan was born at Gargunnock in 1802, and was educated at Glasgow University. He became pastor of the Tron Church in 1833, and at the Disruption he became minister of the "Free Tron," which immediately became a power in the city. He accepted a call to the Free College Church in 1857. The Free Church bestowed their highest honour upon him in 1860, when they elected him Moderator of the General Assembly. The Sustentation Fund, which he was chiefly responsible for, is an enduring monument to his memory. His "Ten Years Conflict" is a record of the church he wrought so nobly for. Great was the grief when he passed away on 30th March, 1875.

**Sir Archibald Allison, Bart.**—The author of Allison's "History of Europe" was born at Kenley in Shropshire, and educated in Edinburgh University. He became an advocate in 1834, was appointed Sheriff of Lanarkshire, and resided in Possil House, on the site of which the Saracen Foundry now stands. The great historian was elected Lord Rector of Glasgow University in 1850, was made a baronet two years later, and three years afterwards a D.C.L. of Oxford University. He was also Lord Rector of Aberdeen University. His biographies of "Marlborough" and "Castlereagh" still remain the "standards" of these great lives. Sir Archibald died on 23rd May, 1867, and was succeeded by his brave and distinguished son, Sir Archibald Allison, K.C.B.

**George and Robert Smith.**—George Smith was born at Saltcoats in 1803. He began a drapery business along with his father, George Smith, and brother, Robert, in 1826. In 1840 they started the well-known firm of George Smith & Sons, shipowners. The younger George took charge of the new venture, and the great success of the famous shipping house proved his aptitude for marine trading. He was a member of the Clyde Trust for fifteen years. On 3rd March, 1876, he "crossed the bar," deeply regretted by an admiring circle of friends. His brother Robert was also born at Saltcoats in 1801. He was better known as a great temperance reformer, and acted as president of the Scottish Temperance League for a number of years. He died at Hofton on 26th July, 1873.

**The Bairds.**—The father of the famous Bairds of Gartsherrie was a small farmer in Old Monkland Parish. James Baird was born in 1803, and, along with his brothers, founded the great firm of the Bairds of Gartsherrie. He represented the Falkirk Burghs in Parliament from 1851 to 1857. He gave £500,000 to the Church of Scotland. He died at his beautiful residence of Cambusdoon on 20th June, 1876. Alexander Baird of Ury was born in 1799, and was a River Bailie in the city. He died in 1862. Robert Baird of Auchmeddan was born in 1806, was Lord Dean of Guild in the city in 1855-56, and died while in that office. Douglas Baird of Closeburn was born in 1808, and died in 1854. William Baird of Elie was born in 1796, and died in 1864. The reputation of the firm is well known. It has done a world of good to the city and West of Scotland in developing the iron industry, and is still a power in the land under their able descendants, who so worthily uphold the family name, both in private and public life.

### Henry Glassford Bell.

Henry Glassford Bell was born in the city in 1805, and educated in the High School and Edinburgh University. While in "Auld Reekie" he associated with Sir Walter Scott, Francis Jeffrey, James Hogg, and all the principal great literary men of the period. When only 23 years of age he became editor of the *Edinburgh Literary Journal*. In 1832 he returned to his law studies and became an advocate. Sir William Hamilton defeated him in the vote for the position of Professor of Logic in Edinburgh University in 1836. He gained great popularity as junior counsel for the Glasgow Cotton Spinners' rioters, and in 1839 he was appointed sheriff-substitute under Sir Archibald Allison, upon whose death in 1867 he became sheriff-principal, which office he filled with credit until his death on 7th January, 1874. His "Life of Mary Queen of Scots" is a valuable record of the unfortunate Queen's career that history could not well dispense with. The better known poem on the same subject is perhaps the most enduring memento he has left of his great genius.

### Rev. Patrick Fairbairn, D.D.

Patrick Fairbairn was born in 1806. His first charge was in North Ronaldshay, which he left in 1836 to come to Bridgeton Church, Glasgow, from where he was transferred to Salton. He went over to the Free Church at the Disruption, and became professor in Aberdeen Free Church College in 1853. Three years afterwards he was appointed Principal of the Free Church College of Glasgow, which post he adorned until his death. He was the author of several standard theological works.

### Robert Dalglish.

Robert Dalglish was born in the city in 1808. After being educated in Glasgow University, he entered his father's firm of R. Dalglish, Falconer & Co., whose calico printing works were at Campsie. He soon made his presence felt, and greatly extended the business. He took an active interest in public affairs. Glasgow returned him to Parliament, along with Walter Buchanan, in 1857. He represented the Liberal interest until 1874, when he resigned. His death took place on 20th June, 1880.

### Professor Rankine.

William John Macquorn Rankine was born in Edinburgh in 1820, where he attended the University, and became a civil engineer. He was appointed Professor of Civil Engineering and Mechanics in Glasgow University. He rendered valuable service in his advocacy of the Loch Katrine water scheme. Dublin University made him an LL.D. He was the first President of the Institution of Engineers in Scotland; and, after a life of much usefulness, he passed away in December, 1872.

### Rev. Dr. John Eadie.

The Rev. Dr. John Eadie was born in Alva in 1813. His early education was got in Tillicoultry, after which he became a successful student in Glasgow University and the United Secession Divinity Hall. In 1834 he was appointed minister of Cambridge Street U.P. Church. Subsequently he became pastor of Lansdowne U.P. Church at Kelvin Bridge, an elegant structure which cost about £12,000. A disappointed member of his old flock wrote on the new edifice in chalk—

This church was not built for the poor and needy,
But for the rich and Dr. Eadie.

On being told of the circumstance, the Doctor remarked, "That is not for *Eadification*." In 1843 he became Professor of Biblical Literature in the U.P. Divinity Hall. Among his many works he published an abridged edition of Cruden's "Concordance," "Biblical Encyclopædia," "An Analytical Concordance of the Holy Scriptures," "Ecclesiastical Cyclopædia of Antiquities," etc. He was a member of the New Testament Revision Committee, LL.D. of his *Alma Mater*, and D.D. of St. Andrews University. He died in June, 1876.

### Alexander Whitelaw.

Alexander Whitelaw was born in Old Monkland Parish in 1823. He was a grandson of Alex. Baird of Lochwood, and was taken in as a partner with the Bairds of Gartsherrie. He devoted a great deal of his time to public life. He was chairman of the first Glasgow School Board in 1873, and had the distinguished honour of being the first Conservative to represent Glasgow in Parliament after the passing of the second Reform Bill, being returned in 1874. His early death, on 1st July, 1879, was looked upon as a great loss to the community.

**John Elder and Charles Randolph.**—John Elder was born in Glasgow in 1824, and served his apprenticeship under his father, David Elder, who was manager to Robert Napier. In 1852 he joined Charles Randolph in the engineering business, and latterly they began shipbuilding at Fairfield yard, where they built some of the largest vessels in the world. On the retiral of his partner, the firm became John Elder & Company, by which name it was known all over the civilised world. John Elder died in September, 1869. His widow gifted the valuable Elder Public Park to the inhabitants of Govan. Charles Randolph was born in Stirling in 1808 and educated in the High School in Glasgow. He became an apprentice engineer with Robert Napier, and commenced business in 1834, being joined by John Elder eighteen years afterwards. They continued in partnership for sixteen years, Charles Randolph retiring from the firm in 1868. He died in 1870. His widow endowed the Chair of Engineering and Mechanics in Glasgow University.

**Principal Caird.**—John Caird was born in Greenock in 1820, and educated at Glasgow University. He was appointed to Newton-on-Ayr in 1847, and two years after was translated to Lady Yester's, Edinburgh, where his fame spread abroad. He removed for a quieter life in 1849 to Errol, in Perthshire. In 1855 he preached before the Queen, the sermon—"The Religion of Common Life"—being published by Royal command, and it was also translated and published on the Continent. Dr. Caird came to Park Church in 1857, and continued there until appointed Professor of Divinity in his *Alma Mater* in 1862. On the death of Principal Barclay in 1873 he was selected to succeed him, a position he adorned until his death on 31st July, 1898.

**Lord Kelvin.**—William Thomson was born in Belfast in June, 1824, his father being Professor of Mathematics in Belfast, and afterwards in Glasgow University, which his illustrous son entered when only eleven years old. He took honours at Cambridge University, and was appointed, when only twenty-two years of age, Professor of Natural Philosophy in his *Alma Mater* in 1846. His discoveries have revolutionised the world. He is best known by his immortal work in connection with the Atlantic cable, for which he was knighted in 1866, and received the freedom of Glasgow, and was made an LL.D. of Dublin, Cambridge, and Edinburgh Universities, and a D.C.L. of Oxford. He was raised to the peerage under the title of Lord Kelvin of Largs in 1892. When the history of the present time comes to be written, Lord Kelvin's name will bulk largely in its pages.

**Sir Henry Campbell-Bannerman.** —Sir Henry Campbell-Bannerman, who was elected leader of the Liberal Party in the House of Commons in 1899, is the second son of Sir James Campbell of Stracathro, who was Lord Provost of Glasgow in 1840. Sir Henry was born in Kelvinside in 1836. He assumed the name of Bannerman in 1872 in consequence of a fortune bequeathed to him by a maternal uncle—Henry Bannerman, of Manchester. The Liberal leader was created a G.C.B. in 1895.

*For other Prominent Men see "Monuments."*

## OLD GLASGOW CHARACTERS.

**"Hawkie"** claims first place among the old characters of the city, seeing there is a book wholly devoted to his life. He was born last century near Stirling, and went with a crutch and stick on account of having a short right leg. His real name was William Cameron. After spending the early part of his life as a "drunken tramp" all over the country he settled down in the city. In the vicinity of the Cross he was famous for his witty harangues and clever repartee when selling "chap" literature. He died in the old Town's Hospital in Clyde Street, in September, 1851.

**"Blind Alick,"** whose name was Alexander M'Donald, was born near Penrith in 1771, and came to Glasgow about 1790. In the daytime Alick diffused music through the principal streets, and Peter M'Kenzie states it is probable the Fiddler's Close in High Street was called after him. In the evening his services were greatly in demand for weddings and dances among the poorer classes. Alick was fond of a "wee drap." The great Dr. Thomas Chalmers was not above patronising the poor fiddler.

**Dougal Graham.**—Dougal Graham was the city bellman. He was in Glasgow when Prince Charlie arrived with his

Highlanders. Graham accompanied the Pretender when he retreated north, and was present at the Battle of Falkirk. He wrote a great amount of doggerel, including a metre "History of the Rebellion of 1745," and is known to posterity as the literary bellman. He is buried in the Cathedral burying ground.

**James Dall** was a city porter, with his headquarters in the vicinity of the Cross. He had anything but a prepossessing face. Mr. M'Kenzie says that, in contemplating the ten Tontine faces, sculptured by Mungo Naismith, the one furthest to the east, No. 3, somewhat resembled the well-known city porter. Anyone who studies the remaining two effigies, now to be seen in Fraser, Sons, and Co.'s warehouse in Buchanan Street, can have an idea what this Glasgow character was like.

**"Feea,"** the idiot, was born in the Stockwell. When about five years of age, he lost his father and mother, and was allowed to grow up almost in a state of nature. He slept on stairs, hay-lofts, or anywhere he could find shelter, and his food was the garbage of the streets, living worms being a favourite tit-bit. Being finely built he was every inch an athlete. Poor "Feea" latterly mysteriously disappeared, and it was thought the resurrectionists had made him a victim.

**"Major" and "Mary."**—The former was a deformed musician who sang on the streets, and accompanied his "bass" melody with two sticks used à la violin. The latter was originally a charwoman, but became partner in life with the street "Paganini." She accompanied him during his "recitals," acting the part of the monkey with the organ-grinder, the terms of the copartnery being halfpennies going to the musician and pennies to the dancer. They were both swept off within 48 hours of each other by the cholera in 1832.

**"Hirstling Kate"** was so named on account of her mode of locomotion along the streets of the city. She leant on her hands, and hirstled along on her knees. Owing to the close proximity of her optics to the ground she picked up the smallest object. All manner of vegetable refuse was carefully stowed away for after use. "Preens" (pins) were, however, her "strong suit." She followed the avocation of a "merchant beggar" between the Cross and Bishop Street (Anderston), "sweeping" the pavements with the train of her dress. On her death she was buried in a corner of the Cathedral burying-ground.

**"Spunk Kate"** was a fishwife in summer and a match vendor in winter. She married a carter nicknamed "Raby Nation," of very diminutive stature. They were both fond of *aqua vitæ*, and as a consequence their domestic relationship was often of a disturbed character.

**The "Reverend" John Aitken** was a street preacher. He was a spare, lean man, and during the cold weather he wore flannel over his ears to withstand Boreas' wintry blasts and the "cranreuch cauld." He plied his vocation on week days at the foot of Stockwell Street or Saltmarket, Barrowfield Toll or at the Burnt Barns, while on Sundays he was always to be found on the Green. A three-legged stool with a pewter plate and a crazy old fir chair served as his furniture, while a comely damsel accompanied him at his services, and read out the line on receiving instructions. His discourses were always of a very "fiery" nature, which were in keeping with the potations he consumed to keep out the cold. He was very fond of touching on local incidents, and consequently drew good congregations, who did not forget the pewter plate. John passed away in his lodgings in the Little Dovehill, and was buried in the Ramshorn Churchyard.

**Jamie Blue** was another vendor of "chap" literature in the streets. He was born in Pollokshaws, and spent a good part of his life as a street singer between Glasgow and Paisley, Burns and Tannahill's songs being his favourites. At the election times he wrote poetical effusions, and was known as the 'Shaws poet. He often wore a huge Kilmarnock cowl. Hawkie and he were rivals in trade, and while generally good friends, they sometimes crossed each other. Both were remarkably "glib o' the moo'." If they happened to meet when the relationship was not cordial, the eloquence of a Cicero or the philosophy of a Plato, not to speak of the maxims of a Shakespeare, paled into insignificance in comparison with the "sparks" which flew from the well-known characters. Jamie ended his eventful career in the old Govan Poorhouse, the site of which is now occupied by Eglinton Street Station.

**Willie White** was a blind whistle player, whose picture is given by Mr. M'Kenzie. On his death, a monument was erected to his memory by public subscription in the Southern Necropolis.

**Wee Jamie Wallace** is in the same position as the foregoing. His likeness shows him to be about 45 years of age, between four and five feet in height, with a long body and very short legs. His headquarters were in the old fruit market in Kent Street, where he constituted himself a self-elected guardian.

"**Bell Geordie**" was the bellman of the city at the close of the last and beginning of this century. His calling made him one of the best known characters in the streets. His name was George Gibson. He was a large, stout man, with a huge carbuncled nose, and proved a worthy successor to the famous Dougal Graham. Geordie was a great wit, and could deliver his orations in an inimitable fashion, and some of his original poetical effusions are carefully preserved to this day. He is buried in the High Kirk burial ground.

"**Blind Angus**" was a midnight minstrel who learned the tunes played by the Tolbooth Chimes, and rehearsed them in the vicinity of the Cross on a tin whistle. He was a harmless mendicant, and met with a fair measure of success.

"**Daft Davie**" lived with his mother in a back house in the Candleriggs. He could not articulate the letter "r" nor the diphthong "th." An attempt was made to teach him shoemaking, but the trial ended in failure. Although poor, his mother would not allow her son to beg. Owing to Davie's pronunciation, originality, and harmless ways he was a very interesting character.

"**Rab Ha',**" whose headquarters were in Paisley, was a well-known glutton, and his gastronomic feats have passed into a proverb.

"**Ru'glen Wull**" was a noted character who frequented the east end of the city about thirty years ago. His eccentric discourses were a fund of amusement to his hearers.

"**Heather Jock**" was an itinerant street vocalist, who used to sing "Annie Laurie" in dramatic fashion. When singing the line "I'd lay me down and dee," he always suited the action to the word.

"**Penny a Yard.**"—This was a well-known character about the sixties. His headquarters were in the vicinity of the Gallowgate and Saltmarket, where he manufactured chains which he sold at a penny a yard, hence the name.

"**Old Malabar**" was an itinerant street juggler, who flourished in the seventies. He appeared in an oriental dress, and a favourite expression of his was: "One penny more, and up goes the ball."

"**The Teapot**" stood at the corner of Ann and Jamaica Streets about the eighties, where he vended the evening papers. The attitude in which he stood procured for him his cognomen.

"**Dungannon**" was a well-known character about twenty years ago to the denizens in the vicinity of the Candleriggs. He went about bare-footed, and was popularly known as the "Boss of the Bazaar."

"**Whistling Geordie**" was a blind *siffleur* who frequented Great Clyde Street, his guide, philospher, and friend being a dog, which was always with him. His favourite music was Scotch airs, and he accompanied himself with bones in Christy minstrel style.

"**Wee**" **Alec Knight** has performed on the tin whistle for over thirty years nightly in Jamaica Street. He is compelled to use two crutches, and is a great favourite with the Glasgow public, who quite recently organised a monstre concert on his behalf.

---

## STATISTICS.

**Provosts of Glasgow.**—The early Provosts of Glasgow were nominated by the Archbishops of Glasgow under the Charters of Barony and Regality granted in their favour by the Crown. The first name on the subjoined list is that of a person who held the Provostship when Glasgow was a Burgh of Barony, to which dignity it had been erected in the reign of King William the Lion.

1268  Richard de Dunidovis.
(Glasgow made a Burgh of Regality
on the 20th April, 1450.)
1472  John Stuart of Minto.
1480  Sir Thomas Stewart of Minto.
1507  Allan Stewart.
1513  Sir John Stewart of Minto.
1528  Sir Robert Stewart of Minto.
1538  Archibald Dunbar of Baldoon.
1541  Lord Belhaven.
1543  John Stewart of Minto.
1545  Andrew Hamilton of Middop.
1553  Andrew Hamilton of Cockney.
1560  Robert Lindsay of Dunrod.
1569  Sir John Stewart of Minto.
1574  Lord Boyd.
1577  Thomas Crawford of Jordanhill.
1578  Earl of Lennox.
1580  Sir Matthew Stewart of Minto.
1583  Earl of Montrose.
1584  Lord Kilsyth.
1586  Sir Matthew Stewart of Minto.
1600  Sir George Elphinston of Blythswood.
(Letter of Guildry agreed upon in
1604, and signed in 1605.)
1605  Sir George Elphinston.
1607  Sir John Houston of Houston.
1609  James Inglis.

| 1613 | James Stuart. |
| 1614 | James Hamilton. |
| 1617 | James Stuart. |
| 1619 | James Inglis. |
| 1621 | James Hamilton. |
| 1623 | Gabriel Cunningham. |
| 1625 | James Inglis. |
| 1627 | James Hamilton. |
| 1628 | John Hamilton. |
| 1629 | Gabriel Cunningham. |
| 1633 | William Stewart. |
| 1634 | Patrick Bell. |
| 1636 | Colin Campbell. |

(Glasgow made a Royal Burgh in 1636.)

| 1637 | James Stewart. |
| 1638 | Patrick Bell. |
| 1639 | Gabriel Cunningham. |
| 1640 | James Stewart. |
| 1640 | William Stewart. |
| 1643 | James Bell. |
| 1645 | George Porterfield. |
| 1647 | James Stewart. |
| 1648 | Colin Campbell, sen. / George Porterfield. |
| 1649 | George Porterfield. |
| 1650 | John Graham. |
| 1651 | George Porterfield. |
| 1652 | Daniel Wallace. |
| 1655 | John Anderson, sen. |
| 1657 | John Anderson, jun. |
| 1658 | John Bell. |
| 1660 | Colin Campbell. |
| 1662 | John Bell. |
| 1664 | William Anderson. |
| 1667 | John Anderson, sen. |
| 1668 | William Anderson. |
| 1669 | James Campbell. |
| 1670 | William Anderson. |
| 1674 | John Bell. |
| 1676 | James Campbell. |
| 1678 | John Bell. |
| 1681 | Sir John Bell. |
| 1682 | John Barns. |
| 1684 | John Johnston. |
| 1686 | John Barns. |
| 1687 | Walter Gibson. |
| 1689 | John Anderson. |

(Free election of Magistrates granted the Town Council in June, 1690.)

| 1691 | James Peadie. |
| 1693 | William Napier. |
| 1695 | John Anderson. |
| 1697 | James Peadie. |
| 1699 | John Anderson. |
| 1701 | Hugh Montgomerie. |
| 1703 | John Anderson. |
| 1705 | John Aird, junior. |
| 1707 | Robert Rodger. |
| 1709 | John Aird. |
| 1711 | Robert Rodger. |
| 1713 | John Aird. |
| 1715 | John Bowman. |
| 1717 | John Aird. |
| 1719 | John Bowman. |
| 1721 | John Aird. |
| 1723 | Charles Miller. |
| 1725 | John Stark. |
| 1727 | James Peadie. |
| 1728 | John Stirling. |
| 1730 | Peter Murdoch. |
| 1732 | Hugh Rodger. |
| 1734 | Andrew Ramsay. |
| 1736 | John Coulter. |
| 1738 | Andrew Aiton. |
| 1740 | Andrew Buchanan. |
| 1742 | Laurence Dinwiddie. |
| 1744 | Andrew Cochran. |
| 1746 | John Murdoch, jun. |
| 1748 | Andrew Cochran. |

| 1750 | John Murdoch, jun. |
| 1752 | John Brown. |
| 1754 | George Murdoch. |
| 1756 | Robert Christie. |
| 1758 | John Murdoch, jun. |
| 1760 | Andrew Cochran. |
| 1762 | Archibald Ingram. |
| 1764 | John Bowman. |
| 1766 | George Murdoch. |
| 1768 | James Buchanan. |
| 1770 | Colin Dunlop. |
| 1772 | Arthur Connell. |
| 1774 | James Buchanan. |
| 1776 | Robert Donald. |
| 1778 | William French. |
| 1780 | Hugh Wylie. |
| 1782 | Patrick Colquhoun. |
| 1784 | John C. Campbell. |
| 1786 | John Riddell. |
| 1788 | J. Campbell, jun. |
| 1790 | James M'Dowall. |
| 1792 | Gilbert Hamilton. |
| 1794 | John Dunlop. |
| 1796 | James M'Dowall. |
| 1798 | Lawrence Craigie. |
| 1800 | John Hamilton. |
| 1802 | Lawrence Craigie. |
| 1804 | John Hamilton. |
| 1806 | James M'Kenzie. |
| 1808 | James Black. |
| 1810 | John Hamilton. |
| 1812 | Kirkman Finlay. |
| 1814 | Henry Monteith. |
| 1816 | James Black. |
| 1818 | Henry Monteith. |
| 1820 | John Thomas Alston. |
| 1822 | James Smith. |
| 1824 | Mungo N. Campbell. |
| 1826 | William Hamilton. |
| 1828 | Alexander Garden. |
| 1830 | Robert Dalglish. |
| 1832 | James Ewing. |

(Municipal Reform Act passed in 1833.)

| 1833 | Robert Graham |
| 1834 | William Mills. |
| 1837 | Henry Dunlop. |
| 1840 | James Campbell. |
| 1843 | James Lumsden. |
| 1846 | Alexander Hastie. |
| 1848 | James Anderson. |
| 1851 | Robert Stewart. |
| 1854 | Andrew Orr. |
| 1857 | Andrew Galbraith. |
| 1860 | Peter Clouston. |
| 1863 | John Blackie. |
| 1866 | James Lumsden. |
| 1869 | William Rae Arthur. |
| 1871 | James Watson. |
| 1874 | James Bain. |
| 1877 | William Collins. |
| 1880 | John Ure. |
| 1883 | William M'Onie. |
| 1886 | James King. |
| 1889 | John Muir. |
| 1892 | James Bell. |
| 1896 | David Richmond |

## Freedom of the City.

—The following have been made Honorary Burgesses of the city since 1800, *viz.* :—

| Oct. | 17, 1800 | Duke of Hamilton. / Marquess of Douglas. / Lord Archibald Hamilton. / Lord Fincastle. |
| Dec. | 24, 1801 | Major-General A. J. Drummond. |
| Feb. | 8, 1802 | Major Stirling. |
| Sept. | 14, 1804 | Earl of Moira. / Major-General Wemyss. |

| Sept. | 1, 1808 | Edward Jenner, M.D. |
| Dec. | 2, 1808 | { Lord Cathcart. |
| | | { Admiral Sir Samuel Hood. |
| Dec. | 15, 1808 | Archibald Campbell, M.P. |
| Oct. | 28, 1809 | James Neild. |
| Aug. | 7, 1810 | Lord Melville. |
| Nov. | 12, 1811 | Edward Earl. |
| Jan. | 8, 1812 | Hon. Henry Cadogan. |
| Nov. | 13, 1812 | Lieutenant-Colonel Grant. |
| March | 19, 1813 | Brigadier-General J. Downie. |
| Oct. | 18, 1814 | Lord Lynedoch. |
| July | 25, 1815 | Lieutenant-Colonel Cother. |
| Aug. | 29, 1821 | Prince Nicolai Esterhazy. |
| July | 6, 1824 | Duke of Buckingham. |
| Nov. | 9, 1826 | Marquis of Tweeddale. |
| Oct. | 13, 1830 | { Hon. Charles Douglas, M.P. |
| | | { Marquess of Lansdowne. |
| Feb. | 20, 1834 | Alexander Thomson. |
| Sept. | 11, 1834 | Earl Grey. |
| Sept. | 20, 1834 | { Dominique François Joan Arago. |
| | | { Robert Brown, LL.D. |
| Oct. | 27, 1834 | Earl of Durham. |
| Nov. | 24, 1836 | Lord William Bentinck, M.P. |
| Dec. | 19, 1838 | Sir James Graham, Bart. |
| Jan. | 11, 1843 | Richard Cobden, M.P. |
| Oct. | 10, 1844 | Dr. Justus Liebig.                    [Bart. |
| April | 15, 1845 | Major-Gen. Sir Henry Pottinger, |
| Jan. | 12, 1846 | Lord John Russell. |
| Jan. | 29, 1846 | Robert Wallace.                    [Bart. |
| June | 26, 1846 | Lieut.-General Sir Henry Smith, |
| Feb. | 9, 1847 | Major-General Edward Fleming. |
| March | 22, 1849 | Thomas Babington Macaulay. |
| Feb. | 27, 1853 | Viscount Palmerston. |
| Jan. | 4, 1856 | Earl of Elgin. |
| July | 1, 1856 | Major-Gen. Sir Colin Campbell. |
| Sept. | 16, 1857 | David Livingstone. |
| Sept. | 21, 1860 | Sir John Lawrence. |
| Nov. | 1, 1865 | William E. Gladstone, M.P. |
| Oct. | 18, 1866 | H.R.H. Duke of Edinburgh. |
| Nov. | 1, 1866 | Sir William Thomson. |
| Oct. | 8, 1868 | H.R.H. The Prince of Wales. |
| June | 3, 1870 | Earl of Dalhousie. |
| Aug. | 28, 1871 | Earl of Shaftesbury. |
| Sept. | 26, 1872 | Robert Lowe, M.P. |
| Nov. | 20, 1873 | Benjamin Disraeli, M.P. |
| Oct. | 2, 1876 | Richard A. Cross, M.P. |
| Sept. | 15, 1877 | General Grant. |
| Nov. | 5, 1877 | Marquess of Hartington, M.P. |
| Oct. | 25, 1881 | Sir W. V. Harcourt, Bart., M.P. |
| Oct. | 5, 1882 | Sir Stafford H. Northcote, Bart. |
| Oct. | 14, 1882 | H.R.H. Duke of Albany.    [M.P. |
| Dec. | 14, 1882 | W. E. Forster, M.P. |
| March | 23, 1883 | John Bright, M.P. |
| Dec. | 18, 1883 | Marquess of Lorne. |
| June | 12, 1890 | H. M. Stanley. |
| Oct. | 10, 1890 | Earl of Rosebery. |
| May | 20, 1891 | Marquess of Salisbury. |
| Oct. | 7, 1891 | Marquess of Bute. |
| July | 28, 1893 | Lord Roberts. |
| July | 17, 1894 | Sir G. O. Trevelyan, Bart., M.P. |
| Jan. | 14, 1896 | Arthur J. Balfour, M.P. |
| Sept. | 23, 1897 | Lord Wolseley. |
| Nov. | 8, 1897 | Joseph Chamberlain, M.P. |

**Rental of Glasgow.**—The rental of Glasgow is only to be had occasionally, previous to 1855-56, when the Lands Valuation Act came into force :—

| | | | | | |
|---|---|---|---|---|---|
| 1712 | - | £7,840 | 1871 | - | - £2,055,388 |
| 1803 | - | 81,484 | 1875 | - | - 2,720,688 |
| 1805 | - | 152,738 | 1880 | - | - 3,400,517 |
| 1815 | - | 240,000 | 1885 | - | - 3,995,800 |
| 1819 | - | 270,646 | 1890 | - | - 3,455,510 |
| 1856 | - | 1,362,168 | 1895 | - | - 4,283,926 |
| 1861 | - | 1,625,148 | 1898 | - | - 4,532,181 |
| 1865 | - | 1,778,728 | | | |

**Population of Glasgow.**—The first figures quoted are merely approximate, but

the others are more or less official. They relate only to the population within the Parliamentary boundaries.

| | | | | | | |
|---|---|---|---|---|---|---|
| 1300 | - | - | *1,500 | 1785 | - | - 45,889 |
| 1450 | - | - | *2,000 | 1791 | - | - 66,578 |
| 1560 | - | - | 4,500 | 1801 | - | - 77,385 |
| 1600 | - | - | 7,000 | 1811 | - | - 100,749 |
| 1610 | - | - | 7,644 | 1821 | - | - 147,043 |
| 1660 | - | - | 14,678 | 1831 | - | - 202,4 6 |
| 1688 | - | - | 11,948 | 1841 | - | - 255,650 |
| 1708 | - | - | 12,766 | 1851 | - | - 329,096 |
| 1712 | - | - | 13,832 | 1861 | - | - 395,503 |
| 1740 | - | - | 17,043 | 1871 | - | - 477,732 |
| 1743 | - | - | 18,366 | 1881 | - | - 510 8 6 |
| 1757 | - | - | 23,546 | 1891 | - | - 565,714 |
| 1763 | - | - | 28,300 | 1898 | - | - †731,675 |
| 1780 | - | - | 42,832 | | | |

\* About.    † Municipal Boundary at June, 1898.

**Relief Funds.**—The following amounts represent the money raised by public subscription in the city for the undernoted objects :—

| | | | | |
|---|---|---|---|---|
| 1877 | St. John, New Brunswick, Conflagration | - | - - | £4,681 16 6 |
| 1877 | Famine in Madras Presidency | 22,374 | 5 8 |
| 1877 | Blantyre Colliery Accident | - | 48,246 19 3 |
| 1878 | Famine in China | - | - - | 3,113 7 3 |
| 1878 | City Bank Shareholders | - | 162,168 5 2 |
| | (This is the sum contributed by Glasgow subscribers.) | | | |
| 1878 | Unemployed, 1878-79 | - | - | 17,463 10 6 |
| 1880 | Famine in Ireland | - | - | 2,719 14 9 |
| 1880 | Famine in Armenia and Turkestan | - | - | 1,031 16 9 |
| 1881 | Henderson St. Gas Explosion | 389 | 8 2 |
| 1881 | Shetland Fishing Fleet Disaster | - | - | 2,096 0 1 |
| 1881 | East Coast Fishing Fleet Disaster | - | - | 5,985 17 5 |
| 1882 | Western Islands Fishing Boats Disaster | - | | 5,143 9 0 |
| 1882 | Russian Jewish Refugees | - | 1,974 6 6 |
| 1883 | Destitution in Western Highlands and Islands | - | 7,209 15 1 |
| 1883 | "Daphne" Disaster on Clyde | 30,722 12 7 |
| 1884 | Unemployed, 1884-85 | - | | 7,205 7 7 |
| 1888 | Lews Destitution Relief | - | | 2,140 5 7 |
| 1888 | Western Highlands & Islands Colonisation Scheme | - | | 1,128 16 3 |
| 1889 | Greenhead Disaster | - | - | 5,368 6 11½ |
| 1891 | St. Johns, Newfoundland, Fire | 2,788 10 3 |
| 1892 | Persecution of Russian Jews | 2,467 16 11 |
| 1892 | Mauritius Hurricane | - | - | 467 9 0 |
| 1893 | H.M.S. "Victoria" Disaster | - | 1,250 2 11 |
| | (Including £1,000 from "Daphne" Fund.) | | | |
| 1895 | Unemployed Distress | - | - | 9,586 1 1½ |
| 1895 | Armenian Distress | - | | 5,023 3 5 |
| 1897 | Indian Famine | - | - | 55,347 13 11 |
| 1897 | Queen's Diamond Jubilee Royal Infirmary Reconstruction | - | 77,659 2 0 |
| | (To Date.) | | | |
| 1898 | Irish Distress Relief | - | - | 2,628 1 1½ |
| 1898 | Gordon Memorial College, | | | |
| 1899 | Khartoum | - | - - | 3,632 5 7 |
| 1899 | Gladstone Memorial | - | | 3,998 6 6 |
| | (To Date.) | | | |

**Executions.**—Hanging for murder was introduced on 30th April, 1630. Previous to that date the punishment was always beheading. Theft and minor crimes were always punished with hanging. From 1765 to 1850, 107 people were executed in Glasgow, seven of whom were women. Only 27 of the executions were for murder. Eighty persons paid the extreme penalty of the law for other offences. The following are a few of the more notorious cases :—

*Executed at the Howgate, where the Monkland Canal Basin is now situated.*

| | | |
|---|---|---|
| July, | 1765 | Hugh Bisland—robbery. |
| Nov., | 1767 | Agnes Dougall—murder. |
| Oct., | 1769 | Andrew Marshall—murder. |
| Nov., | 1773 | William Mitchell and Charles Gordon —robbery. |
| June, | 1776 | George Mactaggart—housebreaking. |
| June, | 1781 | Robert Hislop—housebreaking. |

*Executed in the Yard of the Bishop's Castle, where the Royal Infirmary is now built.*

| | | |
|---|---|---|
| June, | 1784 | James Jack—robbery. |
| Nov., | 1784 | James and William Breadie and John Scott—housebreaking. |
| June, | 1785 | Neil M'Lean—forgery. |
| June, | 1785 | David Steven—murder. |
| Nov., | 1785 | Thomas Vernon—robbery. |
| Oct., | 1786 | John Spence — housebreaking and theft. |
| Oct., | 1786 | Elizabeth Paul—housebreaking and theft. |
| May, | 1787 | Thomas Veitch and Thomas Gentles —robbery. |
| May, | 1788 | John M'Aulay—robbery. |

*Executed at the Tolbooth at the Cross.*

| | | |
|---|---|---|
| Oct., | 1788 | Walter M'Intosh—robbery. |
| Dec., | 1788 | William Scott — housebreaking and theft. |
| June, | 1790 | John Brown—forgery. |
| Oct., | 1790 | James Day—murder. |
| Jan., | 1792 | James Plunkett—robbery. |
| May, | 1792 | James Dick—murder. |
| Nov., | 1792 | Mortimer Collins—murder. |
| May, | 1793 | Agnes White—murder. |
| May, | 1793 | James M'Intosh—robbery. |
| Jan., | 1797 | James M'Kean—murdered Lanark carrier. |
| May, | 1798 | James M'Millan—murder. |
| May, | 1800 | Peter Gray. |
| June, | 1803 | William Cunningham—theft |
| June, | 1806 | David Scott and Hugh Adamson— Ship Bank forgery. |
| June, | 1807 | Adam Cox—murder. |
| July, | 1808 | James Gilchrist. |
| Nov., | 1809 | John Gordon M'Intosh and George Stewart—housebreaking. |
| May, | 1813 | James Ferguson—robbery. |
| Nov., | 1813 | W. Muir and W. Mudie—robbery. |

*Executed at the Jail in Jail Square.*

| | | |
|---|---|---|
| Oct., | 1814 | William Higgins and Thomas Harold —robbery. |
| Nov., | 1815 | John Sherry—robbery. |
| May, | 1817 | William M'Kay—forgery. |
| Oct., | 1817 | Freebairn Whitehill—robbery. |
| Oct., | 1817 | William M'Kechnie and James M'Cormick—housebreaking and theft. |
| June, | 1818 | William Baird and Walter Blair— robbery. |
| Nov., | 1818 | Simon Ross—housebreaking. |
| Nov., | 1818 | Matthew Clydesdale—murdered a man. |
| April, | 1819 | A. Robertson — housebreaking and theft. |
| Nov., | 1819 | John Buchanan—murdered a girl. |

| | | |
|---|---|---|
| Nov., | 1819 | Robert M'Kinlay ("Rough Rab"), Hunter Guthrie, J. Forbes, and Wm. Buchanan — housebreaking and theft. |
| May, | 1820 | Richard Smith—housebreaking. |
| Aug., | 1820 | Jas. Wilson—high treason. (Hanged and beheaded.) |
| Nov., | 1820 | — Grant, — Crosbie, — O'Connor, and — M'Colgin—robbery. |
| June, | 1821 | William L. Swan—forgery. |
| Oct., | 1821 | Malcolm M'Intyre, William Paterson, and James Dyer—housebreaking. |
| June, | 1822 | T. Donachy — housebreaking and theft. |
| June, | 1823 | John MacDougall and James Wilson —housebreaking and theft. |
| May, | 1824 | W. M'Teague—uttering forged notes. |
| June, | 1824 | Francis Kean—robbery. |
| June, | 1824 | George Laidlaw—theft. |
| June, | 1824 | John M'Crevie—housebreaking and theft. |
| July, | 1824 | William Devon—murder. |
| June, | 1825 | James Stevenson—highway robbery. |
| June, | 1825 | James Dollan—street robbery. (First criminal who suffered between 8 and 10 a.m.) |
| Nov., | 1826 | Andrew Stewart and Edward Kelly — street robbery. |
| Dec., | 1827 | James Glen—drowned his child in the canal. |
| May, | 1828 | Edward Moore—murder. |
| Oct., | 1828 | Thomas Connor and Isabella MacMenemy—assault and robbery. |
| May, | 1830 | John Hill and William Porter— assault and robbery. |
| Sept., | 1830 | William M'Feat—murder. |
| Jan., | 1831 | David Little—stouthrief. |
| May, | 1831 | James Campbell—housebreaking and theft. |
| Oct., | 1831 | Jas. Byers and Mary Steel—murder. |
| Oct., | 1831 | William Heath—housebreaking. |
| Jan., | 1832 | William Lindsay—murder. |
| May, | 1832 | Philip Cairney—rape. |
| May, | 1832 | John Barclay—murder. |
| Jan., | 1833 | Henry Buirett—street robbery. |
| Jan., | 1833 | George Duffy—murder. |
| Sept., | 1834 | Hugh Kennedy—throwing vitriol. |
| Sept., | 1835 | George Campbell—murder. |
| May, | 1838 | Mrs. Jeffrey—poisoned a man and woman with arsenic. |
| May, | 1840 | Thomas Templeton—murder. |
| May, | 1841 | Thos. Doolan and Patrick Redding— murder. (Executed at Crosshill, near Bishopbriggs.) |
| May, | 1843 | Charles M'Kay—murdered his wife. |
| Jan., | 1850 | Margaret Lennox or Hamilton— poisoned her sister-in-law. |
| Oct., | 1851 | Archibald Hare—murder. |
| Aug., | 1853 | Hans Smith M'Farlane and Helen Blackwood—murdered a man. |
| May, | 1855 | Alexander Kelso ("Collier Stewart") —murdered a man. |
| April, | 1864 | John Riley—beat a woman to death. |
| July, | 1865 | Dr. E. W. Pritchard—poisoned his wife and mother-in-law. (This was the last public execution.) |

*Executed in Duke Street Prison.*

| | | |
|---|---|---|
| Oct., | 1875 | Patrick Docherty—killed a man with a hoe. |
| May, | 1876 | Thomas Barr—murdered his wife and mother-in-law. |
| May, | 1883 | Henry Mullen and Martin Scott— shot two gamekeepers. |
| Sept., | 1890 | Henry Devlin—killed his wife. |
| Jan., | 1893 | William M'Keown — murdered a woman. |
| June, | 1897 | George Paterson—burned a woman to death. |

# INDEX.